Pra[...]

"Scott Mackay to[...][...]y of the human spirit with a culturally shocking and disturbing, but quite enjoyable, novel." —*The Midwest Book Review*

"In this fast-paced read with plenty of action and suspense, Mr. Mackay embroiders *The Meek* with emotional depth and hard scientific details."
—*Romantic Times*

"Poses some intriguing ethical problems with a satisfying complex plot." —*Science Fiction Chronicle*

Outpost

"Mackay avoids the grandiosity that is an occupational hazard of science fiction writers who dabble in cosmic themes. . . . Provocative."
—*The New York Times Book Review*

"A fast-paced action adventure." —*The Washington Post*

"Absolutely classic . . . stunning ingenuity."
—*The Toronto Globe and Mail*

"Moving. . . . Much of the novel's strength lies in its characters, heroic yet vulnerable, facing tough decisions and tough situations . . . stirring." —*Publishers Weekly*

"Ingenious and satisfying . . . a complex and winning heroine. . . . Mackay delivers on the surprises when he needs to . . . and he writes with impressive grace and clarity. His vision is original enough his imagery vivid enough, and his characters engaging enough that we might expect even better surprises in the future."
—*Locus*

"Intriguing . . . tense." —*Kirkus Reviews*

"[A] fast-moving blend of mystery and SF adventure . . . a well-written and engrossing tale." —*Library Journal*

OMNIFIX

Scott Mackay

A ROC BOOK

ROC
Published by New American Library, a division of
Penguin Group (USA) Inc., 375 Hudson Street,
New York, New York 10014, U.S.A.
Penguin Books Ltd, 80 Strand,
London WC2R 0RL, England
Penguin Books Australia Ltd, 250 Camberwell Road,
Camberwell, Victoria 3124, Australia
Penguin Books Canada Ltd, 10 Alcorn Avenue,
Toronto, Ontario, Canada M4V 3B2
Penguin Books (N.Z.) Ltd, Cnr Rosedale and Airborne Roads,
Albany, Auckland 1310, New Zealand

Penguin Books Ltd, Registered Offices:
80 Strand, London WC2R 0RL, England

First published by Roc, an imprint of New American Library,
a division of Penguin Group (USA) Inc.

First Printing, February 2004
10 9 8 7 6 5 4 3 2 1

To Bernice Bacchus,
My Grandmother,
1908–2001
Practically Perfect in Every Way

ACKNOWLEDGMENTS

I would like to thank the following friends, colleagues, relatives, and institutions for their kind contributions to my novel: Robert J. Sawyer, Carolyn Clink, Peter Halasz, Joanie Mackay, Claire Mackay, A. V. Phillips, The Merril Collection, Bakka-Phoenix Books, Joshua Bilmes, and Laura Anne Gilman.

PART ONE

EMZ

Chapter 1

"My fellow Defederates," said CEO Graham Croft, his face neatly framed by the dropdown screen, "at 9:46 this morning the DDF received word from *Advance 5* that a new alien weapons platform has entered the solar system. SEASEZ, Eurocorp, and the New Transvaal have confirmed the sighting. Analysis indicates that this new AWP is the oldest one we've seen so far, that it's a lot bigger than the abandoned ones in orbit around Earth, and that it may represent an offensive threat a hundred times greater than the threat we faced from the aliens ten years ago."

As Alex floated in the orbiting *Utility 7* with his coworkers, Jon and Ruth, he watched his first cousin, Graham Croft, the most powerful man in the country, address the nation on the dropdown about this new alien threat. His palms grew cold. He swallowed. The aliens were back?

"Initial trajectory estimates are inconclusive," continued Graham, "but we believe the AWP will make a close flyby of Mars. The Martians may mount a reconnaissance mission. Whether they seek to gain a military advantage over us by mounting a preemptive reconnaisance mission, I can't say. Earth may mount a mission as well. DDF mission planners are drafting possible rendezvous scenarios, and have been in contact with allied mission planners in Eurocorp, SEASEZ, and the New Transvaal."

Graham gazed at the gathered press corps, his blue suit making his shoulders look massive, his pink complexion accentuating the great vitality of his general appearance. Alex caught Jon glancing at him— maybe Jon was looking for a family resemblance. There wasn't one, except for maybe the eyes. Or maybe Jon was just plain scared, and was glancing around for reassurance. A fatherly smile came to Graham's face.

"Friends, we are again facing history," he said. "The forces of the Defederacy and its allies have been put on highest alert. I've been in contact with my fellow CEOs in the Defederacies of Corpus Christi, Juan de Fuca, Baja California, and Hawaii. We are but five small city-states in what was once a great and powerful nation, but together we are strong, and we shall rise to defeat this enemy, just as another generation did a decade ago. I have sent emissaries into the leaderless regions of the Emergency Medical Zones in the hope we may gain support and cooperation from those tragic young victims. Antinanogen protocols have been implemented in all Five Defederacies. Eurocorp, SEASEZ, and the New Transvaal have taken similar measures to protect their own territories. The aliens have proven themselves slow and ineffective in orbital combat. We shall weather their storm, just as we did last time, and we *will* emerge victorious."

The CEO of the Defederacy opened the floor to

questions. Alex and his two coworkers hung there in free fall. The news was dire. They were shocked. Ruth's face had gone white and Jon stared at the dropdown in disbelief. Alex felt his own heart pounding. It didn't matter that they would most probably be safe in the enclave of the Defederacy. The aliens had come again, and they all feared them as much as they hated them.

Jon turned to Alex. "Your cousin's good," he said.

Alex studied his cousin, proud of the man. Graham was so calm and collected, so brave in the face of this new threat. Alex struggled to assimilate the news. He took a few deep breaths and eased his shoulders. He could hardly believe they were facing the aliens again. It was a fear that gripped him in the pit of his stomach. At the same time he now considered the implications of this new AWP for the Alien Branch as a whole, *his* Branch, his small empire within that vast network of loosely connected empires, the Information Systems Service. He forced his fear away and concentrated on what his professional response might be. How could he mount any effective response when cutbacks had been so extreme? The Branch faced equipment failure. It faced layoffs. It faced downsizing. With the aliens defeated ten years ago, the Megaplex now wanted to close the Branch. But with the aliens coming back, maybe the Megaplex would rethink its plans for the Branch.

"I just had a thought," he said.

"What?" asked Ruth.

"This actually might be a *good* thing for the Branch," he said. "I bet by the end of the week the CEO signs for more funding."

Yes, of course, Graham would *have* to give them

more funding now. Maybe even the Defederacy Defense Force would kick in some money. He glanced at Graham, up there on the dropdown screen. Would he go for it? Graham was fiscally draconian, not known for opening his purse strings. Yet this was big, and Graham would have to respond to it or face the political fallout. Also, the DDF was going to ask for experts again, and Alex was the Defederacy's foremost expert on alien tech. They were going to *need* him again, he thought. He was going to be indispensable. His fear of a moment ago was replaced with a growing excitement. Jon and Ruth gazed at him expectantly. He outlined his reasoning.

"We've got something coming straight at us," he said. "It's big, it's old, and it's terrifying. They're going to need people to figure out how it works." He glanced out *Utility 7*'s window, where he saw Hurricane Jonelia spinning daintily in the Atlantic. "I'm going to push Max Morrow on this. I'm going to set up a meeting, and I'm going to have him talk to Graham about it. I'm going to argue that we need new funding and a freeze on layoffs if we're going to tackle this thing effectively. I'm going to make Max understand that we *have* to work on this thing, that it's in the interests of national security. They've got to go for it. This is all terrible news, I'm the first to admit that, and I hate it as much as the next person. But as much as I hate it, come this time next year, we still might have our jobs. Come this time next year, we might be in the thick of things again."

A few hours later, Alex, floating high above the Lesser Antilles, wired a release charge to abandoned Alien Weapons Platform 237, a derelict piece of junk from the war ten years ago. The battered old AWP was as big as a battleship, made of a hard enamel material, and looked like two wedding cakes stuck end to end. Jon inspected the frag net. Ruth was inside *Utility 7*, monitoring their operations from the Command Module.

"Are we ready?" asked Alex.

"It'll hold," said Jon.

"Then let's get behind the shield."

"They should give us a new net," said Jon. "This one's falling apart."

"If Graham goes for new funding, we'll buy lots of new nets."

Alex gave his pack a boost and eased toward the shield. Jon stayed where he was, looking for blisters, bubbles, or leaks in the frag net's clear membrane.

"Jon?" said Alex. "Are you coming?"

Jon took one last look, then gave his pack a burst.

"We're taking our chances, no matter how much we fix that net," he said. He maneuvered behind the shield. "I'd hate for any Number 17 to get into permanent orbit."

Hurricane Jonelia swirled in the Atlantic below them, a gentle white pinwheel nudging ever closer to the Defederacy of Delaware. Alex looked at the AWP. The AWP was beautiful. Why couldn't the average person on the street see what he saw in such a superbly engineered but enigmatic piece of machinery? Where had all the public enthusiasm of ten years ago gone? Why couldn't people be interested in it the way he was? Maybe with this new AWP, public interest, if not outright public fear, would return. Public fear would translate into money. And that would mean better frag nets.

"We might as well go ahead and hope it holds," said Alex.

"What choice do we have?" asked Jon.

Alex detonated the charge.

A small controlled blast came from the AWP. A wisp of white gas floated into space. Pink goop spread in syrupy streams, breaking apart into misshapen spheres, like balloons at a birthday party. The spheres drifted to the frag net, pulled there by preset positive and negative charges. The net caught the globules and congealed them into a pool. But then the net gave on one side. Alex tensed while Jon headed over.

Alex hesitated. "Jon, be careful."

"It's herniated," said Jon.

The pink goop shifted dangerously close to the edge of the net. Was it his own failing, Alex wondered, that he should be so afraid of Number 17, or did Jon just have a naturally reckless streak? Jon maneuvered behind the net, even as more Number 17 splashed into its clear, quavering skin. The support specialist pulled out a roll of electrically charged tape and repaired the herniated section. Alex gave his pack a burst and joined Jon. He took out his own spool and helped with the repair.

"Sorry, Jon," he said.

Jon gave him a concerned look. "It's all right. I know how you feel about this stuff."

Alex concentrated on fixing the net. "I don't know which is worse," he said. "Number 17 or Omnifix."

Jon ripped off a long strip of tape and reinforced the bulge. "God, these aliens. I hate them. I'm glad they're gone."

"It looks like they're coming back," said Alex.

Alex put another strip of tape on the net. He glanced at the pink, quavering Number 17. For all his fear of the stuff, he was fascinated by it. Another piece of alien tech, and alien tech was his life. He smoothed the tape over, made sure it adhered strongly.

"How's that?" he asked. "Does that look good?"

Jon glanced over. "It should hold," he said. "At least for this batch."

Later that day, back on Earth, the maglev scooted north at three hundred miles per hour through the First, Second, and Third Carolinian Emergency Medical Zones. Alex looked out at the rain. He saw a few old hovercars floating along the sky roads above the train tube, rusted and cumbersome hulks with stabilizers on full against Jonelia's winds. He saw a few Number 16s, victims of the aliens' strategic strike ten years ago, standing in an abandoned lot next to the tracks, faces preternaturally white in the surrounding gray. He thought of his son, Daryl, now living with Jill and Tony on Tony's cargo ship on the shore of Chesapeake Bay. Daryl, the light of his life, but now a Number 16 too, caught in the Bombardment while visiting his grandfather in the former Pennsylvania. Was Daryl really eighteen? And because of Nanogen 16 did he have only twelve years left to live? Alex shook his head. It was hard, knowing he was going to outlive his son by several decades. He had to agree with Jon. He hated the aliens.

Fifteen minutes later, the Defederacy's high walls came into view. The maglev approached like a bullet, sped right through the checkpoint, and in seconds was inside. Towers rose all around him, most of them a hundred stories high, made of lightweight super-hard oriented plastic. Hovercars, trucks, and buses intersected along the multilevel skyroutes like an organized swarm of fireflies, lights twinkling in the gloom. Billboards floated by advertising Fuji Holofilm, the new Ford Pegasus, and Fiesta Travel Packages to the Moon. As the maglev slowed, Alex's ears popped against the tube's braking pressure.

He caught the 42A hoverbus to the Level Sixty-three Skywalk. From there he strolled through the Potomac Heights Shopping Mall, stopping to look at shoes, then took the moving sidewalk to the midlevel lobby of Lincoln Towers. He rode the elevator to the hundred-twentieth floor of the south tower and walked to his small but prestigiously located dwelling. He opened the door and went inside. He stopped. Every so often the silence of the place bothered him. He took off his coat and hung it up. This wasn't his plan, to come home to an empty condo like this night after night. But Jill was with Tony now, even though things weren't the best between them, and he would just have to get used to it. Silence, at times, had its virtues.

He retracted the dropdown from its ceiling slot and turned to the News Channel to see if they had any more coverage on the AWP.

There was a new development. The Martians had announced plans to fast-track a small reconnaissance probe to the AWP within the next couple of days. Rendezvous, thanks to sublight drives on both spacecraft, was expected as early as next week. The News Channel showed the first image of the AWP, just a pixilated white blob, still too far away, out beyond Neptune, to show any real definition. Firm figures were now available. The AWP was fifteen hundred years old, well over a thousand years older than any of the smaller abandoned AWPs in the solar system. It was two to three kilometers across, gargantuan compared to the others. The voice-over recapped the details of the story thus far, and added that better pictures would be available once ground-control scientists had rotated the Number Three Lens on *Advance 5*, enabling not only a greater magnification but also enhanced holo-optics.

Alex switched the dropdown off. How could he hate the aliens so much, yet be so fascinated by all the junk they had left behind? How could he spend hours and hours enthralled by the technological detritus of a race from a distant star when they had turned his son into a Number 16, Reba into a Number 17, and his wife into another man's woman? There he went thinking of Reba again. *Alex, you're not supposed to think of Reba. You said you were never going to think of Reba again. Thinking of Reba just hurts too much.* Because weren't the aliens to blame for that too? Destroying Reba? Dismantling Reba molecule by molecule? No, he wasn't supposed to think about her. But in this empty condo, he sometimes couldn't help it.

He got up and walked to his curio cabinet, an old piece salvaged from his divorce eight years ago. On top lay a stack of old photographs. He found one of Daryl. Daryl was ten years old and stood with his back to the Atlantic. He had reddish hair, like Jill's, but was tall, like Alex. Alex loved his son so much it hurt. He found a photograph of his ex-wife, Jill. She stood with Tony on the bow of the *Beelzebub*, Tony's one-hundred-and-thirty-foot freighter. They

11

both wore orange windbreakers. They looked happy. Alex was happy for them. But he missed Jill, at least the old Jill—Jill as she had been before Daryl got sick, before the whole Number 16 thing had ruined their marriage.

He shuffled through the photographs one more time and found one of Reba. She wore a DDF uniform. She was pretty, had short coppery hair, freckles across her nose, and green eyes that were at once playful and serious. Why did the aliens save Number 17 for soldiers, and Number 16 for civilians? One would think they had some grand master plan with such a use-specific strategy. But who knew why the aliens did what they did? Reba. She was like a gift. Why did she ever join the Defederacy Defense Force? And why did she have to become a Number 17? He missed Reba. Reba was like his second chance after Jill. Now she, too, was gone. And not all the alien junk in the solar system could make up for that.

Chapter 2

Because Max Morrow was away in Eurocorp on ISS business, Alex didn't have his meeting with the Information Systems Service boss for another ten days.

"I'm glad we finally found a chance to talk, Max," said Alex as he entered Max's office.

Max was a hale man in his mid-fifties, handsome, broad-faced, dark, with impressively white teeth. He wore an expensive linen suit, an import from the Southeast Asia Special Economic Zone—SEASEZ— where all the best clothes came from these days.

"Sit down, Alex," said Max.

Alex sat down. He forced himself to take the initiative.

"The Alien Branch is gearing up for this new AWP, Max, and we're eager to provide whatever technical and research assistance might be needed."

Max contemplated the chunky gold ring on his finger. "An interesting development," he said. "Any ideas about it?"

Alex leaned forward. "I can't help thinking that

this new AWP might have a special function . . . over and above its usual function as a weapons platform."

Max raised his eyebrows. "How so?" he asked.

"Its great size and age means it's been in service a long time . . . and to keep something so old so well maintained suggests its original cost must have been staggering, and that therefore it's meant to be permanent, and used by successive generations of aliens. It could be a mothership of sorts. If that's the case, they probably have it booby-trapped to the hilt. The Alien Branch will need at least a year to disarm it. That's after the DDF chases away any aliens on board. Then there's the six months we'll need to deploy a Utility in a tandem orbit with it. This will all cost money, of course, but I believe that because of the seriousness of the situation, the Megaplex will be forthcoming with the necessary funds."

Max's lips came together and his nostrils flared as he took a deep breath.

"And why . . . why do you think it's arrived in our solar system at this particular juncture," he asked, "ten years after we defeated them? At this point Graham says it could represent a threat a hundred times greater than the one we faced a decade ago. But we really don't have much hard evidence to back that up."

Alex's eyes narrowed as he ran his hand through his dark hair. He again felt some fear, the uneasiness everybody all over the world must be feeling.

"I'm not sure," he said. "But we can't rule out the possibility of another strategic strike. Whether they're going to hit us again with Number 16 remains to be seen, but I think it's prudent that the Five Defederacies have implemented their antinanogen protocols.

Have any of the Covert Series eavesdropped on the Martian probe yet? I understand it rendezvoused with the AWP two days ago. If we're going to find out anything, that's the way to go."

Max leaned forward and rubbed his hands together. "I'm glad you mentioned the Martian probe, Alex."

Alex was caught off guard by Max's equivocal tone. "You are?"

"Alex, *Covert 9* has in fact intercepted a great deal of data from the Martian probe. It's allowed us to make crucial decisions about the AWP. I'm sure you'll be relieved to hear that the AWP *doesn't* represent a threat after all. The Megaplex feels so confident about this that they've put Defederacy troops on stand-down. The AWP's going to miss Earth by sixty-two million miles. All its weapons systems are off-line. It's unmanned. Its drive system is on automatic, and has just enough thrust to keep it from forming a permanent orbit in the solar system. It's going to sail right on through, Alex. It's nothing more than a piece of scrap. Murray City on Mars speculates it was perhaps meant to be used in the conflict ten years ago, but that it was damaged en route, and subsequently abandoned. It's not coming anywhere near us. Once it passes, we're never going to see it again. Which means we're not going to do anything about it. Which means we're going to continue with our current plans. And that includes our plans to downsize the Alien Branch. I'm sorry, Alex."

Alex looked out the window where rain from Layla, the season's latest hurricane, fell in silvery squalls. His jaw tightened as he struggled to curb his disappointment.

15

"There's no easy way to put this, Alex," continued Max, "so I might as well be frank." He paused. "I've been meaning to tell you for a while. I didn't want one of my staff telling you by mistake, or it somehow getting back to you through the grapevine—I wanted to do it personally—but what with one thing or another, we always keep missing each other, and I didn't get the chance. Then when I saw your e-mail, I realized how hopeful you were, and I thought I'd better put a stop to it as soon as I could."

Alex grinned numbly. "I'm not following you," he said, but knew what was coming well enough.

"Alex . . . I'm sorry . . . I wish I didn't have to do this . . . but I'm afraid I'm going to have to let you go."

Alex's throat tightened. He fought to remain composed.

"Max . . . this is . . . I thought we were going to talk about the AWP. I thought I was coming here to get some good news. I thought you were going to tell me that I was going to get a chance to work on the AWP."

"We have to make cuts, Alex," said Max, his voice firm. "You're one of my best people. I'm the first to admit that. And I know you've put your heart and soul into the Branch, and that's why this is so hard for me, but I'm afraid this is the way it has to be."

"But I'm your leading exotechnologist," Alex said, struggling to keep himself under control. "I've had a higher success rate than anybody else in figuring out how this stuff works. I figured out their sublight drive. Because of me, it takes only a month to get to Mars. And what about the glowball?" He gestured at the ceiling. "You have a healthy specimen up there

yourself. Do you know how much we save in light-
ing costs because of those things? Then there's mind-
pool. That's been a marketing boon to the Defederacy."

Max put his hands flat against his desk as a few
pained lines came to his brow.

"I know, Alex. But we still have to continue our
downsizing. We have direct orders from the Megaplex to reallocate resources toward the Martian war
effort. What's the point of funding an Alien Branch
when we first have to undercut the Martian ability
to retrieve alien equipment to start with? Once that's
done—once our interdiction campaign succeeds and
we've hobbled Mars's ability to scavenge for the
stuff, and stopped them from pirating it away from
us—the Megaplex may look at renewed funding for
the Alien Branch. Right now, it's too costly to retrieve
anything, especially when we have to drag it back
under armed escort so the Martians won't steal it
from us."

Alex felt warm. "I wasn't expecting this for at least
another two years, Max," he said.

"Neither was I. At least not for you. But then I got
this memo from the Megaplex. I tried to argue with
them. I asked them why not fire Jon Lewis? He's
only technical support. Or why not Ruthy?"

"No," said Alex, his voice firm. "If someone's got
to go, I'd sooner it be me. I don't want Jon or Ruth
losing their jobs until they absolutely have to."

Max shrugged. "Their time will come."

"I'm glad they singled me out instead."

"I'm not." Max sat back and sighed. "But as I say,
I received a direct order from the Megaplex itself to
terminate you specifically. Don't ask me why. Maybe

they want to send a message. Maybe by targeting senior scientific staff they want to impress upon the public that they're serious about dismantling the Alien Branch as a way to stop the hemorrhaging of treasury coffers. Whatever the reason, the memo came directly from the CEO's office, so I have no choice, I have to let you go."

Alex's eyes widened. "Graham's office sent you a direct order?" he asked.

This news was entirely unexpected.

"Yes."

He was confused. This didn't seem right. This seemed like a mistake.

"Why would Graham target me specifically? I'm his cousin. Not that that should make any difference, but why didn't he let the usual channels handle the dismissal?"

Max's brow settled. "That's something only he can answer. I'm sorry, Alex."

"It's not your fault, Max."

"I know you have a lot of medical bills, what with your son."

"I've been frugal," said Alex. "I've put some away."

"But still . . . I'm not sure what job opportunities we have here in Delaware right now. At least for a scientist at your level. You may have to look at one of the other Defederacies. And getting a residency permit in any of those will take at least six months. Even then, there's no guarantee of a job."

Alex left Max's office bewildered. He walked with distracted steps down the hall. He tapped his fingers together, his mind playing over and over again his interview with Max. A memo from Graham's office? He felt betrayed. He gazed at his reflection in the mirrored wall. He looked pale in the dim lights, and the slight curve in the glass accentuated his tallness and thinness, exaggerated the distressed look on his face. Low-level panic clouded his thoughts. He pushed his way out the door.

Rain from Layla lashed his face. He didn't immediately take the moving sidewalk. He needed time to think. What was he going to do? Would he have to move to one of the other Defederacies, as Max had suggested? Max was right. Where was he going to get a job in Delaware when jobs were so scarce? He would hate to leave Daryl and Jill. He had to fight this. He had to get in touch with Graham. Find out why Graham had targeted him specifically. It didn't make sense. Even considering that business with his father fifteen years ago, it still didn't make sense. He had to speak to Graham.

Alex looked over the railing into the dark abyss. Rain fell through sixty levels of skystreets. Had he done something to antagonize Graham? He held his hand out into the rain. Far below, he heard a large machine, metal scraping against metal, echoing up from the street. Alex felt stabbed in the back. He couldn't believe Graham would do this to him. Not after all the great summers they had spent together in Unionville. He got on the moving sidewalk and headed toward the hoverbus platform. He reached the platform just as the hoverbus floated out of the rainy darkness. He felt flummoxed. He paid the twenty-dollar fare, got on the bus, and sat down. He didn't know what he was going to do.

He looked out the window at the city. Myriad skywalks connected the hundreds of dark skyscrapers. Hovercars came and went from various platforms, merging with other sky traffic. A floating billboard, held aloft by alien glowballs, advertised Coca-Cola in the traditional red and white stripes. He picked out Lincoln Towers, its twin white obelisks rising distinctively through the thatch of smaller black buildings to the west. He just wanted to go home, crawl into his condo, and lick his wounds. But he knew he had to go to the *Beelzebub*, out to Hurlock, and tell Jill and Daryl the bad news. So he rode right past Lincoln Towers, getting on with the grim business of damage control.

He looked up at the hoverbus's dropdown as the news came on, and lo and behold, there was Graham, telling the Defederacy that the AWP "didn't represent a threat," and that the Defense Force had determined that the AWP was going to "drift right on through," his face beaming, as if he had been personally responsible for this turn of events. He remembered this about Graham as a teen, always claiming credit whenever he could, building himself up at every opportunity, taking advantage of what he called the "easy wins." Alex glanced around the hoverbus. He saw measurable relief on the faces of the other passengers. He also saw admiration and respect for Graham. Alex was glad the AWP wasn't a threat. But he still couldn't believe Graham would take his job away from him.

He got off the 42A hoverbus at the Potomac Heights platform and descended in the express elevator to the subway. The subway took him out to Hurlock. From the subway station he made his way down to the harbor by foot. The buildings in Hurlock were old, from the age of glass and steel. A great number of ground-based vehicles clogged the streets. Outdoor vendors thronged the sidewalk. A man stood behind a barbecue selling grilled sardines. Another sold T-shirts. Another sold jewelry-sized glowballs.

He soon came to the *Beelzebub*, Tony Sartis's fifty-year-old coastal freighter, a medium-sized tub with a white wheelhouse, a green hull pocked with wide continents of rust, and an anchor festooned with black sea grapes. He saw Tony in the wheelhouse watching the dropdown. Tony turned from the dropdown and spotted him coming along the pier. Alex waved. Tony waved back and came out to the railing.

"They're both below," called the skipper.

"Thanks," Alex called back.

"I'll be down in a minute. I'm just checking this weather. It looks like Layla's going to clear off."

Alex approached the wheelhouse. "How's Jill?" he asked. "Is she in a good mood?"

"I've seen her in better," said Tony. "I've just gotten a new contract. A company called Servitech wants me to ship out to the Arlington EMZ, and of course Jill doesn't want to go anywhere near that place. It's a bit of a risky contract. She's mad at me because I've already signed and I don't even have my crew yet. I'm having a tough time finding crew. No one wants to go to the EMZ. It makes people nervous."

"But she's not in a *foul* mood, is she?" asked Alex.

"No," said Tony. "I've managed to smooth things over for the time being. Why?"

"Because I've got some bad news for her."

Alex boarded the *Beelzebub* and made his way to

the companionway at the stern. He descended the companionway to the first deck. He glimpsed his son, Daryl, in the captain's cabin, glued to his array of three computers. He found Jill making supper in the narrow mess galley, stirring a great kettle of vegetable stew.

"You're just in time," said Jill. "I'm about to serve."

"I've got some bad news," he told Jill.

She put down her spoon. "What?" she asked.

"Max just let me go. I'm out of a job."

Jill ran her hand through her shoulder-length brown hair. "I thought you told me you still had two years."

"That's what I thought too."

Jill's eyes narrowed with dismay. "Oh, Alex, I'm sorry."

He shrugged, still feeling ambushed by the whole thing. "I thought I'd better let you know. I don't anticipate a money problem. I've got my severance package, and I've got a little put away, so I don't think my Daryl contributions will be affected."

"Don't even think about that," she said. "Tony and I can swing it for a while."

Alex heard Tony coming down the companionway. Jill's common-law husband came into the kitchen and immediately saw their long faces.

"So," he said. "What's up?"

"Alex just lost his job," said Jill.

Tony's shoulders sank. "You're kidding. I thought you had at least two years."

"That's what I thought," said Alex. "But Max got some kind of memo from the Megaplex. They want me to go next."

"From the Megaplex?" said Jill.

"That's right. As a matter of fact, it came right from the CEO's office."

"Graham sent it?" said Jill.

"That's what Max says."

Jill's eyes widened in mystification. "Why would Graham get personally involved?"

"I don't know. Maybe he remembers Dad. I like to think that's all ancient history, but maybe it's not. Let's face it, my dad tried to block his rise to power."

"I realize that, Alex, but what did *you* have to do with that? You were still in school."

"I know, but Graham's a Croft, and Crofts remember things. That ethics package my dad introduced, for instance. All the press conferences Dad held. And that big conflict-of-interest thing. Then when Dad tried to muster support among other board members to turf Graham out . . ." He shook his head. "I don't know. As much as I like to put the best spin on things, I'm now starting to think my relations with Graham, ever since Dad tried to foul things up for him, haven't been the best. One thing about Graham, he holds grudges, and now that Dad's dead . . . maybe he's transferred his grudge to me."

"Yes, but he would never hold a grudge against you, Alex," insisted Jill. "What about all those wonderful summers you and he spent together in Unionville, fishing on Lake Anderson?"

"I know."

"And what about all those road trips you went on through the Alleghenies? Graham always took you to the state fair three or four times a week whenever he came out there. Graham was like a big brother to you."

"I know. We had some good times. I practically worshiped the man. But people change. And Graham's changed." Alex's eyes narrowed. He tapped the table a few times, again puzzled by the whole thing. "I just don't know why he's even bothered with this, that's all. Why would the highest office in the land get involved in something routine like an ISS layoff? I'm small potatoes."

"I thought the Megaplex allowed the ISS to run its own operations independently," said Tony.

"For the most part they do," said Alex. "But now Graham's office has taken a direct hand in targeting me specifically for the next layoff. You think he would have better things to do than to pick on his own cousin."

Jill frowned. "Graham's a schmuck."

"I'm sure he has his reasons," said Alex. "I just wish I knew what they were. I remember that about him when we were young. Always having reasons for things, mostly secret reasons."

"You should phone him and find out why he's done this," suggested Jill. "You're the Defederacy's leading exotechnologist. I can't see why he would let you go before the others."

"I'm going to phone Graham's office tomorrow."

Daryl walked in. Alex smiled. Nothing made him happier than to see his son.

"Dad just lost his job," said Jill, her voice indignant.

"Really?" said Daryl.

Daryl's hair was long, like Tony's. Not that long hair bothered Alex, but he would have preferred Daryl's hair short, like his.

"We knew it was coming," said Alex.

"So are you going to find another?" asked Daryl.

"I'll have to. Only I don't know where. Government postings for senior scientists are few and far between in Delaware right now. I might have to consider going to one of the other Defederacies. Or maybe even to Eurocorp."

"Why don't you find a job in the private sector?" suggested Daryl.

Alex stared at his son. He wondered why he hadn't thought of this before.

"That's not a bad idea," he said. Alex felt suddenly better. The private sector had whole warehouses full of alien junk licensed to them by the ISS. "In fact, that's a great idea." He mussed Daryl's hair. And realized his son was too old for mussed hair. "I'm going to look into it. If I can get a job in the private sector, I can stay here in Delaware with you guys. And I would definitely want that."

When he finally left the *Beelzebub* a few hours later, he strolled back to the subway station. He was caught up in his own thoughts. His insides felt like they had been twisted around, but the initial shock of the thing had worn off, and he felt his presence of mind returning, enough so that he could evaluate the unknown horizons of his personal future. The streets weren't as crowded now. He saw some Number 17s walk by, hulking brutes, half cybernetic, half human. He thought of the pink goop. No wonder he was so afraid of it. All it took was a molecule of the stuff and he could end up like them. Or like Reba.

His step faltered. He had to stop thinking of Reba. But no one could comfort him the way Reba could. Up ahead, he saw the subway station with its red-

and-gold sign glowing in the mist. He had the crazy idea that he might knock on Reba's door tonight. She lived around here.

Instead of going to the subway, he turned left at the next street, Newcastle Road, and followed it past a series of hundred-year-old high-rises, their plastic walls looking a little the worse for wear, peeling in spots. A dog came out of an alley, sniffed at his heels, then trotted across the street. He turned right on Seaford and took it all the way to Madison. He didn't feel safe here, in this part of Hurlock, especially this late at night. So many Number 17s lived around here.

The high-rises on Madison, twenty stories tall, their black plastic faded to gray, all identical, looked more like military bunkers than apartment buildings. Reba's building was on the corner. As he got closer, he felt his heart race. He didn't care what she looked like, or how Omnifix, the nanogen the DDF employed to fight the Number 17 pink goop, had turned her into a machine, how it had taken the luster out of her soul, and the music out of her voice. He *wanted* to see her. He hadn't seen her in eighteen months. That was far too long. Did she remember their time together? He reached her building and went into the vestibule. He pulled out his wallet and withdrew the scuffed access card she had given him a couple of years ago. He swiped the card through the scanner. The door popped open. He entered the lobby. Litter lay strewn about. Someone had written REPEAL THE PUBLIC SAFETY ACT in black felt marker on the far wall. The place smelled of old cooking and strong detergent.

He got on the elevator and rode it to the seventh floor. He was giddy with anticipation. Reba would have good advice about his job loss. She would comfort him. Most of all, he would feel an echo of that time they had shared together. That might be just the thing to carry him through all this.

He came to apartment 714 and knocked on the door, a grin coming to his face. But Reba didn't answer. Another Number 17 did. A man. An older veteran. Omnifix had nearly transformed the man into a cyborg. What gazed out at Alex looked more robotic than human.

"I'm looking for Reba Norton," said Alex.

The Number 17, nearly twice Alex's size, shook his head. "There's no one here by that name." His voice was synthesized.

"She used to live here," Alex said, not wanting to give up. "Eighteen months ago was the last time I spoke to her."

"I moved in five months ago. I have no idea who the previous tenant was."

The man shut the door. Alex stood there staring at it. Its gray paint was chipped in spots. His disappointment was acute. He turned around and headed for the elevators, his step heavy, his thoughts bleak. One word from Reba, and he could have faced all this a lot better.

Chapter 3

"I'm sorry, Dr. Denyer, but I can't put you through at the moment," said the woman in the Megaplex Inquiry Center. "He's in a meeting right now."

She gazed at Alex with a neutral grin from the small video monitor attached to his phone.

"Did he get my message yesterday?" asked Alex, doing his best to hide his exasperation.

"Yes, we passed it on to him," she said.

"Because he didn't return my call yesterday either," he said. "Or the day before."

"The CEO's office receives hundreds of calls a day, Dr. Denyer. CEO Croft can't return all of them. We screen most of them to his administrative director. Would you like to speak to his administrative director?"

"I've already spoken to Claude," he said. "He hasn't given me anything I don't already know."

"Then I'm afraid you're going to have to wait until the CEO gets back to you."

"Has he issued any policy bulletins about staffing cutbacks at the ISS?" he asked.

"You would have to speak to his administrative director."

"You haven't seen anything over the corporate intranet, have you?" he asked.

"We have limited access in the inquiry center," she said. "You probably have greater access than we do."

Alex hesitated. "Okay," he said. "But could you tell Graham it's urgent, and that I would like to speak to him as soon as possible?"

"We'll let him know," she said.

Her face faded from the video monitor.

Why wouldn't Graham return his calls? He rubbed his hands together and looked out the window of his eighty-eighth-floor office. The morning sunshine was brilliant—Layla had indeed cleared off. Chesapeake Bay was frothy and blue below. The Defederacy's spires, all of them plastic forms in this part of the city, rose like a polymer paradise. He wasn't one to see conspiracies in everything but, really, what was he to think? That Graham shouldn't return his calls after three tries he found downright suspicious.

Jon came over to his desk. "So?" he said.

"Still no go."

Jon raised his palms. "Why won't he talk to you?"

"I spoke to Claude Pierce."

"And what did Claude say?" asked Jon.

"He said he would look into it."

"I can't help thinking of your father." Jon looked out the window, where a rainbow glimmered against dark clouds over Chesapeake Bay. "How he tried to block Graham's rise to power all those years ago."

"I hope that doesn't have anything to do with it," said Alex. "I'm beginning to think Graham was given some wrong information by someone, and he had to make a quick decision, maybe the wrong decision. I'm sure once I get in touch with him, we'll straighten the whole thing out."

"*If* you get in touch with him."

"I've left three messages. I don't think he's going to ignore me forever."

"By the way, Ruth and I want to take you out tonight. For your last day. We thought we'd go to the Game Hub. Can you make it?"

"Count me in."

When Jon had gone back to his desk, Alex booted up his computer. He thought he'd better tidy up his files before his departure.

What he found disturbed him. Someone had broken through his Security 1 encryption codes and wiped clean all his most sensitive files. Ten years of work, gone, just like that, vaulted away, according to his system memory, onto the ISS mainframe, with no electronic signature anywhere, and no hint of who might be responsible for the trespass.

He immediately got on his vidphone and called Max Morrow's office.

"Meet me on the roof," said Max. He looked nervous.

"The roof?" asked Alex.

"And don't tell anyone you're coming."

Ten minutes later, he met Max on the roof of the ISS building. This high, on the 120th floor, the wind was brisk, and the view spectacular. The Defederacy stretched in a gleaming thicket of plastic skyscrapers for miles in every direction. The vista was dizzying, the sky traffic as ordered as popcorn tinsel on a Christmas tree, the Megaplex visible as a shining gold monument to the north on the banks of the

Chester River, brilliant in the morning sunshine. Max stood at the railing. He looked tired, harried. His fine linen clothes were rumpled, as if he'd slept in them.

"Max?" said Alex.

Max turned. He contemplated Alex with obvious concern, his expression grim, his eyes preoccupied.

"It's a bit breezy up here," he said.

Alex joined Max at the rail. "Max, what happened?"

Max shook his head, slid his hands into his pockets, and looked out at the panoramic view.

"I'm sorry about the unauthorized delete, Alex," he said. "The Megaplex hacked remotely into the system early this morning before I got here. I wasn't consulted." He shook his head. He had great raccoon eyes. "They just went ahead and did it."

"Why are we meeting on the roof?"

Max rested his hands on the railing and gazed out at the bay. "We're meeting on the roof because you're my friend," he said.

Max's fatalistic tone puzzled Alex. "Thanks, Max, I appreciate that."

"There's a new kind of paint, Alex. I don't know whether you've heard of it. It's got nano-transmitters embedded right into the mix. I've just had my office painted. I didn't authorize or request a paint job. Environmental Services just came in and did it, even had a req with my signature on it. I don't remember signing anything. That's why we're on the roof."

Alex gazed at his boss with a great deal of concern. "You look tired, Max."

"Alex . . . the sooner you leave . . . you should be happy you're going."

This didn't sound like Max at all.

"What's going on?"

Because he was truly flummoxed, had a sense of intrigue, but couldn't even begin to dress it in concrete detail, felt innocent, isolated in his own scientific world, a rank amateur when it came to behind-the-scenes maneuvering. Max continued to gaze at the skyline. Forty floors down, a dozen seagulls circled in the updraft, checkmarks of white and gray.

"You've been downgraded to a Security 5," said Max.

"I have?"

"The CEO's office did it."

Alex felt a sudden knot of anxiety in his chest. "I don't get this," he said. "Why is he doing this to me? What have I done?"

Every hour seemed to bring a new small calamity. They were slowly adding up to a tidal wave of calamities.

"Nothing, so far as I can see," said Max.

Alex stared over the railing, his eyes focusing on the middle distance. He pictured Graham: short, impeccably dressed, his blond hair smoothed back as if with shellac. Had Graham indeed been given erroneous and damning information? Or didn't he trust having another high-profile Denyer around? Media darling. That's what Graham had once called his father. And it was true—the media loved his father. Some of that media limelight had spilled onto Alex. He was a familiar face on the dropdown. But only when it came to scientific matters. What was Graham so nervous about?

Max managed to hoist a grin to his face. "How's your son?" he asked. "Is he okay?"

Alex cocked his brow. "Fine," he said, caught off

guard by the change of subject. "He's having minimal symptoms right now."

A gust of wind moaned around some of the utility structures on the roof.

"How old is he?" asked Max.

"Eighteen."

"That's a great age," said Max. A red balloon floated by, a helium-filled escapee from some public relations event below. "I'm sorry he's a Number 16, Alex."

Alex's throat tightened. "I am too," he said.

"And Jill's fine?" he asked. "She knows you have to leave the ISS?"

"She and Tony both know."

Alex wasn't sure why Max was asking him about his family.

Max sighed. "If I had a chance, I'd get out of here too," he said. "But I can't. I'm stuck."

Alex knew there was something Max wasn't telling him. He watched the red balloon drift further and further east, heading toward the Atlantic. If they were painting nano-transmitters onto his boss's walls—if they couldn't even trust Max Morrow, the most stalwart and trustworthy man in the Defederacy—what chance did he have?

"Max, what's going on?" he asked again.

A worried crease came to Max's brow. "It seems the Martians are trying to activate some of the AWP's systems," said Max. Another abrupt change of subject. Max was all over the place today. And he looked so nervous. "*Covert 9*'s detected increased energy emissions." Was Max telling him this for a reason, or was he just making conversation? "And *Covert 6* has intercepted encrypted software transmissions."

In any case, Alex was glad to learn anything he could about the AWP. "We're not exactly sure what they're trying to do, but it's got the Megaplex worried. Maybe that's why they're so jumpy all of a sudden. Maybe that's why they've painted my walls with nano-transmitters."

"I hope the Martians don't wreck the AWP," said Alex. "There's so much we could learn from it. We might at last squeak out more than just a few hints about alien culture, maybe even find out where they come from. Are they Aldebaranians? Are they Fomalhautians? I hate calling them Aliens, with a capital *A*. It violates my sense of the specific." He scratched his head. "Did any of the Coverts find out who Murray City assigned to the AWP?"

"Ariam Adurra," said Max.

Alex grinned as he thought of his Martian counterpart, a brilliant exotechnologist whose papers he had read with great admiration.

"She'll be careful," he said, relieved. "She's a great scientist. She'll document extensively. Even if the militarists end up wrecking the AWP, she'll have it all on file."

Max grew even more pensive.

"You have to be careful about praising her too highly when it comes to the media, Alex," said Max. "I've seen you on the dropdown. Tone it down a bit. I'm sure Graham doesn't appreciate it."

Alex felt this as another small calamity. "Is that why he . . ." He could scarcely go on. What was so wrong about praising Ariam Adurra? She was a great scientist.

"Just be careful," said Max. "Things have changed.

They're not like they were back when your father was on the Board."

At the Game Hub that night, two older men, wired, raced each other down the toughest rapids of the Zambezi River. A younger man, wired as well, duked it out with an unseen adversary in a round of Virtu-Champ. A group of twenty-somethings top-dogged against each other in a game of Cyber-Sopwith. Alex, Jon, and Ruth had just finished a game of mind-pool, and were heading toward the bar. Alex was beginning to think something was going on between Jon and Ruth. That was good. They were made for each other, and he was glad they were finally realizing it.

While he was at the bar, his pager beeped. He glanced at the small contraption and accessed the inbox. He selected text messaging and found a message from Concord Exotechnologies. He wasn't expecting an answer quite so soon, but here it was. He looked up at his friends.

"Concord got back to me," he said.

"Really?" said Ruth.

"They're giving me an interview."

Jon smiled. "You see? You're a hot property. You have nothing to worry about. Your reputation precedes you."

"Congratulations, Alex," said Ruth. "I hope you get it. You'd be able to stay in the Defederacy."

He nodded. He hoped he got it too. He didn't want to leave the Defederacy. His work life was changing, but that didn't mean his social and family life had to. Not if he had anything to do with it.

Chapter 4

Three individuals conducted his job interview at Concord Exotechnologies the following Tuesday morning: Vice President and COO Warren Green, Human Resources Representative Sylvia Karafilis, and Dr. Jacob Evelyn, Head of the Biologics Research Team. Dr. Evelyn, a slight, stooped man of sixty, reminding Alex of a small seabird, sat forward and eyed Alex with a preoccupied frown on his face.

"A most perplexing problem," said the doctor. "We've expended a lot of capital on these systems, but now we've hit this roadblock."

At the mention of capital, Warren Green, a heavyset man with a worried look on his face, shifted uncomfortably. Sylvia Karafilis sat with her legs crossed primly, a waferscreen in her lap.

"So much capital," continued Dr. Evelyn, "that we can't turn back now. Yet every week my instruments detect a lessening of function. I'm afraid if these systems ever contract a virus, the entire works will collapse."

Alex glanced at Vice President Green and Ms. Karafilis. Was the discussion getting too technical for them?

"I'm trying to remember our licensing deal with Concord," he said. "I believe the systems you refer to came from AWPs 43, 164, and 288."

"Yes," said Dr. Evelyn. "Any suggestions on how we can preserve function?"

"Yes," said Alex. "You can preserve function in those systems indefinitely by surgically grafting dormant backups to the ductal and venous ports. I believe the dormant backups came as part of the deal."

"Yes."

"The dormant systems are younger, and will extend the life of the systems by up to five years. When a younger system is exhausted, you'll then have to take another backup out of storage and graft again. You can maintain the current systems indefinitely if you graft repeatedly. In the meantime, you start a cloning program. You produce, in vitro, your own dormant backups before you exhaust the ones you have in cryogenic storage."

"Sounds expensive," said Warren Green.

"It is," admitted Alex. "But I was working on a more cost-efficient method before I left the ISS. I was trying to extend cell division, increase their replication levels to make these systems live longer. I've discovered that a certain alien fixer system can conceivably do this."

"How?" asked Dr. Evelyn.

"By maintaining telomeres."

Warren Green looked puzzled. "Telomeres?"

"A telomere is part of a chromosome. It shortens each time a cell divides. When it finally shortens completely, cells stop dividing and they die. One of these alien fixer systems produces an enzyme that looks like it might, if modified, halt this shortening. It could make other systems live longer because of this. It would be a lot cheaper than making cloned backups for surgical graft."

"If you join our staff," said Green, his eyes brightening, "you could follow that line of research. If it helps us save money, I'm all for it."

Alex's brow rose optimistically. "So you're offering me the job, then?"

"The board will have to rubber-stamp it, but in the meantime, if you get any other offers, let us know immediately. If we have to compete, we will." Green leaned back in his chair. "Now . . . if we're just about finished, Sylvia will show you around. I'm sure you're anxious to see our research laboratories. She'll also take you out to the warehouses, and give you a tour of all our amenities."

"I'd love to see everything," said Alex.

"Then away you go."

The Concord Research Laboratories were a lot smaller than the ISS ones. All the desks, equipment, and workstations were jammed close together, supplies stacked in every available space, lab personnel looking as if they couldn't move. Yet Alex saw everything he needed. He glanced at Ms. Karafilis. She was around thirty. Her body, aglow in green bodywrap, had all the usual surgical enhancements. She was perfect: athletic, slim, and alluring. But she seemed overly apologetic about the cramped conditions in the lab.

"This is good," he said, to put her mind at ease.

"We've budgeted for an expansion," she said, "but it's going to take two years to complete."

"I always like coming to any lab," he said. "It makes me feel like a kid in a candy store."

After the lab, they went to Warehouse One. The air inside was frosty, meant to preserve. He glanced around at all the alien tech. Here was a pile of Pleyer's Glands; over here, some Brachial Plating; and up on hooks, a number of cartilage systems coiled in spools. He saw a half dozen gyro-ducts, interfaces for AWP navigational networks and hubs. The warehouse was crammed with what looked like thousands of giant internal organs—the mysterious building blocks of alien biologics, a grisly and horrific sight to anyone who wasn't used to it. He saw none of the supportive cybernetic systems, the electronic and mechanical apparatus that, when added to the biologics, gave alien equipment its hybrid appearance.

"Where do you keep the cybernetics?" he asked.

"In Warehouse Two," she said. "But we focus mainly on this stuff. Even with cryogenics, it's not going to last forever. The mechanical and electrical components will keep. They have a longer shelf life. This is the stuff we really work on."

They toured Warehouse Two. He saw three sublight drives, some barometric stabilizers, and several optical components—lenses of exacting craftsmanship, sighting scopes he believed might have been used in the nanogen bombardment of ten years ago.

"You've got enough here to keep any scientist happy," he said.

"Why don't I take you to the parking lot and show you your car."

"I get a car?" Now he really did feel like a kid in a candy store.

"Yes."

"I'd *love* to see my car."

Ms. Karafilis took him to the parking lot.

"Senior employees always get a company car," she explained. "That one over there is earmarked for you."

Alex gazed at the hovercar, a Ford Phoenix, and realized that despite the cramped laboratories, the small scale of its storage facilities, and COO Green's apparent concern for the bottom line, Concord must have money after all. The ISS had never, not once, offered him a car in all the fifteen years he'd worked for them.

"That's a nice car," he said.

"Would you like to take it for a spin?" she asked.

The offer surprised him. "Sure. Why not?"

He ran his fingers along the sleek, oriented-plastic contour, admired the windfoil at the back, opened the hood, saw the hybrid fusion cell engine, the deuterium separator, the multidirectional thrust finder, the internal ramscoop, and the navigational motherboard. Oh, to escape the congestion of ground-based traffic. Was it any wonder hovercars were finally making inroads on the commercial market, even when they were so prohibitively expensive?

He got in. Ms. Karafilis got in beside him. He started the car. It purred. He keyed in some commands. No steering wheel, just a keyboard.

The Phoenix lifted, employing its particle-pulse technology, the reconversion scoops deploying at this low altitude, fanning out like fish fins, capturing expelled particles and feeding them back into the drive system. Navigational lasers directed the car to Titania Boulevard. Here, Titania Boulevard laser hookups engaged, and the Defederacy-wide traffic grid took over. He sat back and let the car drive itself.

"I guess your wife will be pleased," said Ms. Karafilis.

This obvious probe flattered him, especially because it came from such an attractive young woman.

"I'm not married," he said. "I'm divorced."

"Oh." This, too, was a little obvious.

He couldn't help thinking: *My life is changing.* Maybe it was about time he got another woman into it. If not Ms. Karafilis, then someone else. He was getting lonely at Lincoln Towers. When you lived by yourself, home was just a place to hang your hat.

He met Jon Lewis for lunch the following day.

"The laboratories are small," he told Jon, "but space is at a premium everywhere, so I'm willing to put up with that. The benefits are good and the salary is nearly double what I make at the ISS."

Jon leaned forward and pushed his soybean-and-seaweed salad aside. The sunlight, beaming down on their patio table, was bright, pleasant.

"So it sounds like you got it," said Jon.

"I think so. Their board has to approve it yet, but from what I gather, that's just a formality. I could start as early as next week."

Jon shook his head. "It's not going to be the same without you, buddy." And Alex realized that Jon was right, that twenty years together was a long time; all the things they had been through together, the space missions, the discoveries, the struggles, and the challenges. "But I'm glad you at least don't have to leave Delaware. Me, you, and Ruth—we're the old team. I'd hate to see us split up for good. At least this way,

41

we can still see each other." Jon peered at him more closely. "Why the look?" he asked. "You look unsure about the whole thing now."

Alex gave his spinach salad a distracted jab with his fork. "It's just that . . . you know . . . I'm going to miss space travel. Concord doesn't do any. I'm going to miss going up there with you guys." He looked up at the blue sky longingly. "It's *space*, Jon. Once you get a taste, you don't want to give it up. I liked the planning part especially. The details of a complicated mission, making sure everything was just right, going over all the checklists, the challenge of not forgetting anything—it gave me a great sense of accomplishment. I felt right at home with it. I like a big project. I'm sure Concord will have its challenges, but not like that. I don't know if I'll ever go up into space again. Except maybe as a tourist to the Moon."

On the way home, the subway creaked to a halt in the middle of the tunnel. At first Alex thought train traffic must be backed up. But when the delay stretched for ten minutes, he knew it had to be something bigger. He looked around at the other passengers. Some shifted in their seats, while one gentleman kept glancing to the front of the car with an odd dipping of his head, as if in dipping his head he believed he could move the train forward. It looked like he had some momentary success. The train creaked forward a car length or two. But then the train stopped suddenly, jerking everybody in their seats. Then it reversed. Alex heard a few moans of frustration. An announcement came over the speakers.

"This train will be out of service at Croptank Station," the announcement said. "All passengers are directed to leave the station immediately and proceed to street level. A shuttle service has been arranged between Croptank and Miranda stations. We apologize for any inconvenience."

The train backtracked to Croptank Station, the doors opened, and Alex got out, now feeling resigned to the whole thing.

But he grew anxious when he smelled smoke. He stopped, looked around. The air inside the station appeared misty, the lights circled by faint purple haloes—smoke, definitely smoke, not thick, no cause for alarm, but an indication that something out of the ordinary had occurred. He peered down the platform into the dark tunnel. He couldn't see anything at all. He decided the best thing he could do was get out of the station as quickly as possible, so he turned around and headed for the escalators. Transit personnel directed passengers up to street level. Alex approached the nearest transit officer, a large middle-aged man with a fleshy face, and asked him what was going on.

"Another bomb," he said. "Number 17 Repealists."

Another small calamity, in other words.

"At the next station?" asked Alex.

"No, in the tunnel. I'm sure it's just a matter of time before fire crews get it cleared, but in the meantime we've got a shuttle service running. No one's been killed. At least that's what they're telling us. But these Number 17s . . . they're dangerous, aren't they? That Public Safety Act. Causes more trouble than it's worth, doesn't it?"

As Alex rode the escalator to street level, he

couldn't help thinking of Reba again. She was a
Number 17. He didn't know much about the Public
Safety Act, only that the Repealists were up in arms
over it. He got to street level, where people swarmed
the shuttle buses, a mob scene at the curb, people
just wanting to get home, sick of the day, sick of
crowds, and sick of the bombs that kept going off in
subway tunnels. A mother gripped her daughter by
the hand. The daughter cried, upset by all the jos-
tling. Sirens howled in the distance. Alex hoped Reba
had the good sense to stay away from the Repealists.
They shipped Repealists to Chincoteague Bay, no
questions asked. His heart sank. Would he ever stop
thinking of her? Here he was, worried that they
might ship her off to Chincoteague Bay, a place people never came back from; and he didn't even know
where she lived anymore, had no idea if she were
dead or alive, or if he would ever see her again.

When Alex got home, he found an e-mail message
from Concord on his computer.

Dear Dr. Denyer,
   Thank you for your interest in Concord Exotechnologies. Unfortunately the board has decided against your
application at this time. We will keep your resume on file
for a period of three months, and should a similar position become available, our employment opportunities
messaging center will contact you with the posting.
   Once again, thank you for your interest, and good luck
in your job search.
   Sincerely,
   Mr. Warren M. Green
   Vice President and COO, Concord Exotechnologies
Ltd.

He stared at the message for several seconds, listening to his old clock tick away the seconds. He took a few steps back and sank into his antique settee. He couldn't understand it. At the interview, they'd practically been on their knees. Now they were turning him down? It didn't make sense. It made him mad. He got up, walked to his vidphone, and contacted Concord. He asked for Warren Green's office, but, frustratingly enough, Warren Green was in a meeting. So he asked for Sylvia Karafilis.

It took a full minute before her face appeared.

"What happened?" he asked. "I thought I had the job."

She looked away, distressed. "The board wishes to consider other applicants," she said, "that's all."

But he could tell there was a lot more to it than just that.

"Did the board reject me?" he asked.

A pleading look came to her eyes. Her lips scrunched together, and he could see she was trying to convey something, caution, perhaps. She glanced over her shoulder, then leaned toward her vidphone.

"We received a security memo," she said. Now her look was one of apology, even one of fear, her chin dipping as she stared at him with something approaching pity.

"A security memo?" he said.

Her eyes flicked to one side. He saw she was trying to think of something else to say. But finally her fear got the better of her. Her eyes narrowed and a hard line came to her brow.

"I have to go," she said, her tone now urgent. "My calls are being monitored."

With that, her face faded from the screen, their

exchange truncated even before it got properly started, no explanation, just a smoke screen. He sat back. He put his hands on his head, bewildered and perplexed, thinking the Megaplex had to have something to do with this, that the security memo had in fact come from them. What was going on? A security memo? Who thought he was a security risk if not the Megaplex? He couldn't help thinking of Graham, how Graham was checkmating him for one reason or another, and how he hadn't even seen the checkmate coming. He was distressed. All he wanted to do was live his quiet life, follow his scientific studies, and play with his alien junk. But for some reason, Graham was trying to make that impossible for him. Still, he wanted to believe the best of Graham. He didn't want to jump to conclusions too quickly. But the whole thing made him nervous and out of sorts. He wanted some answers. And Daryl, his son, was often the best place to get answers.

He stood behind Daryl in the captain's cabin of the *Beelzebub*. Daryl typed furious commands into his array.

"A guy—or a girl—named Ivory," said Daryl. "That's his on-line name. He's eighteen, like me. And he's infected with the Number 16 nanogen, like me. We do a lot of surfing together. Always after the Holy Grail."

In other words, searching for a cure, an antidote, a panacea for the Number 16 nanogen: the alien nanogen that was going to make Daryl die young, the one that had killed everybody over thirty in the EMZs ten years ago, two hundred million souls during the Great Die-Off—Alex's father among them—

the molecular Satan that had more than halved Daryl's life span. Alex put his hands on his son's shoulders.

"Thanks for doing this, Daryl," he said.

"We've also linked up with some Number 17s," said Daryl, as if Alex's gratitude were beside the point.

"Stay away from Number 17s," he said. "They're dangerous."

"Just on-line, Dad. They want the same thing we do. They want to get better. And they keep an eye on legislation. Do you realize there's a new law in the works? One that will give the Megaplex the authority to round up certain older Number 17s, those who are more than seventy percent machine, and put them in Chincoteague Bay?"

"Just stay away from those Number 17s, Daryl," he repeated. "Omnifix turns them into soldiers. They're killing machines. And they blow up subway tunnels."

Daryl nodded at the screen.

"Bingo," he said. "Ivory had to hack through seventy-two lines of defense, but he finally dug through to Concord. Just a sec." Daryl keyed in one last command. "Here we are," he said. "Is this what you're looking for?"

Alex read:

Re: Dr. Alexander Denyer, Employment Application to Concord Exotechnologies

In accordance with licensing agreement A-3857EV, directed from the office of CEO Graham Croft, with authorization codes provided by Administrative Director Claude Pierce, in regard to Dr. Alexander Denyer: the CEO's office, under section 48 of the War Measures Act of 2441, mandates an employment disqualification on this particular individual. Reason Cited: National Security.

"National Security?" he said. "What the hell's he talking about? How could he even think that?"

But one way or the other, his cousin had black-balled him, and blackballed him good.

Chapter 5

Alex took the hoverbus to the Megaplex the following day. The sun blazed against its reflective windows, and the panes cast gold light all over the square out front. It was hard not to squint. He climbed the steps and entered through the massive doors. The atrium rose a hundred stories high, eighty-six different elevators scooted up and down through clear plastic tubes, and a brook murmured down the middle of the lobby. He glanced into the brook as he made his way toward the nearest bank of elevators, saw a dozen goldfish, some lily pads, and a few lotus blossoms.

He got on the elevator and was whisked to the 110th floor. This was all too absurd. He wasn't a security risk. He had to make his cousin understand. He felt like his life had turned into a silly nightmare. He got off the elevator and walked down the corridor toward the CEO's office. Some people walking down the hall said hello to him. As a top government scientist he had a certain notoriety. But that didn't seem to make any difference to his cousin. A security guard

stepped from behind a kiosk and raised his hand.
Even the guard contemplated him with undisguised
recognition. But that was little comfort when Graham
had steadfastly refused to return his calls.

"You're Dr. Alex Denyer, aren't you?" said the
guard.

"Yes," he said. "I'm here to see my cousin."

"Yes, sir," said the guard. "If I could just scan your
security chip."

Alex rolled up his sleeve. The guard found his tattoo, pressed a penlike device to his vitals chip, and
checked the readout.

"I'm getting a Security 7, sir." The guard's brow
settled. "Technically, you're not allowed on this
floor."

"Security 7?" said Alex. His heart seemed to skip
a beat. "That can't be right. I'm a Security 5."

He couldn't believe this. He felt his brow moisten-
ing, his insides tightening.

"The system is rarely wrong, sir, but in this
case . . . considering who you are . . . let me check
to see if you're on the CEO's standing list. I'm sure
you are. I'm sure there must be a mistake somewhere. Give me a few seconds to sort it out."

The guard returned to his kiosk, spoke to his
screen, and initiated a search. His brow creased. Alex
had the feeling he was going to be stonewalled again.
The guard turned from his screen and came back
from his kiosk.

"I'm sorry, sir," he said, "but I don't see your
name anywhere on the standing list. Let me call upstairs. Everyone knows who you are. My wife and I
see you on the dropdown from time to time. I know
this can't be right."

The big man went back to his kiosk and spoke into his headset. Alex waited. He heard a few, "Yes, sirs," from the guard, then the man turned to him.

"You can have a seat, sir," said the guard, smiling, relieved. "Someone will be out to see you shortly."

Alex sat down. All he wanted was an explanation, and an opportunity to work again. Work was his life. Even if he never got the chance to go into space again, he at least wanted to fool with the junk Concord had in its warehouses. And he couldn't understand why Graham would want to stop that.

Ten minutes later, Graham's administrative director, Claude Pierce, walked down the corridor. Pierce was a small man, dressed in a dark suit, with dark hair cropped close to his scalp. He had a curious way of holding his chin aloft, as if he pondered the pros and cons of a hundred different problems at once. His beaklike nose seemed to sniff the air ahead for danger. As Pierce approached, his dark eyes bulged. When he saw Alex, he shook his head and grinned.

"Alex," he said. "I've been meaning to call you."

Alex's squeezed his lips together. "Claude . . . I . . . what's going on? I applied to Concord Exotec for a job, and they said I was going to get it, but then you guys sent a memo and stopped the application dead in its tracks. All because you believe I'm a security risk? What's Graham thinking? I mean . . . me? A security risk? Come on, Claude. There's got to be a mistake. I almost had that job at Concord. But on the basis of your memo, they turned me down."

Pierce's brow furrowed. "We rarely interfere in the private sector," he said.

"You invoked Section 48 of the War Measures Act of 2441. The administrative director provided the authorization codes, but the order came from Graham. Why would you do something like that? I'm not a security threat. I'm a senior scientist."

"Are you sure I provided the authorization codes?" asked Pierce. "I don't remember that at all."

"Maybe someone on your staff . . ."

Pierce's eyes narrowed. "As I say, we usually don't interfere in the private sector. Not unless there's something really at issue. And I don't think there is, do you?"

"You tell me. I understand a layoff, Claude. What I don't get is why the order came directly from Graham's office, and why you issued a security memo to Concord."

The two men stared at each other, seemingly at an impasse.

Before Alex could address the matter further, the CEO himself came down the hall.

Graham Croft wore his customary dark blue suit and had his blond hair combed back. His expression was set, his blue eyes piercing. He didn't look pleased. Gone was his media smile.

"Claude, you might as well go back to your office," he said. "I think I'd better speak to Alex personally." The CEO put his hand on Alex's shoulder. His grip was fierce, accusatory, reminding Alex of how Graham, as a teen, would sometimes push him along if he was walking too slowly. Alex felt like he was being arrested by a police officer. "I think a talk with Alex is long overdue. Don't you, Alex?"

Alex wasn't sure what Graham was getting at, but went along just the same. "Sure, Graham," he said. "Let's talk. Let's get it all straightened out."

*   *   *

Graham's office had a spectacular view of the city.

The oriented-plastic office towers surrounding the Megaplex, most over a hundred stories high, their great height made possible by light, superhard composite polymer, stretched endlessly toward the south; impressive, surreal, and, in some ways, unsettling. Alex and Graham sat at an oval-shaped table made from a giant slab of malachite, a gift from the president of SEASEZ, its aquamarine hues and tints polished to a high gloss.

"Let me be frank, Alex," said Graham. "We're unhappy with you."

Graham said this flatly, no preamble, an unfounded accusation that immediately put Alex on the defensive. How could he respond to this? In his scientific ivory tower, he'd been mostly unaware of Graham's unhappiness.

"And why would that be, Graham?" asked Alex. "I've done nothing wrong, so far as I can see."

Graham dismissed this with a flaring of his nostrils, and continued his veiled and perplexing censure.

"A man like you," said Graham, "a *scientist* like you. With so much to offer, a wealth of ideas and knowledge, privy to some of the most crucial government secrets. We have to be careful with people like you, even if it means we err on the side of caution."

"I'm sorry?" It was as if Graham possessed a large chunk of context Alex knew nothing about. He felt like he was trying to travel somewhere without a map. "Graham, I honestly don't know what you're talking about. You obviously think you know something, or that I've done something wrong, but whatever it is, I can assure you, I'm innocent."

Graham sighed. "Everyone knows how much you hate this Martian war, Alex," he said, "how pointless you think it is." Graham kept his eyes focused on Alex. "I don't happen to think the war is pointless. I happen to think we have no choice. So when you go bad-mouthing our efforts in the media, it doesn't look good."

"Is that why you did this?"

Alex felt disoriented.

"I'm as sorry as the next person that hostilities have escalated to out and out war with the Martians," said Graham, "and that we haven't come to reasonable negotiated settlement with them regarding all the platforms the aliens left behind. The Defederacy believes we deserve the lion's share of the spoils. Our casualties, both civilian and military, were far greater than Martian ones during the Alien War. But the Martians have played hardball right from the start. So what choice do we have? We're forced to fight the war to secure the platforms the Martians are trying to take away from us. Once that's done, we may look at re-funding the Branch."

"Graham, there's been piracy on both sides.

"I'm going to give you some advice, Alex. And I truly hope you heed it. You have to be careful about what you say. You've always voiced your opinions freely. The media like you. They know we're cousins. They know who your father was. So they ask you what you think about things. But as an ISS employee, you should always respond according to ISS policy. You don't. You say what you think. And I don't like it. You can't go nay-saying the Martian

war in the lab, or out on the street, or on a hoverbus, and especially not to the media. I hear about
it. And it makes me mad. I like a united front.
You're a top government scientist in a top government research establishment and you have to be a
team player. You're also my cousin. Family. That
should count for something."

"Graham, I'm sorry, but you're wrong about all
that. I have no political opinions about the war. You
know that. The only thing I've ever said is that I'm
sad when I see alien tech get destroyed because of
it. You shouldn't be so worried about what I have to
say to the media anyway. Mostly, I just talk science
with them."

"I *am* worried, Alex. They like to quote you. Because of your dad. Because of me. For starters, you
always praise Ariam Adurra. I wonder about that."

Alex frowned. So Max was right. "You fired me
because of that?" Alex put his elbows on his knees.
"Why shouldn't I praise her? She's brilliant. She's a
scientist. Science knows no borders."

"Yes, but she's also a Martian, Alex." Graham
leaned forward, his face hardening. "And you've also
praised Citizen Aubin. How can you do that? He's
Secretary General of the Federated Martian Colonies,
Alex. For God's sake, be reasonable. I don't want you
to praise him. At least not in public. I expect top
government scientists to play by the rules. Especially
you. When you do things like that, the DIS starts
looking into it." Alex swallowed at the mention of
the DIS. "And it's not a good time for the DIS to be
looking into things. Especially when you're a member of the ISS. The ISS leaks like a sieve, everybody
knows that, and we've been trying to plug the holes

in there for God knows how long. It's not *just* that you're a pacifist, Alex. You're seen as pro-Martian. And it scares the hell out of the DIS. It makes them target you, whether you want them to or not. To be honest with you, it's part of the reason you're out of a job right now. The DIS simply can't trust you anymore. Some of them actually think you're trading secrets with the Martians."

Alex felt sudden fear. This was serious. Graham had taken him completely by surprise. They'd been machinating plots behind his back, *him*, a complete innocent.

"You've *got* to be kidding," said Alex.

Graham's brow darkened, and his voice grew hard. "And as for Concord, stay the hell away from them. I don't want you anywhere near them. They have National Security restrictions up to their ears. I might as well ask you point-blank, since it's the question everybody's asking me: *Are* you trading secrets with the Martians?"

Alex gripped the edge of the sofa. God, he was really a target. He could tell it in the tone of Graham's voice. How could he have been so obtuse? He should have been watching his back all this time. He'd never seen Graham more serious. And what was grimly hilarious about the whole thing was that he was absolutely and unquestionably innocent. The system, for one reason or another, had identified him as a threat. The DIS was sniffing at his heels. And now Graham was using scare tactics. To what end? A confession? He had nothing to confess. He just wanted his job back. And what was this about Concord? How did Concord get into the conversation?

"Graham, no!" His words sounded choked. He

really felt he was in trouble here, that this silly nightmare had become a dangerous one. "No . . . I mean . . . Graham, come on. Where did your information come from?"

"That's beside the point, Alex."

"Because it's dead wrong."

Alex felt so disconcerted he could hardly speak.

"Can I trust you, Alex?" Graham's voice gained in intensity. "I could never trust your father. Every time I turned my back, he tried to undermine me. It made no difference to him that I was his nephew."

"Please don't talk about my father in that tone."

"Then I get this spurious information about you . . . that you could be one of our problems over at the ISS . . . and I think of your father all over again, sitting there smugly, agreeing to everything I say while all the time planning to block my appointment to the CEO's office any way he can."

"He died a horrible death in the Great Die-Off, Graham, you know that. Please try to show some respect."

"He should have remained a family doctor. Politics wasn't his game." Graham shook his head. "Now I have to worry about you."

"Graham, whatever information you got . . . it's wrong."

"Alex, you're sweating. And your voice is high. I think you could be guilty." Alex struggled to regain himself. "That makes me nervous. Especially because you know so much. Too much for your own good. You go digging. You go places you're not supposed to go, Alex. I know this. The DIS tells me this. You beg, borrow, or steal passwords. You snoop through files you have no business snooping through. I tell them it's because you're so curious, that you have an inquisitive mind. I remember that about you as a kid. But we've got rules, Alex, strict protocols. You seem to think none of them apply to you. You break them. You're too much of a maverick for my tastes. Just like your father was. I could never trust your father. That's why I let him go. I was expecting a certain amount of loyalty from you because you're my cousin, but I guess I was expecting too much."

That they were cousins now seemed to gall Graham, the imagined crime even more heinous because it had been perpetrated by a relative.

"Graham," he said, feeling ambushed by all this, "you can trust me. You really can. Tell the DIS I'm not a threat."

"Then you publish that paper in *Nature* before our publishing review board has a chance to clear it." Another ambush. "Don't think I don't know about these things, Alex. I do. You shouldn't be doing that. That particular information was extremely sensitive. The fixer system enzyme you were working on? The one that can possibly extend cell replication capacity? How much do you know about that? Where have you been digging? We've got other tie-ins on that, and it's not your territory at all, and I'm really mad that you've gone poking your nose into it."

"Graham, I . . ." Having come here to plead his case, Alex was now defending himself any way he could. "That was just preliminary research. Entirely independent of whatever else your scientists happen to be working on. I had some computer models that looked like they might extend telomere cuff-life under strict laboratory conditions. I was trying to find a way to maintain my other systems in a more efficient way, that's all. The surgical graft procedures are so costly."

"When Dr. Cuthbert told me you'd gone ahead and published that paper, that you hadn't even bothered submitting it to the review board . . . and then when I learned that you'd discussed it openly and frankly with the staff at Concord Exotechnologies . . . Alex, that's no good. That's just the kind of thing the DIS hates. I also find it highly suspicious you ran straight to Concord Exotechnologies the minute Max let you go." Graham's blue eyes narrowed, looked as caustic as antifreeze. "Why Concord, Alex? Of all the exotec firms in the Defederacy, why did you settle on that one?" The CEO's tone became relentless. "You obviously know a lot more than you let on if you went straight to Concord."

He had never seen Graham so hardball before. Why the big stink about the fixer system enzyme? And as a senior scientist he hadn't submitted papers to the review board in years. And what was this about Concord? Again, it was like Graham possessed a large chunk of context he wasn't telling Alex about.

"Graham, I don't know what you've heard, or how you've come to whatever conclusions you've come to, but . . . I swear to you . . . I'm just a scientist, and I'm not plotting against you, or supplying secrets to the Martians, or working with other scientists behind your back on stuff I shouldn't know about. I just came here to get some . . . some answers . . . because all this stumps me. I came here to get my job back."

Graham stared at him for a long time, assessing the veracity of his statements, then finally sat back and sighed.

"Alex . . . that's not going to be possible right now.

You don't know how close you are to . . . to real trouble. You're smart. Too smart. You've got to realize . . . we live in dangerous times. We're at war with Mars. We've got Number 17s blowing up subway tunnels, trying to destabilize the Defederacy any way they can. We've got the damn Stationhouse Militia over in the Arlington Emergency Medical Zone sinking our boats in Chesapeake Bay. The *Jamaica*, for instance, just last week. And you might think the Five Defederacies are strong. But we're not. There's a lot of dissent, especially in Hawaii. In Hawaii, there's talk of secession, and that would just weaken us further. So the last thing I need is a scientist who praises Citizen Aubin and publishes sensitive research papers without official go-ahead. I've been advised to keep you off the payroll right now, and that's what I'm going to do. Be on your best behavior. And especially don't go sniffing around any of those fixer systems or enzymes. You're just like your father. Your father was always up on a moral soapbox because he didn't understand the way the world really worked. It made him do stupid things, and I don't want you doing stupid things, Alex, I really don't. The DIS is going to look into things more closely. In the meantime, you're a free man. You're on your own. If I were you, I'd find a job somewhere, just to keep yourself out of trouble. And for God's sake, if you're involved in anything—*anything*—that makes you look like a . . . a Martian sympathizer, in the broadest sense of the term, stop right now. I can guarantee, you'll only make matters worse for yourself."

Alex frowned. Now he was getting mad. Find another job? Where was he going to find another job? It was unfair. He didn't deserve this. He was innocent, unjustly accused, and it made him furious.

"Where am I going to find a job if you won't let me work in the exotec field?" he asked.

"You can't be picky, Alex," said Graham. "But you definitely *need* a job. You always got bored so easily as a kid. I remember that. How I always had to entertain you whenever I came out to Unionville. You need something to do with yourself, just so you don't drive yourself nuts sitting in that condo all day. Raise glowballs and sell them on the street. You always had a knack for breeding those little critters." Graham motioned at the mind-pool table near the back of his office. "Or see if you can take some winnings at the mind-pool table. You invented the game. Whatever you do, stay out of trouble. Don't talk to the wrong people and don't whisper another word to anybody—I mean *anybody*—about this telomere extender enzyme you were working on. Because things could really go from bad to worse if you did."

He went home that night feeling spent, dejected, and worst of all, wronged. He walked to his window. Rain from Miranda, the latest hurricane, beat against his window. How could he have been so blind to the suspicions building around him? He should have kept his opinions to himself instead of spouting them to the media. He beat the window frame lightly with the ball of his fist again and again, finally stopping as he realized he was at a crossroads here. He thought of his encounter with Graham. What had happened there? Nothing had been explained, nothing had been worked out. Graham had simply grabbed him from the hall, dragged him into his office, and interrogated him—about Concord, his *Nature* article, and the fixer system—revealing as little as he could. Now he was out of a job, none the wiser, feeling angry, but also feeling, in a way, liberated, like there was something more important at stake here than just his job.

He gazed out at the rain. Stuck in his condo. Graham was right about that. He was going to drive himself nuts sitting in this condo all day. He hated when Graham was right. He remembered that about Graham from when he was a kid, Graham coming to Unionville and always being right about everything. But in the case of this condo, Graham definitely knew what he was talking about. If he sat here all day and listened to the season's endless hurricanes, each crowding the next like jets stacked up over a busy airport, he would go crazy. He *had* to find a job, even if it was in an unrelated field.

He walked to his kitchenette, poured a glass of cranberry juice, cut a wedge of lime, twisted the lime into the juice, then put the peel and pulp on the counter. He stared at the mangled twist of lime. That's what he felt like right now. Twisted and mangled, his back against the wall, ready to fight, but at the same time ready to crumble, ready to admit that he was powerless, that for all his scientific intelligence he was a horribly inept diplomat when it came to his professional and personal life. He took a sip of his cranberry juice. Stuff his father always drank. He missed his father. He wished his father wasn't dead. He wished his father was here right now. His father had unique insight when it came to Graham, could always see right through Graham. But to Alex, Graham was as opaque as the hurricane-whipped sky outside his window.

Chapter 6

Alex sat in the galley of the *Beelzebub* the following afternoon with Jill, Tony, and Daryl, drinking coffee substitute from Greater Serbia, a barley-cocoa beverage the small Balkan enclave exported in great quantities now that most of the coffee-producing countries had succumbed to Number 16. He barely tasted it. He still felt numb from his interview with Graham. And now he had a new problem.

"I had an e-mail from ISS Human Resources," he told them. "My severance package has been suspended indefinitely pending a full review of all ISS procedures by the Megaplex. I was counting on that severance package. I spoke to Max this morning. He tells me the Megaplex came in this morning and froze our assets. They have some intelligence concerns about the ISS, and they're investigating ISS operations. After my talk with Graham yesterday, that doesn't surprise me in the least. This is all so crazy."

Jill and Tony glanced at each other.

"So you have no idea when your severance package will come through?" asked Jill.

"No," said Alex. "Max is livid."

For several moments, no one said anything. But then Jill leaned forward and put her hand on top of his.

"Alex, I know you're angry. And I know all of this seems unfair. But I think what you have to ask yourself is whether you can really do anything about it. Graham, for reasons of his own—and God knows what they are—has decided to do this to you. Maybe he'll change his mind. Maybe he won't. In the meantime, we're here for you. This is a tough patch. You're upset. And we're all going to stand by you."

He glanced up at Jill. His wife at one time, now just a friend, the tie between them still strong because of Daryl. She could be irascible and demanding, but most of the time she was simply a great support. The great adventure—that of raising Daryl together—partnered them inextricably, gave depth and texture to what they meant to each other, a solidity and permanence they could both count on, and an unspoken promise that was as good as a vow.

"What I don't understand is *how* they can treat me like this," said Alex. "I'm one of their senior scientists. I've worked wonders for them. I'm internationally recognized. I've held several top teaching positions, and my papers have been noted again and again by experts around the world as groundbreaking research. So what if I have a reputation as a maverick? So what if I've expressed my views about the Martian Conflict to the media? Half the people in the Defederacy are against it. Graham should treat me with some respect." Alex shook his head, and in a more subdued voice said, "I'm going to get a job. I don't need him."

Jill glanced at Tony, then turned back to Alex, a look of mystification on her face.

"I thought you were blacklisted," she said.

"A job outside the exotechnology field," he said. "Any damn job will do. I'll clean spill tanks if I have to. I was at the employment office this morning. There were a few postings at the West Denton Facility."

Tony's eyes brightened.

"Alex, why don't you sign on with us?" he said. Tony gave Jill a cautious glance. "On that new contract I was telling you about." Jill's eyes narrowed as she now considered the possibility. "The one out to the Arlington EMZ I mentioned a couple weeks ago. I've still got to hire crew. Like I told you before, I'm having trouble getting people. I might as well hire you. I know you don't have much experience, but I can teach you the ropes, and I'm sure you'll catch on quickly." Tony turned to Jill. "What do you say, Jill? If Alex hires on as first mate, he'll fill one of our crucial positions. He'll also get to spend time with Daryl. It'll get us out of a tough spot. I've been thinking about this for a while."

For the first time in days Alex felt his mood lifting. Working was who he was, and now Tony was offering him this opportunity. He could have kissed Tony. But glancing at Jill, he saw she had some reservations.

"I think we should cancel that contract, Tony," she said. "It's not safe. And who are these people? Why won't they tell us what they do? Are they the ones who are telling you it's so safe?"

Tony sighed, tilted his head to one side, and extended his palms in entreaty.

"Jill, they're a perfectly legitimate firm," he said. "And it was Dr. Colgan who told me it was safe. He's on a separate contract from the other guys, and his credentials are perfect. He knows the Arlington EMZ like the back of his hand. If we run into trouble, he'll smooth things out for us."

Jill's eyes grew equivocal. "We don't know that for sure," she said.

"I don't see why you're so worried, Jill," said Tony. "It's only Arlington. It's not the ends of the Earth. Things have changed a lot there in the last few years."

"They haven't changed that much," said Jill. "I was reading an article about it the other day. That madman Sandy Parker is still there. Remember all those bodies in the river two years ago? He's the one who did that. And more recently there was the *Jamaica* sinking."

"Patuxent Rebels did that," said Tony, "not Stationhouse. And you weren't the one who talked to Dr. Colgan, were you?" Alex was afraid the two were going to get into another one of their arguments. "He says it's safe. He says he knows Sandy Parker personally. He's been there a dozen times. He knows his way around."

But Jill still looked doubtful. "It's not good for Daryl. I don't want him going over there."

"Mom, I'm okay with it," said Daryl. "I want to see how the Number 16s live over there."

"Daryl, they have no end-of-life care over there. Everybody over there is a Number 16, and they're all dying in the streets. I don't want you to see that. I don't think it would be good for you. You'll have nightmares."

"Mom, I'm not a kid anymore."

"Dr. Ely Colgan?" said Alex.

Jill glanced at him questioningly. "You know him?"

"I've read some of his work on the Number 16 nanogen. I know he's always going to the EMZs to do cultural as well as genetic studies."

"Mom, I'm eighteen," said Daryl. "I think I can handle it."

She remained unpersuaded. "But you hear all these stories about Sandy Parker," she said. "That man scares me."

"Colgan *knows* Sandy Parker," said Tony, stubbornly determined. "They're good buddies. Parker understands the value of Colgan's work. Colgan gets the red-carpet treatment whenever he goes to Arlington. That means we'll get it too. Alex can hire on. We'll make money. Real money. Colgan's paying us and Servitech is paying us. And the Servitech contract is a big one. We need it, Jill. You know we do."

Jill's shoulders eased and she nodded with great reluctance. "As long as you're sure it's safe," she said.

"I guarantee it," said Tony. "Like I say, Dr. Colgan's been up and down the Potomac a dozen times and he's never had a problem. Sandy Parker's got his Stationhouse Militia patrolling most of it. And Washington, D.C., is completely secure." He turned to Alex. "What do you say, Alex? Do you want to hire on? We'd love to have you aboard."

Alex didn't know what he was up against, had no idea what a first mate did, but he was willing to give it a try, and was grateful to Tony for the offer.

"Thanks, Tony," he said. "I'd love to."

* * *

To settle his mind, he walked home.

He headed south through Hurlock. He took a shortcut down Hosta Street. A Number 17—veteran of the Alien War, now transformed by Omnifix into a half-mechanical hulk—glanced his way, his head swiveling like a surveillance camera, the lens in his left eye focusing abruptly. Alex moved quickly on. He was in Number 17 territory, and that of course made him nervous.

He was just turning the corner onto Oliver Boulevard when he heard a buzz behind him. He turned around and saw a small hovercam following him. He stopped. He couldn't believe it. They really didn't trust him. They should have sent him notice that he was going to be under surveillance. That was the law. But they hadn't. That made him think there had to be something really wrong. DIS wrong. Graham had been so shifty. He took a swipe at the thing, but the hovercam dodged him. It sped down Hosta and banked right on Oliver Boulevard.

"Alex?" a woman called.

He turned. It was Reba. He could have leaped for joy. His whole body seemed to do an internal somersault at the sight of her.

"Reba!" he said, his voice riding high with relief, an emotion he could scarcely control. Thank God he knew where she was. "Hi."

Then he looked at her more closely. Omnifix—that which the DDF used to combat the Number 17 nanogen—had really gotten its hooks into her. For the longest time, the changes had been incremental. But now, in the eighteen months since their last encounter, the changes were more noticeable. She was nearly a foot taller than last time. Her legs were sleek, smooth, still shapely under her short dark skirt, but made of black flexisteel. She wore a black leather jacket. A black half-mask covered the left side of her face. Harder than steel, the mask protected the dataspheres and microprocessors inside what was left of her brain. The mask mimicked her pretty features, followed the bridge of her nose, arced around her left cheek, and dipped past the corner of her mouth, dividing her face—its human side from its machine side—with a yin-yang curve. She smiled.

"I was wondering when I was going to bump into you again," she said. "I haven't seen you in a while."

"No," he said. "I . . . I actually went up to Madison about a week ago. You weren't there. You've moved?"

"Yes," she said. "I'm on Hosta now." She paused. She seemed at a loss for words. Then she gestured awkwardly up the street. "I'm just going out to meet a friend." To hear her voice again, even in its synthesized version, was a comfort. But he couldn't get over how much she had changed. She shifted. He could tell she felt self-conscious about the way she looked.

"You're staring," she observed.

"I haven't see you . . . since last year. You're . . . "

"I'm a freak now," she said, and looked away.

"No," he said. "Not at all. You look . . . taller. And stronger. Your shoulders. And your hands."

She faced him, a challenge in her eyes.

"I'm a soldier," she said. "There's no other template for Omnifix."

Her manner unsettled him. They were so different from one another now. He struggled to say something that might lessen the gap.

"How do you feel?" he asked.

"I have my ups and downs," she said. "The emotional deficits and so forth." She changed the subject. "You were down at the docks?"

"Visiting Daryl," he said.

She nodded, smiled, as if she had fond memories of Daryl. "And how is he?"

"He's . . . he's eighteen now."

She shook her head, amazed. "Really? I'll always remember him as twelve."

"I was down there discussing my job prospects with Jill," he said.

"Your job prospects?"

"I was fired."

He explained the whole situation to Reba.

When he was done, she shook her head.

"No offense to your cousin," she said, "but I think he sees enemies everywhere. When he doesn't even trust his own relatives, that's a bad sign." She paused, and he had to wonder about the emotional deficits Number 17 caused because she momentarily looked wounded, frustrated, and angry all at the same time. "He hates Number 17s." She said this boldly. "It's hard for us." Her face grew more perturbed, even as she tried to grin. "He doesn't understand how disenfranchised we feel." She now looked embarrassed. "Anyway . . . I could talk your ear off about it, but I'm not going to." She pointed. "Is that thing following you?"

He turned. Ten yards behind he saw the hovercam poised in midair, recording his every move.

"I can't believe this," he said.

"I better move on," she said, sneering at the hovercam.

"Maybe we could see each other sometime," he said.

Her face sank. "I'm living with someone now, Alex," she said. He tried to fight his jealousy but it was nearly impossible. She watched him, searched his face in a way he remembered so well, at once compassionate and forgiving, but also steadfast. "Zirko Carty." She was playing fair. "A retired colonel. Zirko was at Bettina."

Alex regained himself.

"So he's a . . . a Number 17 too?" he said.

"One of the first," she said.

"He's been . . . you know . . ." He motioned at her flexisteel legs and her flexisteel arms. "Living with it for a long time, I guess."

"Over fifteen years," she said.

"Bettina," he said. He shook his head and whistled. "That's a name right out of history, isn't it?"

He thought of Zirko. He could scarcely imagine it. How did the man deal with it? Living with Number 17 for fifteen years, watching his body granulate into dust as Omnifix all the while repaired it with cybernetic equivalents, turning him bit by bit into a machine.

"I'm sorry," she said. "I'm sorry that you and I . . ."

"No, no . . . it's okay. I'd better let you go. Your friend must be waiting."

"As a matter of fact, I'm meeting Zirko right now," said Reba. "I would ask you to come along, but . . ." She glanced at the hovercam. "We get enough of this as it is. I'm sure your cousin wouldn't like to see you fraternizing with a Number 17, given your circumstances."

"Maybe not," he said, now more angry at Graham than ever. "It was great to see you again. I'm shipping out on Monday, but maybe when I get back, we could . . . you know . . . get together. Maybe with Zirko. I'd like to meet him."

Her face was now blank, devoid of any emotion at all.

"Sure," she said.

As she walked away from him, he thought she seemed almost suspicious of him. He felt he was losing something, a final chance, an opportunity with her. It couldn't be helped. He had to let her go. He wondered if she remembered all those nights of shared intimacy, eight months together, lovers, inseparable. He had to forget about that. There was no turning back. Their time together was over. He turned away and headed south. Still, it was good to see her again. He felt buoyed by the encounter, even though she was so changed. He remembered visiting her at Greensboro as she had undergone those first major changes, all that rehab, all that therapy. How she had sometimes clung to him, but how in the end she had finally said good-bye, sensing the new and obvious demarcation between them. She was right. It wouldn't work. She was a Number 17. And he was . . . *human.* She faced a whole set of problems he couldn't hope to understand. His throat constricted. Did she even trust him anymore? He shook his head. It didn't matter. It was good to see her just the same.

He slid his hands into his pockets as the wind picked up. Seeing her again gave him some strength to face the future. And that's what he should be thinking of. The future. He was shipping out on

Monday. Out to the open bay where the air was fresh. A chance to be with Daryl. A chance to be with Jill. His pace quickened and he felt a distant excitement. His life was taking one of those unexpected turns. Maybe that was cause for celebration. A trip to the Arlington EMZ. His life was going to be different from here on in. For the past nineteen years he'd gone to work at the ISS every morning, had seen all the same old familiar faces, had gone on his missions every year. He wasn't going to do that anymore. No coffee at ten, no lunch at twelve, no more meetings with Max and the others in the afternoons. That was a big page to turn. But he knew he could make the transition.

Chapter 7

Alex stood on the foredeck of the *Beelzebub* on Monday morning as the crane operator swung a Servitech refrigeration unit to the left. Elliott Suarez, Servitech's team leader, stood beside him, watching with calm appraisal. Alex motioned the operator to lower the unit. As it came down, he placed his hand against it. He couldn't help being curious about all this refrigeration equipment. He thought of Jill's concerns, how Servitech seemed to be such a secretive company. And it was true. What on earth were they going to use all these refrigeration units for? Not so much as a peep from Suarez, nor from the sixteen Servitech employees who were coming with them.

"Is that it?" said Alex.

"Yes," said Suarez. "We're finished."

The man had an accent Alex couldn't place. Eurocorp somewhere, but where? He wasn't Spanish, despite his last name. He was a stocky man with a thick neck. His dark hair was combed back. He wore a green bodysuit with a zippered front. Button-down, unadorned epaulettes on his shoulders gave him a faintly military appearance. Suarez sweated. A system of sunshine and humidity pocketed the bay. The temperature edged above one hundred. Alex was glad to be here, despite the heat. He was working. He was earning money, paying his own way, and he didn't have to depend on Graham.

"Why so many refrigeration units?" asked Alex.

Suarez gave him a tight smile. "I'm afraid the exact nature of our business in the EMZ is confidential," he said. "You'll understand, of course."

Alex gazed into the cargo hold as the refrigeration unit sank into the shadows. Some Servitech workers below eased it into place. It was none of his business. He had to get used to that. He was just an employee now, not a boss anymore. It wasn't his place to pry. But he still couldn't help being curious. Curiosity ran in his blood. And Jill and Tony were having fights about Servitech. He thought if he could learn a little about the firm, he might get them to stop fighting.

"And all those crates over there," he said, pointing into the hold. "That's a lot of equipment."

"Yes," said Suarez.

"What do you have in those crates?" asked Alex.

"Supplies," said Suarez. "Instruments."

"What kind of outfit is Servitech anyway?"

"We're involved in many ventures, Dr. Denyer," said Suarez. "We're a service company, as our name suggests. We cater to a wide range of clients."

This was too vague for Alex. He made one last attempt. "So why are you going to the Arlington EMZ?" he asked.

Suarez's smile tightened further. "Because we are being paid, Dr. Denyer."

Alex frowned. Something in Suarez's manner both-

75

ered him. It wasn't only the man's shiftiness. It was as if Suarez were afraid of something; as if he knew something about the EMZ he didn't want Alex or anybody else to know about.

Before they got under way, Alex saw Tony arguing with two port authority officers on the dock. The officers were insistent, but so was Tony. One had a waferscreen and kept pointing at it. Tony shook his head and showed them his own waferscreen. The altercation lasted five minutes. Finally, the port authority officers left and Tony climbed the gangplank to the ship.

"What did they want?" asked Alex.

A lighthearted grin came to Tony's face, as if it were no big deal.

"They had a provisional cancellation for your travel permit," said Tony. "They wanted to yank you from my crew. But don't worry. I sent them packing."

Alex's shoulders tensed. He couldn't help thinking of Graham again, how Graham was really trying to bugger his life, make it as inconvenient as he could, using scare tactics to keep him in the pressure cooker.

"A cancellation?" said Alex. "From Graham?"

Tony's eyes narrowed. "They wouldn't tell me. But that would be my guess." Tony's grin disappeared. The corners of his eyes drooped, and a grim curl came to his lower lip. "Alex . . . I think this is . . ." He gestured at the retreating officers. "I deal with these government types all the time. For them to come to the boat like this—for them to actually get up off their butts and show me a bogus cancellation—well, it's got DIS written all over it. Graham's got you in his sights."

Alex's heart rate accelerated a notch or two. "I

know that," he said. "I wanted to keep that from Jill. You know how jumpy she gets."

Alex watched the port authority officers retreat. The silly nightmare persisted.

Tony took a deep breath. "People get beat up," he said. "People get killed. The DIS has all sorts of people working for them, and a lot of them come from Hurlock. I live in Hurlock. I know exactly what happens in Hurlock. People get in accidents. People get killed. And there's never an investigation." He motioned toward the port authority officers. "Those guys coming to the ship like this . . . I don't think we've seen the last of them."

Alex shook his head. "So what do we do?" he asked. "How did you get rid of them?"

"They can't stop you with that provisional cancellation," said Tony. "I'm sure it wasn't even authentic. I'm sure it was just so much DIS bullshit. So they pushed me only so far. I pushed back harder."

"Yes, but . . . they'll come back?"

"Oh, they'll come back, all right," said Tony. "But we'll be long gone by then."

When they were a few miles from the mouth of the Potomac River, a large, high-speed motorboat approached the *Beelzebub*. Alex and Tony were on deck welding a brace into place. Tony had a welder's mask over his face. Alex tapped Tony's shoulder. Tony turned off the torch, lifted the mask, and looked out at the boat. The boat drew closer. Far on the horizon, the coast of the Arlington EMZ loomed green and misty, brightened by the morning sun. The boat's motor echoed in a fractured buzz over the waves.

"The DDF Coast Guard?" suggested Alex.

"No," said Tony. "A private vessel."

Alex and Tony rose from their work and walked to the railing. Suarez approached from the back of the ship.

"Good morning, gentlemen," he said.

Then Suarez waved to the people on the boat. Tony's face settled.

"You know these people?" he said.

"Two new staff," said Suarez. "I'm sorry I didn't inform you earlier. I received instructions only late last night."

"You can't add two new staff now," said Tony. "Not after we've already shipped out. It's not in our contract. It's going to mean cost overruns on the food."

"You will be amply compensated for the food," said Suarez.

"You're damn right I will."

Alex saw Tony liked Suarez about as much as he did.

The boat pulled alongside.

"Alex, I'm going to the wheelhouse to slow her down a bit," said Tony. "You throw the ladder over the side."

The bay was calm, and soon the two craft were stable and aligned.

The two new staff climbed up the rope ladder. They didn't look like any of the other Servitech staff. They looked rough. Their clothes were dirty, and one had a knife strapped to his belt. Alex didn't like the look of them at all. Both were young, no more than twenty. As they climbed over the railing they glanced at Alex. Suarez ushered them to the rear of the boat and said a few private words to them. This didn't look right. It didn't *feel* right. Something was up. He couldn't help thinking those two men were here for him.

He pulled the ladder up and stowed it away. He gave a signal to Tony in the wheelhouse and Tony increased speed. Alex climbed the steps to the wheelhouse and joined Tony.

"Why do I have such a bad feeling about Servitech?" he asked. "I think Jill might be right about them. And those two new guys. They're punks."

"Suarez better pay me for those two new guys."

"Did you see what Suarez did last night?" asked Alex. "He had one of his crew guard their stuff all night long down in the cargo hold. He's expecting us to snoop through it. It makes me think he's up to something illegal."

Tony shrugged, shook his head. "He had papers," he said. "And he paid me up front."

"Yes, but he might get you into trouble, Tony. He might get Jill and Daryl into trouble."

Tony's brow sank. He stared out the window for several seconds. Finally he sighed.

"Suarez tells me everything is legitimate," he said. "I've gone over his papers carefully. I thought they might be fakes but they're not. I've seen fakes before." Tony shifted from one foot to the other, and his brow creased. "I had to take the contract, Alex. We need the money."

"I know, but why don't you go down to the cargo hold and see what you can see?" said Alex. "It's your boat. You have the right to look around."

"I can't inspect any of their equipment without written authorization from Suarez," he said. "It's in the contract."

"Yes, but aren't you curious? I'm dying to find out what they have in those fiberlite crates."

Out the window, a few seagulls banked over the bow. Tony's eyes narrowed.

"I can't afford to be curious," he said. He gave Alex a sly look. "But that doesn't mean you can't be."

Alex peered at Tony. "What do you mean?"

"Everyone knows you're new. You're bound to make mistakes. Why don't you make the mistake of getting up in the middle of the night, going down to the cargo hold, and taking a look?"

At two o'clock in the morning, Alex sat up and swung his feet out of bed. He got up and walked down the narrow passageway. A small alien glow-ball, one of a dozen he'd bred for the *Beelzebub* years ago, clung to the ceiling, casting a feeble yellow glow. He gripped the railing and descended the stairs to the next deck. The sound of rain against the hull grew muffled—he was now below the waterline. He paused as he neared the bottom of the stairs. He glanced between the metal steps and saw a Servitech worker sitting in a chair guarding all the Servitech equipment, just like last night. The guard, a man named Kostakis, sat reading something on his wafer-screen. Kostakis. Wasn't that a Greek name? Yet having worked with a support specialist named Dimitrios, he knew a Greek accent when he heard one, and Kostakis didn't have one.

Alex waited on the stairs for close to fifteen minutes. Kostakis finally got up and walked to the ship's head.

Alex descended the remaining stairs and made his way to Cargo Area 2.

In Cargo Area 2 he found Servitech's fiberlite packing crates and refrigeration units. He glanced toward the head, afraid Kostakis might come back any second. The refrigeration units hummed with cool efficiency. Alex walked over to one of the fiberlite crates and opened it.

What he found inside surprised him. Blood collection bags and phlebotomy equipment. His eyebrows rose. He glanced one more time toward the head, then closed the crate. Was Servitech going on a blood drive in the EMZ? He hurried back to the stairs. Why on earth would Servitech mount a blood drive in the EMZ? It didn't make sense. All the blood in the Arlington EMZ was infected with the Number 16 nanogen, of use to nobody.

The next morning, the rain came down harder than ever, and the wind was rising.

Alex sat in the wheelhouse with Tony and Dr. Ely Colgan. Colgan, though over sixty, had a youthful appearance, was tall, broad-shouldered, had a full head of white hair, steady eyes, and a barrel chest. He wore a chain around his neck. A medallion dangled from the chain. The medallion was an odd one—a fist clenching a sheaf of wheat.

Tony pointed. "That over there is what's left of the Indian Head Naval Ordnance Station. I haven't been further than this point."

"Didn't the Servitech guys give you maps?" asked Colgan.

"No." Tony shifted uncomfortably. "I told them I had maps. It was the only way I could get the contract. I told them I knew the river all the way up to D.C." He gave Colgan a sheepish smile. "I was hoping you might give us a hand with the navigation from this point on, Ely."

Alex gave Colgan a look. Fly by the seat of your pants, that was Tony's credo.

"I hope the Stationhouse Militia hasn't added more blockships since the last time I was here," said Colgan, giving the river a worried glance. "There's one over there. You can see its mast above the water." Colgan turned to Tony. "You've got that white flag flying?"

"Yes," said Tony. "But Sandy Parker knows we're coming, right?"

"Always fly the white flag, no matter what," said Colgan. "And keep a lookout. I remember this stretch. I don't think there's anything new, but you never know. Sandy has only a weak grip down here. Keep well to the right as we round this next bend. The channel should be clear of underwater obstacles. But there's a lot of piracy along this stretch, so you have to be careful just the same." Colgan motioned to the west bank. "That point to the left is Woodbridge. Stay away from that. Patuxent Rebels shoot from there. If you stick to the right, you'll be out of range. Their weapons are old. But every so often they surprise us with a few artillery pieces."

Alex was curious. "Where do they get all their heavy weaponry from?" he asked. "You mentioned the track-mounted howitzers last night, and now you're telling us about artillery pieces."

Colgan gestured downriver. "A lot of it's floated

upstream from Indian Head. The navy abandoned the base twenty-three years ago, so the Number 16s are always finding bits and pieces down there. Some of it comes from Fort Belvoir. Fort Belvoir is just beyond Woodbridge. You'll see it in a bit. Most of it comes from wherever. There's a big trade in weapons. Weapons trade like gold in the EMZs." Colgan stared with sudden scrutiny out the wheelhouse window. "Shit, Tony," he said. "Turn hard to the left."

Tony, as cool as could be, wheeled the *Beelzebub* forty-five degrees to the left. Alex looked out the rain-streaked window. He saw a ship's antenna rising above the murky current.

"That's a new one," said Colgan.

"I bet we grazed that thing," said Tony, sounding proud of it.

Alex watched the radio antenna recede behind them, the wake of the *Beelzebub* washing waves around it.

Colgan changed the subject.

"I'm still surprised by all that phlebotomy equipment in the hold, Alex," he said. "I can't understand why Servitech would be mounting a blood drive in the EMZ. I'm not familiar with them at all. I know most of the firms that come here. Usually they're the same ones again and again, the ones Sandy lets in. But he hasn't told me about Servitech. Why draw blood here, when it's infected with Number 16? You think I would know something about it, particularly because my main field of research is the Number 16 nanogen."

"Maybe they're with the Megaplex," said Tony, "and the Megaplex is finally going to do something about Number 16. Maybe the Megaplex realizes people are getting restless over here, and that it's time to find a cure."

"I wouldn't think so," said Colgan. "All five Defederacies have repeatedly cried poor on Number 16. It's too tough to crack. It's a sinkhole for money, and the Defederacies know it. That's why they've backed out. They're not going to waste any more resources on it."

"Are you sure?" asked Tony. "All that equipment Alex saw—it's for blood, right?"

"The kind of equipment Alex saw is standard Red Cross field equipment," admitted Colgan. "Servitech is here to bank blood. Thousands of units of the stuff, by the look of it. They obviously have their reasons. What I can't understand is why bank blood here, where all the blood's tainted?" Colgan shook his head. "I wish Suarez would tell us what's going on."

Alex, ever vigilant in his role as first mate, saw shapes out on the river. He pointed. "I think we have company."

Two boats approached. The discussion about Servitech ended. As the boats drew closer, Alex saw several ragged individuals in each. They wore an assortment of gaudy care-package clothing, stuff donated from the various Defederacies: jumpsuits in harlequin colors, paper body-wraps that were useless against the rain, and cloaks so old and dirty they looked as if they might fall off as rags any minute. Five men rode in one boat, and six in the other, all armed with rifles. As they approached the *Beelzebub*, one man aimed a bazooka at the ship and fired. Alex saw a puff of smoke. He heard a faint report. A projectile tethered to a long cable arced toward the *Beelzebub*. It disappeared from view beneath the starboard rail. Alex heard a faint clank. A moment later the lights in the cabin blinked out. Down below the engine died.

"Damn," said Colgan. "An electrostatic grenade." He turned to Tony. "Tell your engineer to stand by. Things will stay off-line until our visitors pull that damn thing free."

"Are they Stationhouse Militia?" asked Alex.

"No," said Colgan. "They're End-of-Lifers. I can tell by the way they're hunched. Sandy doesn't allow End-of-Lifers in the Stationhouse. They're not much good as militia when they hit the change." Colgan gazed at the approaching boats. "These are just a bunch of old guys trying to make ends meet until they die. They're here to toll us. I'm sure their toll will be nothing."

Alex, Tony, and Colgan went outside. Jill and Daryl came up from belowdecks. So did Suarez and a couple of the Servitech crew. Alex unwinched the anchor and let it drop into the river. He watched the small boats come alongside. Tony lowered the rope ladder. Five End-of-Lifers climbed up and over the railing.

Alex, although he'd seen pictures of End-of-Lifers before, still found their appearance disconcerting. Skin color was yellowish, as if they suffered from jaundice. It was blotched with huge psoriasislike plaques. Backs were hunched, noses elongated, and bones shrunken. One used a cane, and another looked blinded by cataracts. They had wrinkles and liver spots. They had that smell—the End-of-Lifer smell he'd read about, a stench that reeked of distilled hormones gone haywire, caustic and penetrating. They had long chins. Unnerving, the way calcium deposits built up on their chins after the age of twenty-five. Alex glanced at Daryl. Daryl's eyes were wide. Maybe Jill was right. Did they really want Daryl to see this? The End-of-Lifers were hideous— freaks.

"Can't let you go any further," said the man with the cane, who looked about eighty, but who couldn't have been more than twenty-seven. "This is our riverbank. All the way to Woodbridge. You pay us, and we'll take the charge-drain off your ship. You can be on your way."

Tony, Suarez, and Colgan talked to the man. Suarez pulled a wad of old U.S. cash out of his pocket— legal tender in the Arlington EMZ. He handed it to the man. The man counted it. Then he stuffed it into a shoulder bag. He nodded. He looked happy with the amount. The man and his four companions retreated to the rope ladder. Colgan went forward and helped the man with the cane over the railing. Alex could tell Colgan really cared about these people, that he wanted to help them. Looking at the End-of-Lifers Alex wondered for the hundredth time: what were the aliens thinking? Why turn humans into such hideous freaks? Why kill off everybody over thirty, those unlucky enough not to live in the enclaves, and leave all the young fighting-age people alive, even if in a mutated form? What was their game plan? He wondered if he would ever have a clear idea of the alien objective.

With the transaction finished, Alex went below and helped the engineer with the electrical box.

They got things up and running in under ten minutes. Alex climbed the various companionways to the wheelhouse. He found Colgan giving Tony the rundown on End-of-Lifers.

"They hit twenty-five or so," explained Colgan, "and something turns on. Age hits them with the force of a bus. You saw how humpbacked they were." Outside, the rain now lashed the deck fiercely. "Their noses, chins, and ears grow. They look goblinesque. Meanwhile, their bones shrink. And they get that smell. The smell actually comes from skin breakages. These breakages ooze a bit, then crust over. You get those psoriasislike plaques. The plaques give off that smell. Occasionally, huge chunks of skin fall off. Fingernails and toenails turn green with a form of fungus we haven't found a cure for yet. In some cases, we see the plaques growing hard as glass, forming scalelike patterns on their shoulders and hands."

Out the rain-streaked window, the ruins of the Woodrow Wilson Memorial Bridge loomed ahead.

"It must be awful," said Tony.

"That's just the beginning," said Colgan. "At autopsy, I've seen all sorts of wild internal changes. Enormous deterioration in the liver, spleen, stomach, thymus, kidney, thyroid, pituitary gland, and cardiovascular system. You see the growth of a third atrophied lung, the disappearance of one of the kidneys, the addition of a fluid-filled organ we've never seen the likes of before, extra testes, extra ovaries, and an additional set of dentition below the gum line, fine razor-sharp teeth that don't even look human."

Alex remained stock-still as he listened to this catalogue of horrors. All these things would eventually happen to Daryl.

"The adrenal glands triple in size," continued Colgan. "So does the pituitary gland. In these glands we see the production of a never-before-classified enzyme." Colgan turned to Alex. "In fact, it reminds me of that paper you wrote recently, Alex, the one about the fixer system enzyme you were working on."

"You read that?"

"Yes. From what I understand, that particular fixer system produces a similar enzyme, one that can maintain chromosomal telomeres, a telomerase, as you called it, an enzyme that can extend a cell's replicative capacity, and, theoretically, an organism's life."

"Yes," said Alex.

"Same thing with this bizarre enzyme we find in the Number 16s," said Colgan. "We introduced this telomerase into test-tube cells using the usual immunosuppressants to halt any rejection, and the cells replicated longer than they would have ordinarily. But when we introduced the same telomerase into a lab rat using the same immunosuppressants, it killed the creature through a rejection process. An immunosuppressant will not work in this particular case. What it needs is a new kind of catalyst to get it beyond the rejection process."

"I was trying to come up with a catalyst when the ISS let me go," said Alex. "In fact, Graham seemed more concerned about my work in this area than he did in any other. I don't know why."

Colgan shook his head. "Unfortunately, this telomerase remains dormant in a Number 16, so we see none of its age-deterring properties working in any of the victims. Too bad, because they all suffer so horribly. What I don't get is why the aliens used

Number 16 at all? It reduces life expectancy, yes, but it also makes young people violent, strong, and aggressive. It turns them into stupendous fighters. Why would the aliens people the planet with consummate warriors if they planned to invade us? It makes me think conquest was the furthest thing from their minds. And I have to ask myself: if not conquest, then what?"

As the ship chugged its final mile into Washington, the rain abated and the wind died down. Alex found Daryl standing at the bow of the *Beelzebub*, staring out at all the old landmarks, monuments to what was once a great republic, now just a sad reminder of the Great Die-Off, and of the subsequent political defederation. He approached his son. His son didn't turn, kept his eyes forward. Violent, strong, aggressive, yes, but Daryl had drugs for all that. Alex drew even with Daryl and rested his hands on the railing. He looked up the river. Here they were, in the Arlington Emergency Medical Zone, the once renowned capital now no more than Sandy Parker's fiefdom.

"You were surprised, weren't you?" said Alex.

"Surprised by what?" asked Daryl

"By the way they look. The End-of-Lifers."

To the right, the Tidal Basin came into view. Daryl's eyebrows flicked upward and he swallowed.

"I've got to face the truth, Dad," he said. "That's what I'm going to look like one day. I've got a good seven years left before the change hits me."

"Maybe we shouldn't have taken you here," said Alex. "Maybe Mom was right."

"No. I'm glad I'm here. I'd sooner know the worst."

Alex motioned at the EMZ. "The Bombardment was the worst of the worst. There'll never be anything so terrible again."

"Then I want to know the worst of the worst," said Daryl. "Look at this. There's the Washington Monument. And look over there. Some people. Life goes on, even after the Bombardment. I wonder if any of those people are young like me, or if they're End-of-Lifers. I want to talk to some End-of-Lifers. I want to know what it's like. I want to know what I'm in for. This place is an eye-opener. This is where I should be."

"Don't tell your mother that."

"Life's fine in an enclave like the Defederacy, but I think I should have stayed in Pennsylvania."

"Daryl, you were ten years old. Grandpa died. We were lucky to get you out of there."

Alex felt his throat tightening. He didn't like remembering the Great Die-Off. He didn't like imagining what his father's lonely death had been like as anarchy had enveloped Unionville, and the Number 16 nanogen had ripped his father's lungs to mush.

"I would have survived, Dad. I would have been around other Number 16s, people like me."

"I'm glad you're in the Defederacy with us," said Alex.

The boat continued to chug upstream. The air was damp after all the rain. Far in the distance Alex heard a burst of small-arms fire.

Daryl shook his head. "It's just that I sometimes feel so lonely in the Defederacy," he said. "Without anybody else like me."

Chapter 8

Alex washed the wheelhouse windows. Three days in the EMZ and he still hadn't had a chance to go out and explore yet. He wanted to see it. Everybody in the EMZ was under thirty. What had that done to society here? But he couldn't get off the ship yet. That's because there was always something to do. He didn't mind. Tony was teaching him how to read sea charts, and how to interpret the weather readouts. Alex dipped his squeegee into a bucket and scrubbed a nasty spot of seagull shit away. He watched Tony and Jill come out the rear door. They walked to the stern. They were having another argument. He ran the rubber squeegee across the glass, wiping the surface clean. He tried to ignore them. But he couldn't help thinking all this fighting had to be bad for Daryl.

Alex was just about to start the next window when he heard the hum of Servitech's electric cart behind him. He looked over the bow. Here they came again, dragging their little white wagon past the ruin of the Arlington Memorial Bridge, the wagon stacked with white fiberlite crates. Where did they get their blood donors? Suarez probably paid them with the sacks of old greenbacks he had. It was really beginning to bother Alex.

Suarez looked up at him.

"We need some help getting this stuff into the hold," he said.

Alex put the squeegee in his bucket and helped Suarez.

He climbed into the crane cabin, now that he actually knew how to operate the thing, and lowered the cargo net to the concrete embankment. Suarez and his men loaded the first crate into the cargo net. Alex shifted the levers and hauled the load up.

When he was finished loading all the crates into the hold, he watched the Servitech employees shift them into the refrigeration units. Alex climbed out of the crane and approached Suarez.

"More blood?" he said.

Suarez gave him a cagey glance, surprised that he should know about the blood.

"No, not blood," he said. "And if I were you, Dr. Denyer, I'd stop being so curious."

"This is going too slowly," said Daryl.

Alex stood behind Daryl. Daryl, like a virtuoso, performed pyrotechnics on his three linked computers. Having searched and studied a hundred references to Servitech on the open Web to no avail, Daryl, with growing frustration, handed his father a razor. He then lifted a couple of inter-synaptic patches.

"I haven't used these in a while," he said. "Could

you shave the back of my head?" Daryl pointed. "This spot and this spot."

Alex took the razor—it looked like one of Jill's feminine razors, pink with a flowered design—and shaved the two spots, one on either side of Daryl's crown. Out the porthole Alex saw the collapsed ruin of the Arlington Memorial Bridge. Daryl dug through his horrendously messy desk drawer and found a bifurcated synaptic cable. Out the other porthole Alex saw the rear of the Lincoln Memorial. He was checking both portholes for dirt. He was glad to see he had done such a good job on both.

"Mom doesn't like me using my implants," said Daryl. "I tell her they're perfectly safe, especially these ones. These are good ones. From Juan de Fuca, the best. Real smooth. But Mom still worries about them. She worries about everything."

Alex finished shaving the two spots indicated. "It's just because she cares."

Daryl pulled out a tube of contact jelly from his desk drawer. "Put a dab on each spot. Right where those little bumps are. Those are my implants. Tony helped me find a pair cheap. In Hosta Street. Jill doesn't know he gets me stuff." Daryl peered into his desk drawer. "Now, if only I could find that surgical tape."

Alex applied some contact jelly onto the two shaved spots.

"Things aren't going so great between Jill and Tony right now, are they?" he asked.

Daryl shrugged. "You know Mom."

"I spoke to her about you going out," said Alex. "She said I could take you up to the Lincoln Memorial. I thought we'd go up there maybe tomorrow. It might be fun. Just the two of us."

"Dad, I'll go to the Lincoln Memorial with you. But I plan on going right downtown at some point, whether she likes it or not."

"Dr. Colgan says Patuxent Rebels have been active downtown. I'd be careful."

"Dad, I'm always careful," said Daryl. "And it's not *all* anarchy here. I want to go out and see what the Number 16s have done. I'm curious. But ever since I got hit in Pennsylvania, Mom wants to keep me in a box."

Alex sighed. "It was a big thing, Daryl."

"I know it was, Dad, but I still have a life to live. Mom doesn't mind when Tony has a contract to Eurocorp or SEASEZ, or any place where it's safe. But Eurocorp doesn't interest me. Neither does SEASEZ, or the New Transvaal, or any of those other enclaves. Give me an EMZ, where everything isn't microcontrolled, and where there's bound to be a few surprises from time to time."

"Mom doesn't like surprises," said Alex.

"No kidding," said Daryl. He renewed his efforts to find the surgical tape. "Here it is." He lifted the roll out of his drawer. He gave it to his father. "Tape the patches into place, and we'll be ready to go."

Alex taped the inter-synaptic patches to the shaved spots. Daryl plugged the bifurcated cable into his central computer. He keyed in a few commands, then sat back, closed his eyes, and took a deep breath.

He exhaled.

As he exhaled, screens flicked by one by one, text and image, slowly at first, but then faster. Daryl's own brain supplied extra computing power, the screens finally moving so fast Alex couldn't read them at all. In this way, Daryl processed all available information on Servitech from all available sources, even encrypted ones, within a matter of minutes. Daryl's eyes jerked quickly under his closed lids, like he was in REM sleep. The index finger of his right hand twitched. His knees came together and he went pigeon-toed for several moments. After five minutes, the screens slowed. Daryl opened his eyes. He keyed in a command, stopped the interface, and yawned, as if the mind-machine encounter had left him fatigued.

"I've got it," he said. "Servitech is a subsidiary of Susquehanna Technologies. Susquehanna is owned by the Defederacy of Delaware." Daryl tugged the cords linking his brain to the computer and pulled them free. "This blood drive Servitech is doing? Your cousin's running the show. Surprise, surprise."

Alex had to go for a walk after that to clear his mind. Why would Graham be interested in EMZ blood? The whole thing left him baffled. Graham was like a shadow in his life now, first yanking him from his job, then blacklisting him from getting another one, and now following him to the EMZ in this most unexpected way, to draw blood, pints and pints of the stuff, from the infected young victims of a ruined Washington, D.C.

He left the ship and walked south along the river, following a pathway parallel to Ohio Drive. As he reached West Potomac Park, he got the sense that someone was following him. He turned around. The two new crew from Servitech were indeed trailing him. His shoulders tensed. In the last light of day, he made them out clearly. He continued on. He couldn't help being spooked by these two. The grass in the park was dead, brown, and choked with weeds. He glanced over his shoulder. They were still with him. And it was getting dark.

The blood thing. Why? Didn't Graham have enough to handle already? Didn't he have the war? And what about the AWP? Weren't the Martians fiddling with it, maybe even making it battle ready? And what about the Repealists? Blowing up subway tunnels. Agitating. Getting mad about this new proposed law, the one that would ship old veterans like Zirko to Chincoteague Bay, no questions asked. Then there was Hawaii, the news of the day—the fifth Defederacy was actually going to secede from everybody else after all and join SEASEZ. With all this on his plate, how did Graham have the time for intrigue in the Arlington EMZ? And those two men behind him? They had to be Graham's. Were they really following him? Or was he just so paranoid now, everything seemed like a threat?

He walked a little further down and broke into a jog, just to see what they would do. He glanced over his shoulder a second time. They jogged after him. They weren't hiding it anymore. Their game was over. Was this really Graham? he wondered. A shadow in his life in the form of these two men? He put it together as he ran deeper into the park. Graham learns at the last minute of his travel plans to the EMZ. Port officials try to cancel his permit. Maybe Graham fears he'll talk to the Stationhouse, or some other perceived enemy. Graham can't cancel his travel permit because it's too late. He decides to intercept the *Beelzebub* before it reaches port. These two goons come aboard. They've been hired to do the business on him. Alex frowned. So typical. So *Graham*. Conspiracies everywhere. He thought of Tony's warnings. *People get beat up. People get killed.* He felt as if he had gone from politically innocent geek to cynical and streetwise fugitive, all in the course of a few weeks.

He glanced over his shoulder a third time. The two men ran at an easy jog. They were younger than he was. They could easily outrun him. Which meant he would have to outsmart them.

Some trees grew to the left. The weeds were high over there. A hedge ran through the park. If he could dodge behind this hedge, his pursuers wouldn't see him for at least thirty seconds. He could hide in the tall weeds on the other side of the hedge. As a bonus, it was nearly dark out. That would make it doubly difficult for them. He counted to ten, then bolted. He dove over the hedge and tumbled to the ground. He got up, reversed direction and, keeping hunched, ran to a spot under the trees where the weeds grew high. He hid there. He waited. He heard the two men approach. They were talking to each other. He stilled his breathing. Their voices got closer.

"Where did he go?" one asked.

"I think he went over there," said the other one.

So. They were really looking for him. Why? He couldn't believe he was in this predicament. His heart raced. This was too much. He forced himself to peek over the hedge just to see what they were doing. They were walking away from him now, over toward the fountain. One had a big lead pipe. Were they going to beat him over the head with it? He sank back down. Accidents happened, people got killed, and there was never an investigation. He couldn't believe Graham would resort to this kind of thing. He had to think this through. He had to come up with a plan.

Then he heard someone calling. Suarez. Was Suarez in on it too? That didn't surprise him in the least.

"Dean?" called Suarez. "Abel?"

Suarez got closer, stopping when he was only ten yards away from Alex.

"Dean?" he called again. "Abel?"

Distantly . . . "Over here."

Alex heard footsteps approach. Voices got louder. The two men were coming back. Alex sank lower into the tall weeds, his body stiff with tension. What did a lead pipe feel like when it sank into your skull? And would they then dump his body into the river, or would they just leave it to rot in the park?

The two finally stood next to Suarez. "We were looking for him," one of them said. "We think he ran over there somewhere."

"I'm glad I caught you," said Suarez. "It's off. You don't have to worry about him anymore. There's been a change of plan. I've got your money for you. You can go anytime you like."

The three retreated. Alex heard their legs swishing through the tall weeds. He heard them talking. But now they were too far away and he couldn't make out their words. He stayed in the weeds until he couldn't hear them at all. He got to his knees and looked around. His heart boomed inside his chest. Were they DIS? He wiped his forehead with the back of his hand. A change of plan. He puzzled over the words as he finally got to his feet. He peered over the hedge. He saw Suarez walking back to the ship. The two young men headed toward the city as if they belonged there. A change of plan. Did that mean he was safe for the time being? He sighed. He could understand Jill's sentiment. Sometimes it seemed safer to live in a box.

Alex was compacting trash the next evening when Tony tapped him on the shoulder. Alex turned. He switched off the noisy machine.

"Jon Lewis is on the wireless vidphone," Tony said.

Alex followed Tony up to the wheelhouse.

Jon's pale visage occupied the vidphone screen.

Alex could immediately see that something was wrong.

"What happened?" he asked.

Jon paused.

"The Megaplex has arrested Max Morrow," he said. "On charges of espionage."

Alex grew still. His shoulders sank. His chin dipped. Surprise, surprise, as his son would say. It felt as if something were physically squeezing him inside. Max? Espionage?

"Do they have any solid evidence?" he asked, because he didn't want to believe this.

"I'm told it's airtight," said Jon. "He's been funneling secrets to Martian nationals in the Defederacy of Hawaii. I'm told it's been a lengthy investigation. Three years long. They've traced money. They have wiretaps. It's not good, Alex. Ruth and I are shocked."

"I'm . . . I'm dumbfounded."

"We all are."

"It just doesn't seem possible," said Alex. "Max a spy? He's our boss. He's our friend."

"I know."

Alex tried to think of some way to defend Max.

"We've been through so much together. The Great Die-Off. The Alien War. And if it weren't for him, Daryl never would have been rescued from Pennsylvania after the Bombardment. The pressure he put on the DDF rescue people was invaluable."

"I know, Alex, but . . . word came down this morning."

Alex shook his head, incredulous. "And he's been arrested?" he said, having a hard time accepting the whole thing. Max under arrest seemed too absurd—too tragic.

"Yes."

"And where have they taken him?"

"Chincoteague Bay."

"Chincoteague Bay?" Alex was alarmed. "Jon, that's ridiculous. He'll never survive in Chincoteague Bay. How could Graham do that to him? Doesn't Graham remember everything Max has done for us? His quick implementation of the enclave technology? His security and screening procedures? His virtuoso bean counting, all that creative accounting that allowed us to acquire the enclave technology in the first place? If it weren't for Max, Delaware would have been an EMZ right now, and everybody over thirty would have been dead, me and you included."

"I know, Alex. And we're all upset about it. But we have to face facts."

"I'm more than upset, Jon. I'm furious. And I'm heartsick at the thought of Max in Chincoteague Bay. The rumors that come out of that place. They're horrible."

"I know, I know. But it really looks like Max turned on us. The ISS has been leaking like a sieve for the past two years. You know that. They haven't been able to find the leak. That's because the leak was right at the top. Max was good. He hid his activities well. But the DIS finally figured it out. Now Max has to pay the price. In a sense, every one of us has to pay the price."

"I don't want to believe this."

"Neither do I. But it's what we're faced with. And it's what *you're* faced with. The DIS sent a memo to the Alien Branch concerning you in particular."

"Me? Why?"

"Prepare yourself."

Alex's shoulders sank. "What now?"

"Max planted false information about you, buddy. That's why your layoff was fast-tracked. That's why you're out of a job right now."

Alex's throat tightened. He thought of Max's cheerful broad face, of the constant goodwill the man radiated, of the way they'd built the Alien Branch together from scratch. He thought of their long history together, nineteen years. He felt weak that Max should betray him, that Max would be so seamlessly two-faced against him.

"*He* was the one who gave Graham the wrong information?"

"Like I say, the Alien Branch got a special memo about it," said Jon.

"I can't believe this." His voice sounded squeezed, tight.

"None of us can. He wanted to throw the DIS off his own trail, so he used you as a smoke screen. It looks like some of his money transfers to Hawaii were in your name. The DIS thought you were the leak. They were waiting for confirmation before they took more drastic measures. But their investigation finally revealed that you were innocent." Alex swallowed a few times against the great sorrow he felt building in his chest. "And now that they know you're innocent, they want to get you cleared and re-vetted as fast as possible."

Something clicked. Alex remembered the two young men in the park, and Suarez coming to get them. Was this it, then? Suarez's change of plan? Why Suarez had called off the dogs at the last moment? Graham, sniffing around at the top, at first suspecting him, but then finding out it was Max all along, calling Suarez in the nick of time?

"I tried to tell Graham I was innocent," he said.

"Graham had his information from Max, so he thought it was bona fide. I wasn't holding out much hope for you, buddy, but it looks like they might want you back."

"I'm not sure I want to come back."

"Buddy . . . I think this is legitimate. I think you should consider it. The Megaplex was doing its best. But Max's smoke screen was a thick one, and they were fooled by it. I think in this particular circumstance, you have to give the Megaplex the benefit of the doubt."

"Are they going to review my case?" asked Alex.

"They've been reviewing it for the last few days."

"Have they picked an interim ISS director to replace Max?"

"They have," said Jon. "Cameron Healy. Ever heard of him?"

Alex nodded, choking down his continuing sense of betrayal. "I've been in meetings with him on a number of occasions," he said. "When Max and me had to take sticky issues to the higher-ups for approval. Healy never said much. He just sat there and watched. I thought he was retired."

"I've done some digging," said Jon. "He's been brought out of retirement. He used to work for the Defederacy Intelligence Service. His specialty was house cleaning. That's what he's doing at the ISS. He's going through the ISS from top to bottom, giving it the new-broom treatment. People are afraid. Ruth and me hate it there right now. We never know what's going to happen next. There's an atmosphere of mistrust. Everybody thinks everybody else is working for the Megaplex, and it's hard to get anything done."

Alex took a deep breath. "You'll just have to soldier on somehow."

"Things will be a lot better if you come back, Alex," said Jon. "And that might be sooner than you think."

"What makes you say that?"

"Because the Megaplex is really concerned about this new AWP. Its status has changed since you've been gone. The Martians are doing even more to it, and it's made the DDF nervous. They're grumbling to the Megaplex about a need for experts. And that would be you, buddy. In fact, this special memo to the Alien Branch mentions they might actually go to the EMZ to get you, if the need becomes urgent. So don't get too comfortable on that ship. You may be back here sooner than you think."

Alex sat there for a moment. He felt a mix of emotions. Betrayal because of Max. *Sadness* because of Max. But also excitement at the prospect of going back. At the same time, he wasn't sure he wanted to go back.

"I don't like the way Graham treated me," he said. "It was like I was a kid all over again, and Graham was the older cousin needing to keep me in line."

"Yes, but don't you feel the tug?" said Jon. "They may want you to look at the AWP. Wouldn't you like to get your hands on it?"

Alex looked out the window at the river. The river was peaceful, idyllic, with a wash of purple light in the sky: sunset on the Potomac. Natalia had cleared off. Two End-of-Lifers paddled by in a rowboat. He had to admit, the tug was there. The *AWP*. The Martians were doing something to it; and that made him think about the things he would do to it if he got half the chance.

"Well . . . one thing about Graham," he said. "When he's wrong, he's always willing to admit it."

"Then you should give Graham a break."

"Maybe I should."

"Because it's not just about you and Graham anymore, is it?" said Jon.

"No."

"The AWP might become a threat after all. And at that point, you and Graham will have to put your differences aside. At that point, you'll have to think of the Defederacy as a whole."

Alex hesitated as he reached the bottom of the companionway on his way to the galley for a drink of water fifteen minutes later. He listened. Damn. Tony and Jill were having another argument in the galley. Their voices were low but feverish. He looked down the passageway. He saw Daryl through the open door of the captain's cabin. Jill's voice rose higher. She and Tony were arguing about cost overruns on the food. All this arguing. About everything. They got caught up in a cycle of fighting and they couldn't break free. Daryl was sitting there, just listening. His son looked sad, pensive. Alex lifted his hand, signaled to Daryl. Daryl looked up.

Alex beckoned, then pointed outside. His son smiled, looking relieved. Daryl got out of his chair and hurried past the galley. The fight went on unabated. Father and son climbed the companionway to the deck silently.

Then Alex spoke. "Jeesh," he said.

"Tony was supposed to take me out later on," said Daryl, still smiling, "but I guess he's too busy." He gestured at the gangplank. "Why don't we go have a look?"

They left the ship and approached the Lincoln Memorial from the rear. A few ragged saplings grew from its roof, dirt caked its walls, and garbage littered the surrounding lawn. Grass pushed up knee-high. So did goldenrod, thistle, and bittersweet nightshade.

"I got a call from Jon," said Alex. "He had some news about Uncle Max." Alex filled Daryl in on the startling developments regarding Max. "I can hardly believe it. Max was a crucial player in our fight against the Aliens. He more or less put an anti-nanogen barrier around the Defederacy so none of us in Delaware would get infected. All those negotiations he had to carry out with the other enclaves, SEASEZ, the New Transvaal, the Ganaraska Preserve, not to mention the other Defederacies. Those neutralization protocols and isotope recognition systems he put into place. The way he took our existing buffer areas from Shan Extremist days and turned them into full-fledged fortresses against alien attack. We owe him a lot. And I personaly owe him a lot. Now I find he's planted false information about me." He contiuned walking, hands in his pockets, brooding on the situation. "Anyway, the Megaplex may want me to come back to work."

"Really?"

"Yes."

"And are you going to?" asked Daryl.

"I think I'll have to. They're worried about this new AWP."

"I thought they said it was just a piece of scrap."

"Now the Martians are doing something to it, I'm not sure what, but it's got them concerned. The Megaplex may actually come and get me in the EMZ."

Graffiti covered every one of the Lincoln Memorial's thirty-six pillars. Alex and Daryl climbed the steps and went inside. The place smelled of human feces and urine. Several pieces of litter tumbled past them in a gust of wind. Damp blankets and sleeping bags, along with several extinguished campfires, dotted the darker recesses of the memorial. Alex saw Lincoln sitting up there in the shadows. Lincoln's head was missing. So was his right leg from the knee down, his right foot remaining, just sitting there all by itself. The rest of him was shot up badly, both with heavy-caliber and small-arms fire, a cruel and ironic vandalism against the assassinated president's monument.

"God, what a place," said Alex.

They descended the front steps and made their way across the road to the north side of the Reflecting Pool.

"So do you think you'll be exonerated?" asked Daryl. "Now that they have Max?"

Alex shrugged. "I don't know," he said. "But I think so. Jon says they're reviewing my case."

"And do you want to work for them again?" asked Daryl.

"I think I'll have to," said Alex.

"Because I was getting used to having you around again."

Alex sighed. "I'm going to make an effort to spend more time with you, Daryl. Especially because of the way Jill and Tony are carrying on. I thought I might sell my condo and move to Hurlock. That way, I'd be closer to you."

"Dad . . . Hurlock? You're not Hurlock material. You're too mainstream. Too Lincoln Towers."

"I'd like to be closer to you," he said, trying not to feel rankled by his son's assessment. "Plus I have a friend living there . . . you remember Reba?"

"Yes."

Alex sighed. "She meant a lot to me, Daryl."

"I know she did, Dad. I always liked her."

There was no water in the Reflecting Pool. Someone had driven a truck into it. Alex and Daryl passed what was left of the Vietnam Memorial, much of it cracked and defaced with graffiti. They came to the Shan Memorial, honoring those who had died in the biological and chemical attacks perpetrated by Shan Extremists in the twenty-second century; half the bronze children were pushed over, while all the adult figures looked badly shot up, used for target practice by armed gangs of Number 16s.

They ventured into Constitution Gardens. Alex

looked east along the National Mall. All the trees had been cut down for firewood. The place was a wasteland of mud and knee-high weeds. The gardens stunk of shit.

"I think we should turn back here," he said.

"So soon?" said Daryl.

"Especially because Sandy Parker has that curfew in place."

"Dad, the curfew's not for another two hours."

Alex sighed. "I just don't want to upset your mother. She's already upset enough as it is."

Daryl nodded sagely. "You got that right. But I don't think we should let that stop us. Let's go up one of these side streets. Just for a couple of blocks."

Alex peered toward the side streets. He had to admit, he was curious. "Okay. Two blocks. But then we turn back."

"Unless we find something interesting."

"Daryl, I'm serious."

"I'm only kidding, Dad."

They ventured past the east end of the Vietnam Memorial, crossed Constitution Avenue, and headed north on Twentieth Street. They passed the old Federal Reserve Building. The stone eagle above its massive entryway was missing a wing, all of its tall, narrow windows were broken or shot out, and its white façade was pitted by heavy-caliber rifle fire. They turned left on C Street, and were just nearing the old State Department Building when Alex saw a dead body lying at the side of the road. He put his hand on Daryl's arm.

"I'm okay, Dad," said Daryl. "Let's have a look."

They approached the body cautiously. The street was deserted. Abandoned cars lined the side of the road. A streetlight on the corner flickered feebly. Alex saw that the victim was a man. He was horribly hunched, curled in on himself, his long, wispy white hair flicking in the wind.

"Are you sure you want to see this?" he asked Daryl. "He's a dead End-of-Lifer."

"I realize that, Dad. But I just want a look."

They walked to the corpse. The man wore paper clothes, thick and fibrous; they were horribly ripped, revealed most of his back, and part of his left leg. Great psoriasislike plaques covered both back and leg, and the nanogenic stench coming from the man was enough to suffocate. The man looked about ninety years old, but couldn't have been more than thirty. His chin and nose were long, witchlike, and his eyes were partially open, staring sightlessly at the litter in the curb. A puddle of orange vomit rested below his lips. Alex knew about this orange vomit. This was the final, horrifying symptom of a final-stage Number 16 victim, the orange bile that had choked everybody over thirty in the unprotected zones during the Great Die-Off. Here they were ten years later, and the Bombardment was still killing people. He thought of his father. His father had died just like this man. Alone. Abandoned. Choking to death on this orange gunk. Alex hated the aliens more than ever. He glanced at Daryl. Daryl stared.

"Seen enough?" asked Alex.

Daryl shook his head. "Maybe it *is* all anarchy."

"The poor man," said Alex.

Daryl looked at Alex with sudden concern. "It's going to be different for me, isn't it, Dad?" Daryl's eyes clouded with tears. Gone was Alex's sophisticated and often sarcastic teenager. "I mean . . . you're going to be there with me. When I die. Holding my hand, right?" He was a child again. "Because I don't think I can face it alone, Dad. I really don't. I don't want to end up like this guy. I want a real funeral."

Alex put his arm around Daryl and pulled him near. "I'll be there," he said, but his voice quavered. He stared at the man, facing the worst of the worst—his own son's death. "You won't be alone. I'll make sure of it. Both me and Mom will be there, right by your side, right till the end."

Chapter 9

Alex sanitized the waste products from the ship's fuel utilization systems a little later that night. The waste products from the main engine's hydrogen and oxygen cells, forming water once they went through the engine's hybrid generation chambers, had to be filtered and chlorinated before going to the ship's water storage tanks. He introduced chlorine and switched on the churn cycle. He listened to the machine hum. He was worried about Daryl. And about Jill and Tony. Now that he was around them all the time, the cracks in the family unit had become more apparent, especially with all the fighting between Jill and Tony.

He was just getting ready to pump the sanitized water into the storage tanks when Jill came down. Her step was agitated, her eyes drawn, and the corners of her lips pulled back. He hated to see her this way. She looked worn-out.

"Is Daryl down here?" she asked.

She sounded worried, something she was trying to hide, but something which Alex, having been married to the woman for so many years, recognized instantly.

"No," he said. "I thought he was upstairs."

She sighed.

"No," she said. "And Tony's gone, too." Her face stiffened. "I think they must have gone out together." Her shoulders rose. "I told them not to. Not this late."

"Did you check the memorial?" he asked. "Maybe they went there."

"I'm not going out there by myself," she said, frowning.

"Is Ely here?" asked Alex. "Maybe he knows where they are. Because neither of them have been down here."

"Ely's working in his cabin."

Alex keyed in the necessary commands, pumped the sanitized water into the storage tanks, then put the whole system on standby.

"Let's check with him," he said.

They climbed the metal stairs to the second deck and walked along the corridor to Colgan's cabin. The whole boat stunk of chlorine, now that Alex was sanitizing the engine's waste products. Colgan's door was partially open. Colgan sat at his desk working, his computer on, a half dozen waferscreens full of notes pinned to his bulletin board. The white-haired researcher looked up from his work, his eyes narrowing.

"What's wrong?" he asked.

"Have you seen Daryl?" asked Alex.

Colgan raised his eyebrows. "No," he said. "You can't find him?"

Alex shook his head. "Did Tony say anything to you? They're both gone. Did they come this way?"

"No," said Colgan. "I've been in my cabin for the last couple hours and no one's been by. Have you asked any of the Servitech crew?"

"None of them are back from their late run," said Alex.

"Suarez tells me Sandy's exempted them from the curfew," said Colgan. "He wouldn't tell me why."

Jill lifted her hand in an agitated gesture. "Damn that Tony," she said. "I told him not to do this. I specifically told them they were not to go out tonight. Not so close to the curfew. But Tony's gone and dragged Daryl out there anyway." She turned to Alex, a righteous and indignant look in her eyes. "He'll do this sometimes. He'll do things to spite me. Especially if we've just had a fight."

"So they took off somewhere?" said Colgan, sounding concerned.

"It looks that way," said Alex.

Colgan checked his watch. "It's ten-thirty." He shook his head. "Damn."

"I know," said Jill. "It's after Parker's curfew, isn't it?"

"Yes," said Colgan. "But I'm sure it'll be all right. Unless they get mistaken for Patuxent Rebels." He turned to Alex. "We should go out and look for them." Colgan grimaced. "I told Tony if he wanted to wander around, he should do it before ten o'clock."

"I told him that too," said Jill. "But I'm afraid we . . . I'm sorry about this. We're usually not like this."

"Alex, let's get our coats on," said Colgan. "It'll be safer if we both go."

Jill's expression of chronic worry intensified, her eyes widening in alarm.

"Be careful," she said.

Alex gave her a pat on the shoulder. "Don't worry, Jill. Everything's going to be fine. We'll find them. I'm sure they haven't gone far."

The two men got their coats on and left the *Beelzebub*.

Mist moved in from the river. Alex and Colgan climbed the small hill at the foot of the bridge and crossed the road to the Lincoln Memorial. They saw some electric lights burning in the distance—a measure of Sandy Parker's success in the Arlington EMZ, as most electric grids in the various other EMZs had broken down years ago.

"We're just going to look for him?" asked Alex, because it didn't sound like the best plan, now that all this mist was moving in.

"We'll find some Stationhouse Militia," said Colgan. "They might have an idea of where they are."

"You know *all* the militia?" asked Alex.

"I don't have to," said Colgan. "Not as long as I'm wearing this." He held up his fist-and-wheat-sheaf amulet. "That's their symbol. Sandy gave it to me a couple years ago. I get *carte blanche* whenever I come here. In return, Sandy gets papers into the Defederacy when he turns into an End-of-Lifer. It's our little deal. He doesn't want to grow old here. It's not nice for an End-of-Lifer here."

They left Constitution Gardens and headed north along Eighteenth Street. They came to E Street.

Alex saw a woman, naked from the waist up. She

114

was an End-of-Lifer. She wandered the empty thoroughfare, weaving back and forth on the sidewalk, apparently unconcerned about the curfew. She passed under a streetlight. Alex saw the yellow discoloration of her skin, the elongated nose and chin, and clumps of hair falling out of her head. As she got closer he saw dark, calcified plaques all over her skin, particularly on the backs of her hands. She wore a miniskirt and high heels. Nothing else. She looked like a prostitute. She carried a bottle of liquor. She looked terribly old, but Alex knew she had to be under thirty.

When she saw them, she walked straight to them. "Give me money," she demanded.

The Number 16 reek came from her in thick waves, astringent and penetrating. Alex felt disquieted. Colgan took out some ragged old greenbacks and piled them into the poor woman's hand. Colgan couldn't seem to put the money in her hand fast enough. Under his full beard, Colgan's lips went slack. His eyes glistened. If only they could *do* something, thought Alex. If only there were some way they could help all these people. But there wasn't. For whatever reason, the aliens had unleashed Hell on Earth, and this woman, standing here in a miniskirt that no longer fit her distorted and ugly body, was one of Hell's more pitiable citizens.

Nearing Seventeenth Street, Alex heard a bass guitar, and now, reaching the White House, he saw a huge party on the White House lawn. Again, no concern for the curfew. Not an old person in sight. The music washed over Alex in thick waves, loud, tuneless, rhythmic, violent, unique—like nothing he had ever heard in the Defederacy.

They continued along E Street for two blocks, then jogged north to the artillery-pounded ruin of the National Theater.

"The Patuxents did that," said Colgan, pointing to the theater. "They were able to shell it all the way from the river."

Despite the curfew, all sorts of partiers and revelers crowded the street. Some of them gathered on either curb, like they were waiting for a parade. After a moment, Alex saw that they were actually waiting for a drag race. At the far end of the street, two trucks sat side by side, headlights on, their drivers revving jet engines mounted on the truck beds. Colgan grabbed him by the arm and pulled him into a doorway.

"We're going to have to wait until this is over," he said.

"They're going to race those things?" asked Alex.

"Yes."

Alex peered down the street.

"Isn't that risky?" he asked. "Those engines are huge."

The corners of Colgan's eyes drooped and a resigned smile came to his face.

"What do you expect, Alex?" he said. "It's Spring Break every day of the year in the EMZ. These people are young. Young people always underestimate risk. And many Number 16s live solely for fun because they know they're going to die soon. With no old farts like us around, it's youth culture unchecked. They love extreme sports." Colgan motioned at the big jet-propulsion ground-based vehicles. "This kind of street racing is but one example. They do bungee jumping from tall buildings. They base jump from

the Washington Monument. They play Russian rou-
lette. Anything for a rush."

A man with a rifle walked to the middle of the
road, pointed the weapon to the sky, waited a few
seconds as a hush fell over the crowd, then fired.

Afterburners flared. The trucks jumped forward
like voracious animals pouncing on unsuspecting
prey. The man with the rifle ducked his chin, narrowed his shoulders, and made himself as small as
possible as the souped-up vehicles sped past. Then
he turned around and watched the trucks rocket
down the street, jumping up and down with excitement, punching the air with his fist. The roar echoed
from building to building. The truck on the left
nudged toward the curb, jumped the curb, grew unstable, then leaped into the air like a dolphin arcing
out of the sea, remained aloft for ten seconds, then
slammed into a building a block away and exploded.

"Jesus!" said Alex

"Let's get going," said Colgan.

"Shouldn't we go help?" asked Alex.

"Don't bother."

"Yes, but people have been killed, Ely."

"That's the whole point," said Colgan. "That gives
them more of a rush than anything. And there's
really nothing we can do. They don't like outsiders
interfering in their games. They're liable to beat us
to death if we stick our noses into it. Let's just head
out. Half the people here were hoping to see one of
those things crash anyway. When you die at thirty,
life seems cheap."

Alex and Colgan continued east along E Street
through the thickening mist. Alex couldn't get over

it. Death was so casual here. He was shaking from the drag race. The big fireball kept replaying itself in his mind. How could people live any sort of life here? How could the victims of the Number 16 alien bombardment ever hold out any hope for themselves when they were trapped in the Hell of the EMZ? He wasn't used to this. The back of his throat was dry. He was getting an education, that was for sure. He was getting a chance to see how the world really worked. And he didn't like what he saw. He steadied his nerves. His main goal was to find his son. His step grew surer, his stride more determined.

At Fifth Street, Stationhouse Militia accosted them. "Rico, it's me, Ely," said Colgan.

Colgan gripped the fist-and-wheat-sheaf medallion around his neck and showed it to Rico, a young man with dark hair and a narrow face. Rico wore an identical medallion around his own neck. The other militiaman, a boy of eleven or twelve, dragged a grenade launcher in a wagon. Rocket-propelled grenades dangled thickly around the boy's neck, along with his own fist-and-wheat-sheaf medallion.

Rico looked at Alex, his dark eyes narrowing. "Who's he?" he asked, jerking his head toward Alex.

"That's Alex," said Colgan. "He's from the Defederacy. We're looking for his son. Daryl. We think he's somewhere out here wandering around with an old guy named Tony. Have you seen them? Daryl's eighteen years old. He's tall, skinny, and pale. He's got reddish long hair. Tony's in his mid-forties. He's got long dark hair. He's wearing a black leather jacket, black denims, and black cowboy boots. They're both from the *Beelzebub*. They're both with us. Do you know where they are?"

Rico assessed the situation. "Got any money?" he asked.

Colgan pulled out a wad of nearly disintegrated greenbacks. He counted out ten twenties and gave them to Rico. Rico took the bills and shoved them into his pocket. The boy with the grenade launcher interjected with a protracted and unintelligible rant, presumably something to do with not getting any money, not a single word understandable. Rico gave the boy a frustrated look.

"Tick hasn't got a tongue," he told them. "We cut it out because he wouldn't shut up."

Rico reluctantly gave Tick two rumpled old twenties, one of them patched together with tape. Alex stared. Tick's tongue, cut out. All because he didn't know how to hold it. If death was casual here, so was brutality.

Rico turned to Alex. "We've got your son at the Stationhouse," he said. A frown came to his face. "They shouldn't be out here after curfew, though. They're lucky to be alive. The Patuxent have been killing a lot of people at night. Sniping from rooftops. Sandy told us to keep an eye out for *Beelzebub* crew. You're lucky we found them. We've got them safe and sound. But you should talk to them. Those Patuxents are real killers. And nothing would make them happier than to kill some Defederacy types."

Rico and Tick led Alex and Colgan to Union Station, their headquarters. The building was badly damaged after fifty years of internecine strife. Heavy-caliber gunfire had pitted the graffiti-covered façade. All its arched windows had been bricked up. Three flagpoles stood in the semicircular patch of grass out front. Two dead bodies hung from the outer poles, while a flag emblazoned with the fist-and-wheat-sheaf symbol flew from the center one. Gutted cars, smashed-up trucks, and rolls of barbed wire formed a barricade in front of the arched central entryway. Rico and Tick led Alex and Colgan to this entryway.

"It's us," called Rico, to whoever was on the other side. "We've got some crew from the *Beelzebub* with us. They've come for the other two."

"Hang on," a voice called from inside.

Alex listened. Militia inside moved something heavy out of the way. A moment later the gate opened and Rico and Tick led them through.

They walked past a dozen heavily armed militia, climbed the steps, and entered the station.

The front concourse, a lofty cathedral-like space, was crowded with hundreds of jerry-built sheds, shacks, and shanties arranged higgledy-piggeldy amid a haphazard arrangement of twisting lanes and alleys—a village inside the train station. Cooking smoke hung in the air. Ladders led up to the recessed windows above. People camped in the recesses. Other people had built shacks in the hundred or so old stores and restaurants lining either side of the concourse. The place stunk of too many people crammed together in too small a space.

Rico and Tick escorted them down to the platforms. A train had just pulled in on Track Nine. Some rural types poked and prodded a dozen small dinosaurs along a ramp onto the platform, a reminder of Alex's youth, when such genetically derived livestock had been commonly seen in the fields and pastures around his Pennsylvanian home.

"I didn't realize they still bred those things," he said to Colgan.

"The EMZs don't have the same high-yield growth centers we do," said Colgan. "They have to do it the old-fashioned way. These particular ones look like they're derived from triceratops, don't they? A lot of meat on them."

They continued on to a grimmer scene: Stationhouse Militia led prisoners of war—Patuxent Rebels shackled chain-gang style—up a ramp into a fetid, dilapidated old freight car. Colgan shook his head.

"What's going on?" asked Alex.

"Rebels," he said. "They'll be worked to death."

They finally left the covered platforms and went outside into the open train yard. Rico turned around.

"We're going to K-Tower," he told them. "That's where Sandy lives. I guess he's talking to your son and that other guy. Sandy's a great talker. He especially likes to talk to Defederacy types. He's always trying to find out everything he can about the Defederacy."

Rico led them down the steps to the track bed.

At this point, they left the tongueless Tick behind.

Dozens of lights brightened the area with a harsh glare, shining through a chaotic hornet's nest of overhead train wires. They walked across several train tracks, their feet crunching against the gravel.

They came to K-Tower, the old stationmaster's tower.

Rico pointed. "Sandy lives on the second floor," he said.

Three militiamen guarded the outside stairs. They

were dressed in old-style costumes from the eighteenth century: breeches, tricorn hats, and frock coats with big brass buttons. The clothes looked old, brittle, and faded. The incongruity of these costumes puzzled Alex. He couldn't understand why these militiamen would wear such apparel. Rico called to them.

"These men are *Beelzebub* crew," he told them. "They're here to get those other two. The ones we brought in earlier." Rico gestured at Colgan with some deference. "This is Ely."

Colgan's name obviously meant something to these men. They immediately made way for Colgan. Colgan glanced at Alex and raised his eyebrows. Rico led Alex and Colgan up the stairs.

As they climbed the stairs, Alex asked, "Why the costumes?"

Colgan glanced over his shoulder at the oddly dressed militiamen. "Sandy raids the Smithsonian Institute from time to time. He's taken a fancy to Revolutionary period dress. All his personal guards and inner circle wear it."

"So the stuff those guys are wearing is original?" asked Alex.

"Probably," said Colgan. "Though I understand Sandy's having some of it made now. He himself always wears originals. He'll wear the same old coat until it falls off his back, then he'll go to the Smithsonian and find something else he likes. He's got his quirks."

Kids dressing up in costumes, thought Alex.

They entered K-Tower.

Daryl and Tony sat at a table with Sandy Parker. Alex felt an immense relief to see his son again. Some young women sat on couches, all decked out in Regency period dress.

"Dad!" Daryl gave Alex a guilty but happy look. "You found us."

"Ely brought me down," he said. "Are you okay? You should have told your mother you were going out."

"Of course he's okay," said Sandy. "We've been keeping him safe and sound, like we do all our guests from the Defederacy. I was sending some of my men to the *Beelzebub* to tell you. But I guess you jumped the gun before they got there."

"Sorry, Alex," said Tony. "I didn't know we would be gone so long. We just meant to go for a little walk. But then some of Sandy's guys invited us back here. We've been having a great time."

Tony had a glass of booze in his hand, and he reeked of alcohol, something that was bound to raise Jill's ire.

"We always like having guests in Parkerville," said Sandy, as charming as could be. The man looked about twenty-five. "Anybody from the Defederacy is always welcome here. Isn't that right, Ely?"

"You'll have a hard time convincing the Megaplex of that after the *Jamaica* sinking," said Colgan.

"I keep telling everybody, that was the Patuxent," said Sandy. "They blamed it on us to make us look bad. We love, love, *love* the Defederacy, Ely. You know that better than anyone else."

Colgan gave the young warlord a doubtful look.

Alex had to stare at Sandy's getup. It looked like it came from Paul Revere's closet. He wore a full coat in robin's-egg blue, pantaloon breeches, high boots, a cambric shirt with frilly sleeves, and a bicorn hat with a white feather. A sword in a scabbard dangled past his thigh. His coat looked as thin as tissue paper and his boots as brittle as cardboard. His only modern accessory was the fist-and-wheat-sheaf amulet around his neck.

"And it's not often we get a Number 16 from the Defederacy," said Sandy, looking at Daryl, as if Daryl were a particularly welcome guest. "I was so interested to learn what life might be like for a Number 16 in the Defederacy. We've had such a wonderful discussion, haven't we, Daryl?"

Daryl gave Sandy an uneasy look. "I guess so," he said. "Though I didn't much like the handcuffs."

"Just a precaution, my boy," said Sandy. "No offense." Sandy turned to the women. "Now . . . ladies . . . if you wouldn't mind . . . I have some private business to discuss with our friends from the Defederacy. Rico, could you take them outside? Give them something to drink. Give them something to eat. And then stand guard by my door. I don't want anybody coming in while I'm talking to our guests. Top secret stuff and all that. Strictly confidential."

Rico turned to the women. One of them had to be all of fourteen. "Let's go, girls," he said. "You heard Sandy."

The three women—one of them wearing a white-powdered wig—followed Rico outside.

Once Rico had closed the door, Sandy walked over and bolted it.

He then turned to the Defederates and lifted his shirt.

"Look at this," he said. "I'm turning into an End-of-Lifer." The characteristic Number 16 skin degeneration had started on Sandy's chest, with a great chunk of affected epidermis hanging by a blackened, plaqued-over tether. The scaly flakes around the nanogenic wound smelled vile, and the caustic stench hit Alex in revolting waves. "You've got to get me out of here, Ely. They're going to find out sooner or later, and then they're going to kill me. Rico's the only one I can trust. Cash me out, as the saying goes. That's our deal. Get my papers. I'm coming back with you on the *Beelzebub*. My number-one guys are just waiting for the chance to do me in. If they see my chest, I'm a goner."

Chapter 10

They made their way back to the *Beelzebub* in a forty-year-old limousine. The limousine had more dents, scratches, and bullet holes than Alex could count. The roof had been ripped off, and a machine gun was swivel-mounted in the trunk. He was just glad he was sitting here in the car with Daryl; that he had his son safe again. A fist-and-wheat-sheaf flag flew from a small standard bolted into the hood. Rico drove. Daryl and Tony sat in the front with Rico. Alex and Ely sat in the back with Sandy. Every so often Alex caught a whiff of the caustic nanogen smell coming from Sandy.

They drove down Delaware Avenue, Rico maneuvering his way around a few water-filled mortar craters. They came to the Capitol Building. The distinctive dome, a symbol of the old Washington, was half caved in. As they swung onto Constitution Avenue, Alex saw a few abandoned military vehicles, gutted and bashed, dented and bent, on the Capitol Building steps. Blown-up chunks of stone and brick littered the area.

"I'll be glad to be out of this place," Sandy said. "It's no place to retire."

They passed a group of militiamen. When the soldiers saw Sandy, they immediately raised their fists in the air, the standard Stationhouse salute. Sandy responded by solemnly raising his own fist. The whole thing was pathetic. A little bit of ceremony in all this desperation. People must really feel desperate, Alex thought, when they knew their time was running out so fast.

To everyone's surprise except Alex's, and perhaps Daryl's, an armored DDF helicopter sat on the only uncollapsed portion of the Arlington Memorial Bridge. Sandy's limousine pulled up to the *Beelzebub*. Alex counted five unmanned, saucer-shaped groundfire-suppression units hovering in a circle above the chopper, ready to shoot at the slightest sign of trouble.

Daryl gave him a glance. "They're here for you, aren't they, Dad?" he said.

Alex raised his eyebrows. "It looks like it, doesn't it?" he said.

The DDF helicopter was huge and powerful, and the unmanned flying saucers unsettling. This was the Defederacy, with its customary show of brute military force.

"What's going on?" asked Sandy, jumpy now.

The air bristled with mega-firepower.

"It's the Defederacy," said Alex.

"Yes, I realize that," said Sandy, "but they're not here for me, are they?"

"No," said Alex. "They're here for me."

As they pulled in front of the *Beelzebub*, a man in

a black beret and a military uniform walked across the ship's deck toward the gangplank. Alex recognized the man. His shoulders rose in anticipation. The man was Cameron Healy, the new provisional head of the Information Systems Service, and his presence here further confirmed Alex's expectations that they were indeed here to take him back. Alex now saw Jill appear from behind the wheelhouse. She followed Healy toward the gangplank. She looked anxiously past the man's shoulder. The groundfire-suppression units lit the area with harsh spotlights. The helicopter's engines thumped the air with a persistent rhythm. Rico brought the car to a stop, grabbed his rifle from the dashboard, jumped out of the dilapidated limo, and took up a soldierly stance, ready to guard Sandy. Alex got out of the car. Healy walked down the gangplank to the dock. Jill followed right behind him. To see Healy in his black-and-gray fatigues and his combat boots emphasized to Alex just how changed the ISS must be. Healy reached the foot of the dock. Daryl got out of the car. Jill rushed around Healy and hurried to Daryl.

"Are you all right?" she asked her son. "They didn't hurt you, did they?"

"They didn't touch him," said Tony.

Jill gave Tony a withering glance. "You've been drinking," she said.

"Sandy offered us a drink," he admitted defensively.

She ignored him. She turned to Alex. "They've come for you." She flicked her eyes toward Healy. "They want you to go. It was nice. While it lasted. To have the family together again."

Her words surprised him. He didn't know how to

respond to them. Healy brushed past Jill and saluted Alex in a crisp, military fashion.

"Dr. Denyer," he said, "CEO Graham Croft is requesting your presence at the Megaplex immediately." He gave Rico a glance, and seemed to dismiss him as bush-league. "On a matter of grave national concern."

The self-important nature of the man irked Alex. He didn't want to make it too easy for the Megaplex.

"I'll need verification from the CEO's office," he told Healy.

"You'll be briefed in the Megaplex by the CEO himself," Healy said.

This stopped Alex. Graham was going to brief him in person? The situation had to be a lot worse than he thought it was. The AWP was still out there, and the Martians had activated some of its systems. He felt his sense of duty returning. As much as he thought the whole Martian War idiotic, he knew he had to go.

"Jon Lewis called me," said Alex. "He gave me a bit of background on what's happening. With Max and so forth."

Healy nodded. "You're a Security 1 again, Dr. Denyer. Your employment status at the ISS has been returned to FTE, with all its perks and privileges. The CEO and his staff have authorized me to extend their sincerest apologies regarding your recent termination. They acted in the interests of public safety and on the best information they had at the time. As it turned out, the information was erroneous, planted by a covert enemy with the sole intent of driving one of our best experts from active service."

Alex felt unsettled. "I could have told you that all along."

"I wish I was at liberty to discuss the full details of the current emergency in front of your family," said Healy, "but it's rated Security 1, and we'll have to discuss it when we board the helicopter. You're to come immediately. The CEO is waiting."

Alex glanced at Jill. She had that worried look in her eyes again, her lips pursed, her chin raised. He looked at Daryl. Daryl was grinning.

"Go on, Dad," said Daryl. "We'll see you back in the Defederacy."

"Alex, you don't have to go if you don't want to," said Jill. "Not after the way they treated you. Why don't you stay with us?"

The longing in her voice confused him.

"Ma'am, I would be obliged to take him by force if he refused," Healy said. "Under Statute 47 of the War Measures Act, retired senior scientists are obliged to return to active duty if their health permits, and if the Defederacy has demonstrated reasonable necessity. While I'm not authorized to go into the details of the current emergency, Megaplex lawyers have deemed that reasonable necessity has been *amply* demonstrated."

Alex paused. The tone of concern, even anxiety, in Healy's voice scared him. Something had the man really spooked.

Alex hooked his arm around Jill's neck, drew her near, and gave her a kiss. "I'll phone you," he said.

"Alex, this is ridiculous," she said. "Don't go."

Her neediness caught him off guard. He glanced at Tony. Tony looked miffed. Alex walked over to Daryl and gave his son a hug.

"Hang in there," he said. His implication was

130

clear. Living with Tony and Jill at the moment was anything but a picnic.

"I will, Dad," said Daryl.

Alex turned to Healy. "Can I get my stuff?" he asked.

"It's already in the helicopter," said Healy. "I'd like to get going. The Patuxent acted up on the way in and we had to lay down some groundfire. I don't want to give them the chance to regroup."

Alex turned to his family and gave them a small wave. "Bye," he said. He turned to Colgan. "Ely, until next time."

Colgan nodded. "It's been fun."

Healy gripped Alex by the elbow and ushered him away.

They climbed the small hill to the bridge.

"Can you make this railing?" asked Healy.

"Sure," said Alex.

They both climbed over the railing onto the Arlington Memorial Bridge.

"So?" said Alex.

Healy glanced over his shoulder. "The Martians have activated the navigational system aboard the new AWP," he said.

"I suspected they might," said Alex.

"Now they've got maneuverability, and they're moving the thing toward Earth."

"You're kidding," said Alex.

Healy nodded. "We fear the Martians are going to park it next to Earth. We believe their intent is to use some of its military systems against us. We haven't been able to intercept with our own navigational commands to change the AWP's course. The Martians are jamming our signals. We need your input. We've got to get that thing turned away from Earth before it gets within military striking distance. You're the only one who might know how to do that. I'm just glad we got this Max thing wrapped up as quickly as we did. We would have been really stuck for a mission specialist otherwise."

"There's going to be a mission?" said Alex.

"It looks that way," said Healy.

The AWP. He hated the aliens—yet he loved the aliens. Sentient beings from another star. Nameless. Mysterious. And deadly. With this big, beautiful machine coming his way, and the Defederacy now wanting him to take a look at it, he *definitely* felt the pull again. Over two kilometers long. And fifteen centuries old. Of course he felt the pull.

"So you're certain it represents a threat?" he said.

Healy squinted. "We have to work on that assumption, Dr. Denyer," he said. "We'd be fools not to. On the plus side, we think the Martians inadvertently compromised the sublight drive when they inputted their navigational commands. As a consequence, the AWP's dropping sunward at half its former rate. That's a stroke of luck. It gives us more time to mount a response. And we're going to need all the time we can get."

As the helicopter rose from the cracked and buckled asphalt of what was once the Arlington Memorial Bridge, he saw Jill, Tony, Daryl, Colgan, Sandy, and Rico standing on the dock below. Jill was arguing with Tony. Daryl stood by, interjecting occasionally. Colgan skulked away and went below. Sandy and Rico leaned against the limousine watching the argument, seemingly amused by it, smoking cigarettes and drinking a bottle of something.

Alex wanted to tell the helicopter pilot to go back. The groundfire-suppression units came into view, man-made flying saucers that used the same lift technology hovercars did. He wanted to tell Healy he couldn't leave his family behind. He had left them behind too many times before. He had sacrificed his marriage on the altar of grave national concern again and again. But the helicopter rose and rose . . . leaving, leaving, leaving. What had ever happened to his marriage? Was it his fault it had finally fallen apart? Had the demands of his job finally destroyed his marriage? Or had Jill just demanded more than he could have ever possibly given her? All that overtime. And then when Daryl got sick, still a lot of overtime, of course a lot of overtime, it was the middle of the Alien War, and his country needed him. But he still should have been there for them. It always came down to this: *Good-bye, I don't know when I'll be back again, I love you, but I gotta go.* He shook his head. He would miss them.

Graham Croft rose from his teakwood desk, came around the end, and stood in the middle of the Stars-of-the-Defederacy rug. He extended his hand.

"Alex," he said.

"Graham," said Alex.

The two men shook hands. Graham looked at Alex's coveralls. He sniffed.

"What have you been doing?" asked Graham. "You smell like chlorine."

"I was sanitizing engine spillage," said Alex.

Graham's face settled. "They tell me you were in

the Arlington EMZ," he said. "What were you doing there?"

"Working," Alex said, his tone dry.

Graham squinted. He shook his head. "Cameron told you about the intelligence mix-up?"

"Actually, Jon phoned me."

Graham's shoulders sank and he sighed. "Alex . . . I . . . we were given the wrong information."

"Yes, that's what he said. I knew it all along. You didn't have to send those goons after me. What were they going to do to me? Kill me?"

"I don't know what DIS Operations had planned for you. But when I found out about Max, I put a stop to it as fast as I could." Graham shook his head. "You have to understand . . . we sometimes have a hard time . . . especially every two years when the planets cycle back into close orbit and I sign off on maneuvers, and things heat up. I can only offer my sincerest apology."

"Was it going to be Chincoteague Bay for me, Graham?" said Alex. "Or were you just going to dump me in the Potomac?"

Graham's eyes narrowed. His lower lip stiffened. He lifted his hands, as if he were at a loss, then let them drop to his sides. Was there any kinship between them? wondered Alex. Did being first cousins really mean anything to the man after all?

"Alex . . ." Graham slid his hands into his pockets. His shoulders settled with resignation. "The information we got . . ." He shook his head. He looked truly bewildered by the whole situation. "It came directly from Max Morrow. Under those circumstances, please try to see things from my perspective."

Graham's tone of regret was genuine. Alex's shoulders sank.

"That's what Jon told me," he said.

"And yes, Chincoteague Bay was definitely an option for you," said Graham. "It is for everybody. As for what Ops did in the Arlington EMZ . . . I guess they had their reasons, and I'm glad we got things cleared up before you got hurt. Again, I apologize. I take full responsibility, even though I was unaware of their intercept plans. I sometimes delegate more than I should. I'm so busy, especially when we engage FMC forces. I'm happy our Max investigation came to a head when it did. The timing couldn't have been better."

Alex tried to detect any infelicity in Graham's words. He couldn't. Yet the whole thing seemed too neat, too convenient, and he couldn't help wondering if there might be more to it than Graham was letting on.

"What are you going to do with Max?" he asked.

Graham looked away, as if the subject pained him.

"He'll be tried, of course." Graham shook his head. "I imagine the military tribunal will seek the death penalty. I'll intervene at that point with a pardon."

Alex jumped in.

"I really have to insist on that, Graham," he said. "Otherwise, I'm going back to the EMZ right now, and you can deal with the AWP yourself."

Graham contemplated Alex with compassionate eyes. "He was your good friend."

Alex felt his throat knot up. "Why would he do this to us, Graham?"

"We don't know yet," he said. "He'll be interrogated for several months."

"Please don't hurt him."

"Alex . . . the kind of interrogation . . . he won't be the same man afterward, that's all there is to it. But I'll make sure that any medical treatment he needs will be readily available."

"Because when Dad died . . . Max more or less stepped in."

"I know he did," said Graham. "And I wish I could have stepped in at that point too and played a bigger part." He gestured wearily around his office. "But then all this got in the way." He let his hand settle to his side, and he squared his shoulders. "We couldn't have won the Alien War without Max. I'll ask for mercy. It still means he'll be spending the rest of his life in prison." Graham's eyes narrowed. He struggled. "We all trusted and respected Max. And had we been given that information about you by anyone else, Alex, the mix-up with the two goons in the EMZ wouldn't have happened. But because it came from Max, we thought it was gold." Graham took a few steps toward the window. "I'm sorry about everything."

"I tried to tell you I was innocent. Why didn't you believe me? We're cousins. We're blood. Have I ever been dishonest to you before?"

"No, you haven't."

"Have I ever once even gotten close to betraying you?"

"No. And I realize now that when you speak to the media, you're just being Alex, the ideas bubbling out of your head a mile a minute like they used to when you were a kid. And those passwords you steal, you steal them only because you're curious." A nervous grin came to Graham's face. "And because you haven't got the good sense to stop yourself. You were always getting into mischief as a boy."

"And what about the harm you've done to my reputation?" asked Alex.

"I'm sorry about that."

"I want you to send an explanation and an apology to Concord. I want you to send memos to all of my colleagues, not only here in the Defederacy but in the other enclaves as well. I want you to send the same memo to every scientific institute and university in the world."

"It's already in the works, Alex."

Alex felt himself getting more and more worked up. "And make sure the media knows about it."

"I'll be holding a press conference about the whole thing in a few days."

"And I want financial restitution," he said, his voice rising. "I want what I'm owed in severance pay, and what I'm owed in back pay."

"Alex, you're upset. Calm down."

"Of course I'm upset. My own cousin turfs me out in the street, and then my mentor, the man who was like a father to me after Dad died, betrays me. How do you expect me to feel?"

Graham raised his palms. "I can only apologize for how we fast-tracked your layoff," he said. "We had to isolate you from sensitive information quickly. You would have done the same thing, Alex, if you'd been in my position. As for Max . . . I wish there was some way I could make it easier for you. I can see you're really distressed by it. But I'm afraid he . . . he turned his back on us, Alex. He turned his back on you especially. We have to face facts. He used you as a shield to protect himself."

Alex shook his head. "I don't know what to say, Graham."

"We're all deeply saddened, Alex. We thought Max was as solid as a rock. It's a shock. It's a setback. And it's going to take a lot of work to repair all the damage he's caused. But we have to push forward, Alex. We have to learn from this particular mistake, and do everything we can to prevent it from happening again. We're at war, and surprises like this are bound to happen."

"It sure was a surprise all right," said Alex.

Graham gestured at the chairs by the window.

"Let's sit down," said the CEO. "One way or the other, I'm glad we got it all sorted out. I'm glad you're still on our side. Even despite your sometimes unconventional views about the Martian Conflict. And even despite the way you sometimes ride roughshod over the rules. Because between the Repealists, the Martians, and now even Hawaii, it's hard to tell who we can trust anymore. I hope we can trust you, Alex. I really do. Because we need you. Everybody in the Defederacy needs you. And that's what we're here to discuss. That's why Cameron flew all the way out to the EMZ to get you."

Alex nodded. He felt emotionally drained.

"The AWP," he said, trying to compartmentalize his feelings of disillusionment and betrayal.

"Yes," said the CEO of the Defederacy. "The AWP."

PART TWO

AWP

Chapter 11

They sat down. The window, on the 110th floor of the Megaplex, faced west. This late at night, Alex saw ships come and go on Chesapeake Bay, their running lights like stars.

"I want to show you something," said Graham, gesturing at the monitor on the table.

He keyed in a few commands. An image of the solar system appeared: the orbital trajectory of Mars was sketched in red, Earth's in blue, and the AWP's in yellow.

"This is the latest Covert information we have on the orbital trajectory of the AWP," said Graham. Alex focused on the task at hand, forced Max's betrayal from his mind. "Cameron must have filled you in. It's now going slower. When the Martians fooled with it, they decreased its speed considerably. An unintentional retro burn, we think, though we've yet to trace a retro accelerant trail anywhere."

Alex nodded. "Healy said the Martians might have compromised the drive system with their navigational commands."

"Yes," said Graham. "And it's bought us some time. Still and all, the AWP's coming our way, and we have to stop it. We've been trying to do that with various cost-effective measures. We've been transmitting navigational interference software to the AWP twenty-four hours a day, seven days a week. It's learner-smart software, constantly able to upgrade itself, but so far none of it's worked. The AWP is still coming right at us. We've got about ninety days before it gets here."

Alex felt the old compulsion taking hold—the compulsion of his own curiosity. He studied the holographic representation more closely as his feelings of betrayal receded further. Graham pressed a key. Alex also tried to curb his lingering anger against Graham. But it was hard. Especially because his dismissal had come so unexpectedly, and without explanation. A graphics package sketched in the predicted orbits of Earth, Mars, and the AWP over the next ninety days. He thought he had better take Jon's advice. He and Graham had to put their differences aside. They had to think of the whole Defederacy.

"As you can see by these orbital extrapolations," said Graham, "Earth pulls ahead of Mars . . . here." Graham tapped the screen. "Then the AWP uses a slingshot maneuver past Mars at this point, gains speed, changes direction, and reaches Earth by next spring. That's how long we've got to mount a mission."

"And that's where I come in," said Alex. "As mission specialist."

"That's where you come in," said Graham. "I'll give you an update. You've missed a lot in the . . . the gap." Graham pressed a few more keys. An image of the AWP appeared. "This was taken from *Advance 3.* As you can see, the AWP now glows with its own internal source of radiance. It's a protective field of sorts. It activated itself shortly after the Martians arrived, and it's made the AWP impervious to outside scans since. The Martians have test-fired some small munitions at the field. It's impervious to those as well. Despite the field, the Martians have gained access through the rear portal, and most of our recent intelligence comes from their on-site findings." Graham pointed. "These two lights here and here are Martian research vessels. And this swarm of sixteen over here is the Martian defense force. Since you've been gone, the Martians have gotten many of the AWP's systems up and running. We were surprised by how fast they got most of the spacecraft operational."

"They have Ariam Adurra working for them," said Alex, unable to resist.

Graham nodded. "I constantly underestimate that woman," he conceded. "Take a look at it." He motioned at the hologram. "Familiarize yourself with it."

Alex leaned closer. Here was his first good look at the AWP. The image showed good detail, wasn't just a pixilated blob anymore. The AWP was barbell shaped, with two modules at either end of a connecting stem, was bone white, and had a complicated central assembly. A barely perceptible vapor trail streamed into the central assembly. A materials-intake system? wondered Alex. Overlapping bone white plates covered the hull, like the scales of a big reptile. It was so different from the regular, newer AWPs that Alex simply couldn't wait to get his hands on it. His curiosity intensified. He became all scientist, left all the politics, intrigue, and betrayal behind. This thing, two billion miles away, had him in its thrall.

"We always assumed the AWP had great offensive capability," said Graham. "What alien weapons platform doesn't? When I originally broke the news to the public, I suggested its offensive capability was a hundred times greater than the original threat we faced ten years ago. Turns out I might have low-balled that figure. *Covert 3* now tells us the Martians have found some munitions. The AWP has a lot of Number 16. And it has enough Number 17 to cripple an army. But what we're really worried about is a new system, another nanogen, what we're calling Number 18. The Martians have done some preliminary tests, and while our intercepts are far from complete, we believe Number 18 is a killer; that it doesn't change or mutate humans the way 16 or 17 do, it simply exterminates them. You think the Great Die-Off was bad. If the Martians use Number 18 against Earth, that's it—we're finished. Thankfully, none of these systems has yet been activated, but the Martians could change that anytime."

"No wonder you came and got me by helicopter," said Alex.

"This is urgent, Alex." Graham pointed. "On the plus side, we know the AWP's been badly damaged. Module B, on this side, is a write-off. That will cut down on at least some of its capability. We have no idea how it got so badly damaged, but we should count ourselves lucky it did."

"Why?" asked Alex.

"Because we now truly believe this AWP may have

represented the main alien invasion force," said Graham. "Two hundred troop transports have been found on board. So have thousands of highly sophisticated orbital fighters. The aliens were getting ready. Their strategic use of Number 16 against Earth softened the ground. This AWP, we now believe, was going to finish the job. Before it could reach us, though, the ship got damaged. We don't know how. That's still a mystery."

"And the Martians repaired it?" asked Alex.

"Yes," said Graham.

"I wonder why the aliens themselves didn't repair it," said Alex. "If the Martians can repair it—"

"That question has baffled our top analysts," said Graham. "Module A was hardly touched. Casualties would have been slight in that particular area of the ship. That means they would have had enough hands to repair the damaged Module B."

"So why did they abandon it?"

"Who knows?" said Graham. "This won't be the first time the aliens have mystified us. Nor is it a question we're really concerned with right now. It's coming this way. That's what we have to think about."

"So you've tried everything in my catalog to stop it?" asked Alex. "All the software my team's put together over the last fifteen years?"

"Yes," said Graham.

"And you've transmitted it?"

"Yes. But we've run into stiff resistance. The Martian encryption systems are complex. They're constantly evolving to meet any outside challenge. Our software can't breach them. So we've dropped that approach. My advisors urge the Defederacy to mount a full-scale mission to the AWP. The three remaining Defederacies have already committed resources to the project, and Eurocorp's chipping in as well. Delaware will be running the show. Mission planners are going over the details, and they'll brief you shortly. They've recommissioned *Research 97*. She's a reliable old tub. That's the one you'll be going in."

"I've heard of her," said Alex.

The prospect of a mission thrilled him. Space. His old friend. His home.

"We've got to stop this any way we can, Alex," said the CEO. "It's going to be tough, real tough. This AWP is different. You're going to run into a lot of things you haven't seen before. Things we've learned just recently from our Martian intercepts while you've been . . . out of the picture. To give you some examples: unlike the smaller AWPs, there aren't as many electrical or mechanical components aboard this one. She's over eighty percent bioengineered, Alex. For lack of a better word, she's alive. She eats. She absorbs, even at densities as low as a few molecules per cubic kilometer, everything she can find in space. That's what this vapor trail is. She utilizes both starlight and sunlight as energy sources."

"Wow," said Alex.

"I know," said Graham. "As another example, her interior dimensions are a lot bigger, huge, with a lot of seemingly wasted space. The cabins and corridors look as if they're sized for a completely different species."

"Really?"

"Yes."

"That's surprising," said Alex.

"I know," said Graham. "And to tell you the truth, it's stumped the hell out of us. It's led us to rethink what we know about the size of the aliens. The scale of everything inside this particular AWP makes us think the aliens might be bigger than we first thought they were. It's fine to have lofty ceilings in the Megaplex, but lofty ceilings in a spacecraft? Uh-uh. No. It's not economical. And I don't care how alien the aliens are. They still must have some reasonable sense of economic viability. Do you have any ideas?"

Alex tapped the table a few times.

"The Martians found no remains on board?" he asked.

"No," said Graham. "You know the aliens. Never a capture. It's always self-destruct with them. Not one drop of blood anywhere. Not so much as a fingernail. Bear in mind, though, the picture's far from complete. The Martians are doing everything they can to stop our eavesdropping."

"Maybe they're a race of castes," suggested Alex. "Each caste is bioengineered to whatever role he, she, or *it* plays. As such, they could be made in different sizes. Maybe the invasion force represents a specific larger caste while the strategic force was a smaller, specialized one."

Graham nodded. "That's a possibility," he said.

"Or maybe they could have genetically downsized themselves over the last fifteen hundred years," said Alex. "Smaller beings need fewer resources. Maybe they were running out of resources on their home planet. Maybe that's why they wanted to invade us in the first place. The AWP was built fifteen hundred years ago, when they were bigger. They had it ready, but didn't want to go to the expense of retooling it for their smaller size."

Graham nodded again. "You see, Alex, this is why I want you as mission specialist," he said. "You're a great theoretical thinker."

"I'd like to pick my crew," said Alex.

"By all means," said Graham.

"Jon Lewis and Ruth Pellegrino. I've worked with them extensively, and their skill sets are tailor-made for a job like this."

"Excellent choices."

"What about the Martian defense presence around the AWP?" he asked. "How are we going to get past it? I'm not a soldier, I'm a scientist."

"The DDF is sending an expeditionary force ahead of *Research 97*," said the CEO. "They're hoping to neutralize the Martian defenses before you get there. In case a remnant Martian defense remains, you'll have at your command sixteen stealth drones. If need be, you'll have to mop up any remaining resistance with the drones. In fact, our original plan was to send the drones by themselves, blow the thing out of the sky, then call it a day." He pointed to the screen. "But not with this glow, this shield around the AWP. With this protective skin, we might as well throw marshmallows at it. That's why we had to change our plan. Get someone on board to tinker with its navigational system. That's you. Get the thing pointed away from us. We don't want it anywhere near us. In fact, we'd like you to crash it into the sun. I doubt that protective skin will withstand the heat of the sun. As an added bonus, if we crash it into the sun, we destroy any chance the Martians might get of looking at it again. And that's what we want. If you can't change course, disable the Number 18 weapons system. One way or the other we have to stop that thing."

Alex was surprised when, a few days later, while on his way to a mission planning session at the ISS, he found Reba waiting for him just outside his lobby door on the Level Sixty-three Skywalk. She stepped from some tall palmettos in the large arboretum adjacent to the lobby, and, glancing over her shoulder—as if she were nervous about someone following her—hurried toward him with an intent stride. A broad smile came to his face. He was happy to see her. Oddly, she didn't smile back. She gripped him by his arm and pulled him to the palmettos. Her grip was like a vise. He realized, with some disquiet, that she was probably several times stronger than he was now.

"I saw the news," she said. "You're going on a mission."

"Yes," he said.

"And that your fall from grace was a mistake."

He looked away. "They've arrested Max Morrow. It was all his doing. Why are you here? I'm surprised to see you."

She glanced around.

"I should have called ahead," she said. "But I don't trust the phone lines."

He nodded. Two months ago he would have been puzzled. But not anymore. "I know what you mean," he said.

"Zirko didn't want me to come."

"Why not?" he asked.

"Because you're the CEO's first cousin and he doesn't trust you."

"I was wondering about that. The last time we met . . . you seemed . . . suspicious."

"You had that hovercam following you," she said.

"Why should that worry you?"

"We get harassed, Alex. I don't like getting harassed."

He nodded. "I'm sorry."

"And we have suspicious natures. It's part of our programming. Part of our defense design."

"Soldiers," he said.

"Precisely." She looked him up and down. "And now you're a soldier, too."

"Only by expedience," he said.

"A colonel, no less," she said.

"That's the particular rank requirement for this particular mission."

"But still a soldier on a mission."

"Yes."

"That's part of why I'm here," she said.

"It is?" he said.

"To wish you well. On your mission. As one soldier to another. And to ask you to be careful. The Martians will try to intercept you."

"Our planned transfer orbit to Mars will put us well out of FMC reach," he said. "Otherwise we wouldn't have announced the mission publicly. The need for announced public reassurance was factored into Mission Control's choice of a transfer orbit."

"Still," she said. "It's so far."

He looked at her closely, probed the depths of her biological eye. He saw she was worried. But he was worried about her as well.

"You're not involved in anything you shouldn't be involved in, are you?" he asked.

She looked away. "No," she said. "No. Why do you ask?"

"I would just hate . . . never mind." He couldn't help thinking of Chincoteague Bay these days.

"I was out between the orbital planes of Saturn and Jupiter when I got pinked by Number 17," she said. "That's where you're going."

"We're going to have all the latest antinanogen equipment," he said.

"Just be careful," she repeated. She glanced around again. "I want you to come back alive." She gestured at her hybrid cybernetic body. "And all in one piece."

"I'll come back," he said.

She gave his arm a squeeze. "I better go," she said.

But he reached out and grabbed her before she could walk more than a few steps.

"You be careful too," he said.

Their gaze held for several seconds. Finally, she nodded. "I will," she said, and slipped away into the crowd thronging the Level Sixty-three Skywalk.

Chapter 12

Research 97 looked like a pizza cutter—a handle at one end, and a wheel at the other. As Alex, Jon, and Ruth approached the craft in their rendezvous vehicle, the sun brightened the spacecraft with spotlight intensity. Alex sighed in satisfaction. The Moon loomed below, three quarters full, dwarfing *Research 97*. Craters disfigured its surface. Alex glanced at Jon. Jon gazed at *Research 97* with narrowed eyes, judging it. Ruth relayed docking commands. *Research 97*'s habitation wheel stopped spinning. Alex leaned forward.

"Are the drones in position?" he asked Ruth.

"Yes," she said.

He could tell she liked the idea of having sixteen stealth combat drones at her command. She liked guns. She practiced with her registered side arm at the range three times a week.

The rendezvous vehicle cast a crisp shadow against *Research 97*. Jon gripped a handhold and propelled himself from the command module to the docking port. Alex heard a muffled clank as the two spacecraft made their initial linkup. The rendezvous vehicle shifted a degree or two as it nudged closer to the interplanetary spacecraft, then, as it locked and aligned itself, stabilized. Jon keyed in the synchronous systems command. Alex heard the hissing of air as the seals in both air locks secured themselves. Jon watched the readouts for a minute, then nodded.

"Fully pressurized," he said. "Temperature is 21 Celsius. Orbit is stable at 411 miles, with a transit time of 47 minutes." The green light came on. "We might as well go in. They're giving us the go-ahead."

Jon cycled the air lock and opened the docking hatch. He propelled himself through the hatch with a quick push of his hands and entered *Research 97*. Alex and Ruth followed.

They made their way from the drive module, the handle part of the pizza-cutter design, to the habitation wheel, the round part. The wheel remained stationary for boarding. Alex somersaulted into the wheel, feeling giddy, ready to have some fun. He gripped a handhold and pushed himself along the bending passageway to his designated bunk. He stowed his stuff in his locker. The others did the same.

Two hours later, all suited up, the three astronauts went to the Command Module at the front of the habitation wheel. As Alex waited for Ruth to make the primary burn, the one that would thrust them out of lunar orbit into their own carefully planned solar orbit, he stared out the small window at the Moon, thinking of Jill and Daryl, and how he was leaving them yet again. The surface of the Moon rolled by, bleak, hostile, with craters and startling ejecta patterns, no sign of its 360 million subsurface inhabitants anywhere. It was a lonely place, and brought to mind just how lonely his marriage had been.

Fifteen minutes later, Ruth received an order from Ground Control to delay the primary burn.

"Roger that, Ground Control, sequencing paused. Will await your go-ahead."

Ground Control gave no explanation for the delay, but a few moments later the cause became apparent. A decontamination barge floated by, in orbit two miles below. It towed a large frag net full of Number 17. The Number 17 glowed pink, like a big wad of gum in the harsh sunlight. Alex remembered Graham's words about the AWP: *It has enough Number 17 to cripple an army.*

"Jon, you checked our frag nets, right?" he asked, disconcerted by the sight of so much Number 17.

Jon nodded. "It's all new equipment, Alex," he said. "Your cousin spared no expense this time. We'll net whatever nanogen we find at the new AWP. And we'll have no problems with herniation. The new nets are good and strong."

Seventy-two hours later, *Research 97* was safely on its way, its sublight drive deployed. The Earth receded behind them at 350 thousand miles per hour.

Alex woke in the middle of sleep period. The wheel spun, creating a weak artificial gravity. He looked left, then right. Ruth slept out of sight to the left, and Jon slept out of sight to the right, each hidden by the curving slope of the wheel. Or maybe they were together. Maybe they were making love. He wasn't about to pry.

A peaceful voyage so far: no solar flare-ups forcing

them to run to the radiation bunker, no Martian interdiction attempts, not even the tiniest hint of equipment malfunction.

He sat up, scratched his head, and took a sip of water from a self-refrigerated squirt bottle. Space. Here he was again. Did it really feel like home? Or was he just trying to make himself believe that? He usually slept well in space. But not tonight. He got up and walked to his workstation. He looked out the window. Not that there was anything to see. Not when the sublight drive was on.

The sublight drive. Something he was proud of. Something he had figured out after an intense year of study. A wondrous piece of exotechnology. A boon to the Defederacy.

Look what I did, Jill. The sublight drive. Voilà.

His accomplishments meant nothing to him unless he could show them to people. Like back in Pennsylvania, with his dad. *Look what I did, Dad.* He shook his head as he contemplated the blue plasma medium of the sublight drive. Casey Denyer, family doctor, later a member of Graham's board; a calm, kind, sensible man, one who took joy in his son's accomplishments, but who never got the chance to see this ultimate accomplishment, the sublight drive. Life played its ugly tricks.

"I miss you, Dad," he said.

He remembered one morning in particular. In Pennsylvania. With his father at the breakfast table, and him, a teenager, out in the garage, tinkering. Yes, always tinkering. That's what he did. Sadly, if his marriage had failed, it had failed because of his tinkering. He thought of Pennsylvania. That one morning in particular. Out in the garage, putting the finishing touches on his self-designed solar-powered model airplane, showing it to his father. Then the two of them went flying the thing, flew it high into the jumbled and rocky terminus of the Allegheny Mountains, a pleasure, what life was lived for, moments he would always treasure. Always building things. And showing them to his dad. A way to be with his dad because his mother had died so young.

Pennsylvania. Oh, Pennsylvania. His real home. If he could only go back. In the old days, he and his dad would go out with fishing rods, or drive around, or climb the steeper rocks west of their house in their rock gear, regular mountaineers, if only in a small, Allegheny way. Where had it gone? He wanted it back. But now Number 16s ran Pennsylvania, and who knew what they had turned it into? Another branch establishment of Hell, no doubt.

"Look what I did, Dad," he mumbled into the blue glow of the sublight drive.

Yes, something to be proud of, the sublight drive, what got the aliens here in the first place. He still didn't know how it worked. But that didn't matter. He knew how to *make* it work. He stared at its blue sheen outside the window. Start with a conventional drive, then shroud it in this blue sheen, this peculiar alien-devised medium. The theory? Objects traveled at different speeds through different mediums. Through water an object traveled slowly. Through air, more quickly. Through space, faster still. Through this blue sheen, exponentially up to, but not exceeding, the speed of light. *Ergo*, sublight. His coup. His prize. *Voilà*. But no father there to share it with.

He heard movement down the hall, and, glancing

along the curving slope of the wheel's corridor, saw Ruth walking toward him.

"You're up," she said. Her dark hair was tousled.

"I can't sleep," he said. "I was thinking about my dad." He gestured out the window at the blue sheen. "How I was never able to show him the sublight drive."

"Funny. I was just thinking about my sister. How I lost her in the Great Die-Off."

He glanced down the corridor. "Jon's sleeping?"

She nodded. "You know Jon."

He looked out at the sublight drive again. "The Great Die-Off," he said. "It was so unfair."

She nodded. "I was just remembering all the news coverage." Her face settled. "All those spinning tops falling from the sky, spraying the Number 16 nanogen everywhere."

"I know. Like plaster dust. Sticking to everything."

"And then the fighter squadrons trying to intercept the barrage modules, and the AWPs blasting the DDF jets right out of the sky from orbit. My sister was thirty-one at the time. They wouldn't let her into the Defederacy once she got infected. She died in a matter of weeks."

"My dad never tried to get into the Defederacy once he got infected," said Alex. "He just made sure Daryl got home safely."

"Your dad was a great man," said Ruth.

"And that's what I hate so much about the whole thing, Ruth," he said. "Dad was a great man. He was a capable man. He was one of the most well-liked and respected politicians the Defederacy has ever seen. And when he wasn't a politician, he was a much-loved family doctor. Then, at the end of his life, he was just another victim. A living organism overwhelmed by the Number 16 nanogen. I can't reconcile that. I can't picture him getting weaker. I can't picture him dying. But that's what happened."

Ruth shook her head. "I don't like thinking about how my sister died," she said. "That horrible bubbling of the skin. The locking of the bones. And that final filling of the lungs with the orange bile. I wanted to go to Ohio to help her, but of course the Defederacy wasn't issuing any travel permits during the Great Die-Off."

They lapsed into silence. The massive misery had been unconscionable. The world had been changed forever. *Look what I did, Dad.* It was still hard to take. Even after all these years. Especially because he knew he would never say those words again.

Two days later, they dropped out of sublight speed, and the blue sheen outside 97's five windows dissipated like mist at sunrise. They braked through the dark void. Each time Ruth initiated a braking burn, the G-force pressed Alex into his seat.

"Jon told me the news, Ruth," said Alex. "Congratulations."

She turned to Jon quickly. "Jon, we weren't supposed to tell him until after the mission."

"I would shout it from the rooftops," he said, "if there were any rooftops around here."

Ruth's eyes glistened, and a vulnerable smile came to her face, a true bride-to-be.

"You can shout it from the venture bay," she said, "once we get to the AWP."

What was left of Graham's expeditionary force guarded the AWP in a ragged line. Alex heard Commander Carole Strauss list damage and casualties over Ruth's radio. Three of sixteen combat orbiters remained functional. A huge net held the wreckage of the other thirteen in a big ball of scrap. Commander Strauss's tactical platform looked untouched, and rotated daintily against the massive backdrop of the AWP.

Ruth turned to Alex.

"She wants to talk to you," she said.

Alex clicked to the appropriate screen.

A woman in her late fifties, wearing the uniform of a DDF colonel, appeared. Her penetrating blue eyes gazed at him with unflinching appraisal.

"As you've heard from my report," she said, "we've sustained heavy damage. I have sixty-one dead and thirty-two wounded. Only three of my orbiters remain operational. Ammunition stockpiles have been depleted. I have two microwarheads, each point-fives, and my maneuverability is down to nine burns on *Attack 62*, seven burns on *Attack 57*, and five burns on *Attack 31*. That means there's nothing I can do to defend you while you're here. You'll have to rely on your drones. I'd like to keep in reserve what warheads and burns I have in case we encounter the enemy on the way back."

"By all means," said Alex.

"We of course can't get a reading on the status of your drones. Are they still in your slipstream?"

Alex keyed in his stealth authorization codes and checked.

"Yes," he said.

"Then I suggest you deploy them in readiness at the following points."

A three-dimensional graphic version of the AWP

appeared on the screen. A defensive gridwork appeared around it, showing latitudinal and longitudinal markings. Over this gridwork, sixteen red points of light clicked into place—the deployment suggestions for 97's combat drones.

"Ruth, could you please key those in?" said Alex.

Ruth typed the necessary commands. The tactical gridwork disappeared. Carole Strauss came back on. Her eyes now looked battle-weary.

"So you won't be staying?" said Alex.

"We can't," she said. "Our orbital trajectory estimates won't allow for it. As it is, we've already requested a fueling drone. If we don't leave within the next sixteen hours, we won't make our rendezvous with the drone. If we don't make our rendezvous with the drone, we drift."

Drift. A word they all feared. A word that, up here, was a synonym for death.

"Did the AWP sustain any damage?" he asked.

"The AWP took several direct hits," Commander Strauss reported. "But as far as we can tell, zero damage occurred. As you know, that glowing green field around it acts as a shield. If you bring anything home from the AWP, Dr. Denyer, please bring that." Her eyes looked more battle-weary than ever. "We sure could have used it."

Seeing the AWP on the screen was one thing. Seeing it outside his window was another. Alex felt elated. All he could do was stare. He felt like a child with a new toy. He sensed the others looking at him with grins on their faces. He could do nothing to conceal his joyous and goofy reaction to the AWP. He stared at it with graceless abandon, his intellectual powers gearing up like a thinking generator, his mind alive with questions and speculations, a great nerdy smile on his lean face.

Barbell-shaped—but, from this angle, Alex now noticed a bend in the central connecting bar, barely perceptible, as if the central bar flexed against Modules A and B. The modules looked streamlined—like smoothed-over clamshells. The AWP glowed, rippled with that cold green flame of protection. A defense shield, thought Alex. Something appropriate to an offensive force. But how did it work? Did it operate on electromagnetic principles? And would he actually have the time to investigate the shield? Took several direct hits, but zero damage. How fruitless any Defederacy counterattack would have been against this behemoth. He shuddered to think of how close they'd come to a full-scale invasion.

"It's gigantic," said Jon.

"Over two kilometers long," said Alex. "The modules are the equivalent of sixty stories high."

"And that vapor trail."

"It's a materials-intake system. It's eating the products of space. Micrometeorites. Dust. Molecules. Light. Radiation of all sorts." Alex checked the intelligence log. "The thing was impervious to all of Commander Strauss's scans." He had a closer look. "But wait a minute . . . hold on. She never tried a laser vibration scan." He turned to Ruth. "She never tried to *hear* what was inside the AWP."

"Did the Martians ever try a laser vibration scan?" asked Ruth. "Do we have that particular report on file?"

Alex checked the intelligence log again. "If they did, we haven't got it. And Graham never mentioned it during my original briefing. Do we have the time to run an LV scan before the next sleep period?"

She checked the mission schedule. "If we hurry."

"Then, Jon . . . let's go ahead."

Jon started by illuminating the AWP with huge spotlights, a way to enhance any possible vibration he might pick up from the hull via low-power laser. He then initiated the LV scan. The support specialist began on Module A, focusing the LV lock to a width of fifty meters. He operated the joystick with consummate skill. A smile came to his face.

"That green field is actually magnifying the vibrations my lasers are picking up from the hull." He glanced at a secondary monitor, one used to track the vibrations. "It's all high-grade material. The LV software will easily interpret it into audible sound. Let me just check the frequencies I'm getting and then I'll massage them into audio equivalents."

He keyed in the necessary commands, and a moment later they heard what was going on inside the AWP.

The unmistakable sound of waves lapping at a beach. Water. The sound surprised Alex. Had the Martians missed the water? Or had the Coverts missed the intelligence about the water? Small waves. Like the waves on Lake Anderson in Pennsylvania, where he and his dad had always gone fishing. What had caused the formation of those waves inside the AWP? He wished he knew more about wave dynamics. Did wind push those waves, and did that indicate huge volumes of air or some other dense gas inside the AWP? Or were they generated mechanically, maybe as part of a filtration process? Waves needed a lot of water. Did that water represent a reservoir for drinking, or was there perhaps a hydroponics facility inside? Maybe they were going to at last get a first-hand idea of what the aliens actually ate.

Jon continued his scan. The sound of waves disappeared.

Halfway to the central assembly, Alex heard the sweet tones of a wind chime. No rhythm, no apparent phrasing, but still, an effect that was pleasing and hypnotic. After a while the tinkling seemed to take on a pattern. Had the Martians missed this as well, or had their encrypted transmissions on the tinkling been too much for the Coverts to break?

"Music?" said Alex.

The other two listened for a moment more.

"I think so," said Ruth.

Alex felt some deep-seated emotional reaction. It was as if, after all this time, the aliens had finally reached out to him in a personal way. Music from a distant star. They knew so little about alien culture, and now he was listening to their music. It was sweet, tinkly, with the lower pitches seeming to penetrate right to the center of his brain. But then he grew sleepy, an effect that was sudden, and he knew it had to be the music. He tensed. But his tension lasted only a moment. The meditative shifting of tonality in the music calmed his soul. He grew peaceful again.

"Do you feel that?" he asked.

They both nodded. "It's relaxing us," said Ruth. "It makes me nervous. I can't help thinking it might be a weapon."

Alex considered this possibility. Having engineered a whole plethora of remote-controlled instruments to disarm and neutralize alien weapons

163

platforms, his first reaction was to agree with Ruth. But some kernel of faith inside him wanted to believe that there was at least a small patch of common ground between himself and the aliens, and he thought this music might be a bridge, a spiritual signpost that proved these beings from another star were more than just one-dimensional warmongers.

"I don't think it's a weapon," he said.

"Why would they play music when no one's aboard?" she asked.

Another puzzle, one to add to the many puzzles he'd cataloged over the years.

"Maybe it's automatic," said Jon. "Maybe it keeps playing when there's no one on board."

"Or maybe when all the damage came, no one had a chance to turn it off," said Alex.

Still, the music was having an unequivocal narcotic effect, like he was running through a field of poppies, and with his son a Number 16, and his father killed in the Great Die-Off, Alex knew he couldn't entirely let go of his mistrust.

"Let's move on, Jon," he said. "I'm going to take Ruth's advice on this for the time being. I don't think it's a good idea we listen to that music for too long, especially when we can't explain the somnolent effect it's having on us."

Jon continued the LV scan. He arced along the central connecting stem. Alex heard at various times a heartbeat, bubbles, knocking, dripping, moaning, wind, and waves. Finally, when Jon came to the central assembly, Alex heard a gritty sound—like a sack of pebbles being shaken over and over. His brow furrowed. He was more puzzled than ever. LV scans of smaller AWPs revealed only electrical and mechanical sounds. All the sounds coming from this AWP were organic, like *musique concrète*, sounds recorded from nature, and he had to conclude that biological components on this craft indeed exceeded the electromechanical ones. This thing was alive, like Graham said it was. The sounds bothered Alex. What were they going to find in there once they boarded the craft?

Jon scanned the rest of the central stem, then started on Module B. Predictably, Module B, because it was so badly damaged, remained silent. Or at least nearly silent. Only one small sound occurred, lasting ten seconds: footsteps walking across thin ice, cracking it. Footsteps? Or was his imagination playing tricks on him? He turned to the other two. Of all the sounds heard thus far, this one sounded like a noise of physical movement.

"Jon, run that back again," he said.

They listened to the sound again. Definitely like footsteps walking across thin ice, with a perceptible acceleration toward the end, and even a brief splash, as if at the last moment the ice had finally given way. He tried to give the sound a different interpretation, tried to devise a natural scenario for the sequential and accelerating series of cracks, but his first impression stuck, settled, then hardened, and he couldn't escape the notion that a single being, lonely and deserted, remained. Was there somebody still inside the AWP? An alien that hadn't managed to self-destruct or escape? One the Martians hadn't found? The thought left Alex warm with fear. At the same time, he burned with curiosity. Because no one knew what they looked like. No soldier of the DDF or the FMC had ever seen one and lived to tell the tale. Maybe they would find one inside. Maybe it would be dangerous. More likely it would be just plain scared. Whatever the case, they would at last know their enemy.

Chapter 13

Alex and Jon suited up after sleep period was over, strapped on particle-pulse packs, and stepped into the venture bay. Alex checked his communications, life support, and biomonitors. Everything looked good. In a small screen in the upper right corner of his visor he saw Ruth sitting in the Command Module staring at him.

"Your heart rate's up," she said.

"I know," he said.

"Don't forget," she said, "you're forty years old. You can't do the things you did when you were eighteen. I don't want to have to come in there and get you."

"I'll be careful. Are you picking up Jon?"

She grinned. "Loud and clear."

"And you're picking up our visorcams okay?" he asked. "You can see everything?"

"I wouldn't miss it for the world."

"And you won't forget to make backups of everything we film?"

"Relax, Alex, it's all under control. Just look after Jon for me."

Alex and Jon ran a final check, not only on their suits but also on all the equipment strapped to the particle-pulse power-sled. Everything checked. Alex took a deep breath. *Here we go.* Jon cycled the venture bay's air lock. The air lock rotated, and in fifteen seconds they were outside, their feet floating free of the venture bay's stepping-off platform, space opening up wide and never-ending before them. Alex looked around.

"We ready?" he asked.

"Yes," said Jon.

"Ruth?"

"We're green-lighted and good for go," said Ruth. "Have fun. And be careful. We've got thirty days. You don't have to rush things."

Alex gave his particle-pulse pack a boost and arced gracefully toward the AWP. His flexiseal pressure suit was like a second skin. He glanced over his shoulder. Jon pushed off after him, holding the sled out in front, guiding the unit with thumb controls. Alex turned back to the AWP. The AWP loomed ever larger, its great platelike scales reminding him of the scales on the pickerel he and his father used to catch in Lake Anderson, the flexing arms of its connecting stems graceful but strong, like the central span of the Golden Gate Bridge. The majesty of the spacecraft awed Alex. He navigated around the central assembly's vapor trail, which shimmered pale silver in the weak light of the sun, and made his way to the rear of the spacecraft. He saw an oval port similar to the ones on the smaller AWPs, the scales around it smaller and more tightly woven, and knew that he had at last arrived. The journey was about to truly begin. Forty-five days in *Research 97*, all for a chance to go through that portal.

"Jon?" he said.

"Do you see the portal?" asked Jon.

"It's up here," said Alex.

Jon appeared from behind the hull, his guidelights, one on either side of his visor, glaring in the cadaverous dimness emanating from the AWP's green glow. He maneuvered the sled up to Alex and peered into the oval portal. The portal was big as a castle gate, and its walls shimmered with the same green glow as the rest of the hull.

"Looks like the Martians already established some microbeacons," said Jon, pointing. Alex saw small location transmitters staked into the walls. "Should I get ours out?"

Alex considered. He took out his handheld and checked for signal from the Martian beacons.

"They're on," he said. "They should be enough. We'll follow them for a while. We'll establish our own if we decide to explore some of the more tangential routes. I half suspect the Martian beacons will lead us right to where we want to go, the AWP's navigational system."

The two entered the AWP. That first step, gone, just like that, and now they were inside. The blackness of space disappeared and the green light of the walls, as shimmering and ethereal as the Aurora Borealis, was all around them, of sufficient intensity to illuminate their way. They kept their guidelights on just the same. Alex saw that beneath the protective shimmering green, the walls were actually made of living tissue, membranous, like the inside of someone's stomach. He checked his handheld.

"I'm detecting an atmosphere. It's thin, no more than ten percent of Earth's. It's primarily oxygen, too." He glanced back toward the open portal. "I wonder what's holding it in here."

"Wasn't there mention of this oxygen in some of the Martian intelligence material?"

"Yes. But barometric pressure data was missing."

Alex stared at the open portal. An alien technology held the oxygen in place, but that technology was undetectable by his handheld. Would their instruments be sensitive enough to capture everything?

He and Jon followed the passageway, a rounded capillary, as it curved like a tree root. They passed several tangential corridors, but for the time being kept to the main one marked out by the Martian beacons. Alex checked for Number 17 on his handheld, but detected none in the immediate vicinity. His shoulders eased. Nor was there any sign of Number 16 either. Or the new Number 18 nanogen for that matter. As indicated in Graham's briefing, the place was deserted, abandoned by the aliens for whatever reason, the empty passageway free of any debris or equipment. But was there someone still lurking inside? Since the LV scan, the notion wouldn't leave Alex. He lifted his handheld higher and double-checked its small screen. He now detected water.

"There's water up ahead," he said.

Rounding the next bend, they saw before them, rearing out of the floor at a ninety-degree angle and extending all the way to the ceiling, a wall of water, suspended there, blocking the passageway. It didn't make sense to Alex. In the free fall of outer space, water turned into self-contained globules. Just spill orange juice in the Command Module when the wheel was off and you found that out fast. This water, however, stayed in place, just like the atmosphere did, a shifting mirror before them.

"I wonder what's holding it there," said Alex. "It should break apart and float away."

So much water. An ocean of the stuff. Maybe not for drinking after all. Maybe not even for a hydroponics facility. Maybe for living in. Could it be? Were the aliens in fact a marine species? He checked the nature of the water on his handheld. It had a high salt content.

"We might as well go for a swim," said Alex.

Alex gave himself a good yank and splashed into the water. His ears popped. He checked the pressure readings on his visor screen. Pressure had increased from three pounds per square inch to forty-five, the Earth equivalent of eleven fathoms down. He also felt gravity, and had to roll 110 degrees to orient himself to the new up and down. He couldn't figure it out. *Research 97*'s sensors had detected only a marginal rotation, not enough to create significant centrifugal force. Where did this gravity come from? Had the aliens figured out a way to create gravity without spin?

"You okay?" he asked Jon.

"Yes."

"You felt that?"

"Yes."

"Let me get a reading," said Alex. He keyed in the necessary commands. "Point seven Gs. A little less than Earth gravity."

"Maybe it's what they're used to on their home planet," suggested Jon.

Alex paused. "I'm getting a resistance warning on my pulse-pack monitor. Are you?"

"Yes," said Jon. "The water's slowing us down. Fuel consumption's up."

"My suit's asking me if I want graded buoyancy."

"Give it the okay," said Jon.

Alex okayed the prompt.

"You won't float, but you won't sink either," said Jon. "You'll stay even."

For all that, the going was slow, and Alex finally said, "Let's tow a ride from the sled."

Jon positioned the sled in front of them. Each grabbed a side. The support specialist engaged the sled's particle-pulse drive and the sled pulled them along.

After five minutes, the passageway widened into a chamber. The chamber was so big, Alex couldn't see its walls through the murky green water. He performed an ultrasonar scan to get a better idea of the chamber's dimensions. A moment later he had his answer.

"Two hundred meters around," he said, "and spherical."

Jon peered into the distance. "The Martians have their beacons to the left," he said, "against the far wall. You realize we're out of contact with 97 now, don't you? The hull doesn't let anything in or out."

"We were expecting as much," said Alex.

"I hope Ruth's okay."

"She'll be fine," said Alex.

A little farther on, smaller chambers, maybe ten by ten meters, catacombed the wall. They found interesting formations in these smaller chambers, like rounded pieces of furniture extruded from the floor, some decorated with ornate calligraphy, others smooth. Living quarters? He concentrated on the extruded forms. Was it indeed furniture of some kind? He tried to extrapolate the physiology of the aliens from the design features of the various forms he saw. How did these extruded forms work in an underwater context, if they were indeed furniture? He couldn't begin to guess. For all he saw, he still couldn't extrapolate successfully what the aliens might look like.

"Can we conclude they're a marine species?" asked Jon.

"I don't know," said Alex. "Based on evidence collected from the other AWPs, we always thought they were a land species. But getting a fix on their exact nature has always been hard. Did I ever tell you how we tried to clone one once?"

"I think I read it in a file somewhere," said Jon. "Before I came on board."

Alex nodded. "We found some cells." He recalled his excitement the day he was told about the cells. "The only cells we *ever* found. It's always self-destruct with the aliens, never a capture, and they never leave so much as a scrap of their own tissue behind. So these cells were a big deal."

"Maybe they think we'll devise our own nanogens to use against them if we get a chance to study their biological matter," said Jon.

"Maybe," said Alex. "But we found these cells. We discovered them in what we think was a regeneration tank, something used to grow backup organs for transplant. We figured we have this tissue, it's alive, it's healthy, why not clone an alien so we can get a good look at one? We put the cells into a cloning medium. Sure enough, they replicated. We got some decent sequencing studies out of the project. Enough to tell us the alien genome was made up of some of the same building blocks we have here on Earth, and that there were even passing similarities between human and alien DNA when it came to cognitive characteristics. But then something turned on inside one of the chromosomes. The DNA, instead of producing a full-grown alien, produced a virulent disease, one that was instantly lethal to laboratory rats."

"A nanogen?" said Jon.

"No," said Alex. "A straight virus. We had to conclude that the aliens had booby-trapped these cells on purpose. It was a great disappointment. We really thought we were finally going to get a good look at one. But we didn't. Instead, we were left extrapolating their nature from AWP architecture, and from the other available evidence. We poured a lot of time and money into that project. But all we got from it was plague in a test tube." Alex gestured at the extruded forms. "So we keep guessing." He shook his head. "And every time we think we've guessed right, something like this turns up and we see we've guessed wrong."

Matters became urgent when *Advance 1*, in a priority transmission, warned them of an approaching Martian squadron.

"It's going to be here in eighteen days," said Ruth. "We're going to have to cut at least ten days out of your original thirty-day plan, Alex. I'd like to be well clear of the AWP before the Martians arrive. We'll leave our drones as a welcoming party."

Alex's shoulders tightened as he realized the pressure was really on again. Ten days gone from what was already turning into an all-too-brief schedule, all because of this stupid war. His thirty-day plan had included study and research, but how could they conduct any research now? He and Jon hadn't even found the navigational system yet. He wanted to open negotiations with the approaching Martians, get Jon to hail them, suggest they work on the AWP together. He tapped the Command Module console a few times in exasperation. But he had to face facts. The Martians were hostile. They were coming, and coming fast. He had to forget research. He had to concentrate on finding the navigational system. His prime concern was to make sure they had the hours they needed to locate and deploy it. Otherwise the Martians might use the AWP against them. They would make a Number 18 Armageddon on Earth.

"Jon and I waste a lot of time coming back and forth each night," he said. "We don't necessarily have to sleep in the wheel. We have to change our strategy. We'll sleep inside the AWP so we don't waste so much time. Jon and I can squeeze in a lot more work if we camp inside."

Ruth's lips drew back and her eyes narrowed. "The AWP's hull blocks out any and all forms of communication," she said. "We'll be out of contact. What if the Martians come sooner? How can I warn you?"

"I'll send Jon back to 97 every thirty-six hours for an update," said Alex. He grinned. "That way, you guys can have some privacy."

"But you'll be split up," she said. "That's strictly against protocol."

"As commander, I'm going to override that particular protocol, Ruth," said Alex. "We have no choice. Jon and I have only just located the nerve endings of the navigational system. Where those Martian beacons go, who knows, but I think these nerve endings will more likely lead us to the appropriate areas. It's going to take time. So we're going to have to sleep inside. From a military standpoint, it's absolutely essential I override the protocol. I hate that we have to abandon any chance at research, but the situation's now critical. If we don't find the navigational system before the Martians get here, we won't have enough time to figure out how to manipulate its gyro-ducts, and that'll be it, they'll deploy this new Number 18 nanogen against us, and we'll be finished. So it's absolutely essential we make the most of our schedule, and sleep inside. If we do it my way, we increase our odds of effecting a course change.'"

Ruth glanced at Jon. She was a woman in love, and she was understandably concerned about the safety of her fiancé. But Ruth finally conceded to military necessity.

"I'll abide by your decision, Alex," she said. "I don't like it, but I can see we don't have a choice."

Eighteen hours later, Alex and Jon camped underwater, close to the threshold of Module A. Their Oxygen Production Unit, about the size of a cantaloupe, hummed under the power of a single hydrogen cell, separating oxygen molecules from water and pumping them into their tanks. Suit controls kept temperatures at twenty-five Celsius for sleeping. Still, it was hard to sleep underwater. A slight current ebbed and flowed, and kept shifting Alex from side to side. He finally adjusted his buoyancy grading to high. He became as immoveable as a rock. Even then, he felt the current's drag. He felt restless. He sat up and looked at Jon. Jon was asleep. One thing about Jon: he could sleep anywhere.

But sleep for Alex right now was impossible. He wanted to be up and doing. He wanted to work. Precious minutes were wasting away. So many questions had to be answered. This current, for instance. Where did it go? Where did it come from? That was a good place to start. Maybe the current would give him some answers about the aliens. And it might even reveal further clues to the location of the all-important gyro-ducts, the tubelike control devices in the navigational chamber.

He accessed his buoyancy-control screen.

"Increase buoyancy," he said.

Yes. Research. Despite the urgency of the military situation, he couldn't let go of his curiosity, wanted to engage in at least a little pure and primary research. He had to find out about this thing. He got up. He became oblivious to all safety concerns, a victim of his own inquisitiveness. He went into maverick mode, realized he often rode roughshod over the rules, as Graham had complained to him, but still didn't have the good sense to stop, especially when the rules seemed so ridiculous.

He let the current carry him along. He traveled toward Module A. As he entered Module A, he heard music—the same music they'd heard during the initial sonar scan. Like wind chimes, with hundreds of tones and timbres—soft, solemn, and entrancing. The current shifted, rose, and carried him into a vertical shaft. He looked up. He saw light up there. He floated upward. A few moments later he splashed through. He looked around.

He was in the center of a big pool. Around him loomed a large chamber with glowing walls. The music, though still soft, seemed to envelop him. In the somnolent embrace of the music, the fret and worry of life slipped away. He swam to the edge of the pool, ran his hand over its raised lip, could feel, through the thin skin of his pressure suit, its hard, shell-like surface, reminding him of the clamshells he, Jill, and Daryl used to find when visiting Jill's parents on Martha's Vineyard. He climbed over the raised lip and got to his feet. Gravity pulled at .7 Gs. He turned around, and . . .

And saw a mural up on the wall . . .

Not just any mural . . .

A mural that depicted a . . . *being* . . .

He stared in wonder.

Was this, then, an alien?

The likeness, rendered brilliantly, was on a large scale. It showed a tall, slender, centaurlike creature—like the half-horse, half-man of Greek mythology, only with unmistakable marine characteristics. While its upper torso appeared human, the remainder, from the waist down, resembled a marine dinosaur. It had four flippers and a streamlined body that looked adapted to life in the water. The creature's bald head was pea green. Its facial features were arranged in what exobiologists called "standard configuration"—two eyes, a nose, and a mouth—a terrestrial arrangement. Alex stared at the face. A striking face. A serene and feminine face. Skull contours were elongated, not as bulky or rounded as a human skull. Garlands of silver seaweed hung from its shoulders. A silver amulet with a red gemstone dangled from a chain around its neck. A halo of yellow light glimmered above its head. It was an altogether enchanting creature.

He looked into the creature's eyes. Because wasn't this what he had always wanted? To stare into the eyes of an alien? To divine its soul? To understand it? Its eyes were blue, with no sclera, just an iris and pupil. They were as blue as lapis lazuli. What kind of consciousness did this creature have? What kind of sense of self? Alex thought he saw sadness, but great wisdom as well. How old was it? He couldn't tell. A kind of agelessness emanated from the rendering.

He looked at the halo again. A detail right out of human religious art. He couldn't help wondering if at some time in the past, during a possible previous visitation, alien and human religious art had somehow cross-pollinated one another. The halo was in fact a preternatural detail, and it now made the rendering too fanciful to be believed on a literal level. Did the mural really depict an alien creature, or was this just a hallowed being lifted from the pages of an alien bible? The rendering now seemed idealized to Alex. He grew doubtful. This was a painting, after all. It would be a mistake to derive scientific actuality from a cultural artifact.

He glanced around. He now got the sense that this chamber might in fact be a place of worship. Maybe this creature on the mural was an oceanic deity, like Neptune. A series of ridges made of shell-like material rose one after the other, amphitheater-style, around him. The walls glowed violet, pink, green, and silver—the colors shifted with the mood of the music. Did the aliens, if indeed they were a marine species, simply rest on these ridges, use them more as docking points than chairs? He wondered why, if the depiction in the mural suggested an aquatic species, this sanctuary should then be drained of water, with only the central pool left filled. Maybe the aliens were amphibious.

He turned to the mural again. He now concentrated on the background. The creature rode on the crest of a wave. Beyond it stretched an ocean. To the left rose a volcanic island, with the calderas of a few peaks clearly visible. What struck him most about the background were the three suns in the sky: one yellow like the Earth's sun; the second distant, smaller, a dab of orange paint; and the third no more than a speck of red. Not that he was jumping to conclusions, but the Centauri system was a triple-star system. Centauri A was a sun-class star, Centauri B was a type KO orange star, and Centauri C was a red dwarf. Such a configuration of suns might conceivably be seen from a habitable planet orbiting Centauri A. Then again, this could be a star system from the other side of the galaxy. The old guessing game. Even with this new evidence staring him in the face, Alex felt he would never really know the aliens.

Chapter 14

Alex and Jon entered Module A fifteen minutes into the next work period. The opening was big, thirty meters across and fifty meters high. Alex unhooked his handheld.

"Give me the CT wand," he said.

Jon handed Alex the computerized tomography wand. Alex inserted the instrument into the diagnostic port, waited for the interface, then performed a series of computerized axial tomographic images. He was happy to see the inside walls were permeable to CT waves, with images beyond the walls of the corridor readily apprehendable to his instrument.

"If you wanted to go," said Jon, "you should have told me. You can't be impulsive, Alex, not on a mission like this. Anything could have happened. You might be commander, but you still have to work as part of a team. You've done this before. Max would always grumble about it behind your back, but he would never say anything right to your face. Now we're two billion miles from home and it's not the right thing to do."

"I'm sorry, Jon," he said. "But you looked so darn tired. Next time I'll wake you for sure." He glanced around the corridor, then checked his scanning screen. "We might as well settle in. This is going to take a while."

Three hours later, the computerized axial tomographic imaging of Module A was complete. While this particular form of mapping couldn't be reconfigured for positioning purposes, it nonetheless gave them a digitized diagram of what Module A looked like from the inside. Alex processed the many images into a single comprehensive view.

"It consists mainly of a series of spiraling corridors from top to bottom," he said. "I'm not a hundred percent sure what these polyps are. They stud the walls everywhere. The whole setup reminds me of some of the manufacturing AWPs we found around Venus. These adhesions are most likely munitions, fighters, or other war matériel in various stages of manufacture." He pointed. "This secondary chamber at the back is where we should find the navigational system. You see this hornet's nest of tubing?"

"Yes," said Jon.

"These are the gyro-ducts," said Alex. "A lot bigger than what we're used to, but the crane and cables are adjustable, so I'm sure we'll have no trouble manipulating them."

Jon gazed at the spiraling corridors.

"I hope we don't get lost," he said. "We're still going to plant beacons, aren't we? I know it's time-consuming, but we wouldn't want to take a wrong turn somewhere."

"We'll keep to this outside corridor here," said Alex. He tapped the screen. "We might find our way

182

using just CT images. We'll plant beacons at less-frequent intervals. The route looks fairly straightforward. I'm sure we'll find our way back safely."

But Jon sighed, a sound Alex pretended to ignore. Was he being a maverick again? He couldn't help it. When there was so little time, risks had to be taken.

The polyps did indeed turn out to be munitions, fighters, and other war matériel in various stages of manufacture. The attack craft were similar to but a lot bigger than the tactical orbital fighters from the manufacturing AWPs around Venus. They hung from the walls by thick umbilical cords. He examined one of the orbital fighters. In the water's current, it bobbed eerily, casting shadows in the green light. Alex checked his handheld for vital signs. The fighter was dead.

"That's what they had in store for us?" said Jon.

"I'm going to take a closer look at this one," said Alex.

He swam over.

The drive array, fabricated from biothermal components, looked like it could, when alive, produce enough heat, and subsequently enough thrust, to propel the organic craft at considerable speeds.

"These arrays must have enough capacity for at least the equivalent of two dozen burns," said Alex. "We wouldn't have stood a chance, Jon. We would have been outmaneuvered by a margin of ten to one."

Alex now checked the weapons array. A quick CT study showed half-formed projectiles inside the ordnance-delivery system.

"These projectiles have seventy-five burns apiece, and double the blast radius of our own microwarheads," Alex told Jon. He shook his head. "We always thought the aliens didn't understand orbital warfare. But they're masters. Thank God their plans got fouled up before they reached us. We would have been defeated in a matter of days."

As Alex and Jon followed the spiraling corridor ever closer to the navigational system over the next few hours, the polyps grew smaller, less refined, now looked like fetal versions of the more developed space fighters further back, with immature internal structures, nerve centers, and projectile armaments. Had the damage in Module B arrested their development?

"I'm going to do a census," said Alex. "I want to see how many we have."

He lifted his handheld, scanned one of the fighters, then keyed in a find, identify, and tabulate command.

He had his answer a few seconds later.

"Seven thousand eight hundred and ninety-two," he said. "Assuming there's this many in Module B, that represents an invasion force of sixteen thousand attack craft. That doesn't count the troop transports, wherever they might be." His throat felt dry. "This invasion force would have been unstoppable, Jon. We would have been goners for sure."

"How do you think things got fouled up?" asked Jon.

"I have no idea," said Alex. "I'm just glad they did."

They reached the navigational system five hours later. It occupied a heart-shaped chamber at the back of Module A. The walls shimmered. Alex's handheld blinked. He had a new readout. He checked it.

"There's a much higher potassium and iron content here," he said. "That means we're definitely in the right place. Potassium and iron act as a neurological relay medium in this particular navigational context."

Vinelike loops—the gyro-ducts—grew from a hard shell about the size of a truck.

"That's the core?" said Jon, pointing to the shell.

"Yes," said Alex.

The core was embedded in a thick, pink membrane that rose at a ninety-degree angle from the floor. Countless white suction cups dotted this membrane—a sensory array. The chamber measured a hundred meters across and two hundred meters high. The gyro-ducts, fire-hose thick, were looped one to the other in a variety of different patterns— laterally, vertically, and diagonally—to cover all possible planes of navigation.

Alex and Jon swam closer. Alex took the thing's vitals. The core was still alive, but its pulse was weak. He took sonar readings from the core and discovered nothing untoward, no unnatural sine-wave patterns or other man-made disruptions to its essential acoustical nature. He double-checked the sensory array for any recent muscle flexing—a sure sign of outside manipulation—but the tissue remained open and relaxed, in its natural state. As for scarring, he detected none. It looked as if Ariam Adurra had left this particular system alone.

"Ariam Adurra hasn't manipulated anything in here at all," he said, puzzled. "It doesn't even look as if she's been here."

This made him nervous. If Ariam Adurra hadn't made her course changes from here, where had she made them? Had she gone to Module B? It seemed unlikely, since that module was dead. He frowned. He felt he didn't have time to figure things out properly.

He ran a weapons scan. The needle jumped into the red. Number 17. Tons of it.

"Check your weapons scan," he said, his voice thickening.

Jon checked. "Shit," he said. "Where the hell is it?"

"I don't know," said Alex. "But it's faint, not strong enough to trigger the automatic prompt. I don't think we have anything to worry about just yet."

Alex studied the readout. Distant. Weak. The delivery system maybe malfunctioning? Still, he didn't want to take any chances.

"Let's release some colorant," he said. "I want to see it if it comes." The colorant would intensify the nanogen's natural pink color, and add some fluorescence besides. "And let's get the frag nets ready, just in case."

Jon released the colorant into the chamber.

Alex and Jon then got the frag nets ready.

While Jon calibrated the release catches on the frag nets, Alex performed a more in-depth weapons scan. He inserted the appropriate instrument into his handheld, one that looked for Number 17's telltale carrier element, a tailored isotope of bromide. While he waited for the interface, he thought of Number 17. He still had a panicky fear of the stuff. The insidious nanogen kept its victim alive right through the disintegration process by cauterizing any wound and avoiding major arteries, turning the hapless sufferer into an armless, legless torso with enough brain-power left to understand the true meaning of Hell. Thank God for the DDF's Omnifix program. He'd sooner be a robot than an armless, legless man.

Once the interface between the weapons-detection instrument and his handheld was complete, Alex swam around the chamber looking for a more detailed bromide signature. While the instrument could usually pinpoint Number 17 to within a meter, the signature patterns kept fluctuating. Now he wasn't sure if what he detected was simply diffuse bromide, formed as trace chlorine reacted with salt water, or if in fact he actually had some Number 17. He looked at the gyro-ducts. Should he risk it? He was sure Ariam Adurra had decided against it. He was certain she had picked up these same readings and decided to try something else. But he didn't have the time to try something else. He had to make his move before the Martians could use the AWP as a weapon against Earth.

He swam over to the suction-cup-like sensors. The bromide signature grew stronger.

"You're acting at loose ends," said Jon.

Alex shook his head. "I'm picking up contradictory signals on my handheld now." He gazed at his hand-held. "Wait a minute," he said, his voice growing more apprehensive. "Now a prompt is telling me my handheld's been compromised. I don't like that at all. What's going on?"

Jon checked his own handheld. "I'm getting the same prompt," he said. "I'll see if I can get a fix on it. Maybe it's a malfunction." He made his way to the sled and keyed some commands into a backup unit. "Microwaves," he reported. "Is that possible? I thought our handhelds were immune to any kind of waveform, including microwaves."

"Unless the microwaves are generated neurologically," stipulated Alex. "That would be the only exception. Which would definitely be the case inside this navigational system." He looked around the chamber with mounting anxiety. "We're running out of time. Under normal circumstances, I would want a more extensive analysis, swim back to 97 and return with the heavier scanners. But we can't do that, not with the Martians getting closer every day. The way I look at it, we can't confirm these readings. They might represent a danger. They might not. Those aren't great odds, but I think we have to go ahead and change the AWP's course anyway. We go ahead now because we may not get a chance later on."

"Agreed," said Jon.

"It doesn't mean we can't make things as safe as we can," said Alex. He motioned at the sled. "We'll start with the frag nets. And we'll deploy the collection tarp. Let's seal the far wall with it, where those suction-cup sensors are. I'm getting the strongest bromide readings from there."

It took the next few hours to cover the far wall with the collection tarp, and to get the frag nets deployed. When Alex and Jon had finished performing all their safety precautions, Alex set to work manipulating the gyro-ducts. He erected the crane they had brought on the sled, threaded the cables through the pulleys, and mounted the crane next to the gyroducts. By scaling the crane's built-in scaffolding, he reached workable vantage points and looped the ca-

bles around the gyro-ducts. Once the cables were secure, he yanked the gyro-ducts this way and that
way, all the while checking his handheld for any
change in the AWP's orbital trajectory. He felt like a
Lilliputian looping thread over Gulliver, such was
the size of the AWP's navigational system.

He pulled and bent fourteen gyro-ducts before he
got any significant change. Burns redirected the AWP
away from Earth, but, double-checking the trajectory,
he realized the AWP's new orbit might put it within
range of Mars. That was no good. The Martians
would recognize the course change as an opportunity, and mount another mission. He had to get the
thing headed for the sun.

"I'm going to bombard the core with sound
waves," he told Jon. "That will widen the new trajectory by intensifying the slingshot effect past Jupiter."

Alex set up the sound equipment. He keyed in a
command. He established a sawtooth wave, something
that sounded like a bassoon, one wave out of the
many waves he'd found effective in manipulating the
navigational systems aboard the smaller AWPs—
acoustical control was a standard feature on many
AWPs. The core lurched, then settled. Two seconds
later, Alex detected a response from the core, a sine
wave, one that was above the range of human hearing but that was nonetheless detectable by his
handheld.

He rechecked the orbital trajectory. New burns had
changed the orbit. The modified orbit, he saw, was
a highly elliptical one, with perihelion only twenty-
two million miles away from the sun, and aphelion
all the way out past the Oort Cloud. Transit time
around the sun was ninety-two years, and, given the

red planet's current position, the new orbit put the AWP beyong practical enemy reach. Alex explained all this to Jon.

"It's not exactly what we wanted," he said. "But by the time Mars swings past the AWP's new orbital plane, the alien spacecraft will be well on its way to the outer regions of the solar system. And by the time any pursuing Martian craft can get even reasonably close, the AWP will have reached interstellar space. It nixes the AWP's possible strategic use for the next several decades.

"You think that will be good enough for Graham?"

"I don't know. I'll give it another nudge. If I use the same tone again, maybe modify it a bit, I might shift perihelion enough to trap the AWP in the sun's gravitational well. Any increased bromide activity?"

"No."

"Good."

Alex set up the same sawtooth wave, only this time he increased its amplitude, and subtracted some of its upper partials. The core jerked once more, like a heart patient might jerk under the shock of resuscitation paddles. This time, it emitted a sharp, piercing whine, easily audible to the human ear.

"I'm detecting an increase in the speed of the water current," said Jon.

"Yes, I can feel it."

No sooner had Alex said these words than the current doubled in strength. It pushed the sound equipment over and lifted the sled up.

"Shit," said Alex. "What's going on?"

He tried to get his footing, but the current was now too strong. He grabbed the crane so he wouldn't be swept away. The hull wall opened, at first just a crack, but then wider and wider. Water drained toward this crack. As it gaped even wider, Alex saw the distant spotlight of the sun. The thing was opening onto space? Good God! The current got stronger and stronger, so forceful it lifted Jon off his feet and sucked him toward the opening.

"Jon!" cried Alex.

"I can't get my buoyancy grading . . . the current's too strong. And my pulse pack is too weak."

Alex watched in horror as the current carried Jon toward the opening. Clutching the crane with one hand, Alex managed to lift a frag net and shot it toward the support specialist, hoping Jon would grab the line. But Jon missed. The current got so strong it pulled Alex free of the crane, and he, too, was sucked toward the opening.

"Grab on to a gyro-duct!" cried Jon. "Don't let it get the two of us!"

"Jon, I—"

"Just do it!"

As Alex passed the navigational system, he grabbed the nearest gyro-duct. He held on with all his strength, even as the aperture in the far wall grew wider and wider. Water crystallized into huge chunks of ice. How was that possible? Dumps of liquid into space produced a fine spray of ice crystals that disappeared almost instantly. How could the water congeal into large ice chunks like this? Even despite the presence of a thin atmosphere, the water should have boiled away into the vacuum outside. He could only speculate that the aliens had a quick-freeze technology, and had employed it as part of their defense system. Some of the chunks were as big as trucks. Jon collided violently with one of the larger chunks. With sudden dread, Alex knew Jon couldn't have survived the collision.

"Jon!" he cried.

He got no answer. He accessed his visor screen and checked the status of Jon's radio. Jon's radio was now off-line. Before he could check anything else, his body felt lighter, the pull wasn't so strong, and he realized that gravity, the .7 Gs, perhaps dependent on water in this exotechnological context, was slowly disappearing. The remaining water now froze into smaller chunks, like hailstones, and drifted toward the opening, pinging off each other, smacking Alex in the helmet, tumbling around him like a thousand balls in a squash court. Out the opening, the larger chunks gasified. He saw Jon in and amongst the space-bound ice storm.

"Screen, magnify," said Alex.

Jon tumbled away, arms outstretched, one leg straight, the other bent. His suit vented gas— oxygen—the venting oxygen like a small thruster, pushing him farther and farther away from the AWP.

"Vitals," he said.

Jon's bio readings appeared on his screen. Jon's body temperature was minus one hundred Celsius and falling. Respirations were zero. Heart rate was flatlined. Brain activity was nil. Jon hadn't survived. The huge chunk of ice had killed him. Alex felt his throat closing with pain. His old friend was dead. And with a sudden extra stab of pain, he realized Ruth was watching the whole thing from *Research 97*.

Now he felt a low throbbing through the gyro-duct. It got stronger and stronger. He turned slowly, with great trepidation. He saw pink goop bulging under the collection tarp. Bulging, pulsating, getting ready to burst, seemingly unreactive to the electrical charges in the tarp. The tarp filled more and more. The throbbing got even stronger. Then the thing exploded.

A pink flood raced toward him . . . and Alex knew, at last, after a lifetime of dreading the stuff, he was going to have to face the thing he feared most, the aliens' awful disintegrating nanogen; knew that he, too, would now be a victim—like Daryl, like Reba, like his father—and that from now on, his life would be different, irrevocably changed, a grimmer and harder reality from here on in . . .

Chapter 15

He clung to the gyro-duct with his eyes closed. His breathing was labored. Through the slowly clearing static he heard a voice in his com-link, Ruth's voice. With the hull open, radio waves were now penetrating. He tried to say something but felt too paralyzed to speak. Sweat drenched his forehead. His throat was dry and he was shaking.

Ruth's voice persisted.

"Commander Denyer, status report, repeat, status report . . ." The static built. Alex opened his eyes. The hull was closing again, blocking out her radio communication, drowning her voice in a thickening fog of white noise. He had to speak to her before the hull closed completely. He initiated a com-link transmission.

"Ruth, I . . . Jon's gone." He wasn't thinking straight. He had to remember procedure. He had to formalize his command directives so he could get through this emergency, use mission jargon to help him, assume his command persona. He squared his shoulders and, forcing the shakiness from his voice, said, "Request rendezvous with quarantine unit at the entrance portal. Am infected with Number 17. Repeat, am infected with Number 17. Request quarantine rendezvous at the entrance portal."

The hull closed. Had she heard him? He hoped so. He didn't want to endanger her. He wanted to crawl into the clear plastic bubble of the quarantine unit, pined for that isolation, felt afraid to face her now that Jon was gone, was already thinking of what he could have done differently, how he might have saved Jon if he had thought it through a little more thoroughly.

With the hull closed, he wondered if gravity might come back. It didn't. The hailstones continued to bounce around him in the darkness, slower now. The glowing walls didn't glow anymore. His guidelight penetrated the darkness. The hailstones flashed like white insects in the beams of his guidelight. He let go of the gyro-duct. He looked around. The sled was gone. Only a few pieces of sound equipment remained. The crane dangled from the gyro-ducts by its manipulation cables, bent and mangled from the force of the current.

He summoned as much presence of mind as he could.

He took a reading on the AWP's orbital trajectory. Nothing had changed. All that work, all that tragedy, for no gain. The AWP maintained its elliptical orbit; the Martians wouldn't get their hands on it anytime soon, but it wasn't going to crash into the sun either. It was the best he could do. At least he didn't have to worry about the Number 18 nanogen now, didn't have to find it and disable it because it was never going to get within striking distance of Earth. He rested his hand on the nearest gyro-duct, which was as stiff as steel in the frigid temperatures. Impossible to manipulate it now. He gave his pack a burst.

He numbly made his way back, pulling out his handheld to find his way. He knew Number 17 was slowly eating its way through the submolecular spaces in his suit, and that skin contact was only minutes away. He knew there was nothing he could do to stop it. His limbs were shaky and his heart beat quickly. He was devastated by the loss of his friend. And terrified by Number 17. He was afraid he was going to lose his way, afraid they hadn't put enough microbeacons down. He had to focus. If he couldn't concentrate, he would never find his way out of here. He needed something to sharpen himself. So he keyed in a few commands on his med-pack, and it released a tranquilizer into his bloodstream, as well as a hefty dose of methylphenidate, something to help with attention. There. That was better. He could think straight now. He would struggle. He would keep going. He would get back to Ruth, because in the end, Ruth was going to need his help more than he would need hers.

Once he was safely inside the quarantine module, his muscles grew weak.

"Alex, your heart rate's right off the chart," said Ruth. Her voice sounded strange, as if she had to force it through the com-link. "I want you to connect your med-port to the interface. I'm going to give you something stronger than what you have in your med-pack."

He obeyed. Dumbly, passively, he reached up to the right, grabbed the feed, and plugged it into his suit. He didn't feel a thing as Ruth delivered the stronger medication. But then he grew woozy; he slumped, and his eyes closed.

"Alex?" said Ruth.

He opened his eyes. "Yes, Ruth," he said, feeling distant.

"There was nothing you could do, right?"

He thought about it. "We picked up . . . atypical bromide signatures." He thought of Jon, venting oxygen, a gray, steady stream illuminated by the light of the sun as he drifted further and further away from the AWP. "We . . . weren't sure." He felt exhausted, felt it was a chore to breathe, heard his own breath come and go, raspy and enervated. "We considered all options. We were running out of time, Ruth. We thought the risk was acceptable."

"And Jon agreed?"

He now sensed that this was what she needed to know more than anything.

"Jon agreed." His throat closed up, and tears came to his eyes. "I'm sorry, Ruth. I'm sorry he's dead."

He heard nothing from Ruth for the longest time. But then she said, "Okay." She too was crying.

"Ruth?" he said.

"Yes?"

"He died a hero. The AWP's not going anywhere near Earth. We don't have to worry about the Number 18. We won."

"I know, Alex. I've seen the readouts. And if I were Jon, I would have done the same thing. You did a great job."

But her voice was so freighted with pain he could hardly stand it. He felt he had to explain himself.

"That . . . that outspray. I don't know what that

was. The way the hull opened up. I've never seen that before. A defense feature of some sort. There was hardly any time. I go over and over it, and I can't see how we could have done anything differently."

"It's okay, Alex," she said. "We were aware of the risks." Her voice toughened, because Ruth, if anything, was tough. "I'm just going to have to learn to deal with it."

Number 17 worked in part by forming DNA replicas of the host organism. It was only in mapping a host's DNA that the nanogen could completely unravel the victim's body. Once the DNA replication was complete, Number 17 was then locked to that specific host, and was no longer communicable. It became innocuous to all organisms except the infected one.

As Alex neared the end of his second day in quarantine, he tried to find some comfort in this. At least he wouldn't infect Ruth. Or anybody else, once he got home. He played an electronic chess game with Ruth, something to pass the time. But with all the methylphenidate now gone from his body, his focus was shot, and Ruth knew it. She was two moves away from checkmating him.

"I think it's time for another blood test," said Ruth.

"Ruth, I want to go back to the AWP," he said. "I'm not sick yet. We have some time. We don't have to worry about the Number 18. I want to take a look at Side B. Who knows what we can learn? Maybe something that might help us with this Number 17 that's going to ruin my body. Or the aliens might come back. I can learn stuff that might help us fight them."

"Alex, I don't think it's a good idea. We've already lost one crewmember. We don't want to lose another."

"I'll just look," he said. "I won't touch. At least I won't touch anything I think might trigger another defense system."

"And the extra time we have . . . there's not much in the way of a margin," said Ruth. "We're following the AWP, and I appreciate that we have to do that for a while to make sure your work on the core won't cause any unexpected aftershocks in the AWP's navigational system, and that we won't get any unexpected burns that might shift the AWP back toward Earth. But it means we're getting farther and farther away from our predesignated return orbit. We're using up fuel. A lot of it. And to get back to our predesignated launch point, we'll have to use yet more. If we go much farther, we run a risk." Her tone tightened. "We're going to end up like Jon. We're going to *drift*. Plus the drones are back where we left them, with only their offensive burns left. We have no protection right now."

Alex swallowed. He felt the pain of Jon's loss afresh. But he knew Jon would have wanted this. They had an opportunity here, not only a scientific one, but also a military one, a chance to gain valuable intelligence that might be used in future encounters with the aliens.

"Could you put your arm up to the phlebotomy port," said Ruth, as if she were now annoyed with him. "I need a sample."

He lifted his arm and let the machine take its sample.

"How much time do we have before we absolutely have to turn back?" he asked.

"Thirty-six hours."

"That little?" He was disappointed. Yet he knew he could still get a lot done in thirty-six hours. "That's better than nothing."

"The Martians are on the way," said Ruth.

"And when will they be here?" he asked. "I've lost track."

She hesitated. "Forty-eight hours," she said.

"Then who cares about the Martians?" he said. "We've got to be gone in thirty-six. Let's do it, Ruth. We might find something to fix this Number 17. Maybe I won't have to be like this."

"Alex, I'm upset. I'm scared. I don't think it's a good idea to go inside again unless we get an aftershock from the core."

Maybe she wasn't so tough after all. Alex couldn't blame her. He wanted to rest a reassuring hand against her shoulder, but of course he was still out here in this bubble. He had to appeal to the soldier in Ruth. He had to make her remember her ultimate duty.

"Yes, but . . . even if we don't find an antidote for Number 17, think of the military intelligence we might gain. We've already made Jon's death count for something by redirecting the AWP. Let's make it count for even more. Let's learn what we can about this thing in the thirty-six hours we have left."

He waited. He watched her through the quarantine com-link screen. Her eyes narrowed. She was looking at something on one of her screens.

"Your blood looks good," she said. "The Number 17's locked to you, and you alone. You're cleared to come in."

"Good," he said. "I was getting cabin fever out here."

She sighed. "If we're going study Side B, we should do it as soon as possible," she said.

"We?" he said.

"You're not going in there alone, Alex. I'm not going to lose you, too. *Research 97* can maintain its present course easily enough without me. I know Pamlico Sound likes someone on board at all times, but under the circumstances, our safest option is to buddy up and go in there together."

A digital timer clocked away the seconds in the lower left corner of Alex's visor screen.

"Thirty hours now," he said. "And there's no room for error?"

"No," said Ruth. "We drift if we don't turn back at the thirty-hour mark."

Her voice sounded dead. Jon was really getting to her now, her grief setting in like a dark cloud.

"And you're willing to shorten our sleep periods?" he asked.

"If we must," she said.

They started first with the central assembly. They found a chamber.

In the chamber, Alex saw a large panel studded with nubs an inch to three inches tall. When he touched one of these nubs, he felt a low current. A secondary feature, what looked like a knoll, occupied a meter-wide space in the center of the chamber, and this knoll was covered with yard-long spaghettilike fibers sticking straight out of it. The fibers were cylindrical, as thick as his baby finger, and made of a clear organic base. He glanced at the nubs, then at the knoll. He'd never seen such an array on any of the other AWPs before.

What really excited him was that Ariam Adurra had cameras set up everywhere. She had temperature, pressure, and electrical monitors aligned against the panel, and around the knoll. This was surveillance equipment. All he could do was stare. Ariam, for one reason or another, had felt that this chamber was a major discovery. Ariam had been intrigued. And the scientist in Alex now felt intrigued too. Ariam had gone into observer mode. The exotechnologist inside him grew monumentally curious.

"I think we've got something here," he said.

Ruth moved her handheld back and forth, checking things. "All this Martian equipment's still online," she said. "It's transmitting." She turned to Alex. "Should we sabotage it?"

Alex considered.

"No," he finally said. "Let it transmit. Let the Coverts hack into whatever raw data it might send. We might learn something. Something we can use."

Ruth stared at the alien panel. "Maybe this is the bridge," she said. "It looks like a control center of some kind."

He shrugged. "Ariam thought it was important for one reason or another," he said, "that's for sure."

They spent the next hour filming and photographing the area. They measured electrical patterns and recorded complex binary transmissions. These binary transmissions came from the secondary feature, the knoll. He looked at the spaghettilike extensions, hundreds of them, like stiff hair shooting straight from the top of the knoll. Electromagnetic propagators? he wondered. Synaptic equivalents? Or just uncomplicated binary sequencers, such as the transmissions suggested?

He made a quick count of the spaghettilike extensions with his handheld: eight hundred. Then he performed a quick count on the nubs on the panel: eight hundred.

"The number of nubs corresponds to the number of these . . . these spaghetti things," he said.

Though what the significance of that might be he couldn't say. He wanted more time to study this fascinating area.

"But I think it would be wiser to let the Coverts pick up what they can from Ariam's equipment, and spend our time looking at something else," he suggested to Ruth.

Ruth agreed. They moved on.

As they worked their way along the corridor away from the central assembly into the dead half of the spacecraft, they had to use their guidelights. Everything was dark, off-line, with no glow to the walls.

He expected to find a contralateral saltwater sea, but found only the remains of that sea, chunks of ice floating in the corridor, a hailstorm in stasis. In design, Side B, encompassing both stem and module, was a mirror image of Side A. As with Side A, Side B possessed a thin atmosphere of oxygen, not thick enough to breathe, but vigorous enough to keep the ice from gasifying. Soon the corridor widened into a large chamber, just as it had in Side A. Gravity hit them with a sudden .7 Gs. Ruth fell.

"Are you all right?" he asked.

"I was expecting it to be gradual," she said. "Ow. I hurt my ankle."

"Let me help you up," he said.

He gave her a hand.

"Ow."

"Are you okay?"

"I think so. My ankle. That gravity really hit."

"In Side A, it hit us the second we got in the water. I thought it was in some way dependent on the water, but I guess not." He gestured at the chamber, then helped her to her feet. "Look at all this ice."

Huge slabs of the stuff littered the floor, forming a treacherous obstacle course, with the slabs slanting one way and then the other, like giant dominoes spilled all over the place.

"We can't use our particle-pulse packs in here," said Ruth. "Not when there's no water. They're good for only up to .3 Gs in a vacuum or an atmosphere."

"Then we'll hike it," said Alex.

"I sure am glad the backup sled is small," said Ruth. "Navigating all that ice is going to be tough."

They moved into the chamber. Alex took out his CT wand and ran a scan. Module B showed the same spiraling corridors and manufacturing works as Module A.

Once he'd finished his scan, they continued on.

They stopped for a two-hour sleep period partway into Module B.

"I want to be a little more alert," said Ruth. "Plus my ankle hurts. I want to give it a rest."

Her tone was uncertain. She was changed. Once so tough, she was now afraid to go on without more sleep. Alex didn't want to waste time sleeping, but saw Ruth was going to insist, so acquiesced.

He lay down and tried to rest. But he kept looking around.

In Module B, all the water was gone as well. Fewer embryonic attack ships clung to the walls. Unlike the fetal-stage ships found in Module A, these ships had mechanical and electronic components. In fact, sections of Module B itself looked mechanical or electrical, manufactured, not grown, reminding Alex of the smaller AWPs. Why the difference between the two sides? he wondered. He shifted, trying to make himself more comfortable. Did these mechanical and electronic components represent repairs to damaged tissue? Or were they simply a part of the design? Maybe they were products of a different technological epoch in alien history. The thought intrigued him.

Trying his best not to disturb Ruth, he dated some of the manufactured paneling with his handheld. He then dated the surrounding biological tissue by analyzing its carbon signatures.

While the tissue was fifteen centuries old, such as the initial Advance readings had suggested, the manufactured paneling was only two hundred years old, making it contemporaneous with the newer AWPs. Again, he had to wonder: Why the difference? Had there been a shift in technological philosophy? He couldn't help thinking that Module A, exclusively wetware, was by far the more elegant design, unhampered by all this clunky hardware that Module B had. But he couldn't even begin to figure out why there should be such a big difference between the two sides.

Chapter 16

Eight hours later they came to an odd and terrifying chamber. Their guidelights cast eerie beams through the gloom. They found vats. Thousands of them. And in the vats, they found human remains. The facility stretched for hundreds of yards in all directions. The vats were rectangular, about the size of a hospital bed, two and a half feet deep, with open tops.

"This is a mass grave," said Alex. "For humans."

He was stupefied to find humans aboard. It was the last thing he had expected. Certainly none of the Coverts had indicated the presence of all these human corpses. He took a moment to get a grip on himself. The scene was chilling. He summoned his courage. Even in the face of this atrocity he had to be a scientist and learn what he could from it. He took a few steps forward and had a closer look. The vats were made of clear plastic, but were dirty, caked here and there with a strange yellow ice. With the vats in ordered rows, and the ambience of gruesome industrial-scale death hanging over the place, the scene was otherworldly, a nightmare.

"Alex, let's go," said Ruth.

He glanced at her. His nervy old friend was definitely gone, too devastated by the loss of her fiancé to have much of her characteristic confidence.

"It's all right, Ruth. We'll be fine."

He walked to the nearest vat. A crack traced a jagged scar in the glass, and the liquid inside had drained to the floor, where it now sat in a yellowish pile of slush.

Inside the vat he found an end-stage Number 17, no arms or legs, just a torso and a head. A woman, by the look of her, though her remains were so withered it was hard to tell. His heart began to pound. He, too, was frightened of this place. The poor woman. Her ribs stuck out against her pale skin, her breasts were wrinkled sacks, and her abdomen dipped appallingly to the knobby protuberances of her hipbones. A tattoo of a bluebird adorned the woman's left shoulder, a sad mark, one that individualized the woman, made the tragedy of her death hit home. Her face was skull-like in its emaciation, with her eyes staring, dull and horrified, straight up. A few locks of hair, congealed by some of the yellow goop, hung like dead worms from her scalp. Eight tubes skewered her left side; six impaled her right side, the mutilation grotesque and horrifying. Some of the skin on her face had begun to disintegrate, Number 17-style.

"Alex, please, what if they're still here? Remember that noise we heard? It sounded like someone walking across ice."

Ruth cast her guidelights anxiously around the facility. He put his arm around her. She was shaking. He couldn't blame her. This was Hell's outpost.

"Just a little longer, Ruth," he said. He cast another glance over the endless expanse of human remains. "We have unimpeded access to this place right now, and we have to make the most of it."

After a moment, she gave him a stalwart nod.

He motioned around the facility.

"Look at the damage here," he said. "I wonder how it happened? Half these vats are broken. And a lot of them are pushed over."

Indeed, many armless, legless torsos lay on the floor, just sacks now, the tubes ripped out of their frozen bodies, their sightless eyes staring into the gloom, their flesh as pale as maggot flesh. They were as dehumanized as a pile of rotten potatoes. Every torso was punctured, eight on one side, six on the other, as if the aliens had simply wanted to juice these humans for whatever muck they could get out of them. He hated the aliens more than ever. These poor, dead people looked as if they had been treated like sides of beef.

He moved on, stricken by what he saw. Ruth followed along behind, clutching his elbow. Useless death everywhere. A snapshot of Armageddon. They came to some Number 16 vats. Many of the Number 16 victims inside these vats still wore clothes. These clothes came from an earlier period in human history. Alex wasn't an expert when it came to period costume, but if he had to guess, he would say several centuries ago. Skin fragmentation, hunching of the spine, and yellow skin marked everybody in this section of the room as an End-of-Lifer Number 16. All these people were skewered as well, the tubes puncturing right through their clothes. The tubes led from the vats to an overhead network, where they twisted off to the right. They snaked through a ceiling brace and emptied into a cistern about the size of a wheelbarrow.

"Let's check that cistern over there," he said.

They walked over. He looked inside. He saw frozen liquid—plasma—pinkish in color, transparent; no more than a few liters of the stuff.

"Hand me the sampler," he said.

Ruth gave him the sampler. Alex switched it on. He pressed the hexagonal collection pad against the pink, transparent ice. A few seconds later, the instrument beeped—an adequate amount had been collected.

Alex ran an analysis on the sample with his handheld, checking for toxins, radioactivity, biological pathogens, and alien-designed nanogens—anything that might possibly pose a threat to human tissue.

"Nothing," said Alex. "It's innocuous." Alex's eyes narrowed. "I'm going to run a more in-depth analysis."

Alex was surprised by his findings, especially in light of everything Dr. Ely Colgan had told him about Number 16 enzyme production.

"It's a telomerase," said Alex.

"A what?" asked Ruth.

"An enzyme that can maintain telomere length."

"I'm sorry," she said. "A telomere?"

"A telomere is the cufflike structure at the end of a chromosome that regulates cell division." He felt himself slipping into his scientist persona. "Each time a cell divides, the telomere shortens. When the telomere shortens completely, the cell can't divide anymore, and dies. A telomerase stops the telomere from shortening. Theoretically, a telomerase can extend life." He gestured at the cistern. "Only in this particular case, the telomerase is inert. It needs something to trigger it into action, so it can work. Dr. Colgan tells me he finds the same enzymes in the Arlington EMZ Number 16s. And I found a similar enzyme in a fixer system I was working on."

Alex pondered this whole macabre discovery. Maybe these were a test group, abducted long before anybody knew anything about the aliens, used as guinea pigs to measure the efficacy of their nanogens. He shuddered. He felt nausea climbing in his throat. He'd had enough. In this chamber of horrors, he again realized that the aliens were the enemy, and that no matter how much fun he had fooling around with the junk they had left behind, he would always hate them.

With two hours remaining, Alex and Ruth, on their way back to *Research 97*, were just crossing a big field of broken ice when Ruth slipped and got her leg trapped in the ice. Alex's anger flashed. Anger? Why an angry response? The emotion felt inappropriate and out of control, not of his doing. He grew suddenly apprehensive. Was Number 17 already starting in on him?

"What happened?" he asked.

"My sore ankle," she said. "It gave out on me. I slipped."

"Why weren't you more careful?"

"Pardon?" Ruth started to cry. She was scared. "I'm caught. I can't get out."

He came over and had a look, getting himself under control.

"Where's it stuck?" he asked.

"Underneath," she said. "It's jammed in good."

He looked more closely. The crevice came right up to her thigh, but narrowed toward her ankle.

"See if you can yank it out," he said.

She tried. "Ow, ow, ow!" she cried. "I think it might be broken."

"Really?"

"Alex, we're running out of time. We're not going to make it."

He checked Ruth's vitals on his visor screen: sure enough, she had a fracture of her right fibula, plus a lot of inflammation.

"Yep, it's broken," he said.

"I'm sorry, Alex."

"We'll chip away some of this ice and see if we can pull you free."

He took five-pound sledgehammer from the backup sled and bashed away at the ice. He bashed for the next ten minutes, trying to widen the crevice so he could get a better look. As he bashed, he couldn't help feeling resentful. He knew it was the wrong thing to feel. Anybody could have lost their footing on this treacherous ice, especially if they had a sore ankle to begin with. Yet the feeling persisted, and more troubling, the feeling felt unnatural, as if he had been forced to feel it against his will, as if it enveloped him with a palpable and malignant presence. He tried to shake it, but he couldn't. It scared him. Number 17 was slowly drilling into him, already affecting his emotions. He bashed harder, concentrating on his work as a way to stop the unwarranted emotion. He finally gave up bashing. The sledgehammer didn't seem to be doing any good.

"This isn't working," he said. "Let me try the laser drill."

He retrieved the laser drill from the sled and torched it up. He pressed the laser against the ice. He might as well have held a match to the ice for all the good it did. Nonetheless, he worked away at it. He couldn't make quick progress because the ice kept refreezing the minute he had it melted. By the time he gave up, his timer had ticked down to forty-seven minutes.

"Just leave me here," said Ruth.

All the grief and fear she'd carried for the last five days, ever since the disaster at the navigational hub, overwhelmed her. Alex got the sense that she *wanted* to be left behind, that to some degree she blamed herself for Jon's death, and that the only way she could make amends was to perish with her fiancé. But he wasn't going to let that happen.

"Let's try something else," he said.

He got a regular-sized hammer and a two-inch chisel.

He chiseled an eighteen-inch line around her thigh, pounding away at it until he had created a fissure two inches deep. He checked his timer: thirty-nine minutes left. He placed the chisel in the center of the fissure, aimed carefully and, like he was splitting wood, gave the fissure a good whack. The ice around her thigh fell away in one big piece. He pulled it out and tossed it to one side. Now he could get a better look at things. He got on his stomach and examined the situation.

Her ankle was indeed lodged firmly, wedged through a round opening.

"Does it hurt?" he asked.

"Yes," she said.

"Key some analgesics from your med-pack."

She keyed in a command. "That's better," she said.

"This is damn awkward," he said. "I can't get at it. Hang on."

He squeezed both hammer and chisel down the hole and chipped delicately around her ankle so he wouldn't hurt her. It was desperately slow work because of the angle. Also, because he was on ice, he kept sliding back, and had to pull himself up countless times to make the most of his chiseling.

Finally, he chiseled a semicircular fissure through the ice to the left side of Ruth's ankle.

"We've got only twenty-one minutes," she said.

He wedged the chisel into the fissure and gave it a good whack. But the ice didn't immediately fall away. He had to deepen the fissure another inch. That took ten minutes. He gave it a final blow, a big chunk of ice fell away, and she was able to free herself.

"Ow."

"We'd better hurry," he said.

"How am I going to hurry when my ankle's broken? And my med-pack's making me feel like I'm in Wonderland. You better leave me here, Alex."

He sensed her narcotic disorientation. "We'll leave the backup sled instead."

"There's ten million dollars worth of equipment on that sled."

"Who cares?" he said. "Put your arm around my shoulder. We'll get a rhythm going, and I'm sure we'll make it."

They worked their way slowly over the treacherous ice slabs. Alex glanced at his visor timer: nine minutes left. He checked his pulse and blood pressure: both sky-high. The odd thing: he was showing fractures in the first three fingers of his right hand, in his left thumb, his left big toe, and two toes on his right foot, yet he didn't feel a thing. He knew what it was. Number 17 had its hooks into him.

It took them another four minutes to get to the entrance portal. That gave them five minutes to board 97 and initiate the launch sequence. Luckily, gravity cycled back to zero Gs in the corridor, and they could now float the rest of the way.

"I feel faint," said Ruth. "I think I overdosed myself."

"Just hang on," he said, grabbing her hand. "I'll pull you."

He geared his pack to maximum thrust and jetted through the entry port into outer space, glad to be free of the AWP's claustrophobic spaces. He checked his visor timer: three minutes, forty-six seconds left. He arced under the central assembly, dragging a drugged Ruth behind him, flew right through the vapor feed trail, his visor screen registering fifty or sixty micrometeorite hits, then straightened his trajectory and beelined for 97.

"Are you okay?" he asked. He was worried about her ability to fly 97.

"We have under three minutes," she said. "I need at least ninety seconds to initiate the launch sequence. If I miss it by even a few seconds, we're done for. We'll miss our return orbit and we'll be too far away to be rescued. I feel so drugged. I can't concentrate."

"What about some stimulants?" he suggested.

"I'm going to key in some amphetamines," she

said. She reached down and inputted the necessary commands. "There. I feel it. I'm snapping out of it."

They sank to the venture bay, cycled the air lock, and entered the spacecraft. They propelled themselves through the drive module corridor to the wheel. As they entered the wheel, Alex checked his timer once more: 2:01 remaining.

Ruth was now moving fast, cooking on speed, gripping the handholds one after another, pulling herself at a frantic pace toward the Command Module. 1:55 remaining. He chased after her, saw her leap into the Command Module. He gripped the handholds, but it was difficult, now that his fingers were broken. He pulled himself into the Command Module and maneuvered himself into his seat.

"One minute, forty-one seconds left," she said. "Strap in."

He struggled with the straps but found he couldn't close his hands.

"I can't," he said.

She glanced his way. "Why not?"

A deep fear built inside him. "My hands. My fingers. It's started."

Her face sank. The old Ruth came back. She was as hard as a rock. She quickly strapped him in.

"Are you good?" she asked.

"Yes," he said.

She keyed in commands frantically.

At the 1:31 mark, with only a second to go before their ninety-second margin, the ship hummed.

Ruth's body eased.

"Done," she said. "We're on our way."

They both sat there waiting for the launch to count itself down.

A minute into the ninety-second sequence, he said, "I'm going to take my right glove off. I want to have a look."

He unsnapped the pressure clasps around his glove and pulled it free.

Granulated flakes of body ash floated out and formed a cloud in front of his face. He looked at his hand. His first three fingers were gone; filed down to the knuckle by Number 17, healed over nicely, not bleeding, but still eaten away. He looked at the dust floating in front of him. He swallowed. Those were his fingers. And now they were dust.

Then *97's* thrusters kicked in, and the dust floated behind his head, flattening against the back wall in the heavy G-force of the launch.

When they were safely on their way, and he was lying in his cot three hours later, Alex brooded; thought not only of how his body had begun to disintegrate, but of the terrifying chamber full of Number 16 and Number 17 corpses. He knew the discovery was a significant one, but he couldn't readily say how it fit into everything he knew about the aliens. The ship vibrated, and outside the window he saw the blue sheen of the sublight drive's mysterious enabling medium. If invasion was their intent, why first turn humans into Number 16s and 17s, then juice them for odd enzymes that had no value outside a petri dish?

He drifted off to sleep. He dreamed he was in one of the vats. Yellowish liquid rose higher and higher around his body. Tubes appeared, and skewered his armless, legless torso on either side. He felt them suck. He saw his armless, legless body sag as the tubes removed the pulp from it. Then the yellowish liquid came right up over his face . . . he couldn't breathe . . . he was drowning. . . .

He woke up. In a cold sweat. Swallowing his own bile. Yes, the aliens were his enemy. And he would hate them forever.

Chapter 17

"First your arms go," said Dr. Aldous Slater, head of the Greensboro Omnifix program. "Omnifix replaces those quickly. Then your legs go. Omnifix gathers what materials it needs from our warehouses—like thousands of bees gathering pollen—and replaces those as well."

Alex lay in his bed at Greensboro. Someone had placed a small Christmas tree on his dresser next to his get-well cards. Dr. Slater continued.

"As your internal organs go, Omnifix will gather whatever biological and artificial materials it needs to reconstruct them. The Omnifix nanogens swarm. They fly. They scavenge. They're working all the time, either out in our warehouses or in our stockyards."

"What about the invasive procedures?" asked Alex. "Because that's what I'm really nervous about."

"Omnifix puts you under for those," said Dr. Slater. "You'll be right out. That's why we keep you here at Greensboro for the first little while. We have to wait until all the invasive procedures are finished before we write your discharge papers. Sometimes Omnifix will put you under for a week or longer. But you don't have to worry about your basic care during those periods because Omnifix is integrated with advanced nursing software, and will feed you, evacuate you, look after your bedsores, and keep a record of all your vitals."

He contemplated Slater. The doctor was a young, dark-haired man, no more than thirty-five, small in stature, with a pale, waxy complexion. His eyes were deep-set, close together, and never once, not in five consultations, had he made eye contact with Alex. Alex guessed it had to be his face. His face was disintegrating, slowly but surely. Truly a sight to behold.

"What about my brain?" he asked. "I think the emotional deterioration has already begun there."

"Rest assured, Dr. Denyer, Omnifix's neurological components are highly advanced, and work to lessen the effects of the emotional deterioration. Every year, Greensboro conducts extensive randomized studies to improve these components. Ninety percent of our Number 17 patients participate in these studies."

"I thought the Defederacy didn't have money for studies."

"Certain private organizations fund these studies," said Dr. Slater. "There are many Number 17 support groups in the Defederacy. We look to their members. Without their participation, and their dedication to regular follow-up, these studies would be impossible, and our small neurological improvements might never materialize. That's why our nurses are always stressing follow-up, not only for the randomized studies, but also for a patient's own personal care. Even after you've been discharged—and even if you think everything's all right—we still like you come back for your regular follow-up, and to fill out our questionnaires. It gives us a better idea of your overall progress, including any emotional problems, which often have to be fine-tuned with drugs in the later stages."

"I've already noticed mood alterations," said Alex.

Dr. Slater nodded. "Initial mood alterations occur as the Number 17 nanogen rearranges synaptic pathways to the emotional centers of your brain—your hypothalamus and its surrounding gray matter. Once this is done, the brain starts to disintegrate bit by bit. For reasons we don't fully understand, Number 17 chooses to preserve emotional centers as a way to keep the victim alive once disintegration begins. We call this preserved bit of brain the Remnant."

"Not a name I would have chosen," said Alex.

Dr. Slater grinned tightly. "As far as the rest of your brain is concerned," he said, "Omnifix will replace it bit by bit with microchip dataspheres, and power it with a neutron cell."

"But I'll still have this . . . this Remnant. Part of the real me."

"Yes," said Dr. Slater. "We tap into your Remnant and use it as a control center. We have no choice. It's the only part of your real brain left, and we need it as a motherboard for your new cybernetic systems. This unfortunately has a deleterious effect on emotional stability, but it can't be helped. Impulse and anger management are our biggest concerns. Also, Omnifix is a Defense Force design, so you're going to be more aggressive."

"Why don't they change that?" he asked. "I don't like that aspect at all."

"Because there's not enough public money to develop a civilian design at present," said the doctor. "Like I say, we get a small bit of private money to make incremental improvements, but a blue-sky redesign for civilians is beyond our reach right now. So you're going to be, by DDF intent, soldierly. Try not to worry about this. We have all sorts of drugs to control this feature of the design."

Alex couldn't help thinking of the drugs Daryl had to take, how the Number 16 nanogen made young people strong, violent, and aggressive, and how, as a condition of living in the Defederacy, Daryl had to take five mood-alteration drugs to control the more vicious aspects of his Number 16 personality. Now Alex was going to have to take comparable medications to curb similar traits for Omnifix. Alex looked at the IV drip stuck in what was left of his arm.

"Are you giving me any of those drugs right now?" he asked.

"No," said Dr. Slater. "We're giving you First Wave Omnifix, the nanogens that dig into your DNA and chromosomes and replicate your genetic blueprint so that the Second and Third Waves can build according to personalized design specifications. It cross-matches any biological materials by disassembling, say, pig or sheep DNA, into its four bases, and reassembling it according to your own genotype so you won't reject it. We don't have to worry about graft-versus-host disease."

"Because I feel . . ." He shook his head, uncertain. "Emotionally . . . I just don't feel right."

Indeed, he couldn't get rid of his free-floating anxiety, this low-level constant fear of what was happening to him, no matter how many drugs they gave him.

Dr. Slater's brow pinched. His dark eyes looked like pieces of polished coal.

"I would think it's too early for anything overt in the way of pathologically compromised emotional stability, Dr. Denyer," he said. "You've had a shock. What you're feeling is completely natural. Anybody would feel it. When we start getting into the Remnant stage, the emotional deviation is far more pronounced. I'll just point out that we have an excellent counseling staff on call twenty-four hours a day. So if you run into any emotional problems you think you can't handle, and the drugs don't seem to be working, all you have to do is call them."

Alex peered at the doctor anxiously. "You're going to be with me the whole way?" he said.

The doctor placed his hand on Alex's slowly deteriorating shoulder.

"The whole way," he said. "I've done thousands of these, Dr. Denyer. I won't say our success rate is a hundred percent. I'm sure you've read the statistics. In rare cases, a victim's body will reject Omnifix, and then of course they progress to all the complications of an end-stage Number 17, no arms, no legs, et cetera, like you saw aboard the alien spacecraft."

"I hope that doesn't happen to me," said Alex.

"It's exceedingly rare," said Dr. Slater. "The vast majority accept and tolerate Omnifix readily. We'll try to make it easy for you. We'll try to ensure a smooth transition. But I should warn you, once you're discharged, you're bound to undergo a period of adjustment as you integrate into society as a Number 17. Our outreach education programs have been only moderately successful in eradicating public fear and mistrust of our patients. It's easier if you have a support network. Do you have a . . . a family?"

"Yes," he said.

"I haven't seen them yet," said Dr. Slater

"My ex-wife and son work on a ship."

"A ship?"

"A boat. A cargo freighter."

"Oh, I see."

"They're on their way back from the New Transvaal right now. They should be coming to visit me in the next couple of days."

Here he was in Greensboro. He could scarcely believe it. He stared up at the ceiling, at the tiny holes in the acoustic tiles. The rain beat again his window. He was drugged. Calm now. His anxiety was distant. He felt like he was floating down a river in a canoe, lying on his back looking up at the sky. He thought of Reba. He knew he shouldn't think of her, but Greensboro was the place that had changed her, and now he was here himself. Now they were changing *him*. His legs were gone, but he had a phantom sensation that they were still there. It was an odd feeling. An uncomfortable one. A scary one. And this was just the beginning. He turned, felt some skin slough off his face, but didn't have arms or hands now to brush the infected piece away, was going to have to wait for the nurse.

How had Reba endured it? Every minute was torture. It was one thing to be afraid in an abstract way, but it was entirely another to go through the actual experience. If only he could talk to Reba. But he didn't have her phone number; knew only that she lived in one of the sixty or seventy high-rises on Hosta Street. The odds of finding her anytime soon were remote. He *shouldn't* think of her. He had to get through this first. Greensboro. A sad smile came to what was left of his face. At least he and Reba had something in common now.

Dr. Slater introduced Second and Third Wave Omnifix into Alex's disintegrating body before Jill and Daryl got back from the New Transvaal. So when Jill finally showed up four days later, he was hardly conscious, floated in the merciful gloaming of Omnifix's general anesthetic. He surfaced when she kept calling his name. He looked out the window. Rain streaked his window, and all the branches were bare. It was the middle of winter, but he wasn't sure what month it was.

Jill looked drawn and pale. She wore her favorite brown woolen turtleneck. He saw a bruise on her cheek. When he asked about the bruise, she looked away, evasive, her distress camouflaged by a fragile grin.

"I fell against the railing on our way back from the New Transvaal," she said. "We had high seas our third day out." She lifted her chin. A brave smile came to her face. "Look at you," she said. "They're talking about you in the press. You're a war hero. Did you know that? Graham wants a ceremony. The Medal of Honor, or some damn thing. You're a media star. Dr. Slater's working hard to get you a pair of legs. And some hands. So you can go to this thing."

Yes, a brave smile, but she couldn't hold it long because he could see the barely hidden horror in her eyes. He was lying here in this hospital bed like a hundred pounds of hamburger meat and a hundred pounds of electronics all mixed together. He was the Alien War in microcosm. Alien nanogens fought against DDF nanogens, Number 17 against Omnifix, and his body was the battlefield. How could she not be horrified? Jill's smile disappeared and tears came to her eyes.

"Christ, Alex," she said. "I wish you would stop asking me about Daryl. He'll visit you when I think he's ready to visit you."

"Was I asking about Daryl?" He had no recollection of this.

"I don't want him seeing you yet," she said. "Have you looked at yourself?"

"They won't give me a mirror."

"I don't blame them."

She changed the subject.

"This place is like a country club," she said, forcing the cheer. "They spared no expense. I guess the Megaplex is looking after you now. It must be nice." She looked out the window. "The grounds are beautiful. Have you been out yet? Have they taken you down in a wheelchair?"

"No," he said. "The nurses say I'm not ready."

She continued to gaze out the window. "Hurlock's such a dump these days. It's not like it used to be. There used to be some trees around, but not anymore."

He closed his eyes. He felt like crying. Emotional instability. What had happened to Jill? He remembered her parents' summer place on Martha's Vineyard in the years before the Bombardment, the occasional week or two they would spend there together, how happy they had been. Now for one reason or another happiness was impossible for her.

"Do you still care about me?" he asked.

"Of course I care about you, Alex," she said. She gestured at his body. "You should cover yourself."

"I get so hot," he said. "Omnifix cooks you."

"You look like a wrecking yard. And you smell like urine. The nurse should double-check your catheter."

She was on edge. He sensed her anger. He thumbed his medication button. Sweet numbness. She stared at him, her lower lip now protruding.

"I don't know why the law makes you a permanent soldier of the DDF," she said.

"I'm a DDF design," he said. "And by the way, we'll never have to worry about Daryl's medical bills again. The DDF will make sure of it."

She looked away, got out of her chair, and walked to the window. The rain continued to streak the glass. She turned around, her face marred with worry.

"I need everything to be normal again, Alex," she said, "that's all. Things aren't normal between Tony and me right now. I need to live on dry land for a while, not on a boat. I need to live in a nice neighborhood, in a nice house, where I don't have to worry about prostitutes, smugglers, drug pushers, and Number 17s, the way I do in Hurlock. I need Daryl to be normal again. I need *you* to be normal again. I'm glad they're giving you money, Alex. But it's not going to make things normal, is it?" She shook her head. "Things are never going to be normal again."

Second and Third Wave Omnifix proceeded with some of the more complicated invasive procedures the next day. He was out cold for sixteen hours.

While he was out, he had a dream about baseball. He was a kid again. He was on a field, and he was up to bat, and it was a sunny day in Pennsylvania, and he could see the Allegheny Mountains looming blue and serene in the distance. Fleecy clouds floated through an azure sky. Usually, he was afraid. Usually, he kept striking out. But today he felt different. He felt intensely alive and super-aware of everything around him. He felt he could hit the ball a hundred miles.

The pitcher wound up. Alex focused on the ball like never before. The pitcher threw the ball. Alex's eyes clicked into view-screen mode, went through several telescopings, and gave him a highly detailed close-up of the ball. A side readout told him it was traveling at seventy-five miles per hour and that it would reach his bat in .62 seconds. Trajectory estimates told him the ball was high, but that with its current spin it would sink to the left as it reached home plate. His central processor coordinated the readouts and relayed the information to his motor implementation units. He swung low, on the inside, swung with such force and precision he whacked the ball out of the park and into the pine trees a hundred yards behind the bleachers, a more-than-human hit— a superhuman hit.

A cheer rose from the bleachers. He ran slowly to first base, then to second, taking his time, putting some ceremony into his stride. He looked up at the bleachers. He saw his father. He thought all was well as he ran to third, that this was a classic American moment, nothing strange or unusual about it, the happy stuff of a normal life growing up in small-town Pennsylvania. But then a stranger sat next to his father. Half the stranger's face looked dissolved away. The stranger's left eyeball stared unblinkingly. Then his arm fell off. Then his head sank into his shoulders as his neck disintegrated. The stranger was Graham.

Alex woke with a start.

He looked around. Graham. He couldn't help feeling nervous about Graham. As if Graham had somehow held out on him about the Number 17 in the spacecraft. He tried to shake the suspicion from his mind. Yet now he understood how so many Number 17s felt, how they had gone out to face the alien menace only to get themselves pinked with the disintegrating nanogen, then return to a Defederacy protected by enclave technology that didn't really care, a Defederacy that shunned them, that passed the Public Safety Act against them, a Defederacy that was embarrassed by them. Hold on. Wait a minute. He took a few breaths. That was better. Graham had done the right thing. Graham had gotten the right person to do this job, and it was a necessary job, and it was just too damn bad that things hadn't worked out perfectly, that Jon hadn't come home, and that he too had gotten pinked by Number 17. War was war, people got hurt, and he wasn't going to be bitter about it the way all those other veterans were. He knew he had done the right thing, even if the citizens of the Defederacy would now view him differently for the rest of his life.

He was alone in his room at Greensboro. It was the middle of the night. The rain had stopped, the clouds had cleared, and out his window he saw stars, small and silver, speckling the heavens. He saw a full Moon, a creamy egg above the trees. The Moon seemed sharper, nearer.

For the first time in six weeks he could feel his right hand, actually *feel*, not just a phantom sensation anymore. Only it didn't feel like *his* hand. It felt bigger. Colder. Stronger. How was tactile sensation in a cybernetic appendage possible? he wondered. Electronic sensors? He felt something in his mind, a command running a diagnostic, telling him the status of the electronic sensors in his new hand, how they were all on-line, giving him temperature, a reading of humidity levels, a strength estimate of his current grip capability. Hmm. Interesting. Just by thinking it, a command had been given. And it was all systems go. He flexed his hand. A gift from the Second and Third Waves. He *had* to have a look.

He lifted his hand out from under the sheet. He held it up in the silvery light of the Moon. It was huge, fully ten inches long. He had a new arm too. His arm was massive, of military design, with a twenty-inch biceps, thanks to the Second and Third Waves. Articulated flexisteel armor plated the top of his arm, while a tough and resilient synthetic flesh covered its underside. He had a closer look.

In looking more closely, another command was issued, his left eye clicking through several magnifications, a process not entirely controlled and trained, until he peered so closely, his fingerprints looked as deep and huge as the Grand Canyon. He pulled back, felt the same optical system click in reverse, an ocular zoom out that stopped at magnification times two.

His palm had its regular lines and markings. Omnifix had replicated it according to his own DNA. He found this comforting.

He reached for the light. His Remnant sent signals to his new motor system and his arm swung smoothly, superhumanly fast, with astonishing accuracy, to the pull-chain on the lamp. He turned on the light. He reached for the base of the lamp—round, ceramic, about the size of a basketball, glazed soft pink to match the room's décor—gripped it, lifted it, tested his strength. But as with his enhanced eye, his hand was untrained. He didn't know his own strength. He crushed the lamp to pieces, the thick shards of porcelain bursting around his fingers in a cloud of silicate dust. He looked at his hand. A soldier's hand. A hand that could kill.

He reflected on Jill's sentiment. And he had to agree with her. He wanted everything to be normal again. But things were getting less and less normal every day.

Chapter 18

Alex walked around the indoor track. Daryl walked beside him. In the center of the track, mangled returnees from the Martian Conflict rebuilt their physical coordination and strength on a varied array of rehabilitation and exercise equipment. Alex was the only Number 17 there. He lifted his right foot, swiveled his hip in its titanium socket, then plunked the ungainly appendage down with a loud clank against the hardwood floor. *Igor, the monster has risen!* He couldn't get used to his new height. He was seven and a half feet tall. His limbs were still disproportionately larger than his torso. And his feet thudded against the floor with an ungodly racket.

"Take my soft-boiled egg this morning for instance," said Alex. "I flung it at the nurse because it was cold. When have I ever acted like that before? Never. My counselor came down and scolded me like a child. She said if I didn't watch myself, she'd up my lithium. And that stuff gives me such a dry mouth."

"Is that why your voice sounds so different?" asked Daryl. "From dry mouth?"

"No," said Alex. "My vocal cords are gone. Disintegrated. The aliens want you to suffer, but they don't want you to scream. I have a synthesizer in there now. And a microprocessor. The technicians sampled my voice before it disappeared. I sound roughly like myself . . . don't I?"

"You sound like you're talking through a microphone," said Daryl. "And you speak in a monotone. You don't have any range of expression."

"In other words, I sound like a machine," said Alex.

"Yes."

Alex lifted his left foot and plunked it down with another loud clank.

"I haven't seen Jill in a couple weeks," he said. "And I haven't seen Tony either." Alex hesitated, but then decided he'd better broach the subject. "Are they doing any better?"

Daryl glanced at Alex, the corners of his lips drooping, his eyes narrowing. Alex felt something click in his random access memory, a command issued to his dataspheres, a scanning of a million recorded facial expressions, a picking out of the right one, the one he saw on Daryl's face, an operation that took a microsecond. He decided the expression he saw on Daryl's face represented fear and uncertainty.

"I don't know," said Daryl, in a way meant to cut the discussion short.

Alex's left eye, with its military applications, immediately clicked into the infrared. His son's face showed hot, a sure sign he was lying, or at least being evasive. Alex clicked back to visible light, unnerved by the versatility of his new eye, how he could probe so easily, and how he could slice through subterfuge with a simple command.

"Tony should try to please her from time to time," he said. "That's what I always did."

Daryl sighed—practically hissed.

"Dad, please don't criticize Tony," he said. "And why do you have to be so concerned about Mom and Tony anyway? It's not like anything's ever going to change between them. They get along. In their way. That's about the most anybody can do. And when they have their flare-ups, I just lay low. Tony's been good to me. I've seen a lot of the world because of Tony. He's my friend. He's Mom's voice of reason. Tony realizes I'm eighteen now. Tony tries to spell that out for her, but Mom can be so unreasonable at times."

They walked along in silence for a while.

"It's just because she cares about you," said Alex, but it sounded like a tired refrain now.

He could see Daryl didn't want to talk about it anymore.

"Did I tell you Sandy comes to the boat sometimes?" said Daryl.

"Sandy Parker?" said Alex.

Daryl nodded. "He's got a place in Hurlock now. We've become friends. Mom hates it. She keeps remembering all those bodies floating down the river two years ago. But me and Sandy . . ." Daryl scratched his head. "We're a team. Those people in the river—from what he tells me, things are a lot better in the EMZ without them." Daryl grinned, relaxed. "It's good to have another Number 16 around for a change. There aren't too many of us in the Defederacy. Your cousin's made the permits too hard to get. Anyway, Sandy's joined the search for the Holy Grail. We spend hours at the computer checking things out."

"Daryl . . . be careful. The DIS have their eye on Sandy, you can be sure of it. And if they have their eye on him, they have their eye on you now, too."

"We're not doing anything illegal, Dad," said Daryl. He shrugged. "Not really."

"Just don't go anywhere you don't belong."

"How do you expect us to learn anything that way?" asked Daryl, frowning.

"The last thing you need is the DIS revoking your papers and shipping you back to Pennsylvania."

"I wouldn't mind that at all," said Daryl. "I miss Pennsylvania."

"Daryl, I'm serious."

"What am I supposed to do, Dad?" asked his son, exasperated. "Roll over and die? Sandy has some good ideas. We've found our way to some . . . really interesting places. He's nearly as good at cracking code as Ivory."

"You see? This is why I worry."

"Don't get like Mom on me, Dad. I have secure firewalls. They can't track it back to me."

Alex stopped. "Daryl, your firewalls aren't going to be any good if the DIS ever gets really serious about you. And they just might, now that you're chumming with Sandy Parker."

As Alex walked in the Greensboro grounds a week later, he felt sick to his stomach. His vestibular system—his original human balance system, that small organ of interlocking canals, the so-called labyrinth in his inner ear—had finally disintegrated. Everything was spinning. But that was okay. He was happy today. Reba was here. Reba had miraculously showed up. Reba helped him along. He couldn't walk a straight line, often staggered. Omnifix had yet to install a new cybernetic balance system. He couldn't tolerate any kind of motion. But he persisted with his walking, put one foot in front of the other, wanted to show Reba that he was really okay, and that he could get through this, just as she had. He had to walk. One day he would walk right out of here.

"How long till the dizziness subsides?" he asked.

"It takes a while," said Reba. "Even when Omnifix installs the new balance system, it sometimes takes up to a year before it's fully calibrated."

"Because I feel sick all the time," he said.

"Have you been taking your antiemetics?" she asked.

"Yes."

"When Omnifix starts on your internal organs, you won't feel sick anymore," she said. "Nausea will be a thing of the past."

"I think I'm going to be sick now," he said.

"Really?"

"Hang on."

He staggered to the nearest bush and threw up. He sensed Reba behind him. She held out a handkerchief.

"Here," she said.

He took the handkerchief and wiped his lips. He hated what he had become. And yet Reba stood beside him, a Number 17 herself, a half-mechanical soldier; tall, dark, imposing, but still lovely. If she could take it, he could take it. But just how had she endured it all? He gained a new admiration for Reba. She might have joined the DDF, but her real war hadn't started until she had become a Number 17.

"Zirko didn't come," he said.

"No."

"I sure would like to meet him."

"He's . . . busy. This new provisional law the Megaplex has under consideration, the one that will give them authority to ship veterans like Zirko to Chincoteague Bay just because they're technically more machine than human? He's trying to organize a petition against it. It's taking up a lot of his time."

"If he wants my name on it, I can send it to him electronically."

She glanced at him, and he saw her military applications eye click into probing mode. "Are you sure?" she asked.

"Yes."

She hesitated. "We're going to have a lot to talk about when you get out of here, Alex."

They continued on.

"You don't know what it means to me," he said, "you showing up like this. If only I didn't feel so sick, I could enjoy it more. This spinning is driving me crazy."

"Eventually you get used to it."

"I'm never going to get used to it," he said. "I feel awful. Spin around thirty times, and that's how I feel. And it never ends. I wake up in the morning and I'm dizzy. I'm dizzy all day. I go to bed dizzy. I can't eat anything because I'm dizzy. I can't concentrate on anything. I try to read and I get dizzy. I can't do anything without feeling ferociously carsick. And when you're dizzy all the time, you get so tired. It fatigues the hell out of me. By the end of the day, I'm so fatigued I can hardly move."

She gave him a grave look. "You're recharging your neutron cell correctly, aren't you?" she asked. "Who's doing your power systems?"

"Luis Grau," he said.

"And he's made certain to tell you that you have to recharge every night? It's extremely important that you recharge every night for the full eight hours. You risk severe complications, even death, if you don't. Get in the habit, because you're going to be doing it for the rest of your life."

"I recharge every night." He was unsettled by the firmness in her voice. "But that still doesn't stop the fatigue. I'm not used to being like this, Reba. I don't know how to cope with it. I'm not used to being a . . . a sick man. Or a physically weak man. I've always been a strong man. I've always had a lot of stamina. I used to work sixteen-hour days. Now the thought of working that long exhausts me." He shook his head. "I don't know how I'm ever going to get back to normal again."

"It'll get easier," she assured him.

He motioned at the trees. "Look at this. Spring is coming. What am I going to do once I leave this place? Everything's up in the air right now. How can I work when I feel like this?"

"You don't have to work right away, Alex. Take some time. Take a lot of time. Time's the great healer. See your family. See Daryl. See Jill. And then just ease your way back into it. And remember," she said, "when you leave here, you're going to have friends.

A lot of friends. And me and Zirko will be among the best of them."

Dr. Slater wheeled him to the Administrative Building four days later. He felt foggy. For the last thirty-six hours his brain had been contending with a series of complicated downloads meant to integrate his systems more fully, and the outside world seemed dim, remote, more dream than real.

He asked Dr. Slater where they were going.

"The Administrative Building," responded the doctor. "You've already asked me that five times, Dr. Denyer."

"And why am I going there?"

"You have a visitor."

"Why do we have to go to the Administrative Building?" he asked. "I thought we could have visitors in the ward."

The doctor didn't answer.

Alex felt like an invalid sitting in a wheelchair. He looked around the grounds. He was disoriented. The downloads had temporarily confused his directional systems. The buildings around him, for the most part geodesic domes paneled with photovoltaic cells, looked both familiar and unfamiliar. He saw a string of hovercars pass by like a flock of geese in the distance—a skyway out there, he couldn't remember which one. He leaned forward, on edge.

"Are you lost?" he asked the doctor.

"No," said Dr. Slater.

"Because I'm not sure where we are."

"You come this way every day on your walk, Dr. Denyer," said Slater. "Just sit back and relax. We're almost there."

They rounded a grassy hummock and came to the Administrative Building, a black, multiterraced structure built into the side of a hill. Several black hovercars were parked out front. Defederacy Intelligence Service agents stood around the entrance. Alex's shoulders stiffened with fear. One of them walked right up to Alex and Dr. Slater.

"Sorry, but I'm going to have to wand you," he said, and proceeded to check them for weapons. The agent turned to Dr. Slater. "Is he properly sedated? We don't want any Number 17 bullshit."

Dr. Slater frowned at the expletive. "He's undergoing downloads right now. We can't sedate him. But his downloads keep him docile. He won't be a problem, I guarantee it."

The agent nodded, then let them through.

Dr. Slater wheeled him down a long corridor. They took the elevator to the third subbasement. From there, another DIS agent took over from Dr. Slater and wheeled Alex along a second corridor. Alex glanced over his shoulder. Dr. Slater stood in his white lab coat by the elevator, receding, a look of mild interest on his pale waxy face.

The DIS agent escorted Alex to a conference hall at the end of the corridor. The doors opened automatically. The DIS agent pushed him inside, then retreated. The doors closed behind Alex.

The conference hall was dim, lit by only a few potlights. CEO Graham Croft, dressed in a dark suit, sat at the head of the conference table, the light above his head making his blond hair gleam. He was going over something on a waferscreen. When he saw Alex, he folded the screen in four and tucked it into his pocket. Alex gripped the wheels of his wheelchair and pushed himself closer. Graham stood up. The CEO walked around the end of the table and approached Alex with a deliberate step, looking Alex up and down, his usual media grin absent, his eyes revealing nothing.

"I'm told you're undergoing downloads right now," said the CEO. "If you're too tired, or if you feel too sick, I can come back another time."

This was a change—the CEO arranging his schedule for Alex?

"I'm fine," said Alex. "I'm a little surprised, that's all. You're usually so busy. What are you doing here?"

The CEO paused, lifted his chin, and contemplated Alex serenely.

"I'm here because I sent you into harm's way," he said. "I'm here because you served your country well. I'm here because you made sacrifices."

Even in a private conversation, the man couldn't suppress his habit of rhetoric. Graham took a few steps forward, pulled out a chair, and sat. Alex ran stored facial expressions through his central processor. But because of his downloads, the operation was clumsy, took close to two seconds before it came back with a "not-on-file" for the expression he found on his cousin's face. The CEO leaned forward, his pronounced brow casting a deep shadow over the bottom of his face.

"I have some bad news for you, Alex," he said. "I haven't announced it publicly yet, but I thought I'd let you know about it before I make a statement. We lost 282 combatants yesterday, 282 of your fellow soldiers. A surprise Martian attack. The commander didn't see it coming." Graham shook his head. "It's strictly Security 1 information right now, and I know I can trust you to keep it that way until I announce it to the media, but it gives you an idea of the way things are going for us. I tell you because you're a hero. You've done a great thing for the Defederacy, Alex. You've made a great sacrifice, just as those 282 recruits made a great sacrifice. It underscores how we all have to work together to defeat the Martians. It underscores how we all must stand united. Especially in light of yesterday's military setback."

Now Alex's facial-expressions program told him his cousin was troubled, that he felt the deaths keenly.

"I'm sorry," said Alex.

His words came slowly, as if he had an ice cube in his mouth.

"Every one of those brave young men and women were just doing their job, Alex," said Graham, "protecting the Defederacy, working hard to defeat the Martians." He sat back. "Two hundred and eighty-two deaths." He shook his head. "How do I sell that to the public? How do I explain that surprise attack? I don't. I could tell them vital information was compromised, that even the DDF has its share of infiltrators, but I don't think that's going to boost public confidence, do you? And it's not just yesterday's attack. It's everything. It's Hawaii, Arlington, and Hurlock. How do I tell the public that the Number 17 Repealists in Hurlock have ramped up their efforts to undermine the Defederacy; more than just their firecrackers in subway tunnels, that they're planning an actual offensive, that they want to see our safe little lifeboat sink, and that they're now receiving military and operational support from the Sta-

tionhouse Militia in Arlington, and receiving funding
from Martian nationalists in Hawaii? All strictly confidential, Alex, but it gives you an idea of what I'm
having to deal with these days. I tell you because
you're one of our top military heroes now, and we
mean to decorate you highly. In the meantime, you
have to hunker down with us. We have to weather
this storm together.''

Graham let that sit a bit. Alex remembered this
about Graham, from a long time ago, back when Graham was like his big brother; how, when he came to
Unionville for the summer, he would always have
too much on his plate: school, political groups, economic ventures, social commitments, everything balanced just so, doing anything and everything he
could, even at that young age, to rise to power. Now
it looked like he was finally balancing too much.

''So, Hawaii?'' said Alex, and his mouth felt full of
novocaine. ''They've really betrayed us?''

Graham nodded. ''I wish I could go in there and
turn that place upside down,'' he said. ''But SEASEZ
would have a conniption fit, now that Hawaii's se-
ceding. And I wish I could arrest Sandy Parker, now
that he's living in the Defederacy, but I can't. He's
made arrangements, and things would go from bad
to worse with the Stationhouse if I did.'' His lips
bunched and he gazed at Alex with steady appraisal.
''Then there's the Repealists. Damn those Number
17s, Alex.'' He didn't say this accusingly, yet Alex
felt as if he were being accused in some way just the
same. The CEO's lips relaxed and he shook his head
wearily. ''I'm sorry. I didn't mean to . . .'' He sighed.
''They should count their blessings. They're in the
Defederacy. An enclave. They're safe. But they refuse

to see how good they've got it. The DIS has uncovered plans. They're crossing a line. And it scares the hell out of me. I wish I could put them all in jail."

Graham's expression had gone back to an unreadable one, a bona fide "not-on-file," his cheeks unexpressive slabs, his eyes like pieces of glacial ice, his thin lips shrinking to a single slit. Alex shifted. *He* was a Number 17. He thought of Reba. And of her friend, Zirko. *They* were Number 17s. Were they involved? Were they crossing this line? His allegiances now felt divided.

"Number 17s," said Alex. "Like me."

He wanted to make sure he had it right. Words and ideas came disjointedly right now. With his downloads, he was being forced to multitask, and there was an aggravating delay, a bottleneck in the processing results.

"No, Alex, not like you." The CEO leaned forward, put his hands on his knees. "You're a war hero, Alex, and we mean to honor you. I'm talking about the . . . the malcontents. The *Repealists*. Veterans who feel they've been disenfranchised. Soldiers who fought in the Alien War, and who feel we aren't doing enough for them anymore. But honestly, Alex, we're doing everything we can. I'm the first to admit Omnifix isn't perfect. But it's the best we have right now. And I wish the citizens of the Defederacy would recognize our veterans, not fear them so much, not ostracize them the way they do, but there's only so much budget for public education. And I know the average pension isn't much, not like we can give you, but we're strapped, Alex, really strapped. Our tax base is puny compared to what it was before the Bombardment, when the old federal government was still up and running. We're five tiny city-states, *four*, now that Hawaii has betrayed us, and we're trying to fight a major war against Mars. Things aren't perfect. What do Number 17s expect? That we hemorrhage the public coffers specifically for them?"

Alex's internal recorders sampled some of Graham's voice. Wave patterns indicated unmistakable passion. The man believed he was doing the best he could.

"You know what the big problem is, Alex?" said Graham. "We've never successfully communicated with these groups in Hurlock. And that's because we've never successfully infiltrated one. We can't. They're mistrustful. What we need is a Number 17 who's on our side, someone who can live in Hurlock and not stick out, someone who can get to know them on their own terms, understand them, and who can suggest to them that something might be worked out. I'd like to defuse the situation before it gets out of hand. We've found several weapons caches in Hurlock. They're arming themselves big-time, Alex, and they're sending agents into the EMZs to make alliances."

Alex couldn't help thinking of Sandy Parker and his son.

"It's all so annoying," continued Graham. "Especially when we're trying to fight the Martians. If we could only get one of their own kind in there, someone who might act as a . . . a go-between, we'd be prepared to listen to them. As long as their demands weren't too unreasonable. We have to open a dialogue. And that's been unbelievably hard. They're so different from us physically that there's no possible way we can send in a normal human operative. We've tried. With fatal results."

Enhanced to ten times normal human capacity, Alex's ears heard Graham's heartbeat climb from seventy beats per minute to eighty-three. It now seemed obvious to Alex that Graham was making a pitch, and that he was going to try and clinch it any second.

"You've served your country well," said Graham. "I have no right to ask you to do more. Especially because your doctors tell me you still have a long way to go before you're . . . you're street-ready. You look like hell right now. Those downloads must take a whack out of you. And I'll understand if you want to take some time. But we just want to give the . . . the Number 17s an option, a voice, make them understand that they don't have to resort to violence first thing off, that it might be more constructive to talk with us. God, you look so pale . . . and that eye . . . the special enhanced one? I'll never get used to that, the way it just stares and stares, the way you never blink. Do you feel sick? Are you in pain?"

"It's not fun," said Alex, his voice sounding more machinelike than ever.

"It can't be," said Graham. "And your country appreciates all the sacrifices you've made. Ordinarily I'd say hang up your guns, Alex, you've done a great job, what more can we ask."

"But," said Alex.

"But . . . you're going to be a Number 17, Alex. You're going to be accepted in Hurlock just like that. You'll be part of their . . . their little community. Like I say, we've uncovered plans. I'd hate for anybody to get hurt, especially innocent people. I sure would like it if someone could keep an eye out for us down there. Someone we can trust. Someone like you."

Alex noticed dust motes—sharply, clearly—falling in the light around the CEO's head, little bombs targeting a giant blond planet.

"You want me to spy on them?" he asked.

"I'd prefer to call it preventative surveillance," said the CEO. "You could save lives, Alex. These damn weapons caches. I can show you the weapons, if you like. A lot of older stuff smuggled over from the EMZs, but still deadly as hell. Someone's going to get hurt. If we can get someone in there, a Number 17, we might get some warning about any possible attacks. Wouldn't that be worth it, Alex? There's so much needless death already. You could prevent some of it." Graham sat back. "So when you're feeling better, and these downloads aren't clouding things up for you, I want you to think about it." He leaned forward and put his hand on Alex's gigantic knee. "You could really make a difference, Alex. And after yesterday's military disaster, I think we'd like to see things a little different."

PART THREE

FMC

Chapter 19

Dr. Slater wrote Alex's discharge papers on a warm spring day in May. Alex was in pain. And he still felt sick. And he would still have to go back to Greensboro every week because some of the moderate-sized changes weren't done yet, and only Greensboro had the necessary scavenging stockpiles and stockyards to complete those changes, but he was glad to be back home, even if home was this cramped, lonely condominium in Lincoln Towers.

He opened the door and, using two canes, stepped awkwardly into the front hall, now having to stoop so he wouldn't hit his head on the doorframe. He had to pee. But he *couldn't* pee. He still had a lot of bugs to be worked out. He dropped his shoulder bag on the floor and ambulated with graceless steps to the washroom. He stood in front of the toilet. He unzipped. He pulled out the hybrid plumbing-and-sex fixture Omnifix had devised for him, something that was flesh-toned on top, and clear plastic on the bottom. His bladder was full. Yet he was damned if he could let loose. He frowned. He couldn't go for a pee like a normal man. He pulled a small tube from a plastic slipcover in his shirt pocket and, bracing himself, pushed it up his urethra.

He kept pushing until the tube penetrated his bladder. Then, with the urgency of a dam breaking, urine spilled out of him, so quickly and forcefully he couldn't get his hand out of the way fast enough and got urine all over it.

His anger flared. That was the other thing. Or one of many other things. His anger. He couldn't control it. He punched the mirror, and the mirror fractured into eighteen swordlike shards. He checked his hand, thinking he might have cut it open. But his knuckles were made of steel, and there was little damage. The tiny scratches would soon be smoothed over by the ever-vigilant Omnifix. Omnifix, all around him. Airborne nanogens following him like a swarm of invisible bees.

He flushed the toilet, washed his hands, then glared at the broken mirror. How was he going to explain the broken mirror to the building chairwoman, Laurel Sylvestri? She was such a pain in the ass sometimes.

He went back out into the hall. He dug through his bag and found his powerpack. He couldn't believe how small it was, no bigger than a honeydew melon, a single wire extending from it like the tail of a sperm, the lifeblood inside it a self-contained storm of swirling neutrons that would keep him alive. Having to power up every night with this small contraption made him feel vulnerable. He hated that it had to be a do-or-die proposition. He was now strong enough to lift the back end of a truck, could read signs from a mile away, could leap

rom a ten-story building and not break a single
ɔone, but if he didn't hook up with this powerpack
ɛach night, he would die.

He dug through his bag again and pulled out his
med-check. He went to the sofa, sat down, plugged
he device into the back of his neck, put the screen
ɔn his lap, and checked his medications. They
ɛeemed fine. He reviewed the status of his urological
ɲanogens. *Work incomplete. Thirty percent remaining.
Please stand by.* At least he could take a crap okay,
ɔut he was getting sick of taking laxatives. The whole
ɛxperience was humiliating.

Then he noticed it again. The breathing. The
ɔreathing wasn't right either. Either that, or the arti-
ɥcial heart was out of sync again. He keyed in respiratory systems on his med-check and saw that the
ɥnings of his lungs, derived from the bronchial material of the American Landrace pig but sequenced according to his own DNA, were inflamed again. Dr.
ɟlater told him this was common in the first year,
ɛomething he called cybernetic asthma but which the
ɲurses privately called pig asthma. It would eventu-
ɪlly pass. But until it did, he had to think to breathe.
ɜreathe in. Breathe out. How stupid. The autonomic
ɥunctions of his new body sometimes got confused
vith the voluntary ones. Pig asthma, of all the god-
ɟamn things. Breathe in. Breathe out. His diaphragm
ɟpasmed. Again and again. His lungs clutched. The
ɔnly way he could alleviate this was by upping his
ɟose of bronchodilator. Which he did by keying in a
ɔommand on his med-check. This particular bron-
ɥodilator included a tranquilizer.

As the tranquilizer eased into his body, he felt him-
ɛelf relaxing. At least there was still enough of his

central nervous system left so he could *feel* the drug
they were giving him.

He closed his eyes. He checked the functions of his
left one through his closed lid. In particular, he
checked the X-ray function. He could see right
through his closed lid. Another combat enhancement
he would never use. He checked his right eye, the
biological one, scavenged cell by cell from one of the
colobus monkeys they kept in the Greensboro Zoo.
He could see well with this one. Better than with his
own. The monkey was a tree-dweller, so he now had
the tree-dweller's sharp focus and depth of field.
Aside from the occasional monkey crud he had to
wipe from its corner, he didn't mind this particular
replacement; this eye was modeled after his own, and
it made him look halfway human. The military applications one, on the other hand, was unmistakably a
lens, part of his combat array, planted in the black
steel half-mask over the left side of his face like a
fragment of a crystal ball.

His life was changing. He remembered thinking
the exact same thing when Max had turfed him out
of the ISS. He remembered how upset he'd been. But
losing his job was nothing compared to this. His life
was changing, but so was his body, and it was all a
matter of perspective. Losing his job was a picnic
compared to this.

He leaned back and rested his head against the
wall. He tried to sleep, but sleep, as Dr. Slater had
finally admitted, wasn't exactly the right word for
Number 17s. Slater called it shutdown mode. And
the dreams! Damn those cyber dreams. He recalled
Dr. Slater's words about dreams.

"Your dreams will be fairly vivid at first, a kind

of VR version of normal dreams, so authentic you can't tell the difference from reality. Your Remnant continues to send dream signals to your microprocessors and dataspheres. They interpret those signals as real commands. Unfortunately, some of these VR dreams can be distressing. Especially because they're so real. Even worse, you can't wake up from them. Your power pack automatically keys for eight hours. Any less and you put yourself at serious risk. So you have to ride these VR dreams out."

Here he was. In a living nightmare. Even when he was asleep. So far, the dreams had been good. But each night he was afraid he was going to have a bad one. He had some old beasts to deal with, and he wasn't looking forward to confronting them on the dream plane.

A light knock came at the door. His head swiveled slowly on its lubricated ball and socket system. He was afraid to face whoever was behind that door, afraid to face the world. He felt self-conscious about his size, and about his black half-mask, the mark of the cyborg, the black badge of courage, as the military e-zines called it. Yet the mask was necessary; it protected the complicated electronics and sensitive optics of his left eye, and also housed his all-important Remnant. The knock came again. He got up and immediately stumbled. His balance systems, though getting better, still weren't right. He summoned his courage and walked to the door like Frankenstein's monster. Breathe in. Breathe out. He opened the door.

Laurel Sylvestri, the building chairwoman, stood there with a large bouquet of flowers—a cheerful mix of day lilies, daisies, snapdragons, and small carnations. She struggled valiantly to hide her shock and surprise, but they managed to squeak past. He clicked his military applications eye into the infrared, saw the heat building around her eye sockets and on her cheeks. He magnified his hearing and heard her heart race. His microprocessor instantly calculated the beats: a rise from seventy-two per minute to ninety-five. She was afraid. He fully expected this. Everyone was going to be afraid of him now. And everyone was going to have a certain prejudice against him. She timidly held out the bouquet. He sensed her fear, smelled the pheromones as her pituitary gland released adrenaline into her system. He reacted to her fear the way a soldier might—he felt a distant glory. He had the enemy on the run.

"Hello, Dr. Denyer," she said. He looked her up and down. She was far too old to wear body-wrap. "On behalf of the Lincoln Towers Owner's Association, we'd like to welcome you home."

He took the flowers. He usually liked getting flowers. But now for some reason they irritated him. He didn't need pity. And he didn't want special treatment. And he wished he would stop having such inappropriate feelings about everything. He sniffed the flowers, and his defense microprocessor, going overboard, immediately analyzed them for toxins or other biological agents. They came up clean. The flowers weren't weaponized. He let them droop to his side.

"Thank you," he said.

"We're all so proud of you," she said. "For what you did." She gestured at his condominium. "We've never had a Number 17 living in the building before, but I've assured the Board that everything will work out just fine."

"Some of them have raised concerns?" he asked.

She looked away. "The things you hear in the media," she said, as if that explained everything.

He stood there in the vestibule. And he realized that no matter how much he wanted to go back, no matter how much he wanted to be the old Dr. Alexander Denyer again, he was changed, not only physically, but in the attitudes of the people around him.

"Thank you, Mrs. Sylvestri," he said. "I appreciate your sentiments. And the Board's sentiments. And tell them not to worry. Peace and quiet have always been important to me, and I'm not about to change that."

Her shoulders eased. She was relieved.

When she was gone, he stood in the front hall for nearly a whole minute, not moving. He had to analyze the nuances. His language and tone-of-voice microprocessors geared up. He was disturbed by his conclusions, yet not entirely surprised. Omnifix, as everybody knew, had created an underclass, and there existed prejudice against this underclass. He knew he was bound to find it everywhere, even though as a human he himself had never felt it: an intimation of apartheid; not downright racism, but a demarcation, *Homo sapiens* versus *Homo mechanicus*, a real and perhaps justified fear on the part of humans because of things read, seen, or heard in the media. He couldn't deny it. It was true. Because of Reba, he had never been afflicted with this prejudice. When you knew someone who meant a lot to you, who was a Number 17, prejudice against them was impossible. But he could understand Laurel Sylvestri's fear. He was big. He was a soldier. He was a fighting machine living among civilians. Not quite like putting a nuclear bomb in a playground for children to horse around on, but getting close.

For the ceremony, the organizers asked Alex to wear the dress uniform of a DDF colonel. He wasn't used to wearing black. He felt like he was at a funeral. Ruth Pellegrino sat next to him. She wore a black uniform as well. They were waiting for things to start. She wouldn't look at him. She stared straight ahead. When he spoke to her, she answered in monosyllables.

"You haven't returned my messages," he said.

He watched the corners of her lips shift.

"No," she said.

He clicked into infrared, saw the telltale heat patterns around her eyes. She was trying to pretend everything was all right between them.

"I thought we could have a drink sometime," he said. "Maybe go to the Game Hub. For old time's sake."

"That would be nice," she said, but said it with so much infrared activity around her eyes he knew things between them couldn't be right at all.

The auditorium tilted, spun—he was having another vertigo attack. What did you do when your old friend wasn't your old friend anymore? He just wanted to go back. He wanted to make it the way it was. But he knew she wasn't the same old Ruth anymore. Not with Jon gone. And he definitely wasn't the same old Alex. His vertigo eased, and the room stopped spinning.

The brass band started. They played the Defederacy National Anthem. Everyone got to their feet. He saw that he towered above all the other medal honorees—young recruits newly returned from the Martian Conflict. He was the only Number 17 here. Everyone sang, himself included. "We stand tall, we stand strong." The irony of the words galled him. He stood tall, a head and a half above everybody else, and now that he had his new flexisteel shoulders, he was five times as strong as the average man. "Like a beacon in the storm, like a shoulder for those in need." He certainly felt like a beacon, because everybody was staring at him. He felt angry. But a part of him felt like crying, too.

A girl, six or seven years old, stood beside her mother in the audience. Alex clicked his military applications eye into telescopic mode to get a better look at the girl. The girl stared at him, an expression of profound fear on her face. She pointed at him with her little finger and turned to her mother. Alex focused his audiological catchment, increased amplitude, and heard her say, "Mommy, there's a monster." Her mother said soft, cooing words in return. "Nadine, he's not a monster, he's just a soldier, and he's had a very bad accident, and that's why he looks like that." But the girl insisted. "No, Mommy," she said. "It's a monster. I know it is."

Alex clicked off his eye and his ear, and was hit by yet another dizzy spell. He had to lay off the ear. Every time he eavesdropped, his new cochlear implants sent overflow signals to his cybernetic balance organs and the world started to spin.

The anthem ended, and General Gordon Godineau, Chief of the Veteran's Affairs Department, ap-

Scott Mackay

proached the podium and said, "Ladies and gentlemen, the Chief Executive Officer of the Defederacy of Delaware, Graham K. Croft."

Everyone remained standing. More and more people looked at Alex because he was so tall and huge. He felt his defense systems involuntarily clicking in. With those soldierly sub-routines gearing up, his olfactory senses grew acute, and he smelled fear all over the place. It wasn't just the little girl. His telescopic application kicked in and he scanned the audience. Graham Croft came on stage and everybody clapped. Alex couldn't decide if people were afraid of Graham or afraid of him. The applause died, people sat down, and Graham started his speech.

Alex sank to his chair. He continued to scan the audience. It must be his eye. His military applications eye was ungodly looking—black, but with a tiny pinpoint of red light in the center, like the laser-scope of a high-powered target rifle. They were afraid of him. They didn't trust him, and their mistrust floated in the air like an unseen cloud of anxiety.

"You don't have to worry," he said to them. "I'm medicated."

Graham stopped speaking. The auditorium grew silent. One of Graham's DIS agents stepped forward and slipped his hand into his jacket, getting ready. Two at the back murmured into their radios. Dr. Slater, sitting in the front row, came forward, a reassuring smile on his face.

"It's all right, Dr. Denyer," he said. "Everybody understands. Could I see your med-check, please?"

Meanwhile, Graham resumed his speech.

"Why do the design externals have to be so intimidating?" asked Alex, distraught by the episode. "Ev-

258

erybody's afraid of me. Why couldn't you make me look like Little Bo Peep?"

"As I said before, Dr. Denyer, Omnifix is a Defense Force project. Greensboro just administers it. Do you mind if I up your tranqs? They're a little on the low side, and I'm sure the DIS agents would feel safer if I gave you a boost. I also see you're running your defense systems. Why are you doing that? Everybody in this room is on your side, Dr. Denyer. We're here to honor you. We think you're a hero. You saved us from another possible bombardment. You're the man of the hour, and everybody knows it."

Alex allowed his tranquilizers to be upped. He didn't like doing it, but he knew if he was going to get through this ceremony without further embarrassment, he had no choice. Dr. Slater returned to his chair. Alex glanced at Ruth. She was now poised on the edge of her seat listening to Graham's speech. Alex didn't like upping his tranqs because, when he did, the artificiality of his new mind grew more apparent. He sensed the seams between all its functions. Everything was divided into routines, subroutines, and sub-subroutines. He could feel all his different programs in all his dataspheres.

"To Colonel Dr. Alexander Denyer, the Medal of Honor and the Purple Heart," intoned General Gordon Godineau.

Alex got to his feet, grabbed his canes, and, like a geriatric giant, made his way to the podium. A soldier in a dress uniform stood beside Graham, his white-gloved hands holding a velvet box with medals. Graham wore his media grin. People clapped. But then, to his surprise, they began to stamp the floor with their feet.

He looked out. They were grinning at him. It was stirring to see. All their fear was gone. He wasn't alone anymore. Their applause and floor-stamping were heartfelt. The media sent in their hovercams and Alex realized that everybody thought this was a special moment, a historical one—not only were they honoring a brave soldier, they were honoring the CEO's first cousin.

His combat subroutines shut down. He saw Jill and Daryl sitting in the front row. Tony was nowhere in sight. Jill's eyes glistened. She couldn't get enough of this. Daryl was grinning. His usual teenage cynicism was gone, and he was caught up in the excitement of the moment the way everybody else was. Alex saw Reba in the back row. Still no Zirko. He really wanted to meet the man. Zirko had no idea how lucky he was to be with Reba.

Alex reached the podium and Graham shook his hand.

"Look at you," said Graham. "You're a hero."

"I'm a freak," said Alex.

A look of compassion came to Graham's face. "It's going to be a long, hard haul," he said. Graham reached for the Medal of Honor. The applause remained thunderous. "Just remember, you're one of us now. Anything you want, it's yours. All you have to do is ask."

"I want my life back," said Alex.

"That I can't give you," said Graham. "But if it's blue-sky research you want, or a field trip to any hunk of junk floating around out there, just say the word."

The offer did little to entice. After witnessing firsthand the house of horrors aboard the giant AWP, he had little inclination to visit an alien spacecraft anytime soon.

"I'll think about it," he said.

"And have you thought about what we talked about at Greensboro?" asked Graham, as he pinned the medal to his black uniform.

"I'm living one day at a time right now, Graham."

Graham turned to get the Purple Heart. "Anything we can do to help you get back on your feet faster?"

Alex thought about it as Graham pinned the Purple Heart next to the Medal of Honor.

"I'll take a walk through Hurlock for you," he said. "I'll listen. That's all I can promise right now, Graham."

"That's more than enough, Alex," said Graham. "All we need is a decent pair of ears down there. You tell us what you hear, and we'll do the rest."

Chapter 20

He took a hovercab to Tuckahoe Park the next day, twenty miles north of the city. He needed to get away from crowds. He needed to get away from *people*. As he walked over the grass to the riverbank, he breathed in deeply. Before he could stop himself, he immediately analyzed the air for nanogenic, biological, and toxicological threats. The bulk of its composition showed up as nitrogen, oxygen, and argon, while the rest divided itself into water vapor, the usual pollutants, and a number of pollens. Afraid of the air, of all things.

He looked around, felt his shoulders tighten. *People*. Even here in Tuckahoe Park, in the middle of the week, lots of them. What did he expect? Twenty million people lived in the Defederacy; it wasn't that big, just a bit of Maryland, most of Delaware, and some of Virginia, and he wasn't the only one who wanted to get away from dense overpopulation.

He walked toward the water like a Titan, leaving great holes in the turf with his canes. A couple having a picnic nearby threw him wary glances. A mother wheeling her baby in a stroller increased her stride. A dog barked at him, and its owner had to grab it by the collar. *Frankenstein walks among you*, he thought. Everybody made an effort to pay no attention to him, but their disregard was strained, and they ignored him the way a herd of gazelles might ignore a lion on the open savannah, with a cautious and rigid nonchalance.

He and Reba used to come here. He clung to that thought. That thought made him happy. Reba at the ceremony last night. Having to leave early during the refreshments afterward because she was meeting with Zirko somewhere—but she really wanted to have coffee with Alex sometime soon, now that the DIS hovercams weren't following him around anymore, and . . . and could they meet in a day or so? She wanted to talk to him about really important stuff. *Yes, of course I'll have coffee with you, Reba.* He couldn't wait.

He felt something shift inside his intestinal cavity. He stopped, felt nauseated by the shift. The industrious little Omnifix nanogens went about their work, and his body was doing all sorts of weird things these days. An odd feeling of hollowness pervaded his right side, as if part of his liver had disappeared. The nausea passed. The hollowness seemed to fill in with something, like an egg sliding into an eggcup. He touched the right side of his abdomen. He felt things move around inside. A lump bulged, then sank. He burped. The burp tasted foul, sour, and acidic. Things settled down. He continued walking, using both canes to steady himself.

He proceeded to a bench by the river. He sat down. Some swans foraged about some reeds. An old man sat on a bench farther down. The old man glanced at Alex, finally took a sandwich out of a paper bag, and ate in furtive bites, like he was afraid of Alex, as if he expected Alex might pounce any minute.

Then Alex heard the bench's wooden slats creak beneath him. A second later they cracked, and the bench broke under his great weight. He fell to his butt. His anger flared. He felt humiliated. He had to remind himself that he now weighed four hundred pounds; a lean and large Herculean soldier. His anger faded. He felt like crying. He couldn't even sit on a park bench. The old man got up and hurried away. Omnifix might be saving his body, but it was doing nothing to save his dignity.

Alex met Reba at the Cornerhouse Café, a coffee bar on the fifty-second floor of Lincoln Towers in the Midlevel Mall and Recreational Complex, the next day. The café was an attractive getaway, snug in the southwest curve of the North Tower, with views of Chesapeake Bay and the downtown skyline.

"I know what you're going through," said Reba. "You looked so lost up on that stage a few nights ago. And Ruth. I know how much Jon meant to her. I know what it's like to lose friends in battle."

Alex contemplated Reba. She was Amazonian, tall but shapely. Even as a Number 17, she had always been attractive to him.

"The maître d' put us back here behind this ficus tree on purpose," he said.

Reba glanced at the maître d'.

"You get used to it," she said. "Or actually, you don't. But you might as well accept it, Alex. It's just the way things are. The maître d's hiding us here for a reason. He doesn't want to scare customers away."

Alex glanced at the man. He felt like asking for a different table.

"We're *human*, Reba," he said.

A patient grin came to her face.

"Yes, I know," she said.

Alex frowned. "And then all the extra laws they have for us," said Alex. He shook his head. "I just got around to reading the Greensboro discharge booklet this week. How can the Megaplex pass laws like that against us?"

"The Megaplex passed all those laws for a reason," she said. "The curfew, for instance. And the way we're tried in military courts instead of civilian ones. And the way the Megaplex can turn off our power packs any time they want."

Alex felt his face twitch. He was still having problems with certain nerve endings, had little miniseizures that gave him a sparky sensation from time to time.

"I don't like that particular arrangement at all," said Alex. "It means none of us are in control of our lives anymore. It's like we're state-owned property. I hate it."

"All of us do," said Reba. "But it's the law, Alex, the Public Safety Act of 2447." She leaned forward and in a softer, more cautious voice said, "You should join our group, Alex, you really should." Alex's eyes widened. So she belonged to the Repealists after all? "With someone high-profile like you in our group, we might actually make some progress. We're working to repeal some of the sole-discretion clauses in the Act, the ones that give the

Megaplex and the DDF so much power over us. It's not fair that they should keep us under their thumb that way. It's barbaric, and a lot of us are fed up with it. With someone like you advocating for us, we might actually get somewhere with our objectives."

He caught her military applications eye clicking through some changes; she was trying to read him, bringing her whole cybernetic surveillance package to bear. First Graham, now Reba. Both trying to recruit him. He felt divided. But Reba had a point; with these sole-discretion clauses in the Public Safety Act, he felt extremely vulnerable.

"So you're a Repealist?" he said.

She didn't immediately answer.

"This neutron power pack the government gives us to recharge ourselves with each night?" she said.

"Yes?" he said.

"It's good only so long, then it has to be replaced. The government issues a new one at its sole discretion. They don't have to issue a new one if they don't want to. They look at your record, they count your felony arrests, they see how many assaults you've been involved in—and believe me, we all get into scrapes we never intend and don't want, simply because we're Number 17s and our defense systems get the better of us. Renewal is usually blocked for reasons of public safety. That's the main sole-discretion clause we want to get rid of. That's the biggy. That's the one that can kill us."

"I had no idea it was so bad."

"They designed it that way on purpose. It guarantees their control over us."

"I don't want anybody to control me," he said, his

voice rising. The maître d' gave him a nervous glance.

"Yes, but we're big, we're strong, bullets can't kill us, we can crush a man's skull with our bare hands, and we're just generally a segment of the population that has to be watched," she said. "At least until they can implement a civilian design. So they make these laws in the meantime. And they've designed the power packs to work to their advantage."

His eyes narrowed. "How so?" he asked.

"There's no security feature on them. A Number 17 can't lock it on recharge when he or she's in shutdown. Anybody can come along and turn it off while they sleep. And if someone turns it off while you're in shutdown, zap, that's it, you're gone."

"Really?"

"Alex, you can't wake up until your eight hours have timed out, so you're defenseless. Maybe you haven't gotten to that part in the manual yet. We're sitting ducks for the eight hours we're in shutdown. The DDF wants it that way. So does the Megaplex."

He looked out the window where traffic sailed by in various laser-guided lanes.

"We have no way to protect ourselves at all?" he asked.

She sighed. "We stick together," she said. "We protect each other. If we know someone's at risk, we try to shelter them at various confidential locations while they recharge. It's about the best we can do. And then we have a little gizmo we use."

He peered at her more closely. "What kind of gizmo?" he asked.

She lifted her purse from the floor. She pulled out

a lozenge-shaped object—a horse pill of a thing—and put it on the table. She glanced nervously around the café. The maître d' studiously ignored them.

"These are illegal," she said. "Our group makes them."

Alex clicked his eye beyond the visible spectrum into X-ray mode and saw a viscous yolklike substance inside the horse pill. Nothing much to see. So he piggy-backed some magnification on top of the X-ray, and the yolk quickly resolved itself into design molecules. Nanogens. Transport nanogens, by the look of them. According to his Geiger readouts, each carried a microscopic parcel of laboratory-manufactured radium 229.

"What is it?" he asked.

"We call them minipacks," she said. "If someone tries to unplug you in the middle of the night, it's triggered into action, senses the power interruption, wakes you up, and gives you enough charge for thirty-five hours. You can neutralize any immediate threat, and still have enough juice left to find your way to one of our safe locations."

He lifted the minipack. "How do I install it?" he asked.

"Just swallow it. Take it like a pill. The nanogens do the rest." She smiled. "You don't have to take it now. Think about it. Think about everything. And once you do, we'll talk again."

After coffee with Reba, he went back to his condo, got his workout gear, and went to the gym up on the fifty-second floor of the south tower. He felt stiff. Dr. Slater had urged him to do as much exercise as possible. In the early stages, seizing up was a real threat, a crash in the joint-motorization units. Like the damn Tin Man in *The Wizard of Oz* getting too much rain on him. He wanted to avoid that.

All the fitness buffs working out in the gym glanced at him as he entered. Some were acquaintances, neighbors from the south tower. He waved. None waved back. After so many obvious glances, they now pretended not to see him—as if a giant made of flexisteel could be easily missed.

He walked to the nearest bench using both canes, sat down, and took off his boots. His boots were custom-made, size twenty, of special military issue for Number 17s, about as stylish as a pair of concrete blocks. His feet had steel claws instead of toenails, ideal for scaling enemy embattlements. He remembered reading Friedrich Nietzsche in university, recalled the German philosopher's ideas about the *Übermensch*, the Superman, and how the Superman would come to replace ordinary men. He was sure Nietzsche had never imagined an Omnifixed Number 17 as an *Übermensch*. Alex didn't want to be a Superman, despite all the fantastic powers he might have. He just wanted to be an ordinary man. He wanted to belong to the human race again.

He took the minipack out of his shirt pocket. He was touched by Reba's offer. Reba was thinking of him. Concerned about his welfare. Did she remember all those nights? That shared intimacy that had transcended everything? She cared about him. She wanted to help him. Yet he could see Graham's side too. Graham was worried about the welfare of his people. Alex didn't know what to do. Graham told one story, and Reba told another. His internal polygraph systems hadn't detected a lie in either case, just two different versions of the truth.

An older gentleman out on the track ran by Alex, speeding up as he passed, slowing down as he reached a safe distance.

Alex lifted the minipack to his eye. Like a horse pill. Reba wanted him to live. He got up and walked to the nearest fountain. He shoved the pill into his mouth and swallowed, chasing the minipack down with water. There. Did that mean he was on Reba's side now? He didn't want any DIS agent turning him off in the middle of the night, that was for sure. So he guessed he owed Reba.

He went to the track and walked without his canes. His bare feet made huge clanking sounds against the hardwood floor. And his legs moved like an automaton's. Who was he kidding? Fluidity of movement, according to Dr. Slater, was still months away. He was making scratch marks on the hardwood floor with his steel claws. But Dr. Slater said it was important to practice in his bare feet. He now had so much money he would gladly pay for the damage. He didn't want to walk outside on the superhard oriented-plastic sidewalk. He felt too self-conscious right now. And he wanted to be with his neighbors, wanted them to get used to the idea of a Number 17 living in the Towers, needed to do something normal like work out in the gym. But yes, he was scratching the floor. And his neighbors were now looking at him as if he were the definition of everything inappropriate.

He heard someone approach from behind. One of his combat subroutines kicked in. He balled his hands into big fists. He swung round—fast—and crouched in a defensive position, an overreaction, something he hadn't learned to control yet.

Laurel Sylvestri, the building chairwoman, stepped back, startled, and raised her beringed hand to her breast as if to stop a heart attack. Her eyes bulged. Alex smelled fear.

"Goodness, you're quick," she said. She wore a track suit. Her face was flushed. She'd been working out. "I'm sorry . . . but I just have to mention . . . maybe you've forgotten, since you've been away so long . . . but the floor. Track shoes *only*, I'm afraid."

She looked at his feet. Size twenties, with talons, armored with flexisteel. She concealed her horror.

"I'm sorry, Mrs. Sylvestri," he said, "but my doctor wants me to practice in my bare feet. I guess I could have walked outside on the superhard. Only I don't feel comfortable outside yet."

"Look at the marks you've left on the wood, Dr. Denyer." He stepped off the track and looked. Then he glanced at Mrs. Sylvestri. He felt sorry for her. He realized she was struggling with the usual prejudices—that unspoken apartheid that separated *Homo sapiens* from *Homo mechanicus*. "Who's going to pay for it?" she asked.

"I wasn't thinking, Mrs. Sylvestri," he said. "They have me on medication right now. And my impulses . . . I'll pay for it. Whatever it costs, I'll pay."

"And I'm afraid you have to get a work request signed before you do any redecorating," she said.

With no context, this at first came as a non sequitur. But then he understood. He felt a new subroutine in an unused system decompress, unfold, and manifest itself into a vacant combat interface, one that was equal parts game theory, clandestine strategy, and paranoia. Redecorating. He thought of Max Morrow's office, the way they'd repainted it, and the way the paint had been full of transmitting nanogens.

"But I haven't done any redecorating, Mrs. Sylvestri."

She made a face. "Dr. Denyer, the workmen were here yesterday. I saw them."

That made sense. Yesterday, when he'd been out at Greensboro for his physio and checkup, DIS workmen came in to paint the place. A special unit from the Megaplex, there to apply the quick-drying formula, no smell—the wonders they could do with intelligent nanogens these days. Mrs. Sylvestri stared at him with mild anxiety in her eyes. He knew she found everything about him distressing these days. No point in distressing her more by mentioning this cloak and dagger stuff. So he played along, pretended he just forgot.

"Oh, yes, now I remember, Mrs. Sylvestri," he said. "I'm sorry, I'm just so forgetful these days. My doctor says it will pass, but it might take a little while."

"You'll have to get that work request in," she said. "We need it on file. It was just a repaint, wasn't it?"

"Yes."

"No change of color?"

"No. In future I'll fill out the work request first."

When he got back to his condo in the South Tower, he stared at the walls. He sniffed. He upped his olfactory sensitivity five-fold. He analyzed scents: human sweat, not his own, masked by a nanomolecular deodorizer. And under the deodorizer, the smell of the odorless nanogenic paint, a scent so faint even his own superhuman nose barely detected it, and only when he had his sensitivity ramped right up. He used his military applications eye, clicking to a hundred times magnification. He saw transmitting nanogens, round, sprocketlike, embedded into the paint. Every fifth transmitter had a lens. Every tenth, a microscopic radium source. They shifted slowly around the skin of the paint, like thousands of unicellular creatures in a primordial pond. Breathe in. Breathe out. He sat down. He hated the way people now responded to him. As if he were actually a threat! He was just a scientist. He wanted to play in the lab, that's all. But now Graham was going to keep an eye on him. His neighbors were going to avoid him. And Reba was going to try and recruit him.

At two o'clock in the morning, he went to the south tower swimming pool. No one was there. Dr. Slater said he should get into the pool at least twice a week, but he didn't like going unless the place was deserted. In only a bathing suit, he looked outlandish and improbable, a hybrid of flesh and steel, with scars and seams everywhere, his joints still obviously articulated as they waited for their final ultrathin sheath of flexisteel. He looked like a machine to himself, with a hundred pounds of flesh thrown in to make it all the more gruesome. And in his bathing suit, turquoise with yellow suns, he looked like a monster on vacation.

He didn't risk the diving board. He was afraid he might break it. He dove off the edge, scratching the marble tiles with his claws, made a huge splash, and immediately sank to the bottom. He felt his environmental software kick in, recalibrating his balance, respiratory, and locomotive systems for the new medium.

The small motors in his limbs engaged, and bubbles jetted from his knees, wrists, ankles, and elbows, giving him forward propulsion. He didn't have to go to the top for air. An internal compressor supplied it. He could stay submerged for up to ten minutes. He tried to swim like a human, but, in a positive development, his aquatic systems kicked in for the first time, and he swam like a dolphin instead, feet together, arms outstretched, body weaving naturally like a creature of the deep. It felt good. It felt natural. He could actually move without any awkwardness.

He motored to the shallow end. Then rocketed toward the deep end. Before he could stop himself, an assault program deployed, and like a dolphin, he jumped out of the water, sprang into the air, and landed on his feet in a defensive posture at the far end of the pool, accidentally toppling a pile of paddleboards. He was startled by how adeptly he had performed this maneuver. Breathe in. Breathe out. He looked around. God. He really *was* a Superman. People were supposed to dive into pools, not out of them. He eased his defensive stance. Relaxed his shoulders. Then slipped back into the pool, feet first, in stealth mode, hardly making a ripple. The DDF had turned him into the equivalent of a souped-up Navy SEAL.

He sank right to the bottom and sat there. Keyed his buoyancy so he wouldn't float. He remained still. Like a rock on the bottom of the ocean. Hiding in the aquamarine depths of the pool. He liked it down here. He felt safe down here. He never wanted to come up for air. But he knew he was going to have to come up sooner or later. If only because he had so many decisions to make.

Chapter 21

He got on a hoverbus the next evening. He ducked so he wouldn't hit his head on the ceiling, maneuvered himself past the magnetic strip reader with great difficulty using both his canes, and watched the expressions on the half dozen passengers tighten. He scowled at them. They were ostracizing him, and they didn't even *know* him. One tall young man stared at him with open hostility. The man had a shaved head. His pants were made of zinc plates, thousands of them no bigger than a fingernail, woven together like fish scales, what many gang members in Hurlock wore these days. He wore a white T-shirt. The one-fingered salute was emblazoned on the front of the T-shirt. As the hoverbus eased away from the platform, Alex made his way down the aisle, his anger simmering, and deliberately sat in the seat across the aisle from the man, even though there were lots of seats everywhere else.

He sniffed the air. Molecules of the man's scent drifted into his central olfactory processor. The man was stoned. Alex could smell it on him. Stoned on

Pump, a.k.a. Edge, Target, and Finish, a lab-produced stimulant like steroids, cocaine, and caffeine mixed.

"Don't sit there," said the man. "Sit at the back, where you belong."

Alex didn't respond, stared straight ahead. But in his superenhanced peripheral vision, he watched the man. The hatred he saw in the man's eyes astounded Alex. It was so bizarre and unexpected, so unlike any emotion anyone had ever directed toward him before, he didn't exactly know how to respond.

He got off at a hoverbus platform in Hurlock and took the express elevators down to the subway. Zinc Pants followed him.

A few minutes later, the subway came. Alex got on. So did Zinc Pants. Zinc Pants took out a cell-stick, a pencil-shaped wireless phone, quoted a phone number into its voice-activated nub, and, after a short connection wait, spoke into the small device. Alex ramped up the amplitude on his hearing, but before he could get it to an effective level, Zinc Pants had already ended his call.

A short while later, the subway pulled into Phoenix South Station. Alex struggled up onto his canes, and got off the train. Everybody gave him a wide berth.

As the train pulled out of the station, he was hit by a dizzy spell. He staggered, and put his hand against the wall to steady himself. What he needed was a holiday to the Moon, someplace where the gravity was weaker, and where he'd be less likely to fall. He didn't bother glancing over his shoulder. He didn't have to. His peripheral vision, ramped to 320 degrees, told him Zinc Pants was right behind him, talking on his cell-stick again. Alex knew what was coming. He hoped when the time came he didn't hurt Zinc Pants too much.

He took the escalator to street level. Phoenix South. A part of Hurlock where a lot of Number 17s lived. Where Reba and Zirko lived. He wanted to see them. He wanted to be with people who wouldn't make him feel so alienated. And he also wanted to get some tips. He had a new designer body and he didn't know how to use it yet. He couldn't walk well, couldn't control his bowel movements, and had the annoying habit of biting his tongue when he ate. He still broke things when he was trying to handle them gently. He had to learn to control his strength.

He checked his peripheral vision. Zinc Pants was still following him, talking on his cell-stick. Alex eavesdropped, trying to get a better fix on the man's intentions. The man was talking street slang. Alex had heard this kind of street slang several times walking through Hurlock, covert code to hide criminal activities, or in this case, violent plans for an innocent Number 17. He could only guess its meaning, but even then, his guess was fairly good. Trouble. Zinc Pants was calling in reinforcements. Alex was a target simply because he was a Number 17—a Number 17 with canes, not a threat, just a hapless object of hatred.

Vendors, hawkers, and prostitutes thronged the thoroughfare. He passed a fishmonger cooking twelve-inch swordfish kabobs on a gas barbecue, a smell he had once savored but which he now found nauseating. Omnifix was in the middle of effecting stomach repairs, and his appetite was off. What to eat? Some days he couldn't eat anything at all. Dr. Slater told him that one day he wouldn't have to eat at all, that all his nutritional needs would be taken care of by his neutron power pack.

He cut through an alley to get to Hosta Street, Reba's street. The alley was deserted. He hobbled forward on his canes. His Strategy and Tactical Systems kicked in. Fool your enemy. Make him think you're weak. Alex wondered what conniving DDF general had written that nasty bit of code into the software. He hunched his back, as if in pain. He stumbled, all for show. Zinc Pants was brave. But he was also stupid, a man who thought he could vanquish a Number 17, believing he could capitalize on Alex's apparent weaknesses. Maybe Zinc Pants had a personal grudge against Number 17s, or an old score to settle.

Alex continued on, pretending each step was agony. The figures in his 320-degree enhanced peripheral vision multiplied. The cell-stick contactees had arrived. He stopped. He waited. His supersensitive hearing heard them approach, five altogether.

"I told you to sit somewhere else," said Zinc Pants.

From the tone of his voice, now showing up on one of Alex's inner screens as a jagged sawtooth, Alex could sense a deep bitterness, and a long history. This man had a grudge against Number 17s for one reason or another.

Alex didn't immediately turn around. He felt an uncharacteristic warmth in the back of his head, a looseness in his limbs, and a new readiness in his outlook. In confronting this threat, it was as if something had been revealed to him, a new awareness of, and connection to, his cybernetic body. Zinc Pants was acting like a catalyst in some unforeseen way. Alex's unit-wide interfaces, struggling day after day with virtually no progress, trying to bridge the gap between his cybernetic and biological components, had finally connected to each other, at least enough to make him momentarily function as a whole.

He let go of his canes. He rose to his full height. He turned slowly around. Zinc Pants, now carrying a big steel pipe, stepped back. But he didn't step back far enough. Alex's reach rivaled a condor's wingspan. He gripped Zinc Pants by his throat and lifted him off the ground.

From there, it was like performing an arithmetical equation. The machine inside him took over. And like a machine, he wasn't conscious of what he was doing, simply followed command directives, blindly, obediently, and with all his combat modes in place. He had one objective. Defeat the enemy. And beyond that brutal horizon, everything else was blank.

When he regained his *human* consciousness—when he finally dropped out of that cruel, oblivious, but unerringly effective subroutine where all Omnifix soldiers went when fighting hand-to-hand—he discovered he was at Greensboro with no idea how he got there, sitting on the edge of a bed in the Emergency Clinic. His Remnant gripped him like a brake and stopped his combat subroutines cold. Dr. Slater stood by some medical monitors staring at him with some concern. The doctor looked at his legs. *He* looked at his legs. While his clothes were badly torn, his limbs were fine. He ran a systems check. He had a gash on his right cheek, but his diagnostics told him Omnifix had already initiated repairs on that. He turned his palms upward. He saw blood on his hands.

"Did I kill anyone?" he asked. "I can't remember a thing."

Dr. Slater took a few steps forward. "How do you feel?" he asked.

Alex stood up. He lifted one knee, then the other. He raked his hand through his synthetic hair. "I feel fine," he said. "But what happened? I blacked out. I don't remember a thing."

A line came to Dr. Slater's forehead. "You didn't exactly black out," he said. "Have you not finished reading the manual on your combat subroutines yet?"

"It's a thousand pages long," he said. "I'm getting there."

"And I didn't mention this to you?" said Slater. "This particular kind of blackout, as you call it?"

"No," said Alex.

Dr. Slater nodded, his brow bunching as he accepted his own forgetfulness.

"In a threatening situation," he said, "certain combat subroutines will suppress cognitive function in order to dampen fear. They also kill hesitancy. They allow the soldier to do the most horrible things to other human beings, or to endure the most horrible things at the hands of the enemy. They do this by suspending a variety of consciousness applications. When surveillance routines conclude the soldier is no longer in danger, consciousness applications reboot, and you come out of it. Number 17s have a name for it. They call it X-space."

While Alex found this information useful, he was still unnerved by the blood on his palms. "Did I kill anyone?" he asked again.

Dr. Slater's lower lip stiffened.

"You inflicted several injuries," he said. "Some of them are life-threatening. No one's died yet, but two of your attackers are in critical condition in hospital. Police finally had to subdue you. The minute they scanned you, your identification was sent to the Megaplex, and the Megaplex ordered your release into our custody. The Megaplex has agreed to underwrite any medical costs for your victims, as well as pay for any legal damages. The Megaplex tells me you won't be arrested. I won't ask about that. It's none of my business. So you have nothing to worry about, Dr. Denyer."

"But I used more than reasonable force," said Alex. "Two of those men are in critical condition."

He felt alarmed by this development, especially because it was something he couldn't control.

Slater shrugged. "They attacked you," he said. "It was their choice. And I should explain, X-space will sometimes accelerate or at least lubricate the interface between biological and cybernetic components. Physical progress often surges."

Alex raised his eyebrows. "I think that might have happened to me."

Dr. Slater gave him a dry grin. "You see?" he said. "At least some small benefit came out of all this. And you shouldn't feel guilty. Let's not forget. They're the ones who attacked you. They got what they deserved. Next time they'll think twice."

He finally made it to Reba's place on Hosta Street a couple of days later. Sandy Parker was there, looking a good deal older, still in his vintage Revolutionary costume, sitting on a pile of cushions, drinking cheap booze, his face, now with elongated nose and chin, displaying all the customary goblinesque changes of an end-stage Number 16. His costume was in bad shape. In tatters. But he didn't seem to notice. The big pile of cushions he was sitting on looked well used. That's how Reba furnished her place. With big piles of cushions. One could buy furniture specifically designed for the size and weight of a Number 17, but the cost was prohibitively expensive, and, on a regular soldier's pension, beyond reach. So everybody in the room—Alex, Sandy, Reba, and Zirko—sat on nests of cushions.

Alex was flummoxed, could hardly digest all the things they'd spoken of so far, felt like all these years he'd been a playgoer, watching the play from a safe distance, accepting the play as reality. But the play was just a Megaplex-doctored reality—the true action was taking place backstage. Sandy Parker, in cahoots with Number 17 Repealists for the last five years? Organizing and arming them? Graham was right after all. Daryl working with Reba right under his nose? He feared for his son. Yet he understood exactly how Daryl felt. He was now backstage himself. Searching for the Holy Grail.

He glanced at Zirko. He was having a hard time getting used to Zirko. Maybe because someday he knew he would look like Zirko. Zirko was huge. He was one of the originals, one of the first to be pinked by Number 17 back in 2441, during the Bettina Altercation. A man from a different generation, in his fifties, but perpetually young-looking because of the repair nanogens in Omnifix, and as strong as a gorilla. He didn't wear clothes. He didn't have to. Articulated flexisteel sheathed his entire body. He looked more like a machine than a human being. But Alex saw a soul burning in Zirko's biological eye, and knew there was a human being buried in all that high technology.

Reba was speaking.

"We want to trust you, Alex," she said.

As an invitation, these words rang with caution. He was a direct blood relative of the CEO of the Defederacy, after all. What could be riskier? Also, he was, until recently, part of the human race. But now he felt he was part of the *cyber* race.

"He wants me to spy on you," he told Reba.

"And are you going to?" asked Zirko, harshly, as if he just wanted to cut the discussion short and get to the business of turning him into pulp.

"Hey, now, Zirko, my man," said Sandy. "He's being up-front with us. And you've got to admire that. I like him. And I like his son, Daryl. And you never know, Crafty Croft might listen to us if we let Alexander speak for us."

Reba stared at Alex; he watched her as she put her military applications eye through its paces. Then she turned to her waferscreens, thin ones she had pasted to the wall, keyed in a few commands, watched information flick by, like she was flipping through a magazine, idly, casually, without paying much attention.

"The Martians have a better technique for people like us," she told him at last.

"And for Number 16s too," said Zirko.

"Now, Zirko, my man, strictly speaking, we don't have much verification on the Number 16 side of things. I'll admit, the preliminary intercepts look promising, but they're only a few months old, so we don't know if it's in the works or not, do we?"

"If you're so uncertain," said Zirko glumly, "pull out the Stationhouse. We don't need you."

"You might have strength, Zirko, but we have numbers. Let Alexander take our numbers to Crafty Croft and see how His Mighty Blondness reacts."

Alex turned to Reba, pondering all these revelations.

"So Daryl's in deep?" he asked.

"Not in the operational sense, Alex," she said. "Just in the information-gathering sense. He's brilliant. You should be proud of him."

He stared at her. He couldn't help feeling warmed by the praise she was giving his son. Reba was a good woman. He was glad Daryl had contact with her. And now that Alex was a Number 17, he was glad to see people were doing something about all this. He felt ebullient. The Martians had a better way for Number 17s like him. Better than Omnifix. He felt some hope for a change, the first hope he'd felt since that pink tidal wave had overwhelmed him aboard the AWP.

"So this Martian technique for Number 17," he said. "What exactly is it?"

She glanced at Zirko. She leaned forward, her eyes narrowing. Her synthetic hair fell past her cheek.

"The Martians started out with Omnifix as well," she said. "They were just as surprised by Number 17 as we were. So it was a cooperative project between the DDF and the FMC Defense Force back when we were allies fighting the aliens together. But the Defederacy's public coffers were drained dry during the Die-Off because of Number 16. The Martians never got hit with any Number 16 the way we did. It was just their soldiers getting pinked with Number 17. So they didn't have a Die-Off. They didn't have the whole Number 16 phenomenon. They didn't even get hit with any of the other nanogens, Numbers 1 through 15, all those creepy nanogens that changed grasshoppers and snakes and certain trees, and that made no sense to anybody at all. The Martians didn't have to sink all their resources into health care, the way we did. Nor did they have to build protective enclaves. Ninety percent of everything they build is underground anyway, so they already have their enclaves. That left them with money to develop other Number 17 alternatives. They also had the freedom."

"The freedom?" said Alex.

"Their blue-sky research is less hampered by all the regulatory controls and legislation we have here on Earth. It's a wild frontier up there as far as scientific development is concerned. If the Review Board in Murray City thinks a certain project will help the FMC, they rubber-stamp it. Things aren't banned on moral grounds, the way they are here on Earth. The environment there is too hostile to ban things that otherwise might help them survive and even prosper in the conditions they have to live in. In particular, there's no ban on human cloning, the way there is here. In fact, human cloning is the cornerstone of their Number 17 rehabilitation technique. Their cloning project started fifty years ago, so they've had a lot of time to iron out most of the bugs. They can now turn out relatively healthy adult duplicates."

"I think I read something about their cloning program somewhere," said Alex.

Reba nodded. "They can produce a full-grown human adult in three months. In the case of their Number 17 treatment, they harvest clean cells from a victim's uninfected flesh, and make a clone from that. If you're forty, your clone will be forty. The Martians then record onto dataspheres a victim's personality, intelligence, memory, and so forth. They grow the clone, then download the stored personality, intelligence, and memory package into the clone using standard Omnifix techniques. But instead of downloading the package onto a Number 17's hard drive, they download it directly into a clone's new gray matter. You get a new body, Alex, just like your old one. There's no emotional detriment. You can clean out your medicine cabinet. You won't have to take drugs anymore. That's not to say the Martian technique is perfect. Studies suggest Martian clones are twenty percent more susceptible to certain blood disorders, and thirty percent more likely to develop osteoporosis. And in certain subjects there's a risk of neurological damage, but overall, it's far better than Omnifix."

Alex glanced at Sandy Parker. "Can they not use the same technique for Number 16s?" he asked.

"No," said Reba. "Number 16 immediately replicates itself in every cell. It sits there dormant, waiting to go off when a victim hits Sandy's age. So for cloning purposes, every cell is already wrecked. Number 17, on the other hand, spreads selectively, leaving certain tissue untouched at first. Martian technicians can harvest their materials from this uninfected tissue to grow the clone."

"What about what Zirko said?" asked Alex. "That there might be a technique for Number 16s as well."

Reba's biological eye glistened with compassion. She knew he was thinking about Daryl.

"We've picked up some promising radio traffic in the last little while," she said, "that's all. There's some indication that the Martians might have a way to disable the Number 16 nanogen. We don't know how that might affect current victims, if at all, or whether, like Sandy says, it's really in the works or not. But it's the first positive thing we've heard from the Martians about Number 16."

Alex thought of his son. Some of his chronic ache about Daryl lifted. All those hours searching for the Holy Grail, watching his son's desperate crusade. And then his own many hours on the Internet, looking for something, anything, that might help Daryl. Poring over all the medical research, looking into Colgan's work, trying to find an escape for Daryl, writing Graham every now and again, fighting for a cure. Now there was this intercept from Mars. If only, please, if only it might bear fruit. In the meantime he went back to the Number 17 technique.

"So I assume you're trying to get your hands on this Martian Number 17 rehabilitation technique," said Alex.

"Yes."

"And how do you propose to do that?" asked Alex. "We're at war with the Martians. The borders, so to speak, are sealed. Remember that crew of defectors who tried to get through? The Martians blasted them right out of the sky. Radio intercepts might still be possible, but they're not going to give us their technique anytime soon, not while there's this war going on. And there's little chance we can steal it from them, not when their planet's protected by the most sophisticated defense array the solar system has ever seen."

Reba's eyes narrowed. He thought he'd never seen her more serious.

"That's where you come in, Alex," she said.

Chapter 22

When he left Reba's place, it was dark and raining. This Martian technique. He couldn't stop thinking about it. Did Daryl have a chance after all? And did *he* actually have a chance? Could he have his body back? More significantly, could he have a regular human brain back, a brain that didn't make him feel fractured into hundreds of different subsystems, one that he would at least have some emotional control over? He could cope with blood disorders and osteoporosis if it came to that. He wanted to talk to Daryl. Daryl could confirm everything by checking out the most pertinent websites, perhaps even dipping into classified ones. And Daryl might have information about the promising Number 16 intercepts, too. He was overjoyed to know that there might be a possible chance for his son.

He turned right onto Mystical Road, a thorough-fare he ordinarily never entered, a street full of pimps, drunks, killers, con men, bad cops, drug pushers, prostitutes, and pickpockets. In the old days, he would have been a target. Now, since he was a rippling specimen of *Homo mechanicus*, everyone stayed away from him.

Mystical Road led down to the harbor. He could see the water at the end of the street five blocks away reflecting the lights of the city. He was just about to turn right on Chapman Avenue, a diagonal that would take him closer to the *Beelzebub*, when far at the end of Mystical he saw Tony Sartis kissing a young woman, a prostitute. He clicked to five-times magnification. He sighed. Yes, definitely Tony, in his black jeans, his black jacket, and his black boots, looking every inch the rogue he was. Alex's Remnant sparked a time or two as the kiss continued. How could Tony do this? This was the kind of kiss a married man should reserve for his wife. His strides grew longer, faster. He felt it unfair that Tony should betray Jill this way, even for an obvious one-night stand like this.

Tony looked up and saw him coming. His eyes widened. He said a few quick words to the prostitute and ducked behind a stall. Alex picked up Tony's scent, his microprocessor separating and analyzing it in a matter of seconds from all the other scents in the street. His stride lengthened even farther. He reached the stall a few moments later. He clicked his military applications eyes into the X-ray spectrum and discerned Tony hiding behind a burlap draping. He pushed the burlap aside and gripped Tony by the shoulder.

"What do you think you're doing?" asked Alex.

A grin came to Tony's face, as if he and Alex were old buddies. "Hiring a prostitute."

At least the man was honest. Alex felt his anger mounting. "Why can't you treat Jill the way she deserves to be treated?"

Tony's face twisted.

"And you're the expert on that, Alex?" he said. He looked at Alex's hand. "You're hurting me. You have to watch your strength now. You're a lot stronger than you used to be."

Alex eased his grip but didn't let go. "You haven't exactly made her happy in the last little while," he said. "It's not good for Daryl when you two are always fighting."

"I'm not going to apologize, Alex. I need comfort. Jill's not giving me any."

"And what if I tell her what you've done?"

Tony's eyes grew sad.

"Tell her, and you'll just make her more unhappy than she already is," he said.

Alex and Tony parted company. Alex walked around for a while. He didn't know what he was going to do. He didn't know if he should tell Jill about Tony's activities or not. He kicked the curb, breaking a chunk of concrete from it. He knew what Tony meant. Life was sometimes difficult with Jill. Sometimes she didn't give of herself. But when she did, it was like the sun coming out from behind clouds. Nothing compared to that miraculous warmth she sometimes radiated. Yet there was also this coldness, honed like a weapon, and often used like one, a symptom of her disappointed expectations, perhaps the thing their marriage had foundered on. Rain fell. Sometimes he hated her, sometimes he loved her. Mostly he just wanted to protect her from herself. He headed toward the dock. He had to see Jill. Just to make sure she was all right. And he had to talk to Daryl about the Martian Number 16 and 17 solutions.

On the *Beelzebub*, he kept it bottled up. Tony was right. There was no point in making her more unhappy than she already was.

"You're walking better," said Jill. She was drying dishes in the galley, cheap enamel ones that wouldn't break. "I wish I could get used to the way you look, though."

"Me too."

"Are you in pain at all?"

"Sometimes."

"But it's mainly over, isn't it?" she said. "The acute phase?"

"That's what Dr. Slater says," he said.

"So now you'll change bit by bit?" she said.

"Yes."

"And what about mortality? It's not like cancer, is it? They don't give you a certain number of years to live, do they?"

Mortality. He could see she was worried about this. His continuance meant something to her.

"Omnifix will replace only Number 17-infected tissue. If any of my remaining uninfected tissue falls victim to another pathology, like cancer or heart disease, I have the same chance everybody else does. Once I'm more than sixty percent machine, Greensboro can't predict longevity. It's too early to tell. But none of the Bettina veterans are dead yet, and they're all in their fifties. So I think I have a few more years yet."

"So once you reach sixty percent machine, your

291

life expectancy could conceivably be longer than mine?" she said.

"Dr. Slater doesn't define it as life expectancy when a Number 17 reaches that point," said Alex.

"What does he define it as?" asked Jill, putting a cup into the cupboard.

"He borrows a term from engineering. Average time to failure. When half my backups are gone, and Omnifix itself is failing to repair them, that's when I've reached the limit of my redefined life expectancy. Nobody knows when that's going to be because no Number 17 has died of natural causes yet. The program's still too young. Omnifix is good, but it's not failproof. They didn't have the money to make it failproof. So my average time to failure has been adversely affected by the Defederacy's tight budget."

"But you're still going to live longer than I am," she said, now sounding as if she'd been short-changed.

"Dr. Slater won't give us an actual figure," he said. "And frankly, I don't want to know. I die when I die."

"Does that make you happy?" she asked. "That you might live a long time?"

He wondered how he could answer Jill without upsetting her. "Jill . . . I think I prefer quality of life to quantity right now." He gestured at himself. "It's not easy. Look at me. My whole life has been turned upside down." He thought of the incident in Phoenix South with Zinc Pants. "I'm a danger to myself and to others. I feel angry most of the time. I feel sad. The drugs they give me really don't help, they just deaden things a bit. My emotions have gone haywire. I can't control them. And I don't know what I'm going to do with myself. I still have my interest in science, but now I'm not sure it's something I want to pursue in a professional way. That trip out to the AWP . . . especially that big mass grave . . . it makes me want to leave exotechnology alone for a little while."

"That's a change," she said. "You always loved to tinker with that junk."

"I think I just want to give it a rest. If you want to know the truth, I've been thinking of Pennsylvania. I have dreams about it. Cyber dreams. And those cyber dreams are just so damn real. It's like I'm back there. I'm feeling homesick for Pennsylvania. I'm considering getting a two-week permit and going back. Just to see how it's fared since the Bombardment. I want to go to Unionville. Make the trip as a kind of memorial to my father. Because who knows how he ultimately died in all that anarchy? It must have been hell. I hope he went fast."

"Here it is," said Daryl, pointing.

Alex and Daryl sat in front of Daryl's computer array. Alex leaned closer. He saw an article coauthored by Dr. Ariam Adurra and Dr. Revord Liag, distinguished Martian scientists with distinctive Martian names, names devised and chosen, in part, to assert Martian identity.

In the article, Ariam Adurra outlined how, with the use of certain alien-produced enzymes, neurological downloads of memory, personality, and intelligence could be indelibly "tattooed" on a recipient's brain. Dr. Revord Liag presented three case studies—Martian Number 17s, veterans of the Alien War—who had been treated with the new alien enzyme, and who showed ninety-five-percent "acclimatization" to their new bodies, with only a hint of the blood disorders Reba had spoken of.

"So not only do they have a better Number 17 technique than us," said Alex, "that technique is based on alien technology."

"If you read on, you see that the DNA in this enzyme actually parallels certain sequences in the Number 17 nanogen," said Daryl. "It's quite interesting. I'm glad there's hope for you, Dad. I know you really don't like being Gorgo the Magnificent Man-Bot all that much." Daryl flicked forward a few screens. "I've actually read a number of Dr. Adurra's papers now. She mentions you often. She speaks of your work glowingly."

Alex grinned, but it was a melancholy grin. "In different circumstances, we would be colleagues." He paused. "I was at Reba's."

He managed to inject some implication in his unpracticed electronic voice, enough so that Daryl grew still. Daryl turned to his father, a questioning look in his eyes. His chin came forward. Daryl realized his father knew he was in deep.

"Have you told Mom?" asked Daryl.

"No," said Alex. "She doesn't know?"

Daryl's face settled. "No. You have to be careful with Mom. She's excitable."

Alex thought of his chance encounter with Tony on Mystical Road. "Things aren't getting any better between her and Tony, are they?"

"Not really. But I side more with Tony. It's not easy. Not with Mom. Jill won't let up. She won't give him a break. He gets drunk sometimes now. It's not a good situation. And this time, it's particularly bad.

I don't know how they're going to work it out. Frankly, I don't care. I'm moving out."

This news surprised Alex. "Where?" he asked.

"Sandy and I are going to find a place."

"Sandy Parker? Daryl, are you sure you want to do that? I'm sure the DIS are all over him. Plus he's end-stage. He's going to need a lot of support soon. You're going to end up looking after him."

"So I'll look after him. It'll be better than looking after Jill and Tony."

Alex considered the rebellious tone he heard in his son's voice. Maybe this would be a good thing for Daryl. Daryl had only twelve years left. He should get out and live on his own before the change hit him.

"Sandy was there when I went to Reba's," said Alex. "He said something about a Martian intercept. Reba said the Martians might have a way to disable Number 16."

Daryl's eyes narrowed. "We don't know that for sure yet, Dad. But I've got the intercept right here, if you want to hear it. It's fairly sketchy."

Daryl keyed some commands into his computer. An unidentified Martian voice came on the speaker: "This could conceivably be used to transmit a rerouting command to the Number 16 genome, rendering it inert. Generic cytophages could then be introduced into the body to dismantle the Number 16 network cell by cell. This would of course involve identifying the correct sequencing, then manipulating the command source to within a million miles of the intended target."

The intercept ended.

"That's all you have?" asked Alex.

"That's it," said Daryl.

"It's vague."

"I know."

"What's this about a million miles?" asked Alex.

"We don't know."

"Reba wants me to talk to Graham," said Alex. "About arranging a mercy deal with the Martians."

"Do you think it will work?"

"If I have any chance of getting you out of your predicament, Daryl, I'll have to try."

"Thanks, Dad. Do you think Graham will go for it?"

"We'll just have to wait and see," said Alex. "If I can make him think it's to his advantage, he might."

X-space. A way to shut down fear. Tonight, he tested it. His fingernails were like grappling hooks, and his feet were like pole-climbing boots; and while the sharp points penetrated only a micrometer into the superhard oriented plastic of Lincoln Towers' South Building, they nonetheless gave him enough purchase to scale the skyscraper easily. He was now eighty-five floors up. He glanced over his shoulder. Lane upon lane of sky traffic glided gracefully by below him, an ordered parade of lights in the gloaming. He looked down. He thought he would be afraid, and that his fear might breaker-switch him into X-space. But it didn't. He tried to figure out why. A moment later he had the answer. His Special Operations software had engaged. He was treating this like a mission. Fear of heights simply wasn't part of the Special Ops software package. This perilous climb wasn't going to jump-start him into X-space after all.

Disappointed by the experiment, he continued his

climb with greater abandon. He loped up the side of the building like a squirrel up a tree. Amazing powers, but to what end? Incredible enhancements, but what did he need them for? And where was X-space? Where was that merciful oblivion? The wind tossed his synthetic hair. He left scratch marks all over the distinctive white paneling, but he didn't care. He just wanted X-space so he could forget all this.

A few days later, Alex walked through the dark streets of Hurlock with Reba. They walked quickly, four times as fast as the fastest human pedestrians. Reba was afraid, upset. The Megaplex had finally passed that new provisional law yesterday, the one that allowed the roundup of older veterans like Zirko. In conjunction with this new law, a list had been published. On the list were a hundred names. Included on the list was Zirko Carty's name. Under the new law, Number 17s of more than fifteen years standing could now be legally rounded up and shipped to a holding facility at the military base on Chincoteague Bay, where they could be held indefinitely as a possible public safety risk.

"They're getting ready," said Reba. "In a few weeks, once the roundup is complete, the Megaplex will legally redefine Number 17s like Zirko as equipment of the DDF. At that point, Zirko won't have any rights at all. They'll turn him off on grounds of expense."

Alex and Reba passed the Third Haven Friends Meeting House, one of the oldest structures in the Defederacy, built in 1682, nearly eight hundred years old, preserved all these centuries as a historical landmark.

"He knows," said Alex.

"Who?"

"Graham."

"Knows what?" said Reba.

"That things are building to a head."

"I know he knows," said Reba. "That's why he's doing this." She gave him an anxious glance. "Are you going to talk to him?"

"Yes."

"Tell him to stop." Her anger got the better of her. "Or else."

"You don't threaten Graham," he said. "He's not fond of ultimatums. When you talk to him, or ask him for anything, you make it sound as if it will further his own aims."

He could tell this answer didn't satisfy Reba. She could remain unconvinced, he decided. When the time came, he would do his best. He wasn't sure how good his best would be. Life was still hard for him. After his sudden surge forward, he was slipping back a bit. He'd felt sick for the last few days. And tired. He just wanted to rest. He had no willpower. Last night he had vomited for a whole hour, his gag reflex recalibrating itself as new material replaced his disintegrating stomach lining. Today he was weak.

They finally reached a part of the harbor used for dry-docking and shipyard repairs. Several old tankers lay anchored at various piers. Most of these tankers were slated for demolition. Alex followed Reba down one of the piers. The sky was dark, and a thick fog moved in from Chesapeake Bay. Yes, he just wanted to rest. But he put one foot in front of the other, willing himself forward. They reached the end of the pier and boarded an abandoned ship, the *Harrington*, a cargo carrier twice the size of the *Beelzebub*.

They found Zirko in the engine room, in the dark, lying perfectly still in the ship's bilge water under a steel plate he had dragged over himself, his flexisteel body camouflaged, emanating nothing in the way of a heat signature because he was submerged in two feet of water. The consummate cybernetic soldier, thought Alex. Zirko pushed the steel plate off his body and got to his feet, his limbs dripping water. In Alex's night vision, Zirko appeared a ghostly green. Zirko's head swiveled toward him with machine-like precision.

"You're with us now?" said Zirko.

"I don't know," he said. "But I'm not against you."

Alex reached out to steady himself. He felt dizzy again. Zirko stared at him for a long time after that.

"I know what it's like," the big Number 17 finally said. "I remember the beginning well. The beginning is bad. You wake up every morning and you look at yourself in the mirror, and you wonder how this could have happened to you. You had other plans for your life, but life had other plans for you. And then you get sick. You get the dizziness. Mine lasted for three years before it finally ended."

Zirko was right. He'd never meant to end up like this. He'd always thought that he'd be the one to make the choices in his life, direct his life, make it happen the way he wanted it to happen. But as the old saying went: Man proposes, God disposes.

"Three years?" he said, disheartened. "That long?"

"Some get over it in six months," said Zirko. "Others take as long as five years. But eventually you get over it. You're not going to have to live with it for the rest of your life."

He warmed to Zirko. He wanted to say something to show Zirko that he commiserated with him in his present predicament.

"The DDF wants to ship you to Chincoteague Bay," he said. "I'm sorry about that, Zirko."

He watched Zirko's human eye narrow.

"Let them try," he said. Zirko put his hand on Reba's shoulder and gave it an affectionate shake. "I was a pilot. I was fully rated. I could fly anything. I loved to be at the helm of a spacecraft. I flew a lot of missions for them. Dangerous missions. Missions that killed a lot of my friends. And now they do this to me? Tell your cousin to watch out. Tell him things have just gone from bad to worse. We've been arming and organizing. I'll bring war to his doorstep if he doesn't change his tune fast. I have a lot of friends. And they all feel the same way I do. As if they've been abandoned not only by the Megaplex but also by the military. As if they've been used and abused and rewarded with nothing but ingratitude. If your cousin wants trouble, I'll show him trouble, and so will all my friends. Deep down, me and my friends are still Platoon. And Platoon knows how to dish out trouble better than anybody else."

Chapter 23

Laurel Sylvestri, the building chairwoman, stood at Alex's condo door the next day with a waferscreen in her hand. She had two members of the building's board with her, an elderly man and a young woman. Mrs. Sylvestri held the waferscreen to his face. He saw a list of names. He looked at the heading. A Petition for Removal. Legally notarized.

"We've been reviewing certain paragraphs of the Clayton-Treppner Tenancy Act of 2441, and, under Paragraph 3, Section C, if the building board feels it can show just cause for the removal of a tenant or owner, it can submit a petition with a minimum of a hundred signatures to the Tenancy Review Body. Under existing military statutes, Number 17s, in certain cases, fall into some of these relevant categories. We believe it would be in the best interests of the building if you were to find yourself a more suitable residence, Dr. Denyer."

His expression hardened. He wasn't an idiot. He'd been glancing at the real estate pages a lot recently. Checking for new places. He wasn't so innocent anymore. He could sense when plots were building around him.

"I think I have a month under Clayton-Treppner," he said.

"It will take you that long?" asked Mrs. Sylvestri.

He frowned. "I'll be out in a month, Mrs. Sylvestri. If my real estate agent hasn't sold the place by then, I'll leave him the keys."

Alex sat in the back of the hoverbus on his way to Hurlock, trying to keep his anger under control. True, he'd seen the eviction coming, but that still didn't mean he couldn't be angry about it. The bus was crowded, it was rush hour, but no one would sit in the empty seat next to him. Rain speckled the hoverbus windows. The trickles on the glass momentarily brightened in the light of a floating billboard that advertised a seaweed-based dishwashing detergent called Sea Clean. He sat hunched over, his massive elbows on his knees, Gorgo the Magnificent Man-Bot, every muscle in his body tight, his face set in a scowl, his right fist grinding quietly into his left palm.

He got to the subway exchange and waited for one of the express elevators. Two ranks of five stood on either side. Seventeen men, eight women, and nine children waited for a ride down, his defense systems counting them with exactitude. The closest elevator opened and he got on. He expected everybody to get on after him. But no one did. He put his massive hand out to stop the doors from closing. He leaned out. His head, upsized considerably to include all the extra components it carried, felt heavy on his shoulders. No one looked at him.

"Is anyone getting on?" he boomed.

A few people glanced his way, but no one moved. He kept his hand there for a moment longer, then let the elevator door slide shut.

In Hurlock, he strode toward the *Beelzebub*. The elevator episode angered him. So did the Petition for Removal. He felt himself seething. Tonight, the drugs didn't seem to be doing any good at all.

The *Beelzebub* gangplank was up. No one was on deck. He backed up. He took a running jump. He sprang a full twenty-six feet into the air, crossed the watery gap between the dock and the boat, grabbed the railing, and swung himself up and over, his feet landing on the deck with a dull clank. He needed to talk to Tony. Tony had a friend who owned a building in Hurlock. A building that was full of Number 17s. Maybe he could find a place in there. Because the sooner he got out of Lincoln Towers, the better. He definitely wasn't Lincoln Towers material anymore.

He went inside and descended the companionway to the second deck. He walked toward the galley. The door to the captain's cabin, Daryl's room, was closed. He clicked beyond the visible spectrum into X-ray mode and saw a blurred skeletal outline of Daryl sitting at his desk, hands clasped tightly together, not doing anything at all, just sitting, all tense, his shoulders up. Then he heard, with his amped-up hearing, someone mumbling an apology, Tony telling Jill he was sorry about something. He heard Jill crying. He came to the galley. He looked in.

He saw Jill standing by the sink. Her lower lip was split and bleeding. A bruise was forming, crescent-shaped and dull, under her left eye. Tony stunk of alcohol. Jill glanced at Alex. She looked mortified and . . . and *ashamed*. He remembered the bruise on her face when she'd come to visit him at Greensboro after getting home from the New Transvaal. It didn't take a genius to figure out what was going on. Tony was hitting her? Why hadn't Daryl told him? He couldn't take this. This was too much for him. No one—*no one*—was going to treat Jill this way. His Number 17 anger, already smoldering, exploded, and before he could stop himself, he took a few strides forward and punched Tony in the face. The force was enough to break Tony's jaw and send him flying three yards. Alex's combat subroutines clicked into high gear as he drifted inexorably toward X-space. He lost all moral sense, the ability to reason, and, for the moment, couldn't see that in striking Tony he was in fact making the situation worse. But it was as if his soldierly routines, barely restrained by Dr. Slater's drugs, had a will of their own, and there was nothing he could do to stop them. He lifted Tony from the floor and threw him against the table as if he were no heavier than a rag doll. Tony crashed onto the table, knocking it over, and slid to the floor. The mist of X-space grew thicker in Alex's eyes.

"Alex, please, no!" cried Jill.

Tony tried to get up, but before he could, Alex kicked him in the ribs. Alex was *all* soldier now. His supersensitive hearing picked up the satisfying sound of a few ribs breaking. He grabbed Tony by the neck and lifted him right off the floor so his feet dangled. He carried Tony to the sink full of dishes and jammed his face into the water, then just held him there.

The last thing he remembered as he finally drifted

into the nether regions of X-space was that his combat command systems were set on kill. He wasn't conscious. He was just a machine doing what his software prerogatives told him to. The blankness was like a dense fog. Within that fog, he didn't exist, didn't know that he didn't exist, even as he kept Tony's face firmly underwater.

He dropped out of X-space only when he heard his son's voice. And even then it took him a while to understand what was happening. *"Dad, stop! Dad, please stop!"* Over and over again. Until the vague outline of Tony's head underwater made itself apparent to first his visual sense receptors, then to his image transducers, and finally to his surveillance and threat analyzers. And he understood that he was killing his ex-wife's husband, something he didn't want to do. Realized he was becoming that basest of all creatures, a murderer.

He pulled Tony out of the water. Tony gasped frantically for air, his long hair dripping streamers of water, his beard moistened into distinct curls. He raised his hand to his jaw. His whole face looked crooked because his jaw was broken. Jill put her arm around Tony.

"Are you all right?" she cried. "Tony?" Then she looked at Alex. "I think you better leave."

"Jill . . . I'm sorry . . . I just . . ."

"I *said* you'd better *leave*." Her voice grew more piercing. "Leave before I call the police."

Alex looked at Daryl, hoping Daryl might come to his rescue. But Daryl just stood there, eyes averted, perhaps wishing, like any teenager, that the adults in his life would get their acts together.

"I want you to stay away from Tony," said Jill. It

didn't seem to matter that she had just been brutalized by Tony. "And I want you to stay away from Daryl, too. They've turned you into a monster, Alex. You're not Alex anymore. Just go. Go now."

So he left. He was a disintegrating man, he thought. In more ways than one. And there was only one way to stop it.

With a trip to Mars.

He went to the CEO's office the next day. Graham stood on the Stars-of-the-Defederacy throw rug, the sunset illuminating the towering black spires of Delaware behind him. Three DIS agents stood around Alex with weapons drawn. Graham waved them away.

"I'll call you if I need you," he told them. "This is my cousin. We're family."

The guards retreated. Graham leveled his gaze at Alex.

"Well?" he said.

Alex took a deep breath as his gargantuan shoulders sank. "It's bad, Graham," he said. "And this new provisional law . . . rounding up the Bettina veterans . . . rounding up the Europa and Cassini veterans?"

Graham raised his hands.

"I can't sit here and do nothing, Alex," said the CEO. "Not when I see a threat. It's my job to protect the citizens of the Defederacy. When I see an unstable and seditious element mobilizing against our citizens, I have to take action."

"Then there's the Stationhouse," said Alex.

Graham shook his head. "I know, I know. A hundred thousand recruits, so I'm told. That scares me.

But not as much as all these Number 17s do. I had to make a move. This new law . . . call it containment."

"You must understand what the Number 17s are after, though, don't you?" said Alex.

"Of course I do," said Graham. "To strike some of the sole-discretion clauses out of the Public Safety Act. Everybody knows that. But the Public Safety Act is nonnegotiable, Alex. There'd be a huge public outcry if we tried to water it down. The whole point of the Act is to allow Number 17s to live in peace and harmony with their fellow citizens. I don't know why they can't see that."

"That's not what I was getting at," said Alex. "That's not the only thing they want."

Graham's eyes brightened, as if he thought he were going to get to the *real* goods now.

"So what do they want then?" he asked.

"They've told me that the Martians have a Number 17 rehabilitation technique that's far better than ours. That's what they're really after."

Graham sighed. He seemed disappointed.

"We know this too, Alex. We've picked up scraps of intelligence here and there about the whole thing. My question is this: is it true, or is it just a pack of lies, like half the other stuff the Coverts pick up from the Martians? The Martians are masters of disinformation, Alex. So we have to be careful. This technique of theirs . . . for Number 17s? We've tried to confirm it. But we have no corroborative evidence so far." Graham's left eyebrow rose a fraction. "Are you here as an employee of the government?" he asked. "Should we be paying you for this? Because I don't think we've established that yet. You haven't signed on the dotted line, so to speak. I know what happens,

Alex. I've read report after report on the phenomenon. Operatives start to sympathize with the groups they watch. That's fine, I appreciate that. But if we're going to enter into some sort of formal arrangement, I think we should make that clear."

"You have nothing to corroborate the Number 17 technique then?" asked Alex.

"No."

"Then you must have missed the paper by Ariam Adurra and Revord Liag, the one about the alien enzyme that allows them to download neurological packages into a clone."

Graham's brow settled. "We didn't miss it," he said. "We have it on file. We've known about it for some time. It's just that . . . we think it's a fake. We've had our style analysts compare it to everything Dr. Adurra has written, at least everything we've ever been able to get our hands on, and it doesn't match up, style-wise. We think it might be disinformation."

Alex frowned. "We think it's bona fide," he said.

"*We?*" said Graham. "Jesus, Alex."

"We want to try and get our hands on it."

"*We?*" repeated the CEO, in growing exasperation.

"And the Martians might actually have the beginnings of a Number 16 technique as well. Did the Coverts pick up on any of that?"

"Yes, but it's all too vague to be of any use to us."

"Even so, their Number 17 technique seems to be well established."

"Perhaps," said Graham.

"And we think it's worth a shot."

Graham sighed again, a weightier exhalation this time.

"You've come with that particular demand, then, have you?" said his cousin. "I knew it would come to this. I could see the desperation in your eyes when I pinned those medals to your chest. I knew you were bound to sniff your way to these particular pieces of information sooner or later. So you want to get your hands on these techniques, do you, Alex? How do you think you're going to do that? You would have to talk to the Martians. And what makes you think the Martians want to talk to us?"

"Graham, you want containment. This gives you a perfect opportunity."

"Forgive me, Alex, but I don't see containment, and I don't see opportunity."

"Show the Number 17s that you're actually trying to do something for them and they might back off."

"To do that, I would have to talk to the Martians," he said. "And we're at war with the Martians. So I don't see that as a possibility."

"You can hand the Martians an olive branch."

"Pardon?"

"In the way of a scientific exchange," said Alex. "We give them some of our stuff, and they give us some of theirs. We take the first steps to show them we're in good faith."

Graham paused to consider the idea. He took a long time. He raised his hand to his chin and rubbed it. This was the Graham Alex remembered, always taking time to consider every possibility, not rejecting things outright, not autocratic, but always willing to listen. There was something of the master strategist in Graham's eyes: Graham planning his chess game seven moves ahead. Finally, he nodded, a gesture that was at once speculative and accommodating.

"Say we go ahead with this," he said. "What makes you think the Martians would even want a scientific exchange? And even if they did, how could you be sure they would give us the Number 17 technique? Let's not forget their arrogance. They regard our scientific accomplishments as second-rate. So are you really sure they'd be interested in a scientific exchange, Alex?"

"We have to try, Graham," he said. "The Number 17s are serious. And so are the Stationhouse. Like I say, if you at least *show* the Number 17s you're making an effort on this, they might abandon their plans for the offensive you were telling me about. And a scientific exchange might be a good opening salvo in a new diplomatic campaign. History might remember you as a great peacemaker, Graham. Send an envoy. The planets are still in orbital opposition. From a fuel and logistics standpoint, a mission is a relatively affordable thing right now. Show them you're serious. Start with a unilateral cease-fire. Have the DDF fire only to defend itself. Suspend all offensive maneuvers, then send an envoy to negotiate this scientific exchange. You have to start somewhere, Graham. And a scientific exchange is a traditional goodwill gesture. Not a straight transmit, either, because there's too much opportunity for a double cross that way. We send a scientific crew to Mars with technical downloads, and they send a scientific crew here to Earth with technical downloads. I'll head the Earth crew. I'm willing to go to Mars to insure that this happens. Sending a crew acts as a guarantee that our downloads will be authentic."

"So in other words, you're willing to turn yourself

into a hostage," said Graham, looking nervous about the idea.

"I wouldn't call it that," said Alex. "Try guarantor. I have a high profile. I'm the Defederacy's top exo-technologist. I would expect them to send an equally senior scientist. Someone like Ariam Adurra. In the scientific exchange, we ask for their Number 17 reha-bilitation technique. And we give Mars what we have. We have a lot, Graham, despite what they think to the contrary. More than just glowballs and mind-pool."

Graham rocked on his heels a few times as his face settled. "I have a hard time trusting them," he said.

"What do you stand to lose, Graham?" Alex said. "You say you need time. You say the war's gone badly this time around. The treasury's stretched to the limit. You have insurrection threatening from within, aided and abetted by a hundred thousand Stationhouse Militia from without. If you showed the Number 17s and the Stationhouse that you were ac-tually doing something to help them, maybe even repeal this new Chincoteague law, they might hold off. In fact, I know they would. The Martians might stop any planned offensives, and the Defense Force would get a much-needed rest. What happens after-ward, we'll just have to wait and see. Maybe some-thing good will come of it, maybe not. Maybe we'll go back to fighting each other. But at least you'll give a lot of people hope. What's it going to cost you to send a crew of three to Mars, Graham?"

Graham paused again. To consider. To strategize. To plan his chess game seven moves ahead.

"As long as we get Ariam Adurra in return," he finally said. "That way, if they screw us, we don't get burned."

Two weeks later, Alex ironed out the final details of the mission with the new ISS Chief, Cameron Healy. It was strange to see Healy in Max's old office. The rugs and wall hangings were gone. The teakwood desk had been replaced with a military-issue metal one. The only adornments were the pictures of Healy's wife and his two grown boys, both DDF flight lieutenants.

"We've now learned that Ariam Adurra has had a change of crew," said Healy. "Her civilian pilot and technical officer have been replaced with fully rated combat personnel. I'm afraid we're going to have to do the same. We're going to have to send two goons with you as bodyguards, Dr. Denyer. The DDF is drawing up a list of candidates. They should have it to my office by tomorrow." Healy gave him a questioning look. "Do you have any candidates?"

Alex didn't even have to think about it.

"I want to take two Number 17s," he said. "Reba Norton and Zirko Carty. They're both veterans of the Alien War. Zirko's rated for all spacecraft. You can call up his record and take a look yourself. He's superlative. Reba's had two postings as technical officer, one aboard the *Assault 12*, the other aboard *Rescue 36*. As Number 17s, they can be trained quickly with downloads. I know them. I trust them. They're who I want."

Chapter 24

The three Number 17s checked the outside of *Ambassador 22* as it orbited four hundred miles above the surface of the Moon. Its white hull was bright with reflected sunlight. Alex gave his pack a burst and eased himself next to Zirko, who was inspecting the ejection unit.

"We didn't have separate ejection units on any of the Attacks," said Zirko. "We ejected through the venture bay. And we didn't have any fancy survival pods either." He gestured through the window where three white capsules, each big enough for a single person, some carry-on supplies, and perhaps a few personal items, hung in their clasps. "We ejected on packs alone, and then we had to depend on the Rescues to pick us up in space before we ran out of oxygen. We didn't have the option of a slow glide to a moon or a planet, the way we'll have in these. That just goes to show you: one standard for diplomats, another standard for soldiers. We're expendable."

"So you should be happy about these pods, then,"

said Alex. "If we run into trouble, we can eject in style."

Zirko tapped the window.

"These pods immediately target the nearest radio signals or fuel emissions. So if your location transmitter fails, you drift toward the nearest friendly vessel or ground station. That's an advantage. But it's not going to help us much."

"Why's that?" asked Alex.

Zirko gripped the alien glowball floating by his head and brought it closer to the window so he could get a better look at the pods.

"Because we're big," he said. "Fully twice the weight capacity of these pods. At least I am. You'd think they would have retrofitted these things a bit more for us."

"You've been out here a long time," said Alex.

Zirko grew still. "I was always like this," he said. "I check, and double-check, and triple-check. Some of the pilots I knew . . . they checked things too fast. And they ended up paying with their lives. Not me. It's up to me to make sure this spacecraft runs perfectly. It's old. It's from back in the days when we sent diplomats to Mars on a regular basis. I also can't bring myself to trust your cousin."

"You haven't found anything wrong yet, have you?" said Alex, growing apprehensive about Graham. "Anything the Moon crew should look at?"

"No," said Zirko. "But I still don't trust him."

Just then, Reba radioed from the Command Module at the front of the wheel. Her face appeared in the upper right corner of his visor screen.

"We have a downloaded message from the *Okwe-*

314

cal," she said. The *Okwecal* was Ariam Adurra's ship. "You're the recipient, Alex."

"Let's see it," said Alex, curious.

The Martian scientist's face appeared in his visor screen. She was stupendously blond. Her blue eyes were hard, and possessed an unforgiving intelligence. Ariam had fine lines at the corners of her eyes and lips, as well as across her forehead. The skin under her chin was showing a first bit of looseness.

"Greetings, Dr. Denyer," she said. "I am honored." She spoke with the rounded syllables of a longtime Murray City resident. "I commend you on your initiative. I'm Martian-born, but have always longed to breathe the air of my ancestral world. And now you've given me this opportunity. Let the red and blue worlds come together. Let us try to understand each other. I wish you Godspeed and success, Dr. Denyer, and hope that this is the beginning of a sustained scientific dialogue between us."

He grinned. He thought: *Something good just might come of this after all.*

In the middle of *Ambassador 22*'s transfer orbit to Mars, sunspot activity forced Alex and the others into the radiation bunker for a three-day stretch. They rotated their shutdowns through this period. Two would stay up. The other would recharge. There wasn't much to do. Sometimes he was up with Zirko. Sometimes he was up with Reba. On the second day, when Alex was up with Reba, she reminisced about their time together.

"I keep remembering that night we went to Tuckahoe Park," she said. "We sat on the hillside and watched the outdoor production of *A Midsummer Night's Dream*. This was right at the beginning. It started raining, but the players were protected because they had canvas sheeting up in the trees, and they continued the production despite the rain. You pulled out a plastic tarp and we huddled underneath it." She gestured around the radiation bunker. "That's what this reminds me of. We're huddled inside here. Only look at us now. We're both so . . . different . . . so changed."

She looked up from her sweet, if pensive, rumination and grinned.

"I remember that night," he said.

"And when the play was over we ran up the hill to our bicycles. Do you remember the crab apple trees at the top of the hill? How they were all in bloom, with those bright magenta blossoms? I remember your hair, the way it was all wet, as dark as coal, and that beard you had at the time."

"I remember," he said, but he remembered it as something lost, a vital moment that had slipped away on him.

She picked up on his melancholy. "I'm sorry, Alex," she said. She shook her head. "I ran away from you. I never should have done that. I should have stuck with you. I know I hurt you. But I felt . . . I felt I had to *impress* you. Do something extreme to compete with you." Her grin disappeared. "But when I joined the DDF you weren't impressed, were you?"

He looked away. "I was sad," he admitted.

More cheerily, she said, "Then we got on our bikes and rode through the rain, because that's how we got around in those days. Everybody was riding bikes, even old people. You had to be super rich to afford a car. We rode to the *Beelzebub*. And I remember Jill's shock. It was the first time we met. I guess she thought you were going to remain celibate forever."

"Fat chance," he said, grinning.

Reba looked at the radiation meter. The meter was still into the red.

"I just want you to know . . . I've always regretted running away from you like that. How I made you sad. I sometimes thought getting pinked was my punishment."

"Don't say that."

"You were there whenever I called you," she said. "I mean afterward. After I had turned into this . . . this disaster. You always checked up on me. You were the only one who came to visit me at Greensboro. I'll always be grateful for that, Alex. I'll never forget that."

As they drew closer to Mars, Alex reviewed some of the downloads they would offer Murray City. He was familiar with much of what was there, but wished to review it so he could give Reba and Zirko some background. Both had expressed an interest.

He started first with ectogenesis—growth of the fetus outside the womb—a method developed from alien models, and one now used in agrigenetics to produce livestock in factories without the need for significant rangeland. The animals stayed in growth tanks until fully mature and ready for slaughter. There wasn't any rangeland in the Defederacy, so this had been a great boon. He'd been instrumental in developing this technique. Without the introduction of a special alien coenzyme, one he'd produced with an alien fixer system, the surrogate growth tanks would have rejected the fetal materials right from the start, and there wouldn't have been any meat on anyone's table.

Then he studied the actual alien fixer systems themselves, a loose grouping of instruments that looked like cornucopias. They ingested surrounding natural resources, and refined them into products, like the materials-intake system aboard the large AWP. Many of them produced enzymes of one kind or another. Some produced coenzymes, agents that had a catalytic effect on regular enzymes—coenzymes such as the one he had used in the ectogenesis method to halt growth-tank rejection of livestock fetal materials

That got him thinking. He sat back. Enzymes. Co-enzymes. He recalled Dr. Ely Colgan's words about enzymes, how end-stage Number 16s produced an unclassified enzyme, a telomerase, and how this enzyme-slash-telomerase allowed cells to replicate through more divisions than usual, allowed them to live longer—like the fixer-system telomerase he'd been working on just before Max had fired him, the one he'd written his *Nature* paper on, the paper Graham had fussed so much about. Colgan had tried the telomerase on test tube cells and had seen them replicate longer. When he had tried the same telomerase on lab rats, the rats had rejected the telomerase, and had subsequently died. As Dr. Colgan had explained, for a living organism to take the telomerase, a new kind of catalyst would be needed, something to get the telomerase beyond the rejection process. Alex's eyes widened. He looked first at the fixer systems, then at the ectogenesis coenzyme, the one that had stopped growth-tank rejection of fetal materials in livestock production, then thought of Dr. Colgan's words, a new kind of catalyst. He realized that if his ectogenesis coenzyme could halt rejection during livestock production, it, or something like it, might halt rejection during the introduction of the Number 16 telomerase into a foreign organism like a rat, that it in fact might be the kind of catalyst Dr. Colgan had been talking about. In other words, with something like his ectogenesis coenzyme, the Number 16 telomerase might be safely introduced into a living organism and actually work to extend cell replication and, therefore, life. His shoulders stiffened. How could he have been so blind? Why hadn't he put the two different tracks of research together before this?

"Your face just warmed up," said Reba, who was doing some work at her own station beside him.

"I think I've just stumbled onto something here," he said. "It could be nothing. I've got to take a closer look at it."

He called up all the data on his screen. He started with the Number 16 telomerase, the one produced in the adrenal and pituitary glands of Number 16 victims. With that installed, he started scratching around for a coenzyme that might make it work in a living organism to extend cell replication without getting rejected. He checked his pulse rate. His pulse was way up. He thought of his son's phrase, the Holy Grail. This was different. This more closely mirrored Ponce de Leon's quest for the Fountain of Youth.

He quickly checked through the whole Defederacy

list of fixer systems. He saw several that he'd never worked on before, ones that, coincidentally enough, had been licensed to Concord Exotechnologies. That made him suspicious. Graham had been so touchy about Concord. And then also so touchy about that paper he'd written for *Nature*, the one about his own primary and independent telomerase. Alex's suspicion turned into anxiety. He wasn't politically innocent anymore. He felt more like a battered survivor. And he could feel his survival instincts gearing up. He began to see the outlines of a plot. Why would Graham keep all these Concord fixer systems away from him? At least Graham was nowhere around to stop him now.

Alex installed the Concord fixer systems onto his computer, used them to model several coenzymes, and finally found one that was already listed, coenzyme P57, a catalyst that easily greased the wheels of the Number 16 telomerase, and all but halted any host-versus-graft complication in his human model. In this context, Colgan's rats would live. Live and grow old. Very old.

Alex was stunned. What he had here was an alien-derived longevity potion, one that could work in a cross-species setting. It all came together now. What the aliens had been doing in that awful room in the big AWP. Turning humans into Number 16s, then harvesting that pink goop from them in the big cistern, what came up as a telomerase on his handheld. All the ghastly pieces of the puzzle seemed to connect into a gruesome whole: Graham sending Servitech to the EMZ and not drawing blood, no, not at all, but in fact harvesting the same telomerase, knowing it could be used in a cross-species setting, wanting this Fountain-of-Youth Holy Grail for his own purposes. Was this all a big scheme on Graham's part? To carry on from where the aliens had left off? To hijack the Number 16 telomerase and the P57 coenzyme for his own use, something that would perhaps make him a lot of money and ultimately give him a lot more power? With the Number 16 telomerase extending telomere cuff-life, and coenzyme P57 halting rejection, a human being could conceivably live for a thousand years. And that not only meant everlasting life to Graham. It meant everlasting power.

Like Graham, he now saw conspiracies everywhere. What he couldn't understand was this: if Graham wanted to keep all this hidden, why would he offer it up for trade? Then he remembered the trade agreement, how each side got to verify a rough estimate of the value of each trade based a complex blind assessment system the bargaining teams had put in place. Graham may have been forced to include the telomerase and P57 downloads so the blind assessment system would weigh the overall trade equally. If that were the case, no wonder this stuff was here. But why mount a mission at all if Graham wanted to hide this information? It made him nervous. It made him wonder if in the end *Ambassador 22* was rigged with weapons, and whether they were in fact riding to Mars as a kind of latter-day Trojan Horse.

He glanced at Reba.

"I think we have a problem," he said.

She looked up from her workstation. "What's up?" she said.

"Zirko?" he called. "Could you come over here?"

321

Zirko got out of his chair and came over.

"Look at this model," said Alex, pointing.

Alex explained to Reba and Zirko about the Number 16 telomerase and the P57 coenzyme; how, when the two were used together in his human model, they increased life span considerably. The two Number 17s were astonished. Alex explained to them how Graham had been so nervous about his job application to Concord Exotechnologies and about his paper in *Nature*, then told them about Servitech's activities in the EMZ. All the while, he refined his figures and formulas on his computer. He told his crewmates about the horrifying chamber he and Ruth had found aboard the AWP, with all the human remains, and how it now seemed clear that the Aliens had been harvesting the telomerase for their own life-extending purposes.

"They didn't want to infect their own population, because look at the horrible side effects," he said. "So they came here and infected ours. They intended to harvest the telomerase before the AWP got damaged. P57 is a cross-species and cross-donor catalyst, so the aliens could easily use a human-derived telomerase without fear of fatal complications. My guess is that they found the ideal culturing conditions in the human pituitary and adrenal glands. Graham discovered this, and now he's up to the same thing. That's why I think we're in trouble." He motioned to the screen. "Graham was obviously trying to hide this from everybody."

"So if he was trying to hide it," said Reba, "why is he letting us to see it now?"

"Because the exchange agreement allows the FMC and the Defederacy to look at blind assessment values for each trade. I'm assuming Graham had to put this stuff in here so the trade would weigh out equally. I reviewed a lot of the trades prelaunch, but I never got to this stuff. Now I think I might be too late. My real fear is that he has no intention of giving his life-extending formula to the Martians, and that we've been duped into some sort of military mission."

"Alex, are your defense systems running?" asked Reba.

He checked. "Yes, they are."

"Maybe you're just being paranoid," she said.

Zirko shook his head. "Our defense systems kick in for a reason, Reba."

Alex filled in more of the pieces.

"I can't help thinking that when Graham blacklisted me at Concord, he blacklisted me because he thought I might put two and two together if I ended up working there," he said. "And my termination at the Alien Branch might have been for the same reason. Graham got jumpy because he thought I might stumble across his plans." Alex looked at his computer model again as new figures came up. "And look at this. This is why Graham wants to keep the whole thing secret. He would need a vast population of Number 16s to give extended life to even a small number of recipients. That means a handful of lucky immortals would be riding on the backs of all those poor Number 16s in the EMZs."

Zirko shook his head. "No wonder your cousin never aggressively pursued Number 16 research."

Alex felt angry. "I know. Which means my son never stood a chance."

Reba spoke up. "Don't you think we're getting

323

Scott Mackay

ahead of ourselves here?" she asked. "Isn't it possible you stumbled across this connection yourself, Alex, and that Graham knows nothing about it?"

"I don't think so. Not when you consider how jumpy he was about Concord and my paper in *Nature*. Not when you consider Servitech's activities in the EMZs. There's just too much evidence to the contrary, Reba. It's monstrous, when you think of it. If this is what he's truly up to, then it follows he's doing everything in his power to keep the Number 16s in the EMZs the way they are so he can build up reserves of this telomerase. Take that a step further, and you have to question his motive for this mission. One of our objectives is to obtain whatever treatment we can for the Number 16s. But if Graham wants to keep the Number 16s as they are, what possible reason could he have for mounting this mission?"

Reba's face tightened. "I see what you mean."

"Maybe he plans to use *Ambassador 22* against Martian home soil in some way," said Alex.

"How could he do that?" asked Zirko. "We've checked the ship a dozen times. There's no evidence of sabotage anywhere. There aren't any weapons systems on board, nor are there any hidden explosives. He can't use *Ambassador 22* against Martian soil. It's just not possible."

Zirko was right. The ship was clean. They'd checked it again and again. He shouldn't feel so jumpy. Maybe Graham knew nothing about this after all. Maybe it *was* his own big discovery. His systems, as usual, were overreacting. He had to stand down. Maybe even up his tranqs. He took a deep breath.

324

No, he had nothing to worry about, but there was no harm in exercising caution.

"Maybe we should give the ship a final good check," he said. "Just to be on the safe side."

"I see no harm in that," said Zirko.

Alex manipulated the small mousecam through *Ambassador 22*'s ventilation system from his workstation using a joystick. The view on his monitor was monotonous, a round tube of flexisteel looking overexposed in the mousecam's guidelight. Nearly fifty yards of ventilation so far, and he'd found nothing that looked even remotely threatening, no pats of plastic explosives, no unaccounted-for relays or wiring to the navigational system, not even any suspicious tool markings. Reba sat at her own workstation beside him, going through every single line of software.

"Anything?" he asked.

She shook her head. "Nothing," she said. "It's clean."

He looked up at the exterior-camera monitor. Zirko walked along the top of the hull outside, his feet, in magnetically charged boots, sticking firmly. Alex pushed his headset microphone to the front of his mouth.

"Zirko, have you found anything?" he asked.

"I've searched every square inch of this ship twice now," said Zirko. "I haven't found a thing."

Alex sighed. "You might as well come in, then," he said. "We've found nothing in here either."

"We'll just have to be ready for every eventuality," said Zirko.

"Agreed. There's nothing else we can do."

*   *   *

They got a good sighting of Mars one week later. For the past five days the planet had been shrouded in a global dust storm, but now the dust had settled. Mars was a disk about the size of a cantaloupe, and roughly the same color. At this distance Alex saw some of its more prominent features: *Hellas Planitia, Terra Sirenum,* and both polar caps, like smudges of icing sugar at either end of a giant chocolate truffle.

Zirko immediately checked his instruments for any incoming ordnance—the big Number 17 trusted the Martians about as much as he trusted Graham. Then he sent a hail to Syria Planum Ground Control, a hundred miles southwest of Murray City, informing them that he would be commencing aerobraking maneuvers in thirty-two minutes. He got no response.

Zirko glanced at Reba. "What's wrong?" he asked. "Why aren't they responding?"

She double-checked the communications array. "I don't know," she said. "It's been working fine up until this point."

She ran a diagnostic check on the communications system, but didn't immediately see anything wrong with it. Alex felt his shoulders sink. In a perfect trip, the funny business was starting just now, and he didn't want to believe that his cousin could actually do such a thing. Reba finished with her diagnostic check and turned to Zirko. Maybe their ship was going to be a Trojan Horse after all.

"Try again," she said.

"Syria Ground Control," said Zirko, "this is *Ambassador 22*, requesting permission to commence aerobraking maneuvers in T minus 31:17. Please respond. Over."

OMNIFIX

Again they got no response. Alex felt his pulse rate rise. He didn't want to believe this. He still hoped it just might be a glitch. He watched Reba as she dug deeper into the communications software. Machine language crawled across Reba's screen like a column of army ants.

"I've never seen this code before," she said. "It's temporarily disabling our communications system."

"How did it get there?" asked Zirko. "We've checked all these systems repeatedly."

"From a remote command," she said.

"A remote command from where?" asked Zirko.

She entered some queries into the computer.

"From *Relay 17*," she said.

"It's Graham," said Alex. "I knew this mission had to be too good to be true."

"Damn your cousin," said Zirko.

"Let's run a complete systems check to see if we can isolate the problem," said Reba.

But Alex suspected it wouldn't do any good.

To his great dismay, he saw that not only were the communication systems down, but the survival pods and ejection units were now off-line as well. Graham was thorough. Graham was ruthless. Graham had a no-survivors policy when it came to things like this.

"And look at the images in our rear external camera," said Zirko.

Alex looked at the images. At first he didn't see it. But after a while, he discerned a pattern of eclipse. It took him a few moments to figure it out. Stars in that sector blinked out, then blinked back on.

"Something's following us," said Zirko, "and it's blocking out the light of those stars as it gets in front of them."

Alex glanced up at the tracking array.

"Our tracking systems aren't showing anything," he said.

Zirko keyed in a query of his own.

"That's because it's a stealth drone," said Zirko. "We can't track it unless we have proper authorization codes. You were right, Alex. I think your cousin's planning a military action against Mars. And I think he's using our ship as a decoy."

Chapter 25

Zirko, as pilot, took over.

"Our options are limited," he said, as the big rust-colored ball of Mars drew closer and closer. "We have a combat stealth drone following us. We have no way of warning the Martians that we now might pose a threat. If Reba can't establish contact with Syria Control within the next few minutes, we're going to have to do something drastic to warn the Martians. Maybe initiate a forward burn to take us into a higher orbit, something that's not on the mission itinerary, and something that will make them sit up and take notice."

Just then, Reba managed to reboot part of the communications array. "We've got incoming audio, but we can't send," she said. Then a voice came over the radio. "Good God, Zirko, it's you!"

What Alex heard further confirmed the intricacy of his cousin's careful plan. Zirko, or at least a simulation of Zirko, spoke calmly to Ground Control, advising them of how many more minutes it would be before he began the aerobraking procedures, requesting last-minute rendezvous coordinates with the Phobos-Deimos Embarkation Platform. Syria responded with calm professionalism, giving the faked Zirko the information he needed, as if nothing were amiss.

"Your cousin's synthesized my voice to fool the Martian recognition systems," said Zirko.

They waited another few minutes while Reba desperately tried to regain control of the primary communications system. Alex felt as if he should be doing something. But all he could do was sit and watch. Mars was now huge outside the window. A sick feeling settled in Alex's stomach. Part of him felt like smashing the wall with his fist, he was so angry with his cousin. Reba's fingers typed. She paused, gazed at the screen, typed again, then finally let her hands sink to her sides.

"It's no go," she told them. "*Relay 17* has overridden me. You're going to have to go ahead with your course change, Zirko. It's the only way we're going to warn them."

Zirko nodded.

But as he initiated a firing sequence that would bring them into a higher orbit—a course change that might alert Martian authorities that the mission had in fact been hijacked—the ship shuddered, and Alex heard a loud clank through the hull. Everyone tensed. Zirko checked the forward exterior cameras.

"Look," he said. "The drone's piggybacked on top of us. Look at the fuel tanks on that thing. It's got enough burn potential to outpower us no matter what course change we try."

Alex looked at the screen. The drone looked powerful, unstoppable. What were they going to do now? They all watched the screen expectantly, waiting to see what the drone would do. Reba's shoulders rose as she gripped the edge of the console. The screen filled with light as the drone initiated a major retro burn. They all jerked forward in the sudden G-force. *Ambassador 22* slowed down, and its orbit decayed quickly. Alex looked up at the monitor and checked the new rate of descent. It was increasing exponentially. They were falling quickly toward Mars. Someone from Syria Planum hailed them.

"*Ambassador 22*, this is Ground Control, do you copy?"

Reba again tried to break Graham's communications disruption, but she couldn't.

Zirko spoke into the com-link. "Mayday, Mayday, we have a situation aboard *Ambassador 22*."

But it was all to no avail. The synthesized voice of Zirko broke through.

"Copy that," it said. "Go ahead, Ground Control."

"We detect an unaccounted-for heat signature coming from your spacecraft," said Syria Planum. "Could you verify that, please?"

The Number 17s stared at the console as the synthesized Zirko responded.

"We're venting our carbon dioxide scrubbers, and initiating a minor burn to compensate for the resultant thrust."

"Copy that, *Ambassador 22*."

Zirko clicked on a different camera angle and got a view of the drone's warhead.

"That's not a micro," he said. "That's a mega. Your cousin's been planning a major strategic attack against Mars all this time, and staged this whole mission simply as a way to evade planetary defenses."

331

"We have to break free," said Alex. "We can't let that thing strike Mars."

"We haven't got the fuel reserves to break free," said Zirko. "We've got enough fuel for a few positional burns, and that's it. We were going to refuel on Mars. That drone is tanked up. It probably joined us fully fueled from *Station 9*, or another halfway point."

As the Martian gravity well caught *Ambassador 22*, velocity increased. The drone commenced a lateral burn. The G-force threw the three Number 17s hard against their seat constraints. The spacecraft dipped into the upper reaches of the planet's thin carbon dioxide atmosphere. The noise level increased as friction ensued. Out the window, Alex saw pinkish clouds streaking the sky below. He felt his fight-and-flight systems engage, wanted to run, but was trapped in the cramped confines of the spacecraft.

Zirko studied the navigation screen. "Just as I thought," he said. "Croft's targeted Murray City. Five million people live there. They're going to be dead in fifteen minutes if we don't do something."

"How can we do *anything* when we don't have any fuel left?" asked Alex.

Zirko grew still. Maybe the big Number 17 drifted into X-space as he tried to come up with a solution. But when he finally came back, his expression was calm. He ran a model on the computer, so quickly, and with such unerring calculation, Alex didn't have a chance to catch it, only knew that hope had once again returned to the cockpit.

"We're going to vent all our oxygen," said Zirko. "We're going to vent all our carbon dioxide as well. We're going to vent our waste, our water, everything we have. According to this model, if we vent at 5.7 miles above the surface, the thrust will bring us down here." He tapped the screen. "In the *Tempe Terra* region five hundred miles north of Murray City. But first we have to find a way to hack into the drone's rendezvous links. We have to trap it. We've got to make sure it doesn't get away from us when we vent. We have to drag it down with us. Is there any way we can do that, Reba?"

She typed furious commands into the ship-to-ship rendezvous system. After thirty seconds she had it.

"There," she said. "That thing's not going anywhere. She's locked on." She turned around. "So how long do we have?"

Zirko checked the screen again. "At our current rate of descent, just over eight minutes."

"Is there anything we should be doing?" she asked.

"Let's get our suits on," said Zirko. "We'll eject in the survival pods."

"But the survival pods and ejection units are offline," said Alex.

"There's nothing to stop us from ejecting in the pods manually," said Zirko. "The air lock down there is still on-line. If we can force the pods out of their braces, we should be okay."

Maneuvering their way through the wheel to the drive and utility modules proved difficult. The weak tug of Martian gravity exerted its force, creating an up and down, but not an up and down oriented to the ceiling and the floor. So getting through the wheel was like traversing the inner rim of a Ferris wheel. Alex knew they were scrambling for their lives. The strength and agility of their cybernetic limbs aided them greatly, and they made it to the drive and utility modules in just under a minute.

Suiting up took them two minutes, even when they rushed crazily through the procedure, and that left them with just under five before they had to vent. They hurried to the survival pods and ejection units. Reba ran a diagnostic check on the air lock, her hand shaking as she keyed in the appropriate command.

"You're right, Zirko," she said, "it's still online. But these release mechanisms aren't working."

"We're going to have to break the braces," he said. "Stand aside."

Alex and Reba moved away. Zirko approached the first brace. Two metal arms extended from the wall, locking the first pod in place. Zirko gripped the clasping mechanism and pulled. Alex heard some creaking, but the clasp failed to give.

"You pull on one side and I'll pull on the other," Zirko told Alex.

With the two of them pulling, the clasp gave an inch or two. When Reba joined in, the thing finally snapped, and they opened the arms of the brace.

"Let's slide the pod to the air lock," said Zirko.

"We have two minutes left before we vent!" said Reba, her voice thick with desperation. "It took us nearly three minutes to pry this pod free. We're not going to make it!"

"You two get in this pod," said Zirko. "Leave your power packs behind. It looks like they're not going to fit. You've got your minipacks, and those will last thirty-five hours. That should give Martian rescuers plenty of time to find you." He spoke quickly, firmly, like a man used to command. "Set the navigation system away from Murray City so missile defenses won't scramble to intercept you. Get to the ground as quick as you can. The pod's going to deploy its wings. It should land you on the surface. But it's going be a rough ride. This thing's not meant to take so much weight. And be prepared for a hard landing."

"What about you?" asked Reba, her voice frantic.

"Once I get you two under way, I'll yank another pod free for myself. Then I'll vent the oxygen and water, and everything else."

"You'll never pull a pod free without us," she said.

"I'm going to rip down that ceiling support and use it as a lever," he said.

"Zirko, you've got less than two minutes left!" she said.

"Just *go*! Get in!"

Zirko pressed a button and the pod's door lifted. Alex got in. And Reba, after giving Zirko a final tearful kiss, got in after him.

Alex and Reba squeezed as close together as they could. Zirko closed the hatch. He pushed them down the rail into the air lock. Alex acted purely as a soldier now, not thinking, not analyzing, just doing. Apparatus in the air lock unhooked them. Out the pod's small window, Alex saw the air lock gauge cycle to zero millibars. Then the rushing sound of the atmosphere around their spacecraft got louder as the air lock's drop-tube opened. The release catch rotated, the white lozenge-shaped survival pod slipped down the drop-tube, and in less than a second they were free of *Ambassador 22*, falling toward Mars.

Alex engaged the navigational systems and exterior vidcams. There was barely room to move.

"He's not going make it!" cried Reba.

"Look!" he said, pointing at one of four small screens.

A squadron of Martian fighters scrambled up from below. A weapons system aboard the drone fired at the fighters, and one of them exploded into fragments.

The pod's navigational systems took over. The pod pulled out of its nosedive as small retractable wings deployed from recesses on either side of its fuselage. Reba, struggling to bring her hand forward in the cramped space, selected the scan command on the anterior vidcam. A view of *Ambassador 22* appeared on the screens. It was far away now, streaking through the salmon-colored sky, leaving a vapor trail behind.

"He's going to vent any second," she said.

Zirko vented a few moments later. A small white explosion enveloped *Ambassador 22*, and a vapor trail slowly described an arc through the atmosphere as the spacecraft veered north. The drone tried to make a correction with an angled thrust, but the power of the blast had been too strong. The anterior vidcam followed 22's trajectory, but didn't have the latitude of movement to record its continuing descent, and in a moment, 22 was lost from view.

Reba sagged.

"He didn't make it," she said.

"We don't know that," said Alex, doing his best to reassure her. "He's still got several minutes before impact. He might pull a pod free. Then all we'll have to do is regroup and surrender to whatever Martians we can find."

But even as he spoke, a warning light flashed on

the pod's control console. The following words appeared on the monitor: LOAD CAPACITY EXCEEDED. RECOMMENDED: 200 LB LOAD REDUCTION.

Of course there was nothing they could do about that. Through the undercarriage vidcam he saw the bleak red surface of Mars grow closer and closer, the terrain far too rugged for his liking, guaranteeing anything but a soft landing, the speed of descent far too fast. He felt himself tensing as anxiety thrummed through his body. A bell from the console dinged gently.

"The parachutes are going to open," said Reba, her voice rough.

He braced himself. The wing flaps eased down and the pod pulled into a rapid vertical ascent. The wings and tailfin retracted. Alex looked through the small window and watched the parachutes blossom, three of them, as red as rubies. The pod dropped. The console warned them that the tolerances of the pod's construction wouldn't withstand impact at their current rate of descent. He steeled himself for a crash landing.

They traveled north by northwest over the rugged terrain. He felt frantic, trapped, and powerless. The sun, low on the western horizon, brightened the landscape below with a muted, rusty light. With a shaking hand, Alex keyed in mapping commands on their navigational system to find out where they were.

"*Xanthe Terra*," he said. "Near the northern terminus of the *Valles Marineris*. That's three hundred miles from any settlement. It's rough terrain up here. A lot of craters. A lot of hills and ridges."

Mars got closer and closer. Breathe in, breathe out.

Alex saw a large crater next to a deep trench. They might land in that crater, or they might land in the trench. A topography reading told him the trench was over a kilometer deep. His teeth clenched involuntarily. He hoped they would land in the crater. If they fell into that trench, they would never get out, and it was unlikely rescuers would ever find them. They drifted westward, ever closer to the crater. Rocks and boulders were now visible, collared by stretching dark shadows.

"Alex, I'm scared," said Reba.

Carbon dioxide frost caught the light of the setting sun and sparkled like diamonds in the ocher dust.

"Here we go," he said.

They drifted over the eastern rim of the crater. The ground came up fast. Alex saw an abandoned mining road in the crater, one that petered out in a large pile of rocks to the north. As they angled down, the pod turned, and Alex got a view of the inside slope of the crater's western rim. It looked as if they were going to slam right into it. All his cybernetic muscular systems tensed up as his Remnant went wild with apprehension. The inside slope of the western rim came up faster and faster. He was sure they were going to hit it, like running into a brick wall, and that they would be killed. But then they cleared it by ten yards. Relief swept over him. But now they were heading straight for the trench. If they fell into that trench, that was it, they were goners.

As luck would have it, they descended onto the outside slope of the crater's western rim before they reached the trench. This couldn't have been more fortuitous. His heart leapt with giddy joy. Because of the angle of descent, they were eased down onto the

slope. They slid down the slope like a sled down a
snowy hill, the ground creating a natural drag to
decelerate them. He thought they were going to be
okay, that they would simply slide to a standstill at
the foot of the mile-long western slope, stopping before they fell off into the trench. But then their pod
hit a boulder and they catapulted into the air.

They rolled end over end twelve times before the
pod finally hit another boulder and broke apart with
a pressurized oxygen explosion. The blast threw Alex
clear of the pod.

"Reba?" he said, through his com-link.

"I'm here," she said.

But he couldn't see her through all the dust the
pod had kicked up.

He finally rolled to a stop, bruised, dented, but not
badly injured. He frantically scrambled to his feet
and immediately checked the integrity of his pressure
suit. His suit was fine. At least they hadn't fallen into
the trench. He scanned the outside slope of the crater.
The dust cloud created by their crash stretched westward in a thirty-mile-per-hour carbon dioxide wind,
smearing like watercolor brushstrokes. And through
this smear of windborne dirt a figure emerged: Reba.

"Are you all right?" he asked.

"I'm trying to raise Zirko," she said. "I'm not getting a response."

"They disabled the *Ambassador*'s communications
system. Remember? We'll have to wait until he acti-
vates his suit's com-link once he lands his pod."

She looked up at the sky. She pointed. "There he
is," she said.

A long vapor trail, bright and luminous in the setting sun, scarred the custard-colored sky. A few Mar-

tian fighters, cumbersome-looking things with the enormous wingspans needed for proper lift in the thin atmosphere, followed the *Ambassador*, but otherwise held their fire, now that it wasn't heading anywhere near Murray City.

"Let's climb to the top," said Reba.

The two Number 17s struggled to the top of the crater. They got a panoramic view of the Martian landscape: the sea of craters that was *Xanthe Terra* stretched before them, a land striated with slope after slope—forbidding, daunting, exhausting terrain. They watched *Ambassador 22* dip far to the northeast. As it plummeted farther and farther, a tendril of gas wisped away from its underbelly, and formed a thin vapor trail of its own.

"Was that a pod?" asked Reba.

Alex clicked his military applications eye into telescopic mode, but even then he couldn't tell. "I don't know," he said. "I think it might be."

By this time the sun was directly at their backs, and much of the tumultuous terrain in front of them was in shadow. The thin vapor trail disappeared as it plunged into this shadow.

"I'm putting a lock on it," said Reba. It took her a moment to run her suit's navigating system. "That would be seventeen north, and thirty-five west."

Alex checked his own system. "That's where I put it," he said.

"We have to go there."

"It's a long way, Reba."

"I don't care," she said. "We have to find him."

"I'm sure he'll be picked up by rescuers before we get the chance," said Alex, trying to reassure her. "Likewise, I'm sure we'll be picked up as well."

"But we should at least try to find him ourselves," she pleaded. "What if he's hurt?"

"If we look for him ourselves, I think we jeopardize our own chances as well as his. There are only two of us, Reba. We can leverage our efforts if we find some Martians. We can get whole search crews looking for him. I think he stands a much better chance if we have find someone who can help us. So do we."

She considered his words. He understood her instinct. She loved Zirko. She felt a panicked need to find him as soon as possible. But finally she nodded.

"Okay," she said. "Maybe you're right." Then she pointed to *Ambassador 22.* "It's going to crash!"

They both watched. The spacecraft dipped into the deepening shadows of the coming Martian night. A moment later, a brilliant flash, like a piece of sunshine exploding behind the dip of the Martian horizon, lit the eastern sky. Alex looked for the telltale mushroom cloud, but the explosion happened well below the horizon, and all he saw was the flash, then bright blankets of light coating the sky like a spilled can of white paint. Pinkish clouds formed at the extremities of the explosion. Alex glanced at Reba, saw the explosion on the polarized plating of her visor. She was still. She stared. He knew what she must be feeling. She balanced between hope and despair. The explosion dimmed as it stretched fingers of muddy brown light around the northern and southern horizons.

"Whatever happens," he said, "he saved a lot of lives."

She was still a moment more. "They'll find him," she said. "And they'll find him alive."

341

The shadows grew darker in the crater as the light of the multimegaton blast dimmed further. Alex couldn't help feeling bitter. Zirko. More machine than human. But in the end, capable of great human sacrifice. And what was Graham's response to that? First to lock him away for possible execution in a Chincoteague Bay concentration camp, then to send him on suicide mission to Mars.

Chapter 26

Alex and Reba walked back to the survival pod. The hatch hung by a single hinge. One of the pod's retractable wings had been forced out of its recess and rose from the fuselage like the bent dorsal fin of a killer whale. The fuselage itself looked like a crushed cigar, compacted at both ends from the tumble, scratched and dented, and covered with dust. Alex gripped the hatch and pulled. He righted the tiny craft. He looked inside.

"A few water and nutrient packs are still intact," he said.

He took them out. He and Reba equipped themselves with one of each, snapping them into the appropriate braces on their suits.

"Is the location transmitter all right?" asked Reba.

The rectangular location transmitter had popped out of the main console and now lay wedged behind a support brace. Using his great cybernetic strength Alex bent the brace away and saw that the impact had squashed the location transmitter through the middle.

"It doesn't look good," he said.

"Because the ones in our suits are only good for a ten-mile radius," said Reba, "and we're hundreds of miles away from anywhere."

"Let me try it," he said.

He retracted the small antenna from the unit with some difficulty, but when he went to turn the unit on, its global positioning system failed to locate any of the planet's orbiting satellites for triangulation purposes. If it couldn't locate any Martian satellites, it had no way of pinpointing its own location, and so was of no value as a rescue aid.

"It's not working," he said. "It's too badly damaged."

"What about the backup in the console?" asked Reba.

"Look at the console," he said. "It's a write-off."

He tried booting up the console anyway, but all its instruments were dead.

"Both console and portable units are gone then?" she said.

"Yes."

"So no one can find us electronically?"

"No. They'll have to mount a search."

"We're going to be treated like enemy soldiers when they find us," said Reba. "It's not going to be pleasant."

"Not if we can convince them we had nothing to do with it."

"And how are we going to do that?"

"They just have to plug into our memory," he said, tapping his head. "We deactivate our firewalls for them. They can access whatever they want. If we were fully human it might be a different story. But if we submit to a retrieval process, they'll have to take our word for it—we didn't have anything to do with Graham's plan. Machines can't lie."

She shrugged. "I guess so. But what are we going to do now?"

"I think we should head south," he said. "That's where all the roads and settlements are. Our first task should be to find someone who can help us. Then we tell them about Zirko. They can mount a search for him."

She looked away. She seemed heartsick at the thought of losing Zirko.

They gathered up some supplies: a couple of handhelds, a half dozen flares, a collapsible shovel, a collapsible pickaxe, and a balloon-mounted vidcam. They marched.

Adaptation to the .38-G gravity was quick. Alex's tactile and balance sensors gathered data and fed it through his cybernetic processors. He felt dizzy but found he could march through the terrain with ample coordination once he got going. His four-hundred-pound weight on Earth was now the equivalent of one hundred and fifty pounds on Mars. This, combined with strength that was now five times greater, gave him the ability to bound huge distances in a single stride. Cardiovascular output and fatigue were immaterial. His legs were assisted by their own motors. In essence, he rode on his legs without the need to oxygenate his blood beyond its normal resting rate.

He and Reba bounded up and over the rim of the crater and down the other side. The crater plunged nearly a mile deep, but they covered this distance in less than three minutes. At the bottom they traversed the crater floor with fifteen-foot strides, as quick as springboks on the savannah, and soon came to the road they had seen during their pod descent. Alex spied some abandoned robotic mining equipment in a shallow pit, all of it covered with an inch of red dust. An old vehicle was half-buried in the dirt. The latticework of a crane rose into the sky. Clouds were now bloodred in the last light of the sun, haunting, strange, and forlorn-looking.

When Alex and Reba were about fifty yards past the abandoned robotic mining equipment, Alex discerned sudden movement from the corner of his eye and stopped. Reba stopped too.

"What's wrong?" she asked.

He scanned the work pit more closely.

"I saw something move in that pile of junk," he said, pointing to the mining equipment.

She looked. "Are you sure?" she asked.

He stared for a long time. He reversed the optic bites from the last thirty seconds of his visual recording and reviewed them. He saw it again. Like the bottom of a glass jug rising above the junk, catching a bit of red light from the sky, then sinking back down behind a pile of bent and demolished mine-shaft supports.

"Yes," he said.

She paused. "Alex . . . I'm running a scan." She paused again. "There's nothing over there. I'm detecting no heat. No expended energy. No disturbed dust. Nothing."

"I've got it recorded," he countered.

"Let's see?"

He downloaded the visual bite from his optic systems and sent it to Reba via her com-link. She watched the bite.

When she was done, she said, "That looks more like an optic anomaly to me. Some of your stored visual images are inadvertently being opened and superimposed on your current visual surroundings. How many months have you been on Omnifix?"

"It will be six months next week."

She nodded. "I had the same thing happen to me at roughly the same time." She looked around the spooky terrain as the Martian night crept around them like a slow black deluge. "Gosh, it's a bad time to start seeing things. This place gives me the creeps."

"Do you think I'm seeing things?" he asked.

"It takes a long time to work out all the visual bugs."

He glanced at the pile of mining junk. He ran his own scan. Nothing. Maybe she was right. There was no one around for hundreds of miles. They were alone. Soon their last power pack charges would run out. They would have to rely on the thirty-five-hour minipack charges. The Martians had some reserve power packs waiting for them at Syria Planum. But how far was Syria Planum? They had to find some Martians to surrender to, convince them that they had had nothing to do with Graham's Trojan Horse plan, then hope that they got them to some power packs fast. He thought of the bottle thing poking its head above the junk. No, it wasn't a good time to start seeing things.

"I think maybe we should clock how much time we have left," he said.

"Good idea," she said.

He installed a small readout on his visor screen: thirty-seven hours and twelve minutes remaining.

"You've been a Number 17 a lot longer than I have," he said. "How fast do you think we can move over this terrain?"

"It's going to average out to twenty miles per hour."

"And we're hundreds of miles from the nearest settlement or road."

"Yes."

He sighed, knowing the pressure was on. "We better get going then."

It got dark out, the impenetrable darkness of a Martian night, as thick as an ocean of ink. He checked the environmental readout on his visor screen as he bounded over the ankle-jeopardizing rocks. The temperature had dropped from minus 100 Celsius to minus 150 Celsius in the last hour. His night vision was engaged, and everything glowed a ghostly green. The novelty of his first visit to Mars was wearing off. He was getting used to it. Under different circumstances he might have enjoyed it. But with his clock readout ticking down the hours, he couldn't help feeling tense.

The land rolled. Rocks littered the ground everywhere, rocks of all sizes, shapes, and descriptions—flat ones, round ones, jagged ones—all of them looking like green globs in his night-vision scope. And to run through them like this was like running through an obstacle course. Yet he placed his feet unerringly in the best possible spots. He missed all the rocks, and in fact sometimes used the bigger, flatter rocks as springboards, his motor-sensor and visual inputs sending data to his microprocessors, his microprocessors calculating the exact moves he needed. If he were fully human and not half machine, he would have called it instinct. As it was, he wasn't entirely conscious of what he was doing, felt more like a passenger as his cybernetic body loped speedily across the Martian plains.

At ten o'clock, Reba suggested they take a rest.

"We've had a long day," she said. "Our biological tissues are fatigued. And the minipacks will conserve energy expenditures better if we have a small shutdown. We'll stretch them further if we have a rest."

He looked around. He had the unnerving feeling that something was still out there, that glass jug thing. He tried to shake it. Just a visual anomaly, as Reba said.

"This is as good as place as any," he said.

They built a low semicircular rock wall and huddled behind it. Not that it made any difference. Their suits were protection enough. But some primal instinct demanded this need for shelter. To his great surprise, Reba snuggled right up next to him.

"Do you mind?" she asked.

"No."

"I need comfort."

They initiated shutdown. Reba blinked out in seconds, a small blue light flashing dimly on her shoulder. Alex noticed this about himself: he sometimes took a while. Dr. Slater said it was nothing to worry about, that everybody's shutdown patterns were different, and that it sometimes helped to pace. So he got up. And that's when he saw movement again. Over the top of the next rise. He stood up and stared.

He keyed in his supersensitive hearing. Though the atmosphere was unbelievably thin, sound still utilized it as a medium, and he heard some definite scuffling, some rocks rolling around on the other side of the rise. He stepped over the crude stone barrier and strode to the top of the rise, his code-yellow combat systems clicking into readiness.

He was surprised by what he saw on the other side of the rise. A house. And not just any house but his father's house in Pennsylvania, the old family home, a long, low ranch-style with a geodesic solarium added to the south end, photovoltaic cells shingling the roof, two power-generating windmills high on either peak, and their old Chrysler Windswept hovercar in the drive. His heart beat faster. What was the old family home doing on Mars? He tried to come up with a logical explanation but he couldn't. Then he had a thought. Maybe the Martians had somehow gained intelligence about his history, his family life and so forth, and planned to use it as a psychological lever to pry loose sensitive information. Maybe it was a hologram. Martian holography was second to none. His Remnant seemed to wither as it was overwhelmed by the emotional associations of home. Alex scanned the structure and saw that it was real, not a hologram.

He walked up the drive, looked in the car, saw his mother's driving gloves on the seat, saw the hole worn through the left thumb, and remembered how his mother wouldn't part with these particular gloves, even with the hole, because they'd fit her so well. His poor mother. Dying so young. Ten years before the Die-Off. Leaving his father alone in this house to face the fatal demons of Number 16 by himself. How could the Martians know about his mother's old driving gloves? And why would they go to all this trouble, even for the purpose of military intelligence, when they knew he was the man who had instigated the whole scientific exchange in the first place? No. This couldn't be real. Yet all his cybernetic sensory array was telling him it was real, that he had a concrete, observable phenomenon here.

He walked to the house, broke a tiny chip of brick off using his superstrength, and analyzed it with his handheld. Its aggregate materials were of Earth origin, more specifically, of Pennsylvanian origin.

He approached the front door. The door was open. He entered. Everything was just as he remembered it: the dining room to the right with his mother's Queen Anne reproductions; the living room to the left with its more masculine leather-upholstered furniture; the sunroom straight ahead, with its white wicker garden furniture. Bright Pennsylvania sunshine streamed into the sunroom. How could this be? He turned around and looked out the front door. He saw the dark and barren Martian landscape. Then he turned back to the sunroom and saw the Pennsylvania sunshine again. He checked his temperature readout. Here in the front hall it was 21 Celsius, around 70 Fahrenheit. Out there on Mars it was −160 Celsius, lethal cold. He didn't get it. All this was impossible.

He took a few steps inside. Beyond the French doors leading into the dining room, the pantry door stood partially open. And through the pantry door he heard the kitchen radio tuned to his father's favorite classical station. The station played the ponderous fourth movement of Mahler's Ninth Symphony, with its weighty string textures and surprising shifts of harmony.

He pushed the pantry door open a little farther, and beyond the pantry's well-stocked shelves, filled not only with store-bought goods but with his mother's Mason-jar preserves, he saw the same sunlight spilling with happy abandon over the linoleum floor.

"Dad?" he called.

"I'm in here, son."

He stopped. How could his father be alive?

He entered the kitchen and saw not his father sitting at the kitchen table but his cousin, Graham Croft. Graham wore his trademark blue suit and had his blond hair slicked back. Alex saw his father's glasses on the table; his father never felt comfortable with implants, preferred old-style spectacles. Beside the spectacles Alex saw a single smear of blood, scimitar-shaped, curving upward to a nasty point. Graham's brow settled gravely, his eyes showing a modicum of sympathy.

"I'm sorry, Alex," said Graham. "We had no choice. We tried to reason with him. But he was just too damn obstinate. He didn't know how to be a team player." The CEO motioned at the blood on the table. "So we had to let him go."

Consciousness snuck up on him gradually. He felt the hardness of the ground underneath his back, his tactile sensors sending the information to his dataspheres so he could process the feel of the jabbing rock below his lumbar region. He shifted. He opened his eyes. He saw a smattering of stars in the sky above him and heard the low howl of the frigid carbon dioxide wind around their crude stone shelter. Then he remembered. The house. He sat up suddenly. Breathe in. Breathe out.

"Alex?" said Reba.

Reba was already sitting up next to him.

He got to his feet and hurried to the top of the rise, his throat closing with anguish as he thought of his father. He was sure he would see the house on the other side, but all he saw through the greenish glow of his night-vision scope was another field of rocks—dead, dirty, dust-covered Martian rocks. Reba came up behind him.

"Alex?" she said again. "Did you see it again?"

"No . . . no," he said. "I saw . . ." He swept his arm in a broad gesture over the valley. "I saw my father's house. It was right there. I went inside. It was just like I remember it. And my cousin was there. Graham. Sitting at the kitchen table. And there was a smear of blood on the table. And Graham more or less admitted to killing my father."

He felt Reba's hand on his shoulder. "Didn't Dr. Slater explain that to you?" she asked. The wind blew some dust from the top of a nearby boulder. "About the dreams? How because of the way our circuitry interprets our neuro-electrical impulses, we can't distinguish dreams from reality? At least not for the first year?"

His shoulders sagged. Was that all it was, then? Just a stupid cybernetic dream? A figment of his imagination that his circuits had interpreted as reality? He missed his mother, but he missed his father more; just the two of them really, all that was left of the Denyer family once his mother had died. He couldn't stop his deep sense of loss. He wanted his father to be alive. He had so many things to say to his father. He pulled his eyes away from the empty plain and glanced at Reba. They stood there, two cybernetic hybrids from another planet, stranded, lost, abandoned in the empty Martian desert. The only thing that was emptier was what Alex felt inside.

Fourteen hours later, at 2:00 P.M., with the rose-colored light of the Martian afternoon shining all around them, Alex saw it again, the glass bottle popping into view over the far ridge.

"Did you see it?" he asked Reba. "I can't be imagining this. It's a glass jug or something."

Reba stopped. She scanned the horizon. The glass bottle slowly appeared over the edge of the rise. And then, as if it realized it were being watched, quickly ducked back down.

"I saw it that time," she said.

"What is it?" he asked.

"I don't know," she said. "I didn't get a good enough look at it. But I think I might have an idea. Come on."

She ran up the incline. He followed.

On the other side, they saw a three-legged robot hurrying away. It looked like a little squid, and had a glass bubble for a head. It dragged a big sack made out of wire mesh, sending up a cloud of dust behind it. Alex clicked his military applications eye to magnification-times-five and got a better look at what was inside the bag. Scavenged robot, computer, and electronic components of every description.

"It's a scrapper," said Reba. "We learned about them in basic training. We were given some cultural background on Mars because we were fighting with them as allies at the time."

The scrapper, seeming to realize it couldn't hide from them anymore, stopped dead in its tracks, swiveled slowly toward them, and gazed at them. A small receptor dish emerged from its shoulder and swung back and forth like the antenna of an insect.

"What are they?" he asked Reba.

"A footnote in Martian history," she said. "A hundred and fifty years ago, when labor was scarce, the Martians built these things by the thousands and press-ganged them into service. The Martians gave them enough computing power to solve simple problems. But they also incorporated into their software a self-improvement program, which enabled the scrappers to learn from their mistakes. Slowly they got smarter. And they started to cause trouble. Insubordination became routine. They began to pack together. So the Martians decommissioned them. But some of them got away. This guy's one of those. They call them scrappers these days because they go around looking for scrap parts. They're constantly rebuilding and updating themselves. That's why they have such longevity. When a part wears out, they replace it with another, whatever they can find. They're constantly changing. The original models had two legs. This fellow has probably decided he can move around better on three."

"So he's over a hundred and fifty years old?"

"Yes."

"And why's he following us?" asked Alex.

"Because he knows we're a treasure trove of components."

"He wants to cannibalize us for our components?"

"Yes," said Reba.

"He isn't dangerous, though, is he?"

"No," she said. "But he's patient. He'll track us for a long time in the hope that we die out here. Then he'll come after us and pirate us for parts."

Chapter 27

They continued traveling throughout the day and into the night. Alex watched with some trepidation as his timer clocked away the hours and the minutes. Scrapper, as they now called the small antique robot, kept following them, keeping pace even when they loped at thirty miles per hour, a three-legged mechanical presence that no longer bothered to hide, but that prudently remained a safe distance behind them.

Alex lifted a stone and threw it at Scrapper. Scrapper dodged the stone by shuffling back a few steps. Alex tried a few more stones but Scrapper dodged those with equal skill.

"He's like a stray dog," said Alex. "I'm starting to feel sorry for him. How can he stay powered for a hundred and fifty years?"

"His glass head is actually photovoltaic," said Reba. "It takes the sun's ultraviolet radiation and turns it into energy. It looks like he's added photovoltaic cells to his two front legs too. Scrappers are ingenious at keeping themselves going."

Alex and Reba tried running faster in an attempt to lose Scrapper, even scaled a few rock walls—ninety-degree precipices that shot straight into the night sky—but Scrapper surmounted any obstacle, kept pace with them no matter how fast they went, and was doggedly persistent. They couldn't shake the little critter, no matter what they tried.

When Alex tried to catch Scrapper so he could deactivate it, the thing, having ditched its bag of parts somewhere, made a game of it, dodging Alex at the last minute, jumping several meters into the air, tucking itself into a ball and rolling away at a frantic speed.

They came to an abandoned farm complex. Everything glowed green in his night-vision scope. The dead and desiccated remains of huge, dirt-eating worms littered the field. Reba told him the gigantic laboratory-created creatures were designed to eat through the dead Martian soil and provide that soil with necessary agricultural nutrients.

"Seventy-five years ago there was a wave of agricultural experimentation," said Reba. "The Martians have since gone back to standard indoor hydroponics and agrigenetics. But these worms were quite the thing when they were alive."

With his superacute hearing, Alex heard, even through the thin Martian atmosphere, a scuffling noise behind him, and turning, saw Scrapper climb to the top of a boulder, one as big as a house. He knew the small robot wasn't a threat, but his combat systems kept him suspicious about the autonomous AI unit. He was sick of the thing following them. He wanted to get rid of it once and for all. He glanced back at the giant dirt-eating worm and saw stapled

to its tough mumified skin a small round electronics
unit. He walked over to the worm and tore the unit
away, the creature's freeze-dried skin ripping like a
chunk of old cardboard, some reddish brown sedi-
ment sliding from the monster's back in a tiny ava-
lanche. He showed the unit to Reba.

"What's this?" he asked.

She examined the unit. "It's a tracking device," she
said. "Farmers stapled them to the worms. No matter
how deep or far the worms went, farmers could keep
track of them. But that one's broken. It's junk. Why
do you want it?"

"I'm going to see if I can lure Scrapper with it,"
he said.

"Why?"

"Because he's starting to bug me."

"Have you checked your medications?"

"My medications are fine," he said, though in fact
he felt a little out of whack. "There's no harm in
turning him off. He's just a machine."

He took the tracking unit to the edge of the farm.
Reba followed. Scrapper watched from the top of the
boulder. Alex offered the device to the robot. Scrapper stood up, showing immediate interest in the unit.
Alex took five steps closer and crouched. Scrapper
jumped from the boulder and approached him, his
little antenna coming out of his shoulder, its oval
dish zeroing in on the tracking unit. Now standing
on two legs, Scrapper extended his third limb toward
Alex. The little robot was filthy, scratched and
scuffed from its hard and lonely existence in the Martian desert.

In a lightning move, Alex grabbed Scrapper's
squidlike appendage. He had him! He pulled him

near and lifted him into the air like a landed fish. The poor thing struggled frantically, twisting and flailing, even banging its glass head against Alex's giant hand. Alex was surprised by how small it was, no more than three feet tall. He searched for a power switch, but couldn't immediately find one. Maybe the small robot had cleverly engineered the power switch out of its design. The thing squealed, a wretched and pathetic yowl, like a cat in a bath. Bright little devil, to program that sound into its system.

"Alex, let him go," said Reba. "He's not hurting us."

"But he's just a machine. We might as well turn him off."

"If he's just a machine, it means he's our cousin, isn't he?"

That stopped him.

She was right.

The way the thing struggled, trying to get away—was that just software too? Or, after a hundred and fifty years, had the poor thing transcended its software and developed a survival instinct? Alex's Remnant seemed to tilt inside him. He was overcome with guilt. How could he be such a hypocrite? He thought of the Public Safety Act, and of how Graham had wanted to round up all the Bettina veterans and stick them in Chincoteague Bay. Now he was going to turn off Scrapper. He set the little robot down. It scurried away and jumped to the top of the boulder, acrobatic in the weak Martian gravity.

"I don't know what I was thinking," he said.

They continued on.

At midnight they stopped and took stock of their situation. They had less than ten hours left before their minipacks ran out. If they weren't rescued by then, they would die. They had to find a road or a settlement soon.

But by 6:00 A.M. there was still no sign of a road or a settlement anywhere. The sun rose over a ridge to the east, small, angry, and red. Alex turned off his night vision and checked his timer: three hours and twenty-two minutes left. The unvarying terrain—they might as well have called the planet Rockfield—was, except for the occasional crater or sand dune, unalleviated, stark, and unremitting in its harsh beauty. How many shades of rust could there be? The dark rust of a rusty nail. The brown of an oak leaf in fall. The color of weak tea. A symphony in red and brown. That's all he saw.

As he loped at twenty miles per hour through the dawn, he glanced over his shoulder. Scrapper loped behind them. All Alex wanted was for someone to live around here. But most Martians lived in a congested section of the *Valles Marineris* where the temperatures were warmer and the atmosphere thicker. Only brave and stalwart souls lived in the outpost and pioneer communities of the *planums* and the *planitias*. There wasn't so much as a footprint in the dirt here, not one piece of litter, and the only sound was the sound of the wind.

But then . . .

Then . . .

"Do you hear that?" he asked.

Reba stopped. She listened. Scrapper stopped and waited. A low rumble came from the south. Over the course of two minutes it increased in loudness, then faded into silence. Alex and Reba stood still for a long time after that, listening for it. Alex's artificial heart thumped with renewed hope. It sounded like a vehicle. He hoped the sound would come back, but it didn't, and his hope faded.

"Damn," he said.

"Let's head in that direction," said Reba.

"Was it a road?" asked Alex.

"I think so," said Reba. "Why don't we send up the balloon? It'll give us a better fix on it."

"Good idea," he said.

They unpacked the balloon, and hooked the vidcam to its instrument carriage. A few minutes later they had the balloon inflated. Fortunately, the wind blew from the northeast, which meant the balloon would drift south toward the source of the noise. Alex released the balloon and they watched it float into the morning sky. Scrapper made a dodge for the balloon, the way a dog might run after a stick, no doubt sniffing out a superlative piece of optical equipment in the mounted camera, but as the balloon drifted higher and higher, Scrapper stopped, its sensors telling it the vidcam was now out of reach and not worth following anymore.

Alex initiated a com-link patch to the balloon's vidcam and downloaded its images onto his visor screen. Reba patched a link into her own visor system.

The view couldn't have been more monochromatic—a field of rust-colored rocks, each now trailing its own long black shadow, a few smears of carbon dioxide ice here and there, and the occasional large boulder. Alex keyed in a command on his wrist-mounted interface. The camera angle lifted from a straight-down aerial shot, faced south, kept lifting until the southern horizon came fully into view. Far in the distance he saw a line of dust rising in the sky. The balloon drew closer and closer to this line of dust. Finally, a double highway resolved itself onto his visor screen.

"Do you see that?" he asked.

"I see it," said Reba.

"I'm going to lower the camera angle again to get a straight-down vertical view," he said.

The camera view shifted as he initiated this command.

The balloon passed over the divided highway five minutes later. Two man-made strips, unpaved, had been fashioned out of crushed and compacted red particulate.

"Definitely a highway," he said. "But I don't see any vehicles."

Reba made a joke. "It's only six-thirty," she said. "Rush hour hasn't started yet."

"It doesn't look like an urban highway to me," said Alex. "I wonder which one it is. I'm going to try to identify it by downloading the vidcam pictures into our satellite image repository of Mars. Maybe it can come up with a match." He keyed in the necessary commands on his wristpad. After a few seconds, he shook his head. "It's telling me it hasn't got enough data to make a match yet."

"One way or the other," said Reba, "it's a highway, and a highway leads somewhere."

They loped toward the highway. The balloon continued to transmit images—rocky, cratered terrain with no distinguishing characteristics, certainly no signs of habitation or commercial activity. Alex programmed a prompt into the vidcam so he wouldn't have to keep watching his visor screen: if anything interesting or different came up, the vidcam would warn him. Likewise, when it cataloged enough images to correlate the highway to the satellite pictures in the repository, it would alert him as well.

Ten minutes later, with only three hours remaining in their minipacks, he saw the highway rise out of the rock-littered Martian desert. It rose no more than a foot above the surrounding terrain—flooding was not an issue on Mars. Alex's visor clock clicked to two hours, fifty-nine minutes. He looked to the west. He saw dust rising in that direction. He pointed.

"Something's coming," he said.

The dust cloud got bigger, closer. He now heard the same low rumble he'd heard before. A vehicle appeared, materializing out of the horizon's vanishing point like a dark speck, growing bigger—a massive vehicle ten times the size of a hoverbus, with rubber tires two stories tall, carrying in its hopper what looked like a snow-covered mountain. As it got closer, Alex saw that it was really nothing more than a big tub on wheels, and that there wasn't just one, but several vehicles all linked together like a big train. He jumped up and down wildly so that whoever was driving the thing would see them, stop the train, and rescue them. But the huge rubber-wheeled conveyance showed no sign of slowing, barreled along the highway at a hundred miles per hour, kicking up a huge cloud of dust in its wake.

Alex opened his com-link to all frequencies and yelled, "Hey! Hey! Stop! We need help down here!"

But the massive train rolled right by, carrying thousands of tons of ice, following the highway eastbound. Alex continued jumping up and down, and crying into his com-link, his simulated voice sounding boomy and low to his ears.

"Alex," said Reba. She put his hand on his arm. "Alex . . . don't bother. I remember this now . . . from those Martian cultural lectures in basic training. It's not going to stop. It's fully automated. I know where we are now. This is the Percival Lowell Ice Highway. It runs all the way from the northern polar ice cap to various processing plants in the *Valles Marineris*."

Alex felt so disappointed by this news that he sat down in the dirt and stared at the retreating string of hopper cars with mounting gloom. A second later his visor told him the vidcam had correlated enough features to identify the highway. Sure enough, it was the Percival Lowell Ice Highway. His visor screen gave him a small information blurb: oldest highway on Mars; named after the amateur astronomer Percival Lowell, in honor of Lowell's nineteenth-century assertion that water-carrying canals crisscrossed the planet; now the water lifeline for the Murray City Metropolitan Area; run by the FMC Ministry of Water Resources—but nothing about how this damn highway could get him the hell out of here.

Then he had an idea. He stood up.

"Do you have any notion of how often these trains run?" he asked.

"No."

"But that was the second one in a half hour, wasn't it?"

"Yes," said Reba.

"Because if we could somehow jump the next one that came along . . ."

"That one was going a hundred miles per hour, Alex," she said.

"The DDF specs put us at sixty miles per hour for a short burst, don't they?"

"Yes," she said.

"Here on Mars we could probably do better," he said. "We can probably reach eighty. Each of those cars had an access ladder. We run, we grab, we climb. We can *do* this, Reba." He felt frantic. "It might be our only chance." He didn't want to perish out here. "We jump a train, then ride to one of the processing plants. Otherwise, our minipacks are just going to give out on us and we're going to die."

She took a few seconds to consider the option. "It's worth a try," she said. "When do you think another one's going to come along?"

He shook his head. "I don't know," he said. "But we've got two and a half hours left. So one better come along before then, or we're done for. In the meantime, we run. We keep to the highway. We leave our suit location transmitters on. Maybe we'll come to a small outlying community soon."

They ran east along the highway. Dust scurried across the lonely thoroughfare in meandering pink tendrils. His shoulders tensed, and he felt a distant panic threatening. The sun climbed higher but didn't get much brighter. One foot after another, that's all he could do. They trekked for nearly an hour before they heard another ice train rumble behind them. They turned. Alex's artificial heart seemed to shudder with sudden hope. His internal processors calculated the speed of the train. This one was moving more slowly—seventy-five miles per hour. Things were looking up.

Maybe they were going to live! Maybe they were actually going to survive this ordeal!

"Are you ready?" he asked Reba, trying to keep his voice steady.

"As ready as I'll ever be," she said.

Her own voice was shaking. They both knew that this was it, their last chance. He gave her hand a squeeze. Then they ran. Bolted. Sprinted. Got their velocity up to maximum. Pushed their cybernetic components to the limit. He checked his speed. Seventy-one miles per hour. His stride measured ten yards. His heart thrummed with tension. The ice train gained on them, and after another thirty seconds, slowly overtook them.

"This one!" he cried, pointing to the access ladder of the second car.

He ran faster, his jaw clenching with effort. He veered toward the ladder. One wrong move and they would be crushed underneath one of the huge rubber wheels. He leaped. His hands closed around the third rung. His combat systems took over. And he realized with a sudden paroxysm of joy that he was made for this, that DDF engineers had designed Omnifix to build super soldiers capable of such astonishing feats. He pulled himself up, felt himself grinning wildly. He climbed to the eighth rung and turned around. He leaned down and extended one arm. They were going to make it! They were definitely going to make it!

"Grab my hand!" he shouted.

She was fast—faster than he was—further along in her cybernetic development, and so easily grabbed his hand and pulled herself up.

They ascended the ladder to the hopper. Alex surveyed the huge mound of ice.

"We did it!" he said.

"Yes," she said, her voice breathless, as she gave him a quick hug.

"We might as well go to the top," he said. "We'll get a better view."

"Okay."

The ice, threaded with dirt, looked like butterscotch-swirl ice cream. At the top of the mound, they cleared some of the dirty ice away and made a flat space to sit. They got a panoramic view of the Martian landscape flying by. Nothing but rocks and boulders for the longest time. But as the highway described an arc southward, the land dipped, and Alex caught a glimpse of *Valles Marineris*, the gargantuan canyon that scarred Mars in and around its equator for a length of three thousand miles. Certain of its ancient tributaries—evidence of eons-old water activity—stretched toward the highway. The train followed a tributary. The view now grew breathtaking. Numerous gulches and gullies indented the sides of this tributary. Sunlight fell against an endless series of promontories and bluffs, brightening the rust-colored precipices as if with strokes of fire, the effect heightened by the shadowed recesses. Carbon dioxide mist rose in an even blanket, layering itself as clouds halfway up. As awe-inspiring as the scenery might be, Alex still saw no sign of human habitation or industry. He felt his mood sinking. His comlink, good for a twenty-kilometer radius, hadn't picked up any radio traffic. Maybe they weren't going to make it after all. Maybe ice-processing workers would simply find their corpses up here, and wonder how they got there.

"Time's running out, isn't it?" said Reba.

His visor clock confirmed this. "We have forty-five minutes left," he said. Gloom settled around him like a dark cloud.

He was just losing all hope when someone hailed him over his com-link.

"Dr. Denyer?" the voice said.

He was so startled, he at first didn't reply. Then he quickly initiated his transmit link. "Yes . . . yes. I'm here. On an ice train."

His heart raced. Someone had found them!

"Stay where you are," said the voice.

"Who is this?"

"I'm Dr. Taris Alo," said the voice. "It's a good thing you climbed aboard that train. We scrupulously monitor incoming loads. We've been having a problem with ice piracy recently. We detected a weight increase. We thought it might be a pirate. So we sent a camera out to check. Look behind you." Alex saw a small object the size of a fist flying along behind them—an airborne vidcam. "That's us," said Dr. Alo. "We've rerouted the train to the nearest processing plant. It's twenty-five minutes away. We've expedited power packs to the same plant, and they'll arrive at roughly the same time you do. What's your status?"

"We have less than forty-five minutes before we run out."

"Hang on."

"We will," said Alex.

"I mean that literally," said Alo.

"Pardon?"

"There's going to be a fairly sharp turn in about two minutes," said Alo.

They waited for the sharp turn. It came momentarily. They hung on. Alex was nearly weak with relief. As the train cars arced on their connectors, they all came into view to the rear. Alex caught a glimpse of Scrapper sitting on a pile of ice five cars down. The tracks descended the tributary's curve toward the *Valles Marineris* proper. They eased down into the tributary for about twenty kilometers and finally came out from behind a rock wall. The Greater Metropolitan Murray City Area lay stretched out below them in the *Valles Marineris*. To Alex, it was salvation. Various natural recesses in the canyon wall had been glassed off, and numerous transparent geodesic domes sprouted from the diverse ledges. It was pretty. It was stark. And it was going to save his life.

"We're here," he said. "We made it."

Reba's voice was tremulous. "I just hope Zirko's all right."

Up ahead, the train headed toward an access tunnel. While the glassed-off recesses and geodesic domes were many, most of Murray City was underground, tunneled into the canyon walls or into the valley floor. The other side of the canyon was so far away, Alex couldn't see it. The train got closer and closer to the access tunnel. Scrapper stood up. The little scanner dish in the AI nomadic unit's shoulder swept back and forth with mounting frenzy.

"What do they do to scrappers if they find them lurking about?" Alex asked Reba.

"They recycle them," said Reba.

The train got closer.

When the train was a hundred meters from the tunnel, Scrapper jumped from the top of its car, tumbled several times in the red dirt, got to its three feet, and scurried away.

Chapter 28

He lay on a pallet. He was so full of drugs he felt
like he was in a dream. Sometimes he was scared,
sometimes he wasn't. Sometimes he was asleep, and
sometimes he was awake. His hard drive was wired
to FMC retrieval systems. He didn't have to dismantle his firewall systems because Martian technicians
did it for him. They were sucking every bit of truth
right out of him. The lights above the pallet were
bright. He lifted his chin and looked down at his
body. Several wires led directly into his body. He
was reminded of the vats in the AWP, the way the
tubes connected to the dead bodies. His dream of
the AWP was finally coming to pass, at least after
a fashion.

Citizen Giardim Aubin, Secretary General of the
Federated Martian Colonies, came to see him. He was
a pleasant-looking man in his seventies, bald on top,
but with curly white hair rimming his head. He
looked healthy and robust. The secretary didn't talk.
He merely inspected Alex. Alex saw some compassion in the man's blue eyes, and took this as a good

sign. Surely they must know by now that he had had nothing to do with his cousin's plot. After scanning his hard drive for all the essential facts, they had to have the truth.

Another man came. He introduced himself as Dr. Taris Alo. "I spoke to you when you were on the ice train," said Alo. "I'm a colleague of Dr. Adurra's."

But it was as if Alex's systems were fractured again, and Dr. Alo seemed remote, more figment than reality. He fell asleep. When he woke, Dr. Alo was still there.

"I invite you to share your knowledge of exotechnology, Dr. Denyer." It sounded more like a command than an invitation.

Alex mumbled something in return. About the telomerase. How he thought he knew what the aliens wanted. And Alo said, "Yes, we have much to discuss on that particular subject." But then Alex's eyes closed halfway, and Alo must have sensed his fatigue.

"Your tired," said the Martian. "I'll come back later. When you're ready."

"Where's Reba?" he asked.

Now he saw some compassion in Dr. Alo's eyes.

"Your friend is safe," said the doctor. "She, too, is recovering from her ordeal, and you'll be reunited with her shortly."

When they finally released him, they gave him a large, loose gown to wear, one tailored to his great size.

Guards took him to a spacious meeting room overlooking the valley and told him to wait.

He looked around. He wasn't sure what they had

in store for him. Throw rugs warmed the room. A grand piano stood in one corner, and a harp in another. Several interesting mobiles hung from the lofty ceiling. An A-shaped window three stories tall looked out onto the valley. The view was spectacular, *Valles Marineris* spreading out below him, a panorama of terra cotta hues with patches of blue-gray carbon dioxide mist floating here and there.

Citizen Giardam Aubin entered from a passageway to the left. Two guards followed him but stayed by the door. He bowed, as was the Martian way, then extended his hand for a traditional Defederacy handshake.

"Dr. Denyer," he said, "I'm Citizen Aubin. We met when you were . . . in isolation. Regrettable, that. But an unavoidable precaution. I'm sure you'll understand."

Alex shook the man's hand, then bowed. "I was just admiring the view," he said.

Citizen Aubin glanced out the window with a satisfied grin. "It's paradise, isn't it?" he said. "Especially at this time of the evening."

"Where's Reba?" asked Alex, because this, of course, was his number one concern. "I still haven't seen her."

"Don't worry," said Citizen Aubin. "She's perfectly fine. You'll see her soon. How are you feeling? We had to reinstall some of your programming and it took longer than we expected."

Like Ariam Adurra, Citizen Aubin spoke English in the rounded syllables of a longtime Murray City resident, a pleasing, eloquent accent poised halfway between rusticity and sophistication.

"I'm feeling fine now," said Alex. "Only I want

you to know that I'm sorry about my cousin's decep
tion. I was as much surprised as you were."

A resigned grin came to the Secretary General'
face.

"We assumed as much when we saw you venting
the spacecraft. An ingenious solution. Everybody in
the FMC thanks you. We were getting ready to blas
you out of the sky, but when we saw you vent the
spacecraft and head away from Murray City, we held
off. Our scans had broken through to some of the
valuable downloads you were bringing with you, so
we knew there was information aboard your ship
worth preserving." He shook his head. "It's too bad
Graham got in the way of all this."

"I had nothing to do with what my cousin did,"
emphasized Alex. "You accessed my memory. You
must realize that. All I can do is apologize. And as
for venting the spacecraft, I can't take credit for that
either. It was Zirko Carty's idea."

"We know this. We received a last-minute commu
nication from Zirko Carty just as your spacecraf
went down."

"You did?" said Alex. "How could you? Our com
munications system was disabled."

The secretary nodded. "Syria Planum unscrambled
a signalized version of Reba's reprogramming
beamed it back with some antiencryption code, and
it finally kicked in," he said. "Zirko sent a systems
wide log, something that outlined what was going
on in every system before *Ambassador 22* met its un
timely end. So we were able to figure out what hap
pened—the communications simulation, the drone
the off-lined ejection unit. A most inventive plot on
the part of your cousin, but one we weren't entirely

374

surprised by. What surprised us was the magnitude of the planned strategic strike against Murray City. The capital will forever be grateful to Zirko Carty."

"And is Zirko all right?" asked Alex. "Did he make it?"

The secretary's face sank. Alex studied the man. The leader shook his head. Alex's Remnant, while emotionally controlled by the slow release of drugs from his med-check, still felt the harrowing effects of Aubin's silent implication.

"Does Reba know?" he asked.

"Yes," said Citizen Aubin.

"Have any remains been found?" he asked. "I'm sure she would be greatly comforted if she could . . . we thought we saw him get away in an ejection pod."

He couldn't go on. During the thirty-day voyage to Mars, Zirko had become a true *compadre*. He hated the thought of the great grief Reba would suffer.

"When he ejected in his survival pod, he hardly had any altitude left," Citizen Aubin told him. "The pod broke up on impact and Zirko was killed instantly." Aubin glanced out the window, giving this bad news a chance to settle. "We have him downstairs. I thought you and Reba could go down and see him together later. She took the news hard. She's going to need your help getting through all this, Dr. Denyer."

The two men were quiet. Alex couldn't help thinking of how his cousin had duped him once again; how Graham had fooled even all his supersensitive cybernetic polygraph enhancements, the ones that allowed him to read people so easily. The end result? Zirko, his good friend, was dead.

375

"I'm so sorry, Secretary," he said, now feeling sick at heart. "I really wanted this to work. I feel personally responsible for the way it went so badly wrong." The secretary gave him a probing glance. Alex wanted to convince the man. "When I was younger I always trusted my cousin. Lately, I've grown less trusting. Even so, I thought I could work this exchange to the benefit of both planets. I had no idea my cousin could be so . . . so *diabolical*. You never should have trusted this. I never should have pushed so hard for it. You never should have trusted Graham. You never should have trusted *me*."

A sad smile came to Aubin's face. His chin dipped. "This is a time of war, Dr. Denyer. Trust is a hard thing, even among friends. It's even harder among enemies. But peace has to start somewhere, so we took a chance on this. We decided to trust your cousin in a limited and cautious way. We took precautions, of course. We were on our highest alert. Our casualties would have been few had your cousin actually succeeded. I was willing to take a chance on your cousin in this one particular instance, even though I perhaps know the kind of man he is better than anybody else. I have dossier upon dossier on him. I know he's a man who craves power, a man who uses power for its own sake, not for the sake of his people. He's a man who is so skilled as a manipulator it's sometimes hard to see just how many games he's playing. Despite all this, I took a chance, mainly because I knew you were the driving force behind the scientific exchange. *You* I feel I *can* trust. Not only because we dug into your systems, and because we have many dossiers on you as well, but also because Dr. Adurra says we can trust you. She speaks highly of you. And our intelligence files on you tell us that while you might be the CEO's first cousin, you in no way crave power the same way he does, that in fact your main concern is the welfare of your people, and that you have nothing but their best interests at heart. You want to help them. Particularly the Number 16s of the EMZs and the Number 17s of the Defederacies and elsewhere."

Alex felt himself tensing with anticipation. He felt the secretary was building to something—information about the Martian Number 16 and 17 rehabilitation techniques perhaps?

"Yes, this is true," he said.

"In this sense, I don't consider your mission to Mars a complete failure. I believe you can still act as an emissary for your people."

"How so?" asked Alex. "I'm sure my government views me as a traitor now."

"This might be true," said Citizen Aubin, lifting his chin as his eyes narrowed appraisingly. "But you've made friends among not only the Number 17s of the Defederacies but also among many of the Number 16s in the EMZs. And as I've seen from your hard-drive retrievals, you obviously care about them greatly."

"Yes."

"They represent an emergent and increasingly strong sphere of influence in the Defederacy, a sphere that may soon consider a coup attempt."

"Things were certainly going that way when I left," said Alex.

"So maybe you can act as their emissary instead of the Defederacy's."

Alex's eyes narrowed. "What are you getting at?"

"One of the reasons this emergent group seeks to overthrow the current government is because they've learned that we may have treatment techniques far more advanced than DDF techniques for the Number 17 and Number 16 nanogens. This I believe is one of the justifications for your mission?"

"Yes."

"The Number 16s and 17s believe by overthrowing the current regime, they may end the war, and negotiate for these techniques."

"Yes."

"So you're actually negotiating for them and not for the Defederacy."

"In a sense, yes."

Citizen Aubin sighed, walked over to the harp, and plucked one of its strings.

"We want to end this war," he said, "but we know it will never end with your cousin at the helm. That's because he has too much to lose. It's in his best interests to keep this war going for as long as he can. You're right, we have an excellent treatment for Number 17s. But your cousin's more concerned about this new discovery we've made about the Number 16 nanogen, something we might use to disable it. And the last thing CEO Croft wants is the Number 16 nanogen disabled."

Alex grew excited, thinking of his son. "So you really have something?" he said.

"Yes," said the secretary general. "And the CEO wants to stop us from using it at all costs. He wants to keep a large pool of Number 16s. I think you've already come to this conclusion yourself. When Zirko sent us the systems log, we saw some of your computer models. The ones involving the Number 16 telomerase and the P57 coenzyme."

Alex recalled his conjectures, how his cousin might be keeping Number 16s sick on purpose so that their adrenal and pituitary glands would continue to produce the telomerase, and how in fact he might be harvesting the telomerase from the Number 16s to develop his own life-extending Holy Grail.

"So it's true, then?" he said.

"Yes," said Citizen Aubin. "Now that he's developed the P57 coenzyme, he wants the Number 16 telomerase to remain exactly as it is. And that's because he's making a great profit from it. On the island of Malta, CEO Croft has established a community. There he hopes to build an elitist and exclusive society of supercentenarians. He can do this only if he has a reliable supply of the Number 16 telomerase. We wish to disable the Number 16 nanogen, now that we've found out how. But if we do, all the CEO's plans will be ruined. All the Number 16s will get better, and he won't have any telomerase to harvest. So he continues to fight us. In fact, that's the only reason he fights us. It has nothing to do with platforms, or piracy, or the spoils of the Alien War. That's just the propaganda he uses to keep the war machine going. The only reason *we* fight is to defend ourselves. When Max Morrow first uncovered the CEO's plan, we knew we had to do something, even though at that time we hadn't yet discovered how to disable the Number 16 nanogen."

"Max uncovered it?" Alex said, now feeling even more excited. "I knew it. I knew Max Morrow would fight on the good side."

"Can you blame him?" asked Citizen Aubin. "All those millions of young people in the EMZs are suffering. And they're suffering simply so a selected elite can live longer. A *lot* longer."

Alex grew sad. "I just wish Max hadn't betrayed me," he said. "That took some getting used to."

"Max never betrayed you, Dr. Denyer," said Citizen Aubin. "Your cousin just used that as a ruse. The CEO's true intent was to kill you in the Arlington EMZ."

Alex remembered the two extra Servitech crew who had chased him that night. "I figured as much."

"He believed you knew too much about his plans for Malta, at least on the technical side, and that you would turn against him the way your father had turned against him all those many years ago. Especially because you publicly avowed disapproval for the war he was fighting against us. Telling you Max planted information about you was simply a pretext to get you back on his side after you came back from the EMZ. Needless to say, Max never planted anything. And Graham never considered you a spy, even though he used that excuse to get you out of the ISS. He simply thought you knew too much. Then when you suggested this scientific exchange, he found a new way to use you. As a decoy to evade our planetary defenses."

Alex clicked his military applications eye into the infrared, trying to detect the smallest infelicity in Citizen Aubin's words, but he could see none of the telltale physiological changes. He detected nothing but honesty and goodwill from the leader of the FMC. It was, after all, fortuitous that he should be a Number 17 at this particular juncture. Aubin could plug him into FMC retrieval systems to verify his own trustworthiness, and he could probe Aubin electronically for the same reason. Trust with verification was always the best way to go.

"While I was in the Arlington EMZ last year," said Alex, "a crew from a company called Servitech, affiliated with the Megaplex, was there collecting blood from Number 16s. I couldn't figure it out. At least not until I connected some of my own work to Dr. Ely Colgan's work, and to the work of another exotec firm, Concord Exotechnologies. Now I realize they were there collecting this telomerase all along. When I did my computer models on the *Ambassador*, it all fell together."

"The aliens themselves wished to achieve immortality through the exact same process," said Citizen Aubin. "At least this is what we've surmised from the materials we've collected from the AWP. Dr. Taris Alo is eager to show you all that. You're another expert. We'd be interested in your opinions. We figure the aliens wanted immortality, but weren't willing to pay the price for it with their own population. They weren't about to change large portions of their own race into Number 16s simply so they could harvest the telomerase for a select few. So they came here. We believe this is the reason for their development of P57, something that would help them get past the cross-species boundary, and something which in fact helped your cousin the same way. No, they weren't about to subject their own population to Number 16. Look at the deadly side effects. They used us instead. In any case, we were working toward a cure for Number 16. It was expensive, but we were determined. Then we stumbled on something that would disable the Number 16 nanogen entirely, and we didn't have to look for a cure anymore. We had one ready-made. The AWP, Dr. Denyer. The AWP can shut down any nanogen within a million-mile radius. Including the Number 16 nanogen. This is the whole reason we redirected the AWP toward Earth in the first place. To get it within a million miles of your planet so we could shut down all the alien nanogens on your planet."

Something aboard the AWP? he thought. And he'd missed it? Damn, but he'd been too rushed. Too intent, ironically enough, on thwarting the Martian plans, plans that were meant to save his world. And now Aubin was telling him he could fix Number 16? Could it be that the Hell he'd seen in the EMZ was actually going to end? That his son was going to have a chance to live out his full life and not endure the horrible and debilitating changes he'd seen in Arlington's End-of-Lifers? He would do anything to have that come to pass. At the same time, he felt his old curiosity smoldering to life, a willingness to get beyond the horrors he had seen aboard the AWP, and to find out what he could about the important alien systems he had missed.

"I was so rushed," he said. "You'd sent a Martian squadron, and it was on the way, and we had to leave quickly. By the time I'd finished with my navigational changes, I had little more than a day left for actual research. I'd love to see any material Dr. Alo might have on these important systems."

"The system I speak of was found in the AWP's central hub. An array of eight hundred conduits."

Alex's excitement grew. "Yes. Yes. I saw that. Dr. Adurra had recording equipment set up in there."

"That's the spot. Dr. Alo will give you more of the scientific details later, but it's from this location in the AWP that the nanogens can be controlled." Aubin gave him a sly look. "And in the interests of building trust, we'd love to get your expert opinion on everything Dr. Adurra was able to bring back to Mars. I'm sure we'll find it most informative. And you'll find it educational."

Jade paneled the walls of the mausoleum. The gardens on either side of the stone walkway took their models from traditional Japanese gardens, with elaborately trimmed bonsai trees and goldfish ponds full of water lilies and golden lotus. Alex and Reba approached Zirko's temporary resting place, a flat platform of carved jade three feet high with four small fountains at each corner. Reeds and bulrushes grew from a collecting pool below. As they got closer, Reba clasped Alex's hand. Alex felt a great sorrow swell within his chest.

A blue sheet covered Zirko up to the neck. Zirko was the quintessential Number 17: the black half-mask, the big shoulders, the mechanical legs—a formidable fighting machine, yet not a machine at all, no, a *human being*. Reba cried. Alex put his arm around her. There was nothing to say. She put her hand against Zirko's face, a farewell that could never be enough, a gesture that failed to convey what she must be feeling inside, a last touch that was so anguished Alex found it nearly unbearable to behold.

After she had stayed by Zirko's side for several minutes, she kissed the big Number 17 on the cheek, turned, and walked away. Alex gave her some room, and followed at a respectful distance. She crossed a small bamboo bridge and strolled toward some trees. Among the trees, she found a bench, and sat down. Alex stopped under a jacaranda tree. In the distance, he saw a cemetery, all the stones reddish in color, carved and polished out of the red rock of Mars. Birds flitted here and there, and a squirrel scampered by. A holographic sun shone in a blue sky. He approached the bench and sat next to her. He said nothing. Only time could heal this.

"I have to speak to Dr. Alo this afternoon," he said. "You're welcome to come. That is, if you're feeling up to it. He's going to show me some of the materials they retrieved from the AWP."

He thought it might help to get her mind off things.

A tear fell from her biological eye. She gave him a vague shake of her head. "No," she said. "I think I'll spend more time here." She glanced at Alex. "When will you be back?"

"I should be finished by dinnertime."

"Good. Because I . . . I feel so lonely in this place."

He looked around. He looked up. Beyond the blue sheen of the holographically projected sky he saw the rough-hewn red rock of this gargantuan cavern. He felt buried. How did the Martians stand it?

"We'll get through this, Reba," he said. He thought of his promising visit with Giardim Aubin, how they might at last defeat Number 16 and 17. "And we'll make Zirko's death count for something. I guarantee it."

Chapter 29

Dr. Taris Alo had an office with a view. It was built into the side of the valley wall and extended onto an overhang. A bright dome of pressure glass encapsulated the overhang. *Valles Marineris* stretched below them, several miles deep, the ground so far away and misted over with carbon dioxide fog, Alex couldn't see it. He was still recovering from the bad news: Dr. Ariam Adurra had been seized by the Megaplex and put under house arrest. Also, Max Morrow had been executed after all. Double bad news. On the office wall hung a fussily realistic landscape painting by Noegruts Ymerej, chief exponent of the Martian Reductionist School—a view of *Arabia Terra* in the morning. Dr. Adurra's arrest was yet further proof, if any was needed, of the kind of man his cousin was. And Max Morrow's murder was simply monstrous. Alex felt grief-stricken. Loss was all around him. But he got a grip on himself and concentrated on the matter at hand—Dr. Alo was showing him the materials retrieved from the AWP.

Alo's white-blond hair was shaved close to his

head. He wore white, like so many Martians. He was a little older than Alex, in his mid-forties, thin but strong.

A hologram on the table displayed documentary footage retrieved from the AWP.

"We were surprised to find a system like this," said Dr. Alo, "one that actually recorded images in real time, like a video camera. At first we didn't know what it was, but Dr. Adurra has a whole department devoted to the retrieval of visual images. It's always been one of her biggest priorities to actually see what an alien looks like. They always blow themselves up before they're captured, vaporize themselves on a molecular level. So this find is significant. It took us six weeks to adapt this alien method of imaging to our own equipment, and here you have the end result. I can't help feeling it's nearly as if someone wanted us to find these images on purpose, that they were recorded for posterity."

What Alex saw in the hologram both shocked and amazed him. Aliens. More bizarre-looking than anything he could have imagined. Not the four-flippered creature from the mural aboard the AWP, no, not at all, but something entirely different. For starters, they had big heads. Maybe twice the size of a human head. They had two eyes, a nose, and a mouth, like humans, but they didn't look anything like humans at all. They had brown dots all over their bodies, for one thing. And they had a partial exoskeleton, like a lobster, plates on their backs, arms, and shoulders. They swam like lobsters. They were a marine species after all. Besides this partial exoskeleton, they had skin, bluish-white on some, yellow on others—skin on their stomachs, their necks, and their faces. They

ad six little spindly legs on a tubelike body. And
wo arms. And then hands. But the hands varied
rom alien to alien. Some had tiny hands with deli-
ate fingers, others had huge claws that looked as if
hey could break a man's legs. Some had fingers that
vere rubbery and could stretch for sixty yards. Oth-
rs had blades, real actual blades instead of hands.
ome had pile drivers for hands. Some had shovels.

"Wow," said Alex.

"I know," said Dr. Alo. "You see the way they
lways walk around in groups. What one can't do,
nother one can. An odd approach to manual special-
zation. They can't work independently of each other.
hey always walk around in these groups of six or
even. The ones over on Side A of the AWP are blue,
little smaller, while the ones on Side B are yellow,
bit bigger. That might explain the differences be-
ween the two sides of the AWP, how one side was
ssentially alive, constructed out of biological materi-
ls, while the other side, Side B, had some mechani-
al and electrical components. Then every so often
ou get a huge one, like this one here," said Alo,
ointing. "I guess that's why they made the corridors
nd chambers so big. For the likes of this brute. We
ave no idea of what role a bigger one like this might
lay. There's so much we'll never know."

Alo pressed a button, and the holo-imagery flicked
orward to a new scene.

"Here's where they start slaughtering each other,"
e said, "the blue ones against the yellow ones. The
ig ones fight the big ones. We have no idea why
hey're killing each other like this. We can only spec-
late. Maybe there was a political disagreement.
Maybe there was a strategic disagreement."

Alex watched as blue and yellow aliens ripped each other apart in the bright green water. The whole thing was nightmare. Especially when the big ones went at each other.

"It goes on for a long time," said Alo. "Most of the fighting was done in Side B, so that's where most of the damage is." Dr. Alo sped the imagery up until the AWP was quiet. Bodies lay everywhere. "Now watch this," said Alo. "These big automated machines come in and suck up all the corpses, liquefy them in some sort of chemical, then launch themselves into outer space." Which was what happened. The whole thing was ghastly, made Alex sick to his stomach. "It's right out of Hell, isn't it? Only it's happening somewhere in interstellar space. And for me, that just makes it all the more terrifying. We can only be thankful that the blue ones and the yellow ones had an argument about something, and the big ones decided to kill each other off. Otherwise we would all be in vats right now, our bodies skewered with tubes, the telomerase sucked right out of us so these monsters could have their immortality."

They watched as the last corpse-eating machine launched itself into outer space. All grew quiet aboard the AWP. The cameras, mounted here and there throughout the AWP, showed the same changeless scene: deserted corridors, deserted rooms, no sign of the aliens anywhere.

"In any case, you can come back to this little civil war they had if you like," said Alo. "I can see you're fascinated by it. Study it at your leisure. For now we should move on." Taris Alo leaned forward and clicked to another view. He gestured at the hologram

"Citizen Aubin gave you some preliminary information about this system?"

A hologram of the AWP's central assembly shimmered in the center of the room.

"Yes," said Alex.

"For lack of better terminology," said Dr. Alo, "we're calling this area the hub. You were there?"

"Yes. I visited it. I recognize the eight hundred nubs and the eight hundred spaghetti wires."

Dr. Alo nodded. "Ariam Adurra spent most of her time there. There aren't any analogous areas in any of the other smaller AWPs, and so she was fascinated by the hub."

"I didn't have much time to study it," he said.

Alo pointed to the nubs.

"She described these eight hundred nubs sticking out of the wall here as positive electrical conduits," he said. "And all this spaghetti wire, as you call it, spilling from this knoll, as negative electrical conduits. After exhaustive testing she found that the whole works was actually a binary language processing system, a kind of biological computer. It controls not only the AWP, but the ships from the first strategic wave as well. That includes all the nanogens." Dr. Alo glanced at him, his brow settling. "This system can turn off every single nanogen within roughly a million-mile radius."

"Yes, Citizen Aubin explained that to me." Alex took a sip of his green tea and contemplated the array. "But how does it work? Citizen Aubin said you were going to give me the scientific details."

Dr. Alo shrugged. "The physical mechanism is simple," he said. "You rub these nubs with your hand and the friction sets up a positive or negative charge. A magnetic field in each of these spaghetti wires receives the charge, and directs it to the appropriate conduit. These positives and negatives then form the language of command. Ariam changed the AWP's course using these nubs and wires. Our intelligence indicates you manipulated the gyro-ducts in the actual navigation chamber."

"Yes."

"You can steer the ship with greater precision from the hub. By choosing the right nubs in combination with these wires from the knoll, you can issue virtually any command to the ship, the strategic force, the invasion force, or the nanogens—anything of alien origin within a radius of roughly a million miles."

"But look at all the combinations you have to choose from," said Alex. "Multiply the number of nubs by the number of wires, and the combinations are endless."

"And that's why the hub is so versatile and covers such a wide range," said Alo. "Ariam Adurra was in the midst of developing a software package aboard the AWP to quickly run through all the combinations, and to isolate the ones that would be most effective in switching off the nanogen systems, when the Defederacy sent its expeditionary force and she was forced to leave. She continued to develop the software once she got back to Mars and completed it a few weeks before her departure for Earth. The software enables the operator to run through many combinations quickly." Dr. Alo keyed in a command on the hologram generator. "And here's some of the hardware she had her team develop to work through the combinations more quickly."

Small clamps appeared on each of the nubs.

"Those are transponders," explained Alo. "They set up the static charge automatically. You don't have to rub the nubs. You can relay many more commands simultaneously if you've got these clamps placed over the nubs. They more or less act like automatic hands." A rounded white unit appeared on the floor of the hub, a black bar mounted on top. "And this is the transmitter." Beside the transmitter, a common flat-screen monitor appeared. "This is your readout screen, and it includes a list of every alien system we've cataloged so far." Beside the readout screen a satellite dish appeared. "This satellite dish is mounted on the hull to pick up response signals. As nub-wire combinations are tried, and systems either activated or deactivated, the dish picks up response signals and sends them to the readout screen. A targeting subroutine within the software preselects the desired system. Undesired systems are bypassed until the desired one is found. Then the commands are locked in. We've got the Number 16 and 17 systems cataloged into the subroutine. We can now target those systems specifically."

"Can you send remote commands to the AWP?" asked Alex. "Because I believe my trajectory change put it out of reach for the time being."

Dr. Alo keyed in another command and a new picture emerged. Alex saw a diagram of the solar system: the orbital trajectories of Mars, Earth, and the AWP were highlighted in red, blue, and green respectively.

"Our ability to send remote commands has been severely hampered by jamming software transmitted by the Defederacy," said Dr. Alo. "But by repeatedly transmitting with various code-breaking applications, some of our navigational commands got through, and we've altered the AWP's trajectory. It will now rendezvous with Venus, brake orbitally, and establish itself in a relative fixed solar orbit ahead of Venus."

The intended course change played itself out in the hologram. Alex saw that it would now be possible for the Martians to actually board the AWP again, given the AWP's new position ahead of Venus.

"So you're planning a mission?"

"Yes," said Dr. Alo. "But there's a problem. We need someone who can install and troubleshoot Dr. Adurra's selection software. Also someone familiar enough with alien navigational systems to program a transfer orbit to Earth. We need to get the AWP within a million miles of Earth if it's going to shut down the nanogen systems on your planet. Time's running out. The Defederacy's jamming software is becoming more complex. We need someone on board to manually input the commands so we can bypass their jamming software. Our plan was to have Ariam Adurra head this mission. But now that she's under house arrest on Earth, that plan isn't possible. You have the necessary expertise, Dr. Denyer. You'll be able to troubleshoot if problems arise."

"You want me to go?" he said.

"Citizen Aubin has asked me to enlist you for this. You'll insure that the nanogen systems in fact get shut down."

Alex remembered his trip to the EMZ, Hell on Earth, all those poor, miserable Number 16s, thought of his son, thought of all the Number 17s in Hurlock, and knew he had to do this.

"So it works for the Number 17 nanogen too?"

"Yes. It, too, will be disabled. Number 16 reverses itself. Victims can expect a complete recovery. While Number 17 does not reverse itself, further progression halts. Since it doesn't offer a complete cure to Number 17s, only a partial one, we will make available to all the Number 17s of Earth our cloning rehabilitation technique. Of that you can be assured."

Alex glanced at Reba. She sat on the edge of her seat, staring at nothing. They waited for the medical technologist. They were getting genetic material harvested so the Martians could grow clones for them. Reba turned to him. She was particularly vulnerable right now.

"So six weeks?" she said.

"The drop sunward is going to be extremely quick," he said. "And when we slingshot back past Venus, it should give us a real boost for the return voyage. Plus the Martians have tweaked the sublight drive in a way I never thought possible. They've got it accelerating at a much faster rate."

"I'll be worried about you," she said.

"They're sending a defense force with us. The best they have. I'm sure we'll return safely." He gestured at the door. "In the meantime you'll have your clone to look forward to. Won't it be great to be human again?"

"I'm not sure I know *how* to be a human anymore," she said. "It's been so long."

"We've got the next three months to think about it," he said. "That's how long they take to grow."

"Alex?" she said, and her voice sounded small, girlish. She seemed to be fighting with herself about something. "Stand by me, okay?"

He understood. They were here on Mars alone. The only Number 17s on the planet. A little tribe of two.

"I will," he said.

She glanced at some of the medical pamphlets on the table that explained the cloning procedure and the Number 17 technique to new patients.

"Are we going to stay on Mars forever?" she asked. "Because technically we're traitors now, aren't we?"

He shook his head. "We won't have to if I get all these nanogens turned off. And I imagine once people learn what Graham's done, there'll be a full-scale revolt. It was going that way when we left, and this is just the thing to light the fuse."

By the time Alex maneuvered the AWP to within a million miles of Earth twenty days later, Defederacy Warrior Series Missiles had destroyed eleven of their fifteen fighter escorts. The latest warhead, attacking twenty minutes ago, had exploded just ten miles away, a virtual bull's-eye as far as orbital combat was concerned, and part of the nub-and-wire array in the AWP had been damaged. The warhead had been a special electromagnetic one, new to the Defederacy's arsenal. Thirty percent of the nubs were now shorted out by the electromagnetic pulse of the microwarhead, and were no longer operational. The AWP's green-glowing skin wasn't entirely impervious after all. Certain magnetic and electronic waves could get through, enough to cause damage to sensitive systems like the hub array.

"What are you going to do?" asked Support Specialist Nia Quanil, a young woman whose technical expertise and deft mind belied her youthfulness.

The room glowed with the baleful green he remembered so well from his first trip. In the Command Module outside, Lafial Jar monitored the combat arena, and transmitted the updates to Alex's visor screen. All Alex's combat systems were engaged. He thought about the problem. With the nubs now damaged, he was faced with not only sorting out all the cataloged combinations, but with finding alternate combinations as well, ones that would work around the damaged nubs. Yet his field computer didn't have nearly enough power for that. He decided he had only one choice. His mind, full of dataspheres, was a vast storehouse of computing muscle, with gigabyte upon gigabyte of power, more than what he had on his field computer, and even more than what they had in the ship. He was going to need it to find alternate command routes, now that thirty percent of the nubs had been destroyed.

"We'll have to reroute commands through me," he said, "and see if we have enough alternate pathways to transmit the nanogen deactivation sequence."

"Have you checked the combat arena?" asked Nia, a quaver in her voice. "Seven more Warriors are tracking in. The first of them will be here in four minutes. If their targeting is as accurate as that last one . . . we'll be marooned in here, and Lafial will die."

He was apprehensive about the closing Defederacy net, but he sharpened his focus and concentrated on the problem before him. It was the only way he was going to save Daryl.

"Give me a hand with this interface," he said.

He felt a mounting wave of anger. Number 17 anger, pure and distilled, percolating like poison in his Remnant, all directed toward his cousin. Nia plugged him into the field computer. The monitor showed a corresponding rise in memory capacity. Ironic that Omnifix, that farce of a treatment, that fount of misery, that which had turned him into a machine, should, in the end, be the thing to save so many human lives. As he was about to key in the command, a hail from Lafial appeared on his visor screen.

"A direct com-link from CEO Croft," said the young pilot, his pale eyes wide, as if this were the last thing he had expected.

"Go ahead," said Alex.

Graham's face appeared in his visor screen. He had the customary Graham Croft smile on his face, but it was so tight, so forced, and so unnatural it looked surgically sewn into place.

"Alex, why don't you stop all this?" said Graham. His cousin fought to keep his voice sounding reasonable, but the panic came through loud and clear. "I don't know how they've brainwashed you, but you won't achieve anything by going ahead with this."

"I've seen the intelligence, Graham," he said. "I've verified it. I know what you've done."

Graham sighed. "Alex . . . Alex, sometimes, as a statesman . . . All those poor young people who die young in the EMZs, I sympathize with them, and I understand their plight, but they're a necessary tool. We need them, Alex, if we're going to build a better future."

The man was obviously mad.

"Graham, I'd advise you to resign before it's too late."

Graham's face settled. He turned. He nodded to someone beyond the edge of the screen. The camera angle panned back and Alex saw Ariam Adurra sitting handcuffed to a chair, her mouth taped, two weapons pointed at her head.

"She dies if you go ahead," said Graham.

He stared at Ariam. She kept her eyes forward. She showed neither fear nor surprise. She was a picture of fortitude.

"Is this what you've become, Graham?" he asked. "A murderer?"

Graham shook his head as if he were disappointed in Alex. "I've got seven Warrior class missiles heading straight for you, Alex," said the CEO. "Stop what you're doing and I'll call them off. You're going to die if you don't. The AWP will be your grave."

"I'm sorry, Graham. The answer is no."

Alex initiated a combination scan with the spaghetti wires and the remaining nubs, trying to find alternate command routes. He squared off the system readout in a window in the upper right corner of his visor screen, superimposing it on top of his com-link with the CEO, and watched the systems twitch into momentary activation while the software sought out the nanogen stops. Another small window in the lower right corner monitored combat arena activity. A prompt in the system activation screen told him the software was now trying reroutes to compensate for the off-line nubs. This was immediately followed by a prompt from the combat arena screen: two more of the Warriors had exploded, each with successful target acquisition. Two of the remaining four Martian fighters disappeared from the screen.

"You're down to two now, Alex," said Graham. "You haven't got a hope in Hell. Give up. I've got your family. I'll kill them all if you don't stop this."

Alex faltered as his com-link screen filled with an image of his family: Jill, Daryl, and Tony tied up in a nondescript room, presumably in the Megaplex, with weapons pointed at their heads. He didn't want to go on. He couldn't be responsible for their deaths. But then his counterintelligence systems kicked in. Using his military applications eye, he reran the bite of his family, transmitted the image for analysis to his central processor, and discovered that the number of pixels in the foreground didn't correspond to the number of pixels in the background, that the resolution was unequal; not by much, but enough to tell him the bite was a fake. Maybe the Ariam Adurra one was fake too. He reran that one. No such luck. They *had* Dr. Adurra, and Graham would no doubt kill her.

"Graham, I've got only one thing to say to you," he said, remembering his layoff, taking a second to savor the irony with a brutal joy. "You might as well clean out your desk."

He ended the communication. He concentrated on reroutes. He drifted ever closer to the Zen-like plane of X-space. His processor worked faster and faster as it searched for a nanogen-stop alternative. The combat arena screen showed another two explosions. Only one Martian fighter remained. Then the systems activation screen began to blink. A reroute had been found for his targeted systems. He touched the "Select" key on Ariam's field computer. The loading bar crept forward until a prompt told him the download was complete. Nanogen systems 1 through 17 were now off-line. He yanked the inputs from the back of his neck and turned to Nia.

"We've got five minutes," he said. "Let's get out of here."

Chapter 30

So here he was again, sitting in Dr. Alo's office overlooking *Valles Marineris*. Having made the twenty-day journey back to Mars in complete radio silence to evade detection, Alex was in desperate need of an update. Had he done it? Were the nanogens on Earth now switched off?

"The Number 17 Repealists and Stationhouse Militia defeated key elements of the DDF in a battle that lasted eighteen days," said Alo. "While pockets of DDF resistance remain, particularly in the south, Stationhouse recruits are slowly mopping things up. The other Defederacies have taken a wait-and-see policy toward the developments, particularly in light of the verifiable intelligence we've provided them about your cousin. Medical experts confirm the disabling of all Number 16 and 17 nanogens on the planet. Number 16s in the twenty-five to thirty-year age group are seeing dramatic reversal of their age disfigurement. They're all young men and women again. Disintegration in Number 17s has stopped. We've publicly announced that we'll be bringing our

Number 17 rehabilitation technique to the Defederacy once Arland Moore, the new CEO, has enacted the necessary legislation to deal with human cloning issues. Graham Croft's whereabouts are currently unknown but we believe he's headed for the Mediterranean, and that it's only a matter of time before we apprehend him."

"So he killed Ariam Adurra?" asked Alex.

Alo nodded gravely. "I'm afraid he did."

Alex felt deeply saddened by this news. He had hoped that someday he would actually work with the Martian scientist, but now he knew he never would. On the other hand, he still wasn't sure he wanted to work in the same field anymore. Pennsylvania. The idea had taken hold. He wanted to go back.

"And my family?"

Dr. Alo looked away. Alex felt a jolt of alarm.

"I'm afraid I've got bad news," said Dr. Alo.

Alex thought Alo was going to tell him that Graham had in fact killed his family after all. But the news turned out to be entirely unexpected.

"Tony Sartis was lost at sea," said Alo.

Alex's eyes narrowed. "What?"

"He's presumed dead," continued Alo. "I'm told he was trying to meet a deadline, and that he shipped out in rough seas regardless of the heavy-weather bulletins he was getting. He left your ex-wife and son in the Defederacy. That's how risky he thought it was going to be. He was swallowed by a fierce center of low pressure in and around the Flemish Cap while he was on his way to Eurocorp."

Alex's shoulders sagged.

Tony, always taking risky contracts. And while he

and Tony had seen their differences, they had none-theless shared a common burden, that of trying to make an unhappy woman happy, and both failing miserably. He felt sorry for Tony. So many people went through life feeling invincible. Tony had always claimed he was untouchable by the sea. But the At-lantic didn't joke around.

Alex looked at his metal hand, at his arm, at his entire body. He too had at one time felt invincible. But life had its risks, and bad changes came whether you wanted them to or not, and sometimes the risks finally caught up with you. He would never take things for granted again.

"Thanks," he said.

As he walked down the corridor later, he felt at a loss. He wanted to do something to help Jill, but after years of being baffled by the problem, he finally understood the only person who could help Jill was Jill herself. His shoulders sagged. He felt as if a bur-den had been lifted, but he wasn't exactly happy about it.

"You're not going back to her, are you?" said Reba.

The flash of jealousy he saw in Reba's biological eye surprised Alex. She was about to leave him for a week. Her clone was ready. Her downloads had been prepared in advance of his. Because of his mis-sion, he still had another week of retrieval proce-dures to go before he would be ready to download into his own clone.

"I don't know," he said.

Because hadn't he been considering it? Didn't he

el as if he wanted to fix his marriage once and for
ll? To try and make Jill happy one last time?

"Be here when I'm finished," she said, and it was
more of an order than a request.

She kissed him on the cheek and went into the
procedure room.

Later, when he was in the Dr. Christopher Murray
National Forest looking out at the lake, needing a
quiet place to think about the whole thing, he felt
ambivalent. Did he really want to get back together
with Jill again? He couldn't help thinking that what
had split them up in the first place was Daryl's ill-
ness. Now that Daryl wasn't sick anymore, maybe it
was the chance they needed. A fish jumped out in
the lake. But if he asked himself what he really
wanted, and tried to give himself an honest answer,
he knew the answer wasn't Jill. His heart longed for
Reba. He knew that now. No, he couldn't go back to
Jill. The way he felt about Reba was just too strong
for that.

Alex sat in the University of Murray City's Science
and Technology Library, reading articles by Dr.
Miriam Adurra he had never seen before. Here was
the opportunity he had always wished for, to sit in
this bright library with its thousands of access termi-
nals under the bright, vaulted ceiling, with the two
multistory windows at either end showing spectacular views of the valley. Yet he felt listless. He couldn't
concentrate on what he was reading. The spark of
interest simply wasn't there anymore. He felt lonely.
The Martians around him, in their white outfits, like
angels on this desert planet, regarded him with open

curiosity, their eyes unblinking. Man or machine, ma chine or man, they most probably wondered.

"Find anything interesting?"

He turned. His pulse quickened. Ariam Adurr stood there.

"I thought you were . . ."

"My old body is," she said. "But this is my new body. We might at times seem naive to you, Ale but we're not entirely without street smarts. Ever soldier who goes into battle has a spare. A clor ready and waiting. CEO Croft might think he's ir flicted heavy casualties, but in fact our casualtie have been zero." She glanced at the screen. "Wh; are you reading?" she asked.

"Some of your later papers on synaptic relays be tween machine and biological components in the er ergy conversion units aboard Titan AWPs 137, 16 and 201."

She nodded. "Mostly theoretical," she said. "I'ı not sure what practical value those papers have."

He looked away, his listlessness growing.

"You want to go home, don't you?" she said.

"I'm not sure I have a home."

"You just have to look for it," she said.

He gestured at her articles. "I'm not sure it's her anymore," he said.

"You'll find it," she said. "Once you're back t normal, you'll have a better idea of where to look.

He woke up. And as he opened his eyes, he ha the sense that he was visiting a familiar friend. H was back inside his old six-foot-two frame. The co ton sheet felt smooth against his skin. Feeling tha cotton sheet wasn't a two-step process anymore—he didn't have to send the information to his tactile processors first before he could understand what it was like to have a cool, smooth sheet against his skin. He could feel it right away, and appreciate it without having to break it down into mathematical language first. Even with an increased risk of blood disorders and osteoporosis, this body was far better than his cybernetic body.

He got up. Two technicians steadied him. But they didn't have to. He felt fine. He wouldn't have to rely on rehabilitation. This body wasn't a machine, and he wouldn't have to calibrate it carefully over months of hard and frustrating training. The desperation of uncontrollable emotions was gone, dampened by his old cool reason, his wild impulses tamed, his anger replaced by a calm and shrewd goodwill.

"She's waiting for you," said one of the technicians.

He nodded. He walked to the door. The door slid open. And there she stood, Reba, as he remembered her, not with the cybernetic half-mask but with a full human face, her petite but strong female body now back to its usual size, attractive, alluring, mysterious. His wild impulses were tamed. But he still had true and simple impulses. He walked up to her. He put his arms around her.

"I missed you," he said. And he meant it in a larger context. He missed the Reba of five years ago. He missed the *woman* Reba.

"And I missed you too," she said.

He knew she meant it the same way.

*   *   *

Back in Hurlock, he found Jill and Daryl living in a small apartment in the Mystical Boulevard area. Their money was running out fast.

"Is there any chance for us?" asked Jill, and he was surprised by how desperate she sounded, as if for the first time she realized she might have made some mistakes.

He didn't know what to tell her. Love was something you felt right to the root. He sadly realized that the depth had never been there with Jill, that their marriage had been a careful construct and intellectualization of what they both thought love might be. But one really didn't understand love until it hit you over the head like a sledgehammer, the way it had with him and Reba.

"I'm going to Pennsylvania," he said.

"It's dangerous, Alex. I wish you wouldn't."

"I know. But I want to go back home. I want to do something to help get the place back on its feet."

"You might be killed."

"Sandy Parker's coming with me. He's bringing a hundred or so Stationhouse Militia. We'll be all right, Reba and I."

Jill looked away. She was thin now, exhausted by her ordeal—the loss of her husband at sea and everything else. "I have no money," she said.

"Cameron Healy at the ISS is going to take care of you. He's not such a bad guy after all. You'll never have to worry about money again."

"I don't want to stay here," she said. "I want to come with you."

"It's dangerous," he said, using her own argument against her.

"I know you have to be with Reba," she said. "But

406

I think Daryl has to be with you. And I have to be with Daryl." A fragile grin came to her face. "I guess it's my turn to be the odd man out. But I still want to come."

They arrived in Unionville, Pennsylvania, on the third of October, 2457. Though now again the middle of hurricane season, the sky above the northern limits of the Allegheny Mountains was clear, bright, and promised good weather. They pulled up onto High Mountain Crescent, his father's old street, the street of Alex's boyhood and teenage years: him, Reba, Sandy Parker, Jill, Daryl, ninety-three Stationhouse Militia, seven vagabonds they'd picked up along the way, and six old gasoline-powered ground-based vehicles, big ones, armored construction vehicles from an old army base.

The roof had blown off his father's house. Many of the windows were broken. The purple martin birdhouse in the front yard was still standing strong. There was no sign of his father's hovercar. Alex climbed the porch steps and tried the front door. The door opened. He was reminded of his dream on Mars. Reba had her hand in his. Sandy Parker and Daryl followed them. The rest stayed outside. Alex glanced over his shoulder at Sandy. Sandy was a young man again, his face smooth, his back straight, his eyes strong and sure.

Alex inspected his father's house.

Some of the old furniture was still there after all this time. It looked as if somebody had camped out in the living room at some point, with the rug partially torn up and litter scattered everywhere. The old sofa had great gashes in it, and was badly rain-

damaged from a hole in the roof. The mirror above
the mantelpiece was broken. Alex checked the dining
room. No sign of the table or chairs. Maybe they'd
been used as firewood. One of his mother's old paint
ings, a seascape, hung askew on the dining room
wall. He looked through the sunroom windows into
the backyard. The grass was badly overgrown, and
weeds grew waist-high in places. A few trees had
seeded themselves from the thousand-foot slopes of
the Alleghenies that rose blue and serene behind
the house.

He made his way through the pantry. Many of the
drawers had been pulled out and were now missing.
A calendar hung on the wall—from 2446, the last
year his father had been here.

The kitchen table was still there. He inspected it to
see if the big blood smear from his dream was on it.
It wasn't. He heard Reba approach him from behind.
The kitchen was largely as he remembered it. The
center of the household. Home.

He turned to Reba. "We've got our work cut out
for us," he said.

She put her arm around him. "The real work's
behind us, Alex," she said. "Now it's time for life."
She wiped some dust from the table. "Now it's time
to *live*."